Time Enough for Murder

How far would you go to save your family from murder?

A New Science Fiction Murder Mystery

By

Manuel Rose

$30.99 USD
$40.99 Canada

DEDICATION

To my family,
thank you for all your support
in my writing.

Published by MMRproductions.com &
Ingram Spark a Lightning Source Company

Copyright © 2023, 2024 By Manuel Rose
MMRproductions.com
815 Route 82 # 51
Hopewell Junction, New York 12533

Cover designed by Robynne Alexander of Damonza.com © 2024

Illustrations by Robynne Alexander, Manuel Rose, Pexels and iStock
© 2024

Edited by Mark Meyer

Printed in the United States of America

Books and audio books can be ordered.
For information, please write to:
MMRproductions.com
815 Route 82 # 51
Hopewell Junction, New York 12533

FORWARD

Scientists have experimented with time travel with several devices for many years, with no success. Albert Einstein's theory states that massive objects can bend space-time; he also stated that the stronger the gravity, the slower time will pass. Maybe someday, time travel will become a reality, and not just science fiction, but until then, we can all dream.

I wanted to write a science fiction novel, but with a twist. I decided to include a murder mystery in my story, also. This story can easily be enjoyed by groups of nearly all ages, especially anyone with a vivid imagination, like me.

Without further ado, I now present to you my latest creation: *Time Enough for Murder*. I hope you enjoy it as much as I did writing it.

M. R.

AUTHOR'S NOTE

This novel was not intended to insult, discriminate, embarrass, or degrade any group of people in any way. This novel was written purely from my own imagination, and from experiences around me.

CONTENTS

For Melissa Rose

"…may you always remain young at heart."

ACKNOWLEDGMENTS

To my wonderful daughter, Melissa Rose, thank you for all your inspiration; and to Mark Meyer for his crafty editing. I also want to thank Robynne Alexander and Damon Freeman of Damonza.com for the fabulous cover design.

MANUEL ROSE

TIME ENOUGH FOR MURDER

HOW FAR WOULD YOU GO
TO SAVE YOUR FAMILY FROM MURDER?

CHAPTER 1

NATHAN HARRIS

On a cold winter evening, Saturday, January fourteen, multimillionaire American scientist and inventor Nathan Harris was down in his spacious laboratory working on his new invention. Nathan was oblivious to the blizzard that was heading toward his town of Solville. The town was about a hundred and fifty miles north of New York City. Nathan loved New York, but he didn't want to be close to the congested city. "Upstate New York is just fine by me; I want some countryside for my money," he would often say.

Nathan had just turned forty-five, but he looked younger than his real age. The man made sure he took time to work out in his own gymnasium that was conveniently located near his laboratory, in the basement of his home. The scientist wanted to remain thin and fit. Nathan was also very tall; at six foot five inches, he towered over many of his colleagues.

Photo courtesy of Mikhail Nilov

Being a renowned scientist and inventor of many devices, Nathan was doing really well in his five-million-dollar, six-bedroom, historical colonial mansion, which was brick faced with white trim. The building was surrounded by over thirty rural acres of plush and secluded property, at 1 Imperial Road. He and his family had almost all of the amenities they could ever need and want, including a horse stable, but the horses were both gone now and he didn't feel the need to replace them. Nathan often gave seminars at prestigious universities when he was away from home.

"Darling, are you coming up for dinner?!" his wife called out over the intercom that was built into the back wall.

"I'll be up shortly, sweetie," Nathan replied.

Photo courtesy of Pixabay

Nathan brushed his black wavy hair away from his brown eyes and started shutting down all of his equipment, including his new experiment. The inventor hated leaving something when he was on the verge of a big breakthrough, however, he made sure to back up all of his settings in the computer and in his notebook. Nathan would also be recording everything that was going on in the lab; he had a digital camcorder facing him up on a tripod.

*
**

A few hours later, Nathan was right back in his lab working on his new invention. The scientist was sure his new machine would transport him back in time. He wanted to go back to the instant just before his mother had passed away in the hospital, almost twenty-three years ago. Nathan had always felt guilty about not being at the hospital before his mother had passed away from pancreatic cancer; he was giving a seminar at MIT University in Massachusetts at the time. By the time Nathan had arrived back in New York, his mother, Alice, was already gone. *I never got to say goodbye to her; I never got a chance to tell her how much I loved her,* he thought.

The scientist and inventor was not interested in going into the future, just the past. He played around with the settings on his equipment until the lights went out. The storm had already arrived and was knocking down power lines along the way. The one thing that Nathan didn't have in his posh mansion was a standby generator. The man didn't want to spoil the classic charm of the old colonial mansion by adding too many modern appliances. He now pondered the idea of having a backup generator installed, especially one that was capable of running all of his equipment in the lab, so he wouldn't be interrupted by service disruptions like this.

*
**

The next morning, Heather Harris was waking up to an empty bed again, wondering what the hell had happened to her husband.

"This is bullshit. I know he's working on another damn invention, but I'm sick and tired of waking up all alone in the morning," Heather said to herself.

Heather thought her husband was taking her for granted. *Always a new invention,* she thought. *To the devil with that. I need my man here with me now in bed.*

"The electricity is still out. We've got no power whatsoever. What could he possibly be doing downstairs in that dungeon of his with no power?" Heather asked herself.

The frustrated woman looked at her bedside battery-operated alarm clock; it was seven thirty in the morning. Heather went to the bathroom and looked at herself in the mirror. *You know, I'm still young and attractive,* the thirty-five-year-old petite woman thought to herself, while admiring herself in her white negligee. *I still have all of my blonde hair and a pretty face. I still have my nice figure. What's down there in that damn laboratory of his that's more important than me? I need someone that appreciates me. I need attention too.* Heather decided to go downstairs with her flashlight to find out what her husband was up to. She slowly walked down the three flights of stairs to her husband's laboratory. All of the doors were open and unlocked downstairs. Heather was surprised to find Nathan asleep in his chair wearing his red robe, near his equipment counter, with papers on the floor right next to him. Apparently, they had fallen from his hands when he fell asleep.

"Nathan, honey, wake up. Nathan, come on," Heather softly said to him.

"Wh-what? Oh, it's just you, babe," he said groggily.

"I'm sorry if I startled you, honey, but you weren't in bed, so I came here looking for you."

"Is the electricity still out?"

"Yes, it is. You know, this wouldn't happen if we had our own auxiliary power. We really need a backup generator, honey. That's the second time this year we've lost power. Big ole mansion without a generator, and yet you have all these inventions of yours; there's something wrong with that."

"Yes, I know, Heather, you're absolutely right; I'll get right on it, babe."

"Do me a big favor and just call a professional to have it installed, darling, it'll be a whole lot quicker; you know you don't have the time to take on a project of such magnitude as that."

"I know, you're right, sweetie. I really don't have the time, but it'll have to wait till I get back from Oregon."

"Oh, that's right, you're giving that seminar at the university;

when is it?"

"The day after tomorrow. I have to be there Tuesday early morning to set up my presentation."

"Sure, now are you coming back to bed, or what?" Heather anxiously asked him.

"What time is it?" Nathan asked.

"It's about seven forty-five in the morning."

"I might as well, there's not much I can do around here without power."

"Why do I now feel like I'm second best around here?"

"I meant to ask you something, hon; where did you go off to yesterday?"

"I was visiting a close friend."

"Anyone I would know?"

"No, honey, you wouldn't."

"I just wondered. You were out rather late last night," Nathan asked her in an accusatory tone.

"Oh, darling, stop it. I was out with an old friend I knew from the university; you don't need to be jealous of me."

"Really?"

"Yes really. Now, that's all there is to it. Come, let's go off to bed, shall we?"

The two of them went off to bed. Nathan knew she seemed distant to him lately. He really wanted to continue working on his project, even though the inventor knew it was physically impossible without any power. Heather thought Nathan was on to her. *I'm going to have to be more discreet next time. I hope the power stays out for the rest of the day and night, it would serve his ass right,* she angrily thought while walking up the stairs with him.

*
**

Two days later, on Tuesday morning, January seventeen, Nathan had left for his seminar in Oregon. Nathan regretted not being able to say goodbye to his wife, Heather, and his thirteen-year-old daughter, Alice. It was five o'clock in the morning and he didn't want to wake any of them.

Alice was his only child; they had named her after his late mother, although she resembled his wife a little, with the exception of her having a slightly smaller nose and her hair color was different. Alice was a strawberry-blonde, while Heather had golden-blonde hair. Nathan was happy that Alice was a straight-A student in school and he loved his daughter dearly. *She is the best thing that Heather's ever given me,* Nathan thought to himself.

Nathan had left his wife in the middle of the night to go over some notes in the lab. He liked it down there since it was peaceful and quiet with all of the soundproofing he installed. *A man can think more clearly with peace and quiet and no interruptions,* Nathan thought. The scientist fell asleep, again, in the lab and decided to leave from the lab's separate entrance, without ever going back upstairs. Nathan was relieved that the power had been restored, and that most of the roads were now fairly clear from the nearly two feet of snow that the blizzard had left everyone. He was happy to see that the man he hired to clean the driveway had already come by. Although the scientist favored the ride of his Bentley, he decided to take his Lincoln SUV out instead, since he felt safer in the snow with it. Unfortunately, the phones were still out.

*
**

Wednesday afternoon, January eighteen, insurance agent Jonathan Mitchel was at the front door of the Harris residence. The young insurance agent had an appointment with Mrs. Harris to amend her husband's life insurance policy. Mr. Mitchel was short and stocky, with light brown hair. Mitchel wore a gray pinstriped suit and a gray derby. He loved his job but hated using his car to travel to the clients. *I hate putting all this mileage on my own car. I don't want to burn it out before I finish paying for it,* he thought. Jonathan rang the doorbell several times, but he got no response. *Maybe the doorbell isn't working, I don't hear it,* the young agent thought. Jonathan was cold and he didn't feel like hanging around there much longer, so the agent decided to knock hard on the front door.

"Mrs. Harris, it's Jonathan Mitchel from J&J Insurance. We had an appointment!" the man shouted.

This time, Jonathan knocked harder on the solid maple wood door. Suddenly, the door slowly crept open; apparently, it wasn't closed all the way. The agent decided to walk into the vestibule, while still calling out his client's name.

"Mrs. Harris, it's Jonathan Mitchel from J&J Insurance. We had a twelve o'clock appointment, remember?!"

Jonathan slowly walked into the rest of the home. He had the feeling that something was not quite right there in the mansion. Then, the young man looked up at the mahogany-colored, antique grandfather clock standing by the staircase and near a plush green chair. The massive clock stood at a height of over eight feet tall. The only glass panel it had was on the clock's face; the rest of it was all solid wood. Jonathan noticed that the clock had stopped at 4:49, but since it was a nineteenth-century, antique mechanical clock, there was no way to tell if it was a.m. or p.m.

Photo courtesy of Pexels

Jonathan remembered that the Harris's had a maid the last time he was there, about a month ago. *Where is she, and why was the door unlocked?* Jonathan wondered. The insurance agent slowly walked into the parlor and looked around. Mr. Mitchel was horrified when he looked up at the family portrait that hung above the brick fireplace. The painting displayed Mr. and Mrs. Harris with their daughter; however, the face of Mrs. Harris was visibly slashed up. Jonathan also noticed that the painting was askew. The man was now literally shaken with fear, thinking that something dreadful had happened to her, and possibly the rest of the family. Jonathan Mitchel decided to call the authorities on his cellphone.

*
**

One hour later, the police had arrived at the Harris residence, led by Detective Juan Gonzalez. Gonzalez was a forty-one-year-old man of Puerto Rican heritage. He was average height with a slender build. The detective also had curly black hair and was looking a bit unkempt today, since he forgot to shave this morning and his black suit was a bit wrinkled. Gonzalez was with the police force for over fifteen years, moving up steadily through the ranks. He was also known to be tough on criminals and he did not take any shit from anyone, except of course from his boss, Captain Paul Martinelli. The insurance agent had waited for their arrival. Jonathan had greeted Detective Gonzalez and the two officers at the front door of the home.

Photo courtesy of Rein Krijgsman

"Hello, I'm Detective Gonzales with the Solville Police Department. We got a call about a missing person and also vandalism here."

"That was me, Detective, I called it in," Jonathan replied.

"And who might you be, sir?" Gonzalez asked.

"My name is Jonathan Mitchel, I'm an insurance agent for J&J Insurance."

"Do you live here, Mr. Mitchel?"

"No sir, I just came—"

"So, you don't live here, right?"

"No, I just came by—"

"So, you're trespassing on the property, right?"

"No, Detective, I'm not, I just—"

"Are you related to the Harris's, Mr. Mitchel?"

"No, I had an appointment here with Mrs. Harris at twelve o'clock."

"Who let you inside the residence, Mr. Mitchel?"

"No one sir, the door was open, so I just let myself in."

"That's trespassing in my book, sir."

"Listen please, Detective, would you just come inside and investigate?"

"May I see some ID? I just want to verify who you are and your intentions of being here in the first place, Mr. Mitchel."

Jonathan Mitchel showed the detective his insurance identification card. Mitchel thought the detective was arrogant. *The nerve of him treating me like this,* he thought. *He's acting like I'M the criminal.*

Gonzalez carefully scrutinized the insurance agent's identification.

"Ok, so you claim you came over here because you had an appointment with Mrs. Harris at twelve o'clock, right?" Gonzalez asked him.

"Yes, that's correct, sir," Mitchel replied.

"The door was open, so you just waltzed right in here, correct?"

"Not exactly, Detective. I *did* ring the doorbell, then I knocked on the door."

"You said the door was open, right?"

"Not at first. After I knocked on the door, hard, then it just started opening all by itself. I began calling Mrs. Harris's name while I walked in."

"I see," Gonzalez said in a suspicious tone of voice.

"I just found it strange that no one was at home, not even the maid."

"You said something about vandalism, Mr. Mitchel."

"Yes, that's the creepy thing, Detective. There's a family portrait hanging over the fireplace in the parlor. The face of Mrs. Harris is visibly slashed completely. You could see it for yourself, Detective."

"All right, come on boys, let's go check it out!"

Detective Gonzalez and the two police officers finally walked into the Harris residence to investigate. Jonathan was feeling relieved. *Man, I thought he'd never come in here. It's as if he thinks that I had something to do with their disappearance,* Jonathan thought to himself.

Gonzalez looked at the security alarm panel near the front door, and he noticed it was disabled. The detective also thought the mansion was cold inside, as if the thermostat was deliberately set at a low temperature, which is usually done when no one's going to be home. *Yet, the insurance agent claimed to have had an appointment with Mrs. Harris at twelve this afternoon, interesting,* Gonzalez thought. The kitchen telephone started to ring, and after the second ring, the answering machine picked it up.

"Hello and thanks for calling, no one is currently available to take your call at this time. Please leave your name and number and we'll return your call as quickly as possible. Thank you and have a pleasant day," Nathan's recorded voice had played over the machine's loudspeaker.

"Hello Heather, pick up the phone please. Heather are you there?" Nathan Harris asked over the machine's speaker.

Detective Gonzalez briskly walked toward the machine hanging on the kitchen wall to answer the phone.

"Hello this is Detective Gonzalez from the Solville Police Department, who is this please?"

"Juan, is that you?" Mr. Harris asked over the phone.

"Nathan? I didn't recognize your voice, how are you doing?"

"I'm doing fine, but what are you doing in my home and where's my wife and daughter?"

"We got a call from your insurance broker, who's standing right in your home, a Mr. Mitchel from J&J Insurance; you know him?"

"Yeah, I do; how did he get into my home?"

"He claims the door was unlocked, sir."

"That sounds like my wife, always forgetting to lock up."

"I haven't seen your wife and daughter yet. Do you happen to know where they might be?"

"My daughter's probably still in school. As for my wife, she's almost certainly socializing with her friends. I'm at Oregon University. I just called to let her know I'll be home tomorrow morning; I got an earlier flight."

"Ok, I was just wondering because your insurance guy here claims that he had an appointment with your wife at twelve."

"My wife has a habit of losing track of time; she probably forgot about her appointment."

"All right then, Mr. Harris, I guess we're done here."

"That's good, Juan; oh, and do me a favor, just close the front door when you guys leave, I know you can't lock it but…"

"Don't worry about it, Nathan. I got you covered."

"Great. Say hello to Paul and Winston for me, will you?"

"Sure thing, have a safe flight back."

Detective Gonzalez hung up the phone and turned toward the insurance agent.

"We're done here, Mr. Mitchel," Gonzalez told the insurance agent.

"Wait! You didn't even check out the house, or the painting I told you about," Mitchel said with a concerned look on his face.

"Do you even know who Nathan Harris really is, sir?"

"Yeah, I know, he's a multimillionaire scientist and inventor."

"More than that, I might add. Mr. Harris is a well-known philanthropist. He gives to *all* charities, including our police force. Nathan is good friends with our captain and the mayor of this town; he even knows them on a first name basis. So, before you start anything, just be careful what you say. Remember, *you* walked into his home, unauthorized."

"I'm not trying to start anything; I'm just saying to at least look around, especially in the parlor. You've got this guy so high up on a pedestal that you won't even do your job to see if anything's happened to his wife; yet, you're quick to accuse me of—"

"Watch it, Mr. Mitchel, don't push me into doing something you'll regret later."

"I'm just saying to take a look around, sir, that's all."

The detective gave Mitchel a dirty look, and begrudgingly took the officers around with him for a quick inspection of the premises, starting with the parlor. Detective Gonzalez didn't find anything in disarray around the room, with the exception of the mutilated family portrait above the fireplace. Gonzalez took his men quickly around the main level of the mansion, noting that everything was in order.

"Well, that's it boys, we've wasted enough time here. Let's go and close up shop," Gonzalez stated.

"Wait! Aren't you going to check the other levels?" Mitchel asked them.

"For what?! There's no sign of forced entry here. Everything appears to be in order. No evidence of foul play or anything. Oh, and by the way, for your information, Mr. Mitchel, just in case you're not aware of it, the law states that a person has to be missing forty-eight hours before being legally declared missing. Just so you know."

"I'm very well aware of that, Detective."

"Good! Now let's *all* leave the premises, shall we?"

"What about the slashed painting above the fireplace? You *did* see that, didn't you, Detective?"

"Yes, I did. I know for certain that their daughter plays with her drone inside and outside of the house; I've seen her with it. She could have accidentally flown it into the picture and tore it up. Those drones have some *sharp* propellers; they could hurt you *really bad* if you get near one, you know."

"I guess it is possible."

"Sure, it is. Now, let's all get out of here."

Detective Gonzalez escorted the two police officers and the insurance agent, Jonathan Mitchel, out of the house, while closing the front door behind him. Gonzalez did wonder why the front door was unlocked in the first place, even though Mr. Harris claims that his wife probably forgot to lock it up. He also recalled that the alarm system was disabled. *Maybe we should have taken a quick look upstairs, just to be sure,* he thought in the car ride back to the station.

If Detective Gonzalez *did* take the time and the initiative to inspect the rest of the mansion, he would have found bloody evidence of foul play upstairs in the master bedroom suite.

CHAPTER 2

THE MURDERS

Thursday morning, January nineteen, Nathan Harris had just returned home from his seminar in Oregon. He walked into his home and was suddenly hit with a foul odor. Nathan immediately thought it was another field mouse that met its fate. *I guess the exterminator didn't do such a hot job after all,* he thought. The scientist noticed that the grandfather clock by the staircase had stopped at 4:49, and he wondered why his wife didn't wind it up. *It's 9:30 in the morning, it must have stopped last night. She knows how I feel about that clock; why did she let it stop?* Nathan asked himself. He was getting upset. Nathan knew that his daughter, Alice, was at school by now, but the inventor wasn't sure if his wife, Heather, was home and in bed. He knew that Heather wasn't very good at keeping appointments; she would always check with him, since he was well organized.

"Heather, I'm home!" Nathan called out.

Nathan kept calling his wife while walking around, but he got no response. *That smell! Where the hell is it coming from? I've got to call the exterminator again,* he thought. Nathan started walking up the curved staircase toward the master bedroom suite, searching for his wife.

"Heather, where are you?!" Nathan asked.

Nathan walked down the hall until he reached the master bedroom on the right. He wondered why the door was closed. *Maybe she's tired and doesn't want to be disturbed,* the man thought. Nathan slowly opened the bedroom door and was immediately horrified. The room looked like a crime scene of a horrific murder. There was blood everywhere. The king-sized bed and its sheets and pillows were all soaked in blood. The white carpeting surrounding the bed had large blood stains on it. The walls were also sprayed with blood, and so was the cloth-covered lamp shade, which sat on the nearby nightstand. Some blood had also sprayed onto the tan-colored curtains that were hanging on the ornate windows. It was enough to make anyone cringe with fear. However, there was no trace of Heather.

Nathan screamed and ran out of the room so fast that he caused a breeze strong enough to shut the bedroom door. Nathan ran right into the downstairs bathroom to vomit in the toilet. He could have used the private bathroom in the master bedroom suite, but Nathan wanted to get far away from the scene in the bedroom. He slowly stood back up and cleaned himself off. The hairs on his neck were standing up at complete attention. Then, the man took out his smartphone and called the police.

*
**

A half-hour later, Detective Gonzalez was at the residence of Nathan Harris, ringing his front doorbell. Gonzalez had brought along Officer Cheng with him. Cheng was relatively new to the force, but the young Asian was dedicated to his job, he worked really hard, and he strived to move up in the police force. Officer Cheng was a little shorter than Gonzalez, but he was in better shape. Cheng had just gotten himself a new haircut, sporting a feathered look of his short black hair.

Gonzalez was worried about the Harris's. *They're good, kind, and generous people. I hope everything is all right with them,* Gonzalez thought. The detective remembered what Mr. Harris said when he called: "You'd better come right away, Gonzalez, there's blood everywhere and I can't find my wife," Nathan had told him over the phone. Gonzalez feared the worst for Nathan's family.

"Who is it?!" Nathan asked while coming toward the front door.

"It's Detective Gonzalez!" the detective shouted back.

Nathan opened up the front door. Gonzalez could see that Mr. Harris was visibly shaken by what had happened.

"Come on in gentlemen," Nathan replied while letting them inside.

"It smells like something died in here," Officer Cheng said while walking inside the home.

"Yes, it does," Gonzales added.

"Follow me upstairs and I'll show you what I found," Nathan told them.

*
**

Nathan took both Detective Gonzalez and Officer Cheng upstairs to the master bedroom suite that was practically saturated with blood. He opened up the bedroom door and led them both inside the room.

"*¡Ay Dios Mío!*" said Detective Gonzalez.

"Whatever that means, I'm with you on that," added Officer Cheng.

"It means, oh, my God, in English. What the hell happened here?"

"I don't know and I'm really scared to find out," Nathan replied to Gonzalez.

"Ok, this is now officially a crime scene investigation. No one comes in or out of here. Cheng, go call the captain and have forensics come on over here, pronto," Gonzalez told him in an authoritative tone.

"Is it my wife's blo—" Nathan tried to ask.

"I don't know yet, Mr. Harris. We have to do a DNA analysis to find out," the detective replied.

"Oh, my God."

"Come, let's all go back downstairs. I have a gut feeling we may find the body down there where the smell is," Gonzalez said.

*
**

The three men all went back downstairs. Officer Cheng was still on his smartphone with the captain. Detective Gonzalez helped Nathan down the stairs, after seeing how shaken he was. They all noticed how strong the stench of death had become, as they walked down toward the source.

"Yo man, we got to check this place out. I got a feeling there's a body down here to go with all that blood splattered upstairs," Gonzalez told Cheng.

Detective Gonzalez followed the scent into the parlor with Officer Cheng and Nathan Harris behind him. Gonzalez noticed a few drops of dried blood on the base of the sofa. He turned around and faced Nathan.

"You never did find your wife, did you, Mr. Harris?" Gonzalez asked him.

"No, no, I didn't," Nathan fearfully replied to him.

Detective Gonzalez cautiously walked over toward the tan-colored sofa. He put his latex gloves on and proceeded to remove the cushions. Gonzalez noticed that there was a black pull handle on the sofa.

"Is this a convertible sofa?" Gonzalez asked Nathan.

"Yes, it is," Nathan replied.

Detective Gonzalez tried to pull up on the handle, but he just couldn't open the sofa. Gonzalez kept trying until the fabric handle snapped, sending him on his butt, on the floor.

"*¡Coño!*" Gonzalez shouted.

Officer Cheng finally got off the phone with the captain. He tried really hard not to laugh at his superior after watching him fall on his butt. Gonzalez gave the officer a look that said, *you better not laugh, or else.*

"*Mira,* Cheng, come here and help. I can't open this shit up," the detective said.

"Sure thing, boss," Cheng stated as he went over to help him out.

The two of them tried really hard to pull up on the bar of the sofa bed.

"Man, this thing is tight," Cheng replied.

"I know. I have a feeling it's not empty," Gonzalez replied.

Detective Gonzalez and Officer Cheng kept pulling up on the bar until the sofa bed finally started opening up. The stench of death was getting worse as the two men began to unfold the rest of the bed. The mattress was missing, leaving only the springs of the bed. There was a big black garbage bag in the center of the bed. Some of it had been torn from the springs as blood started to ooze from the openings. Detective Gonzalez noticed some blonde hair protruding from the top of the bag as it became snagged in the mechanism of the sofa bed.

"I think we may have found your wife, Mr. Harris," the detective grimly stated.

"No, no it can't be," Nathan struggled to say as he fell down onto his knees.

Gonzalez took out his pocket knife and gingerly started to cut open the bag containing the body. The detective slowly began to expose the head of the corpse. The once beautiful deceased young woman was dressed in a peach-colored nightgown. Heather Harris had several knife lacerations in her, mainly in the mid-section area. Her body was covered with most of her blood.

"¡Ay Dios Mío! Yeah, that's her all right," Gonzalez said while shaking his head from left to right.

"Oh, God no! No, no, no!" Nathan cried out.

"Where's the mattress?" Officer Cheng asked.

"The killer obviously took it out to make room for the body.

Even though Mrs. Harris was petite, removing the mattress made it a lot easier to store the body in the convertible. Find the mattress and maybe we'll find our killer," Gonzalez stated.

"Forensics are on their way, Gonzalez," Office Cheng stated to him.

"Good. Mr. Harris, you can't stay here, at least not until we complete our investigation. Oh, and for whatever it's worth, I'm sorry for your loss," Gonzalez sincerely told him.

"Thank you. I feel like it's my fault," Nathan added.

"How's that, sir?"

"Well, if I hadn't gone and left her alone, maybe—"

"No man, you couldn't have known that would happen to her, unless, of course, did you know if Mrs. Harris had any enemies?"

"None that I can think of, Juan."

"Do you mind if we go downtown for some questioning, Mr. Harris? You can't stay here anyway."

"Sh-sure, Juan, anything if it would help find my wife's killer, but, you are aware of the fact that I've been away and I just returned home to this."

"Yes, I know that, Mr. Harris."

The two of them started walking toward the front door, until Nathan stopped right in front of the grandfather clock by the staircase.

"Wait; that bugs me," Nathan said as he looked up at the huge wooden clock standing in the hall.

"What, the clock? Yeah, I know, it's not running," Gonzalez said.

"Yes, it stopped at 4:49. That was one of the reasons I was going upstairs; to get the key to wind the clock, until I got sidetracked with—"

"Did you ever get the key?"

"No, like I was saying, I got sidetracked seeing all that blood in our bedroom."

"I think you should get the key and open it up, Mr. Harris. There's a foul smell coming from it. Come, let's go back upstairs and get the key for the clock."

*
**

Detective Gonzalez escorted Nathan Harris back up to the master bedroom to find the key for the clock. Gonzalez watched him intently as Nathan went toward the wall near the dresser to acquire the key. There was a small wooden plaque hanging on the wall by the dresser, near its mirror, with the words "HOUSE KEYS" engraved upon it. There were six hooks with keys on them. One of the hooks had an old-fashioned brass key, which was tarnished with age, hanging from it. The key had a tag on it that read, "CLOCK."

"Hold it! Put on these gloves before you touch anything, Mr. Harris; there may be prints from the killer here," the detective stated.

"Sure, Juan," Nathan replied as he took the latex gloves from the detective and put them on.

Nathan continued to walk over to the wall where the wooden plaque was hanging. He looked at the keys that were on it and grabbed one of them.

"Here it is!" Nathan said while grabbing the old-fashioned brass key with its tag.

"Ok then, let's go back downstairs, Mr. Harris," Gonzalez told him.

*
**

The two men went back downstairs to the antique grandfather clock. Nathan approached the clock and inserted the brass key into the keyhole of its door. He tried to turn the key, but it wouldn't budge.

"It's stuck!" Nathan shouted.

"I think there's something in there pressing on the door. I can see a slight bulge in the wood," Gonzalez stated.

"Well, what are we going to do? It's a valuable antique and I don't want it damaged."

"I'll tell you what we're gonna do, I'll push in on the door while you unlock it, all right?"

"Ok that sounds logical."

Detective Gonzalez slowly pushed in on the door of the clock, while Nathan turned the brass key until it clicked.

"Ok Juan, it's open," Nathan said.

"Ok, here goes nothing," Gonzalez stated.

Gonzalez slowly released the pressure on the door as the clock started to gong its hourly chimes. Then, the two men looked in shock at the clock's horrific contents. The body of a young girl, dressed in pink pajamas, with a bloody gash on the back of her head, was all scrunched up inside the mechanism of the old clock. Nathan Harris collapsed down on the floor in front of the old clock. Detective Gonzalez stared at the once beautiful adolescent girl with long strawberry-blonde hair; he knew in an instant who it was.

"*¡Ay Dios Mío!* Hey Cheng, come here, now!" Gonzalez shouted.

"What's up, boss!" Officer Cheng shouted back.

"We got another body here!"

"Are you serious?"

"Yeah, I'm serious, get your ass over here, now!"

Officer Cheng briskly walked over to where the detective and

Nathan Harris were. Cheng stared in awe at the body that was stuffed inside the clock.

"Who was she?" Cheng asked.

"*That* was his daughter, Alice," Gonzalez grimly replied back to him.

"Wow, what a waste; she was beautiful."

"She was only thirteen years old," Gonzalez replied while giving Cheng a disgusted look.

"What happened to him?" Cheng asked while pointing at Nathan laying on the floor.

"He passed out after seeing his daughter in the clock."

Nathan Harris was gradually waking up with the sound of the two men talking in front of him. Nathan slowly sat up on the floor and gazed up at the open clock. Tears started to stream down his face as he stared at the now lifeless body that once was his beloved daughter, Alice.

"My baby. My beautiful baby girl. Why, why oh, why Lord, why—" Nathan tried to finish but he just broke down and wailed.

The forensics team was at the front door, ringing the bell; Detective Gonzalez went over and let them in. Gonzalez showed the two bodies to the forensics team of two. Then, the detective took them upstairs and showed the men the blood-stained bedroom.

✲
✲✲

An hour later, Detective Gonzalez was at the Solville Police Department with Nathan Harris. Officer Cheng had stayed behind at the Harris residence with the forensics team. Captain Paul Martinelli came by to greet them, not knowing the entire circumstance of the situation that was going on.

Captain Martinelli had just returned from a one-week vacation in Florida with his family. The fifty-eight-year-old captain was happy to be back, since the man had been bored to death for the last few days. Martinelli was of Italian heritage, had been battling obesity, coupled with the loss of most of his hair, and he had lost a lot of his self-esteem. Martinelli hated to see his big belly overhanging on his belt buckle, and because of that, the man buried himself in his work, sometimes putting it in front of his family life. Captain Martinelli had extended his right hand out to his friend, Nathan Harris.

"Mr. Harris, I want to personally thank you for that very generous contribution you gave us for this police department," Martinelli said while shaking Nathan's hand.

"The pleasure's all mine, Paul, but this isn't a social visit," Nathan responded.

"Yes, I know. Come, step into my office, you too, Gonzalez."

Detective Gonzalez escorted Nathan Harris into Captain Martinelli's office. Nathan sat down in the chair that was in front of the captain's desk. Martinelli pressed the record button on his microcassette tape recorder; Martinelli informed Nathan that he had to record their conversation.

"Gonzalez, did the forensics team finally arrive at his residence?" Martinelli asked the detective.

"Yes, Captain, but there's been some recent developments since then. We now have two bodies," Gonzalez stated.

"What! Two bodies?!"

"That's right, Captain. One is his wife, Heather Harris, and the other one is his daughter, Alice."

Nathan Harris had begun to cry in his seat, hearing the detective state the news to the captain.

"Mr. Harris, I'm so sorry for your loss, but we do have to ask you some questions. It's just routine, you know," the captain informed him.

"I understand, Captain. Just so you know, I just returned back from a seminar in Oregon, only to be kicked out of my mansion, after finding my wife and daughter murdered in my own home," Nathan stated in between his tears.

"When exactly did you leave for Oregon, Mr. Harris?" Gonzalez asked him.

"Tuesday morning, January seventeen," Nathan replied.

"About what time in the morning was that?" Martinelli asked him.

"I left at around five o'clock for the airport."

"And you just got back today?"

"That's right. I walked in the door at 9:30 in the morning."

"And then, what did you do?"

"I started looking for my wife. I kept calling her name while I was going upstairs. Finally, I walked into our bedroom; that's when…"

"That's when you saw the blood and called us, right?" Gonzalez asked.

"That's right, Juan. I just can't believe it's true. My wife and daughter are both dea—" Nathan couldn't finish, he was visibly distraught.

"Mr. Harris, I didn't notice the maid or the groundskeeper present there; is it possible that they may have seen or heard something?"

"No, I let them both go last week. They weren't working out. I caught both of them trying to steal from me. I was going to hire some new help when I returned, and now this happened."

"I know it's hard for you right now, but do you or your wife have any enemies that you know of, Mr. Harris?" Captain Martinelli asked him.

"None that I can think of, except I'm sure there are some people that may have some animosity toward us."

"None that you can think of offhand, Mr. Harris?" Gonzalez asked.

"No sir," Nathan replied.

"What about your daughter? Does she maybe have a jealous boyfriend or something?" Martinelli asked him.

"She had a boyfriend, but she broke up with him about three months ago."

"Ok that's a start. Do you know his name?"

"Yes, it's Charles Nolan. He's in her class, but he's only thirteen, like her."

"You'd be surprised at how young some of these killers are today, Mr. Harris. Why, just last year we arrested a twelve-year-old boy for murdering his mother and her new boyfriend. Apparently, the boy was jealous of his mother's new beau, so he killed them both with an axe."

"Yes, I remember seeing that story on the news."

"Did any of you notice anything else out of the ordinary, other than the blood and the bodies?" Martinelli asked the two men.

"Captain, when Cheng and I got there, we immediately noticed the smell of the bodies. Also, it was cold in the house; as if the killer knew to turn down the thermostat to preserve the bodies and keep the odors down as long as possible, sir," Gonzalez stated to the captain.

"Ok, Mr. Harris, I think you should go check yourself into a hotel until the forensics team is done with their investigation. We'll let you know if there's anything else that we may need from you," Martinelli told him.

"Can I please just get my luggage that I left by the front door of my home?" Nathan asked.

"I'm very sorry, Mr. Harris. But until this crime scene investigation is complete, no one or nothing goes in or out of that house, not even your car."

"My *Lincoln? Why?*"

"What if someone planted a time-bomb in your vehicle to get *you* out of the way *too?* I don't want that hanging over my head, would you?"

"No, I suppose not," Nathan somberly replied.

"Good, now that that's settled, Detective Gonzalez will drive you to whatever hotel you want to go to in town," the captain stated.

*
**

Detective Gonzalez took Nathan Harris out of the police station and back into his car. Nathan got in the back seat and asked Gonzalez to take him to the Solville Hotel. Nathan knew the accommodations were acceptable there, but he had a feeling the captain and the detective both suspected him of murdering his wife and daughter. *They always suspect the spouse first, that's a given,* Nathan thought to himself.

CHAPTER 3

THE BASEMENT

eather Harris was completely naked, straddling Nathan, with her breasts hanging right over his face. She was riding him like a top jock riding a prized racehorse in the Belmont Stakes. Nathan was enjoying the ride, but his exhaustion was slowly getting the best of him. The scientist and inventor was gradually falling asleep while his wife was making love to him. Heather became furious after seeing her husband close his eyes to her. Then, Nathan started to snore.

"Nathan! Wake up! How could you fall asleep on me?! You sonofabitch! Do I bore you that much?!" Heather screamed at him.

"Heather, I, I'm sorry, but I'm very tired," Nathan replied while yawning.

Heather was so hurt that she slapped her husband in the face, got off of him, and cried herself to sleep. Nathan had tried to console her, but she just pushed him away from her. The man had so much on his mind that he simply succumbed to his own weariness and fell asleep.

**

Nathan Harris had just woken up in his hotel room from his very vivid dream. *Was it just a dream? Is Heather still alive?* Nathan mentally asked himself. However, after looking around at his surroundings, the man tried to come to terms with the reality of what *really* happened to his family. Nathan *did* know that he was in a hotel room while the police investigation continued, but Nathan *still* couldn't process the fact that he would never, ever see his beloved wife and daughter again.

"Are they really dead? Was my whole family brutally murdered? No, it can't be. I cannot believe it. I mustn't believe it. They'll be back; I must have faith in that," Nathan said to himself in complete denial.

Nathan quickly understood that the dream he just had was a flashback of a scene that actually transpired; that night was the last time he had seen his wife alive. Nathan never did see his wife again before he left that morning for his seminar in Oregon. *I left so early in the morning and from downstairs in the lab; she was probably still sleeping when I walked out the door,* he thought to himself. Nathan looked at the digital clock on the nightstand and noticed it was eight o'clock in the morning. Suddenly, the hotel desk phone started ringing.

"Hello," Nathan asked while picking up the phone.

"Good morning Mr. Harris, this is Detective Gonzalez, how are you making out?" Gonzalez asked him.

"I'm surviving," Nathan replied.

"Good. Listen, we would like to conclude our investigation in your house, but my team can't get into one area of your home. Can you please give us the keys or the combination?"

"What area of the house are you talking about, Juan?"

"The basement, Mr. Harris. We need access to the footage from your security cameras."

"My laboratory? I'm afraid it doesn't open up like that, Juan. I have to be physically present to open it up for you. My lab is fitted with a lot of hi-tech security measures to protect all my research and experiments. All of my top-secret inventions are down there, so, I keep it off limits to everyone."

"Well, we *still* need to look down in there, Mr. Harris."

"Ok Juan, I understand, but you won't find the DVR from the security system down there. I'll have to show you where it is. Let me just get dressed and then I'll call a cab and meet you there in about an hour.

Is that fair enough?"

"Ok Mr. Harris, we'll be waiting for you," the detective said before hanging up.

Nathan hung up the phone, went to the bathroom, and started to wash up. He didn't have any other clothes except what he came there with. *I've been stuck in this hotel for about two days now, I thought they were done, damn,* the scientist thought to himself. Nathan brushed his teeth, got dressed, and called for a taxicab.

*
**

About an hour later, Nathan was getting out of the yellow cab in front of his mansion. He tipped the driver and walked up his brick pathway. Nathan noticed how warm it had gotten outside. *It's nice out, the sun is really shining bright for a January morning; a far cry from all that snow we've been having,* he thought. Nathan assumed that Gonzalez was off on Saturdays, but he was obviously wrong about that. *Maybe he's working some overtime,* the scientist wondered. Detective Gonzalez was waiting there for him at the front door.

"Hello Mr. Harris, we've been expecting you," Detective Gonzalez stated.

"Good morning, Juan. It pains me to come back here, but I know I have to face it sooner or later. How's it going?" Nathan asked him.

"We're getting there, slowly but surely, but we need access to downstairs."

"I know, that's what I'm here for."

Nathan walked into his mansion with the detective close behind him. Gonzalez noticed that Mr. Harris was still wearing the same navy-blue suit he wore two days ago. Gonzalez thought that Mr. Harris would have stopped by a store to pick up some new clothes while he was staying at the hotel. *I guess he's too devastated to even think about that,* Gonzalez thought. The detective was wearing his new dark-gray business suit; he had just picked it up on sale at the local department store in Solville.

Nathan decided to go to the ground-floor bathroom to relieve himself first; he noticed the bodies of his wife and daughter were gone from where they were. Tears started to flow from his eyes as he relieved himself. *They can't be dead. I remember seeing their bodies, but I still can't believe they're really gone forever,* Nathan sadly thought.

***

A few minutes later, Nathan Harris, Officer Cheng, and Detective Gonzalez were down in the basement near a large steel door. There was an electronic control panel next to the door with a handprint scanner attached to it. Above the control panel was a retina scanning device with a closed-circuit TV camera and microphone right above it. The area was also equipped with thermal heat sensors. Detective Gonzalez marveled at the hi-tech security system that was present there in the scientist's home.

"I would expect this kind of security equipment in a bank or some kind of secure headquarters, but not in a home, Mr. Harris," Gonzalez stated.

"This is my place of business; it's my laboratory, Juan," Nathan replied to him.

Nathan placed his right hand on the handprint scanner and waited for the computer to respond. The security system sounded an approval tone with its accompanying message on the screen that said, "PLEASE SCAN YOUR EYES." Nathan looked into the scanner and waited for the machine to respond.

"Good morning Mr. Harris, please verify your name and code number for voiceprint analysis," the computer said in an electronic female voice.

"My name is Nathan Harris, code number 917661212," Nathan replied to the machine.

"You may enter now, Mr. Harris," the computer said while unlocking and slowly opening the heavy steel security door that was motorized.

"Wow, all that just to get inside here," Gonzalez said.

"I told you I had to be present to open up my lab," Nathan told the detective.

The three men walked through the open door and down the hallway. When they arrived at the gymnasium, the detective stopped to marvel at the facilities. Gonzalez looked like a little boy on Christmas morning. The detective admired all of the workout equipment in the large, brightly lit room. He stared at the four huge professional treadmills, the four exercise bicycles, and the four rowing machines. There was one type of exercise equipment for each family member, plus a spare unit, just in case. The room also had an assortment of weights, four elliptical trainer machines, and a host of some other equipment he never even knew existed. Truly, the personal gym would rival any sports center in town.

Photo courtesy of Denys Gromov

"Man, you've got *everything* down here! All the same equipment that the local fitness centers would have in their facilities. Where do I sign up?" Gonzalez said jokingly.

"I take it that you approve of my private gym," Nathan replied.

"Approve, are you kidding? I love it, but, where's the lab, Harris?"

"Down this way, gentlemen."

The three men left the gym and kept walking down the long hallway. They finally came across another steel door that was locked with another hi-tech electronic lock. Nathan placed his hand on the hand scanner and waited for the computer to respond. The security system sounded an approval tone with its accompanying message on the screen that said, "PLEASE SCAN YOUR EYES." Nathan looked into the scanner and waited for the machine to respond.

"Good morning Mr. Harris, please verify your name and code number for voiceprint analysis," the computer said in an electronic female voice.

"My name is Nathan Harris, code number 917661212," Nathan replied to the machine.

"You may enter now, Mr. Harris," the computer said while unlocking and slowly opening the heavy steel security door that was motorized, with a loud buzzer alert sounding.

"Right this way, gentlemen," Nathan said while he escorted the detective and the police officer into his laboratory.

"*¡Ay Dios Mío!*" Detective Gonzalez said in complete wonder.

"*Man,* this is sick," Officer Cheng added.

"Welcome to my lab, gentlemen. This is where all of my inventions are created."

Gonzalez was shocked at all of the expensive equipment the scientist and inventor had acquired over time. The large, light-gray room had everything a fully loaded machine shop contained, plus elaborate computer and robotic systems. There were large computer monitors mounted on the front wall, resembling a modern television studio control room.

Photo courtesy of TommL

A sophisticated vision system, complete with two robotic arms were on one bench. A large computer numerical control router was in the left corner of the room. The scientist also had a computer-controlled laser cutting and shaping machine.

Photo courtesy of Tima Miroshnichenko

There was a large chemical vat that stood in the right corner of the room. Nathan also had an assortment of test tubes with chemicals in them. Detective Gonzalez noticed a camcorder that was up on a tripod near an equipment counter. In the middle of the back wall stood Nathan's newest invention, his time travel machine.

Photo courtesy of SpicyTruffel

"What's that contraption, Mr. Harris? It looks like something from the TV show *Star Trek*," Detective Gonzalez asked with extreme curiosity.

"It's my latest invention, Juan, but I'm afraid it's top secret," Nathan replied.

The time machine took up a great portion of the back wall in the room. The contraption, which was shaped like a tube, stood from the floor up, almost touching the ceiling. It featured retractable cylindered doors that were made of stainless-steel and were powered by powerful motors. The machine had a circular step-up platform with built-in lights and sensors. There was a touchscreen computer panel with a hand scanner mounted on the back wall of the machine. The ceiling of the unit had electrodes protruding from it. Various cables and hoses were attached from the unit to a computer console located directly in front of the machine. The entire unit was made from stainless-steel and a composite compound. Detective Gonzalez got closer to the machine and tried to analyze it.

"That's some piece of equipment you have there, Mr. Harris," Gonzalez stated.

"Yes, I know," Nathan responded.

"So, you can't tell me what it does?"

"You'll be the first to know, when it's functioning, but right now, it's just a non-functioning prototype."

"Come on now, Mr. Harris, you've *got* to give me more than *that*. After all, I *am* investigating a double homicide here."

"All right then, Juan, you've twisted my arm, it's a time travel device," Nathan begrudgingly said, knowing he really didn't have much of a choice.

"A time machine? Come on now, what are you playing here, Doc Brown?" Gonzalez jokingly asked him.

"Who's Doc Brown?" Officer Cheng asked.

"You've never seen *Back to the Future*, Cheng?" Gonzalez asked with a chuckle.

"No, I haven't. Is it a new movie?" Cheng asked inquisitively.

By now, Detective Gonzalez and Nathan were both trying their best not to laugh at the young police officer, but unfortunately, the two of them were losing their composure, fast.

"No? I guess it's before your time, man. Those movies came out over thirty years ago. The first one, which was the best, came out in 1985. Why don't you go stream it, Cheng?" Gonzalez said laughingly.

"It came out in 1985? Shit, that's before I was even born. Was it in color or black and white?" Cheng asked.

"You better stop, man. Come on now, black and white in 1985, really? Shit, you don't get out much, do you? So, Mr. Harris, do you really think that gizmo will take you back in time?" Gonzales asked while turning his attention over to Nathan.

"I hope so, Juan, but so far it's been a miserable failure," Nathan answered.

"Well, you let me know if and when you've got it up and running; I'd sure as hell like to see it in action," Gonzalez said with a chuckle.

"I'll let you know, but It'll be a while, there's a lot of bugs I've got to get out of it. Oh, and by the way guys, this *is* a top-secret experiment, no one knows it exists, so keep this under your hats, will you please?" Nathan pleaded.

"You've got it, Mr. Harris, no one will ever know about it, at least from us. By the way, that camera over there, is it recording anything?" Gonzalez asked while pointing to the camcorder up on the tripod.

"I only put it on when I'm down here documenting my work."

Detective Gonzalez went over to the camcorder and checked it out. He searched for the compartment that would hold a tape cassette.

"Where's the tape?" Gonzalez asked.

"There is no tape. It uses a flash memory card," Nathan replied.

"Well, where is it?"

"Like I said before, Juan, it's only on when I'm down here working, after that I take the card with me."

"I see…"

"You forgot? I was away for a couple of days, Juan. Why would I leave my work camera on? Nobody can get in or out of here without me—I'm sure you know that by now—and even if they could, I would have gotten a text from my security system, and you would have gotten an automated robocall from it."

"Your insurance man said the front door wasn't locked and the security system was unarmed, at least when we arrived here."

"Yes, that's true, however, my lab has a separate security system that arms itself automatically whenever I leave here. These doors down here are all six-inch-thick steel vault type doors with three-inch-thick locking bolts on all sides, including the ceiling and the floor. Also, if you noticed, there are no windows down here. So, you see, gentlemen, it's almost impossible to break in here; for all intents and purposes, my lab is impenetrable."

"You've thought of everything, haven't you, Mr. Harris? Everything except the safety of your wife and daughter," Officer Cheng said sarcastically.

"I beg your pardon, officer, are you saying my work here is more important than my family? How rude!" Nathan said while raising his voice and feeling insulted.

"All right gentlemen, cool it! We're not here to pass judgment about how you protect your family, Mr. Harris, we're here to gather all the facts, right, Officer Cheng?" Gonzalez added.

"Yes, Detective," Officer Cheng solemnly responded, knowing he was way out of line.

"Ok, well it looks like we're done here, except just one more thing, Mr. Harris," Detective Gonzalez said.

"What's that, Juan?" Nathan asked him.

"I noticed you have security cameras on the main floor of this house, also outside the perimeter of it. Are those cameras active? Also, are they hooked up to the recording device you mentioned earlier?"

"The cameras are functioning, but the recorder isn't. I was supposed to call it in for service, but with my trip and the preparation for my seminar, I guess I forgot."

"Where is the recorder located? I thought you'd have it down here."

"It's upstairs in my bedroom closet, hidden on a shelf."

"May we see it, Mr. Harris?"

"Sure, Juan. Come on gentlemen, let's go back upstairs, shall we?"

*
**

A few minutes later, Nathan Harris, Detective Gonzalez, and Officer Cheng were all upstairs in the master bedroom suite of the mansion. Nathan escorted the two men toward his closet and opened up the door. Nathan tried his best to ignore the blood that was still all over the place. He pressed a hidden button behind the molding and a small, motorized shelf came down from the ceiling. Nathan pointed to the digital video recorder up on the shelf of his closet. Detective Gonzalez looked at the machine and the small LCD monitor that was next to it.

"Wow, no wonder we couldn't find it. We need to see all of its footage, Mr. Harris," Gonzalez told him.

"I told you it doesn't work; it hasn't worked in a while," Nathan stated.

"Mr. Harris, I want to take that machine downtown with us so my guys could have a look at it. It's possible there might be some footage on it, possibly footage of our killer," Gonzalez told him.

"Ok, but I don't think you'll get anything worthwhile from it, since it won't even boot up."

"Let us be the judge of that, please."

Detective Gonzalez reached up to the shelf in the closet and grabbed the security DVR. Gonzalez unplugged all the cables from the machine and handed it over to Officer Cheng.

"How come you don't have that recorder locket up downstairs in your lab with all the other stuff you've got down there? Wouldn't it be

41

more convenient to you?" Officer Cheng asked.

"It would be more convenient, but not practical. You see, Officer, I'm the only one here that has access to the lab, as you very well saw for yourselves. If I'm not present here, then the security techs wouldn't be able to service the system; that's why it's up here, instead," Nathan responded.

"Your wife didn't even have access to the lab?"

"No one did, not even my daughter, but when we were both home and I was down there, I usually left the doors open for them, just in case any of them wanted to come downstairs to see me. My wife or the maid would usually just call me on the whole house intercom system for dinner, or anything else, unless of course I told them that I didn't want to be disturbed."

"I see," the officer responded.

"So, gentlemen, when may I be able to return to my home? I've got a lot of work to catch up on," Nathan said while looking at the detective and the police officer.

"Probably by tomorrow, Mr. Harris. We'll let you know," Detective Gonzalez stated.

"I'm gonna need time to bury my family, too. Where did you take them?" Nathan asked him.

"The bodies are down in the morgue being examined, Mr. Harris, I'm sorry."

"You're performing an autopsy on them?"

"That's correct, Mr. Harris, given the nature of their deaths, it had to be done."

"I completely understand, Juan. So, am I still considered a suspect?"

"No sir, not at this time. You *are* a person of interest, though, and I *do* advise you not to leave town, Mr. Harris."

"Understood, Juan. Don't worry, I'm not going anywhere."

"You may return back to the hotel, for now, Mr. Harris. Would you like me to call you a cab?"

"Thanks, Juan, I'd appreciate that," Nathan replied.

Nathan didn't believe the detective. *If I'm not a suspect, then why can't I leave town?* Nathan mentally asked himself. The scientist was upset; he wanted to return back to his home. *If I could just get that damn Time Transporter running, maybe, just maybe I could go back in time and find the real killer,* Nathan thought. *Perhaps I could save them.* He missed his wife and daughter dearly. *Now I have no one, no one at all. My beautiful wife and daughter are both gone. I still cannot believe it.*

The scientist and inventor wondered why his family had been targeted. *Who knows, the killer could have really been after me? Why didn't the murderer just ask for a ransom? I would have paid anything to spare their lives, especially my only daughter, Alice,* Nathan sadly wondered. The scientist felt guilty for leaving them all alone. *Maybe if I were here instead of being at that seminar, this could have all been avoided and I would still have my family with me.* The scientist sat down on the chair in the vestibule and waited for the cab to come pick him up; as he waited, the tears started to stream down from his eyes.

CHAPTER 4

EVIDENCE OF MURDER

𝕸onday morning, January twenty-third, Nathan Harris was finally allowed to go back home to his mansion. Detective Juan Gonzalez had called him earlier and gave him the okay. Gonzalez had also reminded him about not leaving town. Nathan was relieved he was able to go back to his home, however, the scientist and inventor was also worried about being accused of murder. *They're going to be watching my every move,* he nervously thought to himself. *How the hell am I supposed to get on with my experiments with that hanging over my head?* Nathan asked himself. He finished washing up in the bathroom and was getting dressed to leave the hotel.

*
**

Across town at the Solville Police Department, Detective Juan Gonzalez was in Captain Paul Martinelli's office. Gonzalez suspected Nathan Harris of murder, but the captain could not believe it.

"You've got this guy so high up on a pedestal that you won't even consider the fact that he may be guilty of murder," Gonzalez angrily stated.

"You'd better have all of your damn facts right, before you go and accuse the richest and most well-respected man in town of murder. Nathan Harris is also the most generous philanthropist I know. Why, just look at all he's done for this town and this here police department," Martinelli shot back in disgust.

"I know all about that, Captain, but—"

"You also forgot the fact that the man wasn't even in town, or even in this *state*, when the murders occurred, Gonzalez."

"Captain, his daughter's body was locked up in an antique grandfather clock, which *he* had the keys for, upstairs in his bedroom on a hook. Do you think a perpetrator would have gone through all that? How did the murderer even know where the key was?"

"You said so yourself, it was out in the open, labeled and on a plaque with other keys. The killer found the perfect hiding place for both bodies to buy him some time," Martinelli said in Nathan's defense.

"Did you even see the autopsy report on the bodies, Captain?" Gonzalez asked him.

"I just got it on my desk this morning; I didn't get a chance to read it yet."

"Well, *I* did. Mrs. Harris was stabbed sixteen times. She had multiple stab wounds on her right breast, stomach, both legs, and then, the final blow that killed her, a twisted stab in her heart, as if the killer was trying to cut out her heart while it was still beating. This was no ordinary murder, Captain, this was a crime of passion and pure hatred for the woman."

"Jesus H. Christ!"

"It has all the earmarks of a murder from someone very close to her, someone that despised her, someone that really wanted her out of the way, like, her spouse."

"There you go again, accusing Mr. Harris."

"Look at the report if you don't believe me, Captain; it's all there in black and white!"

"What about his teenage daughter Alice?"

"According to the autopsy report, she died from blunt force trauma to the back of her skull. Forensics found some blood and hair on the armoire dresser that matched hers. I think she simply just got in the way, probably trying to protect her own mother from the perpetrator. When Alice was trying to defend her mother, the killer must have thrown her toward the wall, but instead, she struck the corner of the armoire, killing her instantly."

"Shit, what a shame, what a waste; she had her whole life ahead of her," Martinelli said in sorrow.

"It sure is, Captain, it sure is."

"I *still* don't believe Nathan Harris killed his own family. That man doesn't have a nefarious bone in his body, at least none that I've ever seen. Nathan loved his wife and daughter. I've seen them together plenty of times and you could see the love they had for each other. I'm not trying to sound corny here, but, if you've seen them together, you'd know what the hell I'm talking about, Gonzalez," Captain Martinelli said empathetically.

"Anyone's capable of murder if they're pushed too far, Captain, anyone."

"What about that DVR from his house; was there anything on it?"

"The last recording on that machine was on January 7, over a week before the murders, Captain."

"What was the estimated date and time the two females were killed?" Martinelli asked him.

"The medical examiner had stated—going by postmortem, lividity, rigor mortis, and the decomposition of tissue—that both, Heather and Alice Harris, were murdered between fifty-four and fifty-seven hours from the time he arrived at the Harris's residence. That puts it in the timeline that Mr. Harris may *still* have been home, before he left for his trip to Oregon."

"That means that they were probably already dead when you first arrived at the scene."

"Yeah, when that insurance broker was there. Also, it appears that Mrs. Harris had sex before she was killed. There was evidence of semen in her reproductive tract; we sent it out for DNA testing. Both bodies were moved downstairs almost immediately after they were killed."

"I guess we're going to need a DNA sample from Mr. Harris," Martinelli said while looking down to the floor of his office.

"That's for sure. Now here's the other thing, Captain, the grandfather clock had stopped at 4:49, probably the time young Alice Harris was stuffed into the clock."

"Nathan Harris claims he left the house around five o'clock Tuesday morning, January seventeen. There are still a few variables here, Gonzalez."

"Such as…"

"Well, for starters, the grandfather clock is an antique; being an antique and not modern or digital, it's a twelve-hour clock. It stopped at 4:49, but that doesn't tell us if it was a.m. or p.m. Also, since it's an antique mechanical clock, we don't even know how close it really was to the actual time. We don't know its accuracy. It could have been off an hour or more. I still can't see Mr. Harris killing his wife and daughter, taking the time to stuff one of them in a sofa, the other in a clock, and then rushing to catch a plane to Oregon without any remorse whatsoever."

"I think the evidence of the murders speaks for itself, Captain. We have to go by what the medical examiner stated and the timeline he gave us," Gonzalez added.

"If that's the case, then we have to assume that the grandfather clock did *indeed* stop at 4:49 in the morning; the time poor young Alice Harris was stuffed inside the old clock," Captain Martinelli added.

"Which means that Mr. Harris could have murdered his wife and daughter before leaving for his trip to Oregon."

"Let's not go jumping to conclusions until we have all the facts in. Remember, we're talking about Nathan Harris here; the biggest philanthropist in town, and one of our biggest benefactors. Bring Mr. Harris back in here for a DNA sample."

"Ok, Captain, you got it," Detective Gonzalez said before he left the captain's office.

*
**

A few miles away, Nathan Harris had just arrived back at his home. He stood there in the large vestibule and looked right up at the staircase.

"Honey, I'm home!" Nathan announced himself in the empty mansion.

Nathan walked into the parlor, still not coming to complete terms of the murder of his wife and daughter. He stared at the family portrait that hung above the fireplace. He particularly noticed the face of his late wife, which was slashed up in the painting. *Who would do such a thing?* Nathan thought as the tears welled up in his eyes again. The scientist was recalling happier times with his family until he heard the unmistakable sound of his front doorbell playing Westminster chimes through its large tubular bells.

Someone's at the door; I wonder who that could be? Nathan asked himself.

Nathan walked over toward the front door. He looked out through the sidelight window and noticed Detective Juan Gonzalez standing there. *What's he want from me now?* Nathan asked himself. The scientist and inventor begrudgingly opened up his front door.

"Hello Juan, what can I do for you?" Nathan asked.

"Hello Mr. Harris. You can call me Detective Gonzalez."

"Detective Gonzalez? Wow, I see things have changed, haven't they?"

"Let's just keep it professional and respectful, Mr. Harris, ok?" Gonzalez asked.

"Ok, Detective Gonzalez, what may I owe the pleasure of this visit?" Nathan asked him with suspicion on his mind.

"I need you to come downtown with me to give us a DNA sample, please," Gonzalez stated in a matter-of-fact tone.

"Wow, you really *do* suspect me."

"We just want to cover all bases, Mr. Harris, nothing personal."

"All right then, let me grab my coat and we can go."

*
**

A while later, Nathan was back at the police station, giving them a DNA sample. Captain Martinelli personally came over to thank Nathan for his cooperation in this matter. The captain also assured Nathan that he wasn't a suspect as of yet, but he was only a person of interest. Nathan, however, wasn't buying it, at all. The scientist knew he was going to have to consult with his attorney, even though Captain Martinelli told him that it wasn't necessary as of yet.

"Look, I swear to you, I didn't kill my wife and daughter. I wouldn't harm one strand of hair on them. I loved them both very much with all my heart, you both know that, don't you?" Nathan sympathetically asked the captain and the detective.

"Nathan, I personally don't believe you would be capable of doing anything wrong to your family, but we have to follow our protocols, you understand, *right?*" Captain Martinelli asked him.

"I suppose so. You're only doing your job. Please, don't stop looking for the *real* killer."

"Don't worry, Mr. Harris, we won't," Gonzalez said.

*
**

49

A little over a week later, Wednesday morning, February first, Captain Martinelli was in his office looking at the DNA reports that had just arrived. The captain was stunned at what the report from the lab had stated. He decided to call Detective Gonzalez into his office.

"Gonzalez, come into my office please," Martinelli asked over the intercom on his desk.

"I'll be right in, Captain," Gonzalez replied.

Martinelli kept staring at the findings in the report. He couldn't believe what it had revealed. The captain kept flipping through the pages until Gonzalez walked in.

"You wanted to see me, Captain?" Gonzalez asked him.

"Yes, Gonzalez, I've been looking through the DNA report on Mrs. Heather Harris," Martinelli stated, while he was still feeling shocked.

"When did it come in?"

"Just a little while ago."

"How come I didn't get a copy?"

"Because *I'm* the captain and you're a detective."

"Touché, Captain. So, what does it say? Was I right about Mr. Harris?"

"I think you'd better bring him in again, Gonzalez."

"You got it, Captain, I'll go get him," Gonzalez happily stated while leaving the captain's office.

*
**

Later in the morning, Nathan Harris was in his laboratory working on his newest invention, the Time Transporter. All of a sudden, one of his closed-circuit television monitors on the wall lit up with an image of Detective Gonzalez, ringing his front doorbell.

Oh, shit, what the hell does he want from me now? Nathan asked himself.

The scientist reached over the console to press the intercom button.

"I'll be there in a moment, Detective," Nathan said over the intercom.

Nathan started shutting down his equipment. He took the flash memory card out of the camcorder and put it in his pocket. The scientist and inventor walked out of his laboratory while the motorized doors started closing behind him. He walked up the stairs and went toward the front door. Nathan casually opened up the door and was greeted by Detective Gonzalez.

"Good morning Mr. Harris, I'm afraid I have to bring you back downtown again," the detective stated in a matter-of-fact tone.

"What is it this time, Juan? Did you find the *real killer yet?*" Nathan asked him.

"I think we did, Mr. Harris. The captain wants to see you at the station."

"All right, let me grab my coat and we can go."

*
**

A few minutes later at the police station, Detective Gonzalez escorted Nathan Harris into Captain Martinelli's office again. Nathan took a seat in front of the captain's desk and anxiously waited for him to speak. Martinelli put the DNA report he was holding back down onto his desk.

"Mr. Harris, besides you, did you know if your wife had another lover?" Martinelli asked.

"What?! What are you saying, Captain?!" Nathan shouted.

"I'm saying, Mr. Harris, there was evidence of semen in your wife's reproductive tract. We sent it out for DNA testing; it's not yours."

"My God, are you saying what I think you're saying? My wife was cheating on me?"

"I'm sorry, Mr. Harris, but please, just answer the question. Did your wife have an affair—"

"No, not that I know of," Nathan angrily interrupted.

"Ok, also, the blood that was all over Mrs. Harris wasn't all hers. There was some blood and tissue on her fingernails that matched with her lover. Mrs. Harris could have either tried to defend herself, or she could have clawed her lover's back during sex."

"Excuse me, Captain, are you saying that there was someone else present during the murders?" Detective Gonzalez asked.

"I'm saying that Mrs. Harris knew who her assailant was. I don't know if her daughter knew him; I think she just got in the way, unfortunately," Martinelli replied.

"Do you know what the killer's motive was, Captain?"

"I think that maybe Mrs. Harris was going to break it off with her lover, but he wasn't quite ready to let go of her. The two of them probably started arguing, and then it became heated. Alice must have heard them, and knowing her mother was in danger, she tried to break it up. Our killer, in a fit of rage, simply just threw poor Alice toward the wall, except she missed the wall and went straight into the corner of the armoire dresser, cracking her skull and killing her instantly. At least that's the way I see it."

"Captain, what about the timeline the medical examiner gave us?" Gonzalez asked him.

"I thought about that, Gonzalez. The killer could have already been around the Harris residence, waiting for Mr. Harris to leave for his trip."

By this time, Nathan Harris had buried his head into his hands and began to weep. Detective Gonzalez didn't expect this outcome. He thought for sure that Nathan Harris was the murderer. Martinelli and Gonzalez both knew that they had a vicious killer on their hands who had to be found and brought to justice.

"Mr. Harris, I think I owe you an apology," Gonzalez somberly stated.

"You sure do, Gonzalez," Captain Martinelli added.

Nathan Harris picked his head up from his hands, wiped his tears, and looked at the detective.

"It's all right, Juan, you were just doing your job," Nathan tearfully said to him.

"Mr. Harris, can you possibly think of anyone that was really close to your wife, anyone that she might have invariably mentioned to you?" Martinelli asked him.

"My wife knew a lot of people, Captain. I can't say for sure who she was really close to; I thought it was me. I thought I knew her well. I guess I was wrong, dead wrong," Nathan painfully replied.

"Ok, Mr. Harris, I see how painful this is to you. No one ever wants to hear about their spouse having an affair," Martinelli sincerely added.

"I thought she was happy with me. I let my work get ahead of me. I guess I should have spent more time with her and my daughter. This could have been prevented," Nathan softly said as the tears were beginning to fall again from his eyes.

"No one knows for sure why these things happen, Nathan. You're a well-known scientist and inventor. You've got plenty of obligations on your plate. You can't split yourself and be in two places at the same time. Listen, I'll let you know if I come up with anything and you do the same."

"Thanks, Paul. If I can think of anybody, I'll let you know."

"Ok. Gonzalez, take Mr. Harris back home, please."

"You've got it, Captain," Gonzalez replied.

Detective Gonzalez escorted Nathan to his white Ford Taurus and they both left the police station. Captain Martinelli was relieved that the new evidence had now presumably found Nathan Harris innocent of the crimes. The captain didn't really want to implicate Nathan in the murders of his wife and daughter. Now, the question was, who *really* killed Mrs. Harris and her daughter?

*
**

Shortly after, Detective Gonzalez was pulling up into the long circular driveway of the Harris mansion. Nathan was sitting in the back of the white four-door sedan, not quite ready to leave yet. Gonzalez stopped the car and looked up at the sky.

"It looks like it's going to snow again, Mr. Harris," Gonzalez stated.

"I sure hope not, Juan. I need to hire a new groundskeeper," Nathan replied.

Nathan got out of the car and closed the door. He thanked the detective and walked toward his front door. Nathan thought about going back to his laboratory, but he decided to change his mind. *I'd better not go down there right now*, the scientist thought. *I'm not really in the right frame of mind. I might screw everything up.*

Nathan kept thinking about how his wife had cheated on him. *I gave her everything I owned. How could she have done this shit to me?* Nathan mentally asked himself.

The scientist opened up his front door, walked inside, and closed the heavy wooden door behind him. Nathan looked around the empty mansion, expecting his wife and daughter to greet him. Suddenly, the loneliness crept up on him, as tears welled up in his eyes again. Nathan finally realized that his wife and daughter were never ever coming to greet him again.

CHAPTER 5

THE TIME TRANSPORTER

Thursday morning, February second, Nathan Harris had just woken from a very nice dream about his late daughter, Alice. It was more of a memory from the past than just a dream. Nathan had recalled the day that he and Alice were trying to crack open geode stones on his workbench, down in the basement. Nathan remembered how hard it was for them to crack open the pretty rocks, as his daughter would call them, but it was *still* quality father-daughter time spent together. *That was such a fond memory; I wish I didn't wake up,* Nathan thought. He went to the bathroom to relieve himself and then Nathan decided to go downstairs to the kitchen, while still in his pajamas, to make some coffee and breakfast. The phone rang, but Nathan wasn't in the mood to answer it; he let the answering machine get it.

"Hello Nathan, it's Doctor Berlin. I heard about your family and it's been a while since we've talked. Please call me at your earliest convenience," the doctor said over the answering machine before hanging up.

I'll call him back later; I've got to get out of here, Nathan thought. The police had finally released the bodies of his wife and daughter to him and Nathan was going to the funeral parlor to say goodbye to them for the last time before the double funeral. He finished his breakfast, washed up, got dressed, and left.

*
**

Later that morning, Nathan Harris was out in the cemetery, listening to the sermon from old Reverend Hollis. He noticed it was a pretty big turnout, despite the cold weather. Light snow had started to

55

fall, and there was a gloomy sky, which made it even more depressing. Nathan noticed that his father-in-law was walking toward him with his wife.

"Hello Nathan," Richard Stevens, Heather's father, said to him.

"Good morning, Mr. and Mrs. Stevens," Nathan solemnly replied.

"I just want to say one thing to you, Nathan."

"What's that, Mr. Stevens?"

"If I ever find out that *you* had anything to do with the death of my daughter *and* my granddaughter, I'll kill you myself," Mr. Stevens seriously told him before grabbing his wife and leaving.

Nathan couldn't believe that his father-in-law accused him of murdering his own wife and daughter. *Wow, I guess I'm guilty before being proven innocent,* he thought. Nathan knew deep down inside that he never had a good relationship with his in-laws.

Nathan noticed a tall and very attractive young blonde looking at him from the back; it was Nancy, his sister-in-law. Nancy was Heather's younger sister, although she was taller than Heather. Nancy always had a crush on Nathan, even before he married her sister. *Uh-oh, time to go,* he thought. Nathan briskly walked over toward his car and left, wanting to avoid another unpleasant confrontation.

*
**

A few hours later, Nathan was back in the laboratory making some modifications to his new invention; he named it the Time Transporter. Nathan made sure he had his camcorder on in front of him to document everything. Nathan figured out that using lasers would facilitate his idea for time travel. The scientist's theory relied on German-born theoretical physicist Albert Einstein, who's theory was that massive objects can indeed bend space-time. Nathan knew that Einstein stated the stronger the gravity, the slower time passes. He figured if you could bend space, you may also be able to twist space. Nathan knew that space also involves time; that's why it's called space-time. Nathan's machine was designed to twist time into a loop, that way, he would be able to travel from the future back into the past, and then, Nathan could go back to the future.

This was his idea of the wormhole; the tunnel would essentially have two openings in it. Nathan had studied the gravitational field that was produced by a halo laser, which utilizes a circulating beam of light. The scientist knew it was the halo laser that could make time travel possible by creating a circulating beam of light that would twist space and time. The heart of Nathan's machine was the halo laser, located in the chamber that was shaped like a tube, with its retractable cylindered doors. The transporter would demolecularize the subject's molecules during transportation and remolecularize them back into the same order upon arrival at the destination. The scientist and inventor also realized the fact that it would take a considerable amount of energy to make everything work as designed.

Nathan Harris idolized Albert Einstein. He knew the German-born theoretical physicist, who died on April 17, 1955, at the age of seventy-six, was a genius. However, Nathan did not want to wind up like him. Nathan could not grasp the fact that the genius had his brain extracted from him by pathologist Thomas Stoltz Harvey during the autopsy, without the permission of his family. *I hope his family sued his ass to the fullest. Imagine doing that just to discover what made Einstein tick, shit,* he angrily thought.

Nathan fired up all of his equipment and set the date dials to January 6, 2000, the day his mother died of pancreatic cancer in a New York hospital. He then set the location to City Medical Center, down in New York City, and the arrival time at 3:15 p.m., just two hours before his mother had slipped into a coma and passed away. Nathan wanted to make this his test journey, before going back to when his family was murdered, a little over two weeks ago.

The scientist and inventor had also devised a remote controller and radio transporter link for his machine in the form of an electronic belt with a built-in halo laser that he would wear. Nathan put on his new, specially designed navy-blue suit with its retractable hood. He had outfitted the suit with an antenna system sewn right into the lining to help the controller belt communicate with his laboratory computer and to facilitate time travel. The remote controller would be able to send and receive location and control signals via satellite to his laboratory computer. The computer would then communicate to the Time Transporter.

The suit and hood, coupled with the controller belt, was really an extension of the transporter chamber; a portable version of the apparatus, but not independent. The belt still needed the laboratory transporter to function. The system also had a fail-safe application that was built in to it. If for whatever reason the Time Transporter lost its signal with Nathan at the preset return time, which he had set for 5:15 p.m., the machine would attempt to initiate his return back to the present.

Nathan walked into the transporter chamber and waited for the retractable cylindered doors to close on him. He powered on his controller belt, reached behind his collar, and pulled up on his retractable hood to cover his head. Nathan placed his hand onto the touchscreen that was mounted on the back wall of the machine.

"Hello Mr. Harris, and welcome aboard," the machine announced in a female robotic voice that eerily sounded like his late daughter Alice.

"Hello Alice, initiate time travel sequence," Nathan replied to the computer, as he put on his dark glasses to protect his eyes from the powerful lasers in the machine.

"Affirmative, Mr. Harris, initiating time travel sequence in ten seconds."

The Time Transporter began its countdown.

"Ten, nine, eight, seven, six, five, four, three, two, one, zero," the computer stated while displaying the numbers on the LCD screen.

The overhead electrodes began to energize, followed by the halo laser that was circulating powerful light rays around him in the tubular chamber. The transporter sounded like the engines whirring on the spacecraft Jupiter 2 from the 1960s sci-fi TV show *LOST IN SPACE*. Nathan Harris felt strange as his body began to demolecularize within the chamber. Within seconds, Nathan's molecules were being transported back to January 6, 2000.

Photo courtesy of Guillaume Meurice

When all of his molecules arrived in the past, they began to remolecularize back in the same exact order. It was like being disassembled and reassembled, all within seconds, and with great precision. The whole process took fifty-five seconds to complete.

59

*
**

Nathan Harris found himself back in the year 2000, over twenty-three years ago. The scientist was standing in front of City Medical Center, down in New York City. Nathan retracted his hood back into his collar and walked into the entrance.

The hospital lobby was painted a sterile white with a décor that was modern for its time. There were no LCD screens on the walls, showing information and ads, like in today's hospitals. He noticed a beautiful young woman with short blonde hair at the information counter. Nathan walked over toward the garbage can by the entrance doors; he noticed that it had a newspaper sticking out of it. Nathan pulled the paper out of the can and read the headline, "APPLE'S INTERIM CEO MAKES IT PERMANENT." Nathan read on to find out the reporter was talking about Steve Jobs announcing that he's back at Apple for good. *Steve Jobs has been dead for over twelve years, now,* he thought. Nathan also noticed some articles about y2k, how everyone was *still* worrying about their computers. Then, the scientist and inventor noticed the date that was printed on the paper. The newspaper had the date of Monday, January 6, 2000, on it.

"Holy shit, I made it! My transporter finally works!" Nathan exclaimed to himself.

Nathan wanted to be sure. He walked on up toward the information desk to ask the young lady at the counter the current date. Nathan had to wait for the woman to get off the phone. While he waited, Nathan noticed the time on the digital wall clock above her. It read 3:17 p.m. The woman finally got off the phone and smiled at him.

"May I help you, sir?" the receptionist asked him.

"Yes, miss, can you please tell me what day it is today?" Nathan asked her.

"Today? Today's Monday, sir. Is there anything else I can help you with?"

"I need the date, miss."

"It's the sixth, January six."

"More importantly, the year, miss, what year is this?"

"Sir, are you feeling all right?" the lady asked him with a concerned look on her face.

"I'm fine, miss, now please humor me and tell me the year," Nathan asked, while running out of patience with her.

"Ok sir, it's 2000, The New Millennium. Are you satisfied now, sir?"

"Yes, yes, I am. Now, can you please tell me what room Alice Harris is in?"

"Are you a relative, sir?"

"Yes, I'm her son."

The receptionist typed a few keys on her computer. She waited for the machine to respond before answering him.

"She's in room 305, but I'm afraid Mrs. Harris isn't doing very well."

"I know, that's why I'm here to see her," Nathan told her.

Nathan thanked the young woman and took the elevator upstairs to the third floor. He looked at the countdown display on his electronic belt. Nathan noticed that he only had one hour and forty-five minutes left before the Time Transporter would initiate his return back to his time, back to the future. *I've wasted too much time already. I have to hurry,* he thought while riding up in the elevator. The elevator stopped on the third floor and opened up its door. Nathan walked out into the corridor and looked for room 305, the room the receptionist said his ailing mother was in.

*
**

61

Back in the future, in Captain Martinelli's office, Detective Gonzalez had just walked in. Gonzalez *still* had a bad feeling about the Harris murders. Something just didn't sit right with him.

"Morning, Captain," Gonzalez said.

"Morning, Gonzalez. What's with the long face?" Martinelli asked him.

"Something's wrong, Captain. This case just seems too cut and dry; I don't buy it."

"You're not talking about the Harris murders again, are you?"

"Yeah, that's right."

"Oh, come on now, don't tell me you still suspect Nathan Harris of murdering his wife and daughter."

"Something's just not right. The pieces don't fit, Captain. For starters, don't you find it a little bit strange that Mr. Harris fired both his maid and his groundskeeper exactly one week before the murders?"

"The thought did come across my mind, Gonzalez, but he explained that. Nathan said—"

"I know, I know, he said they were stealing from him," Gonzalez interrupted him.

"Why don't you go find his maid and groundskeeper and find out what the hell *really* happened? There are two sides to every story, you know."

"I'm right on it, Captain. I'm glad to see we're on the same page."

"Hey, wait, before you go, you were in Nathan's lab, right?"

"Yeah, I was."

"Well, you never told me all the details, like, what's he working on now?"

"Captain, if I told, you wouldn't believe it, besides, he swore me and Cheng to secrecy."

"Oh, come on now, Gonzalez. There are no secrets in this department, especially when it deals with a murder investigation. Now, what the hell is it?"

"All right, Captain, but don't say anything about it to anyone."

"Yeah, yeah, now what the hell is it for Christ's sake?!"

"Well, Harris claims he's working on a time machine," Gonzalez said with a chuckle.

"A what?! Who the hell does he think he is, H. G. Wells?"

"Who's H. G. Wells?"

"I guess that's a little before your time, you young whippersnapper," the chief said with a snicker.

"Now you know how it feels, Detective. I didn't forget when you and Mr. Harris made fun of me in his house," Officer Cheng added while walking into the captain's office with his coffee.

"Oh, shut up and mind your own damn business," Gonzalez said while leaving the captain's office.

"By the way, I watched *Back to the Future*, it was all right!" Cheng shouted as Gonzalez left.

*
**

Back in the past, in the year 2000, Nathan had just entered his mother's room. Alice Harris was hooked up to an IV for fluids. She was also connected to heart monitoring equipment to check her vitals. Nathan looked at his mother laying on the hospital bed in a semiprivate room. Alice had grown thin as her cancer had spread over to her liver. Alice's dyed red hair was going gray, fast. *My God, she looks so frail,* he thought.

"Hello, Momma," Nathan softly said to her.

"Na-than," Alice barely said.

"How are you feeling, Momma?"

"I'm dying; how do you think I feel?"

"Oh, stop it Momma."

"Good Lord, what the hell happened to you? You look like you've aged about twenty years since I last seen you. I don't remember you having crow's feet around your eyes. And do I see some gray hairs on your head?"

"It's stress, Momma. I'm worried about losing you."

"Well, Son, I hate to have to break it to you, but I am dying, you know."

"I know; you've already told me."

"They got me on pain medication. Pancreatic cancer is very painful. I thought you said you couldn't come see me? You said you were giving a seminar at MIT in Massa-chusetts," she struggled to say to her son.

"I was, but I, I left early to, to see you, Mom," Nathan barely said while chocking back the tears.

"Don't cry, Son."

"I love you, Mom. I just wanted to make you proud, that's all I ever wanted to do."

"You've made me very proud, Nathan. I wish your father could have seen how successful you've become, but his heart gave out long ago."

"I know, he died when I was little. I don't remember him as well as I do you, Momma. I do remember one time you two were really fighting, you pushed him up against the wall, it was about William."

"William? Don't you ever mention his name to me again!" Alice hissed and was visibly upset.

"All right, Momma."

"Did you run into your girlfriend? She was just here."

"Heather? Heather was here?"

"Who's Heather? Have you got ano-ther girl-friend? I was talking about Sheryl."

Nathan had to think. He forgot all about Sheryl Fletcher. Nathan lost two important women in his life on that day in 2000. The scientist not only lost his mother, but Nathan had also lost his girlfriend, Sheryl Fletcher. Sheryl got run over by a grief-stricken driver in a freak accident in the hospital parking lot. The driver lost his wife to cancer and was not paying attention to where he was going. Sheryl was hit by him while walking to her car; she died instantly. It took a very long time for Nathan to get over Sheryl's death and to start all over again. Now, Heather and his daughter Alice were both dead too.

"Sheryl was here?" Nathan asked with tears in his eyes.

"That's what I just said, Na-than," his mother faintly responded.

Nathan went over toward the room's window, hoping it would give him a view of the hospital parking lot. Nathan witnessed a bunch of people running over toward a car that was partially overtop someone's body. *Oh, no, I'm too late,* he thought. By now there were doctors and nurses running out into the hallway, with an emergency code being announced over the public address system.

"What's going on, Nathan?" Alice asked her son.

"Nothing, Momma," Nathan said in a soothing voice while returning toward her bed, with tears forming in his eyes.

"Momma, I want to tell you something."

"What is it, Son? I don't think I have much time."

"I just wanted to tell you that I love you, Mom."

"I love you too, but there's something I have to tell you."

"What is it, Momma?" Nathan asked.

Nathan kissed his mother on her forehead, waiting for her to reply. Then the nurse walked into the room. He felt his mother's arms and legs. Nathan turned around toward the young nurse.

"Why is she so cold, nurse?" Nathan asked her.

"Her body's shutting down, sir. Are you her relative?" Nurse Coleman asked him.

"Yes, miss, I'm her son."

"Oh, all right, then I guess you're aware of her condition. Your mom's a very sick woman."

"I know; she's terminally ill. My mother is dying of pancreatic cancer."

"Yes sir, that's right, and it spread to her liver. There's nothing we can do for her except try to keep her as comfortable as possible. I'm sorry."

Nathan looked into the eyes of the attractive young African-American nurse; he could see that she was very sincere in what she was saying. Nathan knew that there was nothing he could do for his ailing mother or his girlfriend. He knew that changing anything in the past could have serious repercussions for the future. Nathan turned back around to face his mother and noticed that her eyes were closed.

"Momma? Are you awake? Can you hear me?" Nathan asked.

"I think she just slipped into a coma, sir," the nurse replied.

Nathan looked at the countdown timer on his remote controller belt. The Time Transporter was set to send him back to the present in two minutes. Nathan knew he didn't have much time left. He kissed his mother on the cheek and whispered, "I love you," to her. Nathan ran out of the hospital room and went down the stairs, knowing that he didn't have time for the elevator. Nathan never found out what his mom was trying to tell him.

The scientist went back outside, to the exact same spot in front of the hospital that the time machine had sent him. The countdown timer started on the remote controller belt. Nathan pulled up on his collar and covered his head with the retractable hood. He stood there, listening to the machine's electronic female voice counting down over the remote controller belt's built-in speaker.

"Ten, nine, eight, seven, six, five, four, three, two, one, zero," the computer stated while displaying the numbers on the belt's LCD screen.

The female receptionist was stepping out for a cigarette break. She watched in awe as Nathan slowly disappeared, right before her eyes. The woman collapsed to her knees and fainted in front of the entrance doors. Nathan had completely dematerialized and was sent back to his time and place in the future.

*
**

Nathan Harris had arrived back to his present time and his laboratory. The scientist was standing in his transporter chamber. Nathan waited for the retractable cylindered doors to reopen. He powered off his controller belt, retracted his hood, and walked out of the transporter chamber.

"I made it back, all in one piece. The Time Transporter is a success!" Nathan happily said to himself.

Then, the scientist and inventor noticed that his equipment was overheating. All of the gauges were in the red-hot zone, especially the transporter itself. He quickly started powering down everything that was associated with the time travel apparatus. Nathan found out that the high-voltage rectifier board was fried. He also noticed smoke was billowing out of the transporter's power supply. *I guess that's fried too,* he thought. Nathan went over to the camcorder up on the tripod.

"Operation time travel to the year 2000 was a complete success. Unfortunately, it appears that some of my equipment may have become damaged due to overheating. I guess I'll just have to install some additional cooling chambers in my time travel controller unit," Nathan said to the camcorder.

Nathan turned off his camcorder and removed the flash memory card. He placed the card in his wall safe where the other ones were. Then, the scientist went over to his black notebook on the counter. Nathan jotted down some notes into his book and then he placed his notebook in the safe and spun the dial to lock it. Nathan picked up the painting of his mother and hung it back up over the wall safe to conceal it. After that, the scientist left the lab and went to take a shower.

While Nathan bathed, Nancy Stevens was ringing his front doorbell.

"Nathan, it's me Nancy, can we talk?! Open up, Nathan, please!" Nancy desperately shouted while pounding on the door.

However, Nathan never heard a word. The scientist decided to take his shower all the way up on the top floor of his mansion. Nathan liked it better up there since that bathroom had a built-in sound system on the wall. Nathan bathed while listening to Bach, oblivious to Nancy's calls.

CHAPTER 6

WHO KILLED THEM?

Monday afternoon, February six, it had been over three days since scientist and inventor Nathan Harris had gone back into the past in the year 2000. He had to do some repairs on his Time Transporter, since some of the components had fried from overheating. The scientist had to locate replacement parts for his transporter. Nathan also needed to add additional cooling to the machine to prevent that from ever happening again. Nathan had replaced the lab circuit breakers in the panel to automatic self-resetting types. He didn't want to be left stranded in the past because of an overload.

∗∗

Detective Gonzalez was back in Captain Martinelli's office. Gonzalez had not yet been successful in interviewing the Harris's maid and groundskeeper.

"Well, what did you get from the hired help over at the Harris residence, Gonzalez?" Martinelli asked.

"Nothing. I can't seem to get ahold of Mr. Harris to ask him where they live," Gonzalez miserably replied.

"Maybe he went away for the weekend, keep trying."

"I've been ringing his doorbell for the past three days, Captain."

"Have you called his house?"

"Yeah, done that too, no answer."

"Offhand, you wouldn't know their names, would you?"

Martinelli asked him.

"I only know that he called the maid Consuelo once when I was there."

"Why don't you try to get ahold of him again today, Gonzalez."

"All right, Captain, I'll give it a shot," Gonzalez said as he exited the captain's office.

*
**

Later that afternoon, Gonzalez was back at the Harris mansion. He got out of his car and was greeted by light snow falling down from the sky. *Shit,* the detective thought. Gonzalez was not keen on driving in the snow. He briskly walked up to the front door and rang the bell. Nathan had just come down the stairs and was heading toward the front door. He looked at the small video monitor that was mounted on the wall near the door. *Oh, shit, he's back. When will he leave me alone?* Nathan asked himself before opening up the front door.

"Juan, what brings *you* back here?" Nathan asked with a surprised look on his face.

"Hello again, Mr. Harris, may I come in?" Detective Gonzalez asked him.

"Sure, Juan, come on in."

Nathan escorted the detective into the parlor, wondering what this was all about. He asked the detective to have a seat on the sofa, but Gonzalez decided to stand instead.

"So, Juan, have you found my wife and daughter's killer yet?" Nathan asked him.

"That's why I'm here, Mr. Harris. I need the names and addresses of your hired help," Gonzalez stated.

"You mean my maid and groundskeeper?"

"That's correct, Mr. Harris. They may have seen something that could point us to our killer."

"I told you and Captain Martinelli that I let them go, before my wife and daughter were killed."

"I know that, but they may still know something, Harris. I have to follow up on any and every lead."

"All right then, let me get my notebook and I'll be right back."

Nathan walked out of the room to get his notebook. Detective Gonzalez looked around the parlor with its dark green carpeting. *Still looks the same,* he thought to himself. *He still kept that torn up picture of his wife; I would have thrown that shit out.* Gonzalez wondered why the scientist really fired all of his help at the same time. It bothered him that Nathan let them both go just before his wife and daughter were brutally murdered. *It's as if he knew something was going to happen to them and he didn't want anyone around to witness it,* the detective thought. Gonzalez also knew that he had to find Mrs. Harris's lover, since he would probably hold a key to her murder. The blood on Mrs. Harris's fingernails would help them identify him, using a DNA analysis.

✳
✳✳

A few minutes later, Nathan Harris came back to see Detective Gonzalez in the parlor. Nathan had a big black notebook in his hands. He opened the book to show Gonzalez the names and addresses of his maid and groundskeeper.

"Here you go, Juan. These are the two people that used to work for me," Nathan said while handing the book over to the detective.

"May I take this with me, Mr. Harris?" Gonzalez asked him.

"No, I'm sorry, Juan, but I need the rest of the information in that book. I can copy that page for you on the Xerox machine I have downstairs, if you want."

"No, that won't be necessary, Mr. Harris. I'll just take a picture of it with my smartphone."

Detective Gonzalez took pictures of a few pages from Nathan's book, and then he handed it back to Nathan. Gonzalez told him he would keep in touch before he walked out the door. Nathan was relieved that he finally left. The scientist was appalled that the police still suspected him. *How rude. After all that I've done for them and the rest of this town, they have the nerve to still interrogate me, instead of searching for the real killer,* Nathan angrily thought to himself.

*
**

Detective Gonzalez was on his way to the home of Consuelo Hernandez, Nathan's ex-maid. The snow was starting to stick, which made the roads a little slippery. Gonzalez was not happy about that.

Consuelo lived in a garden apartment complex on Cranberry Drive, in Cortland. The detective looked at the picture of Nathan's book on his smartphone. *Here it is, 15 Cranberry Drive,* he said to himself. Gonzalez parked his car in the lot and walked over toward the door labeled fifteen. The detective rang the doorbell and waited.

"Who is it?!" Consuelo asked behind the door.

"It's Detective Juan Gonzalez from the Solville Police Department. I'd like to ask you some questions if you don't mind!" Gonzalez shouted through the door.

"Ok, *un momento* please."

Consuelo Hernandez opened up her front door and innocently looked at the detective with her soft brown eyes. Gonzalez never really noticed her, until now. The detective was taken aback by her beauty and charm; he thought she was sweet and petite. The thirty-two-year-old Mexican immigrant had beautiful, long, lustrous black hair and a soft, sweet face. Consuelo also possessed a very shapely but thin body. Gonzalez thought she was very sweet and innocent looking; certainly not the thief that Mr. Harris had recently portrayed her to be.

"May I please come in, Miss Hernandez?" Gonzalez gently asked her.

"*Sí señor,* come in," Consuelo said while smiling at him.

Consuelo ushered the detective into her apartment and closed the door behind him. She led him into the kitchen and sat him down at the table.

"Do you want coffee, I make for you," she said in her broken English.

"No, thank you," the detective replied.

"Ok, we talk."

"You used to work for Nathan Harris, right?"

"*Sí,* used to."

"What happened there?"

"He fire me. He say I steal from him. I no steal from no one, *señor.*"

"Did you ever see Mr. and Mrs. Harris fighting?"

"Only one time, he think she have boyfriend."

"Did you ever see Mrs. Harris with another man?"

"Sí, but she say he just a friend."

"Do you know this man's name?"

"No, I only see him maybe once or twice."

"Can you describe him for me?"

"I no pay attention, not my job, but he young, blond hair, and handsome."

"Do you think you could identify him if you saw him again, or maybe if you saw a picture of him?"

"I think so, but you know, I no think Señora Harris would do anything around me. Maybe she think I tell her husband, you know?"

"*Sí, señora,* let me know if you remember anything, anything that could help us locate him or anybody that was close to Mrs. Harris."

"I see on TV what happen to her. Is very bad what happen to her and her daughter. I hope you find killer," she said with a concerned look on her face.

"I hope so too. Have a good day," the detective said while leaving Consuelo's apartment.

*
**

A half-hour later, Detective Gonzalez was arriving at his next destination, the home of Hector Delgado, the groundskeeper that used to work for Nathan Harris. Gonzalez remembered Hector Delgado; the detective had asked him for advice on planting bushes. Gonzalez recalled what the handsome, young Mexican immigrant looked like. Hector was in his late twenties, with short black hair and a muscular build. *He certainly didn't have blond hair, like the description of the man that Consuelo just gave me,* Gonzalez thought. The detective got out of his white four-door sedan and scanned the seedy urban neighborhood he was in.

"Low-income housing, that's for sure," Gonzalez said under his breath to himself.

He walked into the graffiti-laden courtyard of the old tenement. The detective noted the building number, it was number 60010.

"Yeah, that's it all right, 60010 Maiden Street, in Oakwood," he said to himself.

Gonzalez knew he had to go all the way up to the top floor for apartment 6I; the apartment that Hector Delgado lived in. Gonzalez walked into the lobby of the building. He noted the nice marble and decorative tiles on the walls, with one wall having rows of built-in brass mailboxes for the tenants. *This looks like it was a pretty ritzy building at one time,* he thought. The detective went toward the green elevator door; he pressed the call button and waited. A middle-aged female tenant was coming down the stairs from the second floor. The woman looked at the detective with a smug look on her face.

"Hey mister, don't you know it's out of service, again?" she asked him.

"No, I didn't. I don't live here, miss, but thanks for the tip," Gonzalez angrily stated, knowing he was going to have to walk up six flights of stairs.

*
**

Detective Gonzalez was tired and pissed off. He had climbed up six flights of stairs in the old apartment house.

"*Shit,* the least the superintendent could have done was to put an *out of order* sign on the elevator door," he muttered under his breath.

Gonzalez walked down the corridor looking for apartment 6I. He heard the sound of Merengue music coming from one of the apartments. An old woman stepped out of one of the apartments.

"*Mira, señor,* elevator working?" the old lady asked him, hoping it was.

"No, *señora,*" Gonzalez replied.

He watched the gray-haired old woman slowly begin her journey down the stairwell, wishing there was something he could do for her.

"*Señora,* you need some help?" Gonzalez gently asked her, feeling sorry for her.

"*Gracias, señor, pero,* I ok," the woman said as she continued to walk down the stairs.

The old woman reminded him of his late mother. Gonzalez resumed walking down the hall, looking for apartment 6I. Finally, the detective came across the apartment he was looking for; 6I was further down on the right side of the hall. Gonzalez rang the doorbell and waited.

After waiting a few seconds, he rang the bell again. Gonzalez was getting impatient. He rang the bell a third time while knocking on the door.

"Mr. Delgado, it's Detective Gonzalez from the Solville Police Department! I want to ask you some questions, please!" Gonzalez yelled at the closed door.

Gonzalez rang the doorbell a few more times, and then he gave up. *Sonofabitch, he's not home. I came all this way and up six flights of stairs for nothing,* Gonzalez angrily thought to himself. *I guess I'll have to come back. Hopefully, next time the elevator will be working.* The police detective walked down the hall and took the stairs back down to the lobby.

*
**

Back at the Harris residence, Nathan was back in his lab. The scientist and inventor was rummaging through his spare parts cabinet. He had searched all of the shelves, looking for replacement parts for his new invention, the Time Transporter. Nathan needed components for the high-voltage rectifier board and the power supply. *I think I should replace the heat sinks with larger ones, also larger fans for better cooling,* the scientist thought. Nathan couldn't find everything he needed, so he decided to go online with his computer and shop for electronic parts.

"I sure miss Radio Shack. I used to love to go downtown to that store and get whatever I needed. Now I've got to go on the internet, search for whatever I need, and wait for them to ship it to me," Nathan sadly said to himself.

Nathan continued to search the internet sites for electronic distributors. He finally came across one that looked promising. Nathan started placing items in the shopping cart of the website. When he was through, the total came to $390 plus shipping and tax. Nathan pulled out his credit card and started entering the information into his computer.

"You have *got* to be kidding; these parts are shipping directly from China?! *Man,* it'll take forever to get here with this pandemic still going on!" Nathan yelled out in the laboratory.

Clearly, the scientist was highly upset. Nathan looked at the estimated delivery date. The website said in fine print, on the bottom of the page, that shipments from China take three to four weeks to get to the United States.

"I don't like this one bit, William won't either," Nathan said to himself.

Knowing there wasn't anything else he could do about it, Nathan began cleaning up. He began putting all the parts he didn't need back into the spare parts cabinet. The scientist and inventor methodically started shutting down all of his equipment and left the laboratory.

*
**

On the other side of town, in the Solville Police Department, Detective Juan Gonzalez was back in Captain Paul Martinelli's office. The captain was getting ready to go home. He was shutting down his computer, putting stuff away, and getting his coat. Martinelli was tired; it had been a long day and he just wanted to go home, but unfortunately, Gonzalez was now holding him up.

"Make it fast, Gonzalez. It's after six and I want to get my ass home," Captain Martinelli stated while sounding snippy.

"Ok, Captain. I just want to give you a heads up on my investigations," Gonzalez told him.

"Well, out with it already! Did you interview Mr. Harris's maid and groundskeeper?!"

"The maid, yes. However, I couldn't get ahold of the groundskeeper."

"Oh, come on now, Gonzalez; why the hell not?"

"He wasn't home, Captain."

"Well, keep trying until you find him, all right?"

"You got it, Captain. But don't you want to know what the maid had to say?"

"Well, what did she say, for Christ's sake?"

"Consuelo Hernandez, Mr. Harris's maid, claims she never stole anything from them, and you know what, Captain?"

"What?"

"I believe her, Captain. She seems genuine to me."

"Why, cause she's pretty?"

"She is, but Consuelo just doesn't look like the type that would jeopardize her job for some bullshit. I know temptation's a bitch, but I don't believe that she would be the type to do something like that."

"Well, did Consuelo ever see Mrs. Harris with another man and can she identify him?"

"Well, Consuelo claims that she saw Mrs. Harris once or twice with a young man with blond hair. She said she'd be able to identify him."

"Anything else, before I get out of here?"

"Yeah, Consuelo also stated that she caught the Harris's fighting one time. She thought that Mr. Harris was jealous or something. You know what I think, Captain?"

"What, Gonzalez?"

"I think that Mr. Harris could have caught his wife in bed with her lover and then killed them both in a fit of rage."

"Purely speculation on your part, Gonzalez. You forgot several things in that mix. For starters, if it were true, where's the body of her lover? Also, why would Mr. Harris kill his own daughter? Harris adored his daughter. I've seen them together several times, and a real parent like me could tell there was nothing but fatherly love from him toward his daughter. The other thing is, I don't believe that Mr. Harris knew his wife was having an affair. You saw the way he acted when we told him that.

Harris looked genuinely surprised and shocked. Now, I've got to get the hell out of here. You let me know when you get ahold of his groundskeeper and some real proof, all right?"

"All right, Captain. I'll see you tomorrow," Gonzalez told him.

Detective Gonzalez walked right out of the captain's office and back to his own office. *I can't say shit about Harris to him, boy. In his eyes, Harris is a friken angel,* Gonzalez angrily thought. He started writing some more notes in his notebook. The detective noticed the captain leaving his office with his coat on. *I guess I should be getting ready to go, myself,* Gonzalez thought to himself. Gonzalez grabbed his black winter coat and his black bowler hat, while he left the police station to go home.

"Well, tomorrow's another day," he said to himself while walking out the door.

CHAPTER 7

THE GROUNDSKEEPER

𝕿uesday morning, the seventh day of February, Detective Juan Gonzalez was heading out to the old apartment complex again to see if Mr. Harris's former groundskeeper, Hector Delgado, would be at home. Gonzalez grabbed his gray winter coat and black derby hat as he left the police station. Gonzalez noticed that the roads were finally cleared from the six inches of snow that had accumulated. *Sure, they clean the shit after I struggled to get here this morning,* he angrily thought. The detective decided to stop at the local Dunkin' Donuts to pick up a large coffee and a jelly doughnut to go.

*
**

Detective Gonzalez had finally arrived at the old tenement where Hector Delgado resided. Gonzalez parked his car on the street and then he walked straight through the courtyard and into the lobby. The detective went to the elevator and stopped; there was a sign on the door that read, "Out Of Order."

"Shit! At least this time the asshole has a sign on the door," he angrily said to himself.

Again, Detective Gonzalez had to hoof it and walk up six flights of stairs. The man started to climb up the stairwell while mumbling to himself. *I'm getting too old for this shit,* he thought.

*
**

A few minutes later, Detective Gonzalez had made it up to the top floor. He tried to catch his breath after the six-story journey; clearly the good detective was out of shape. Gonzalez walked past the green elevator door as it started to open. An old man with a cane got off the elevator and looked at him.

"It's working?" Gonzalez asked the man.

"Been working since early this morning," the man replied.

"There was a sign on the door downstairs that said it was out of order."

"That's our super for you, he probably forgot to take it down," the man said while walking down the hall.

This infuriated the detective; the fact that he had to walk up six flights of stairs for absolutely nothing. Gonzalez started walking down the hall again, looking for apartment 6I. As he got closer toward the apartment, the detective heard an angry man yelling and banging on a door.

"Mira señor, you a week late on the rent, let's go!" the man hollered.

Detective Gonzalez overheard the man yelling as he approached Delgado's apartment. Gonzalez got close enough to see that the angry, middle-aged Latino man was banging on the door of apartment 6I, the home of Hector Delgado.

"You're looking for him, too?" Gonzalez asked.

"Sí señor. He a week late on the rent, *Señor* Gomez no like that; he ask me to tell him. You know him, *señor?"* the man asked him while brushing his black hair from his brown eyes.

"Señor Gomez?" Gonzalez asked him.

"No, *Señor* Delgado, the man who live here," the man said as he unzipped his black leather jacket.

"No, I don't. I'm Detective Gonzalez with the Solville Police Department. I came here to question him," Gonzalez stated while showing the man the police badge that was hanging down from his neck.

81

"Oh, is he some kind of trouble?"

"No, it's just routine questioning, that's all. So, you must be the super, right?"

"Si, super. My boss is *Señor* Gomez, the landlord."

"Can I get your name, *señor?*"

"Si, Jose Garcia," he answered while pulling his pants up over his bulging belly.

"Ok, Jose, when was the last time you've seen Mr. Delgado?"

"Maybe three weeks ago, *Señor* Detective," Jose told the detective.

"Ok, it's obvious he's not home. Do you have a key to get into his apartment?"

"No, I don't. Everyone put their own lock on apartment door. They supposed to give me a key for emergency, but not everyone do."

"Ok, here's my card; if you find out anything, including whenever you do see him again, please, call me," Gonzalez told him while giving the man his card.

"Ok *señor,* I will call you when I find him," Jose told the detective.

Detective Gonzalez left the supper and started walking back down the hallway. He went to the green elevator door and pressed the call button. *I've got a bad feeling about this,* Gonzalez thought while waiting for the elevator.

*
**

Nathan Harris was enjoying another vivid dream about his late daughter, until he was rudely awakened by the ringing of the phone on his nightstand. He rolled over on his bed to see the time on his bedside alarm clock.

"Eleven thirty; man, I can't believe it's that late," the scientist said while picking up the black desk phone on the nightstand.

"Hello," Nathan said over the telephone in a very groggy voice.

"Hello Nathan, it's Doctor Berlin. How are you doing?" the doctor asked.

"I'm doing fine, doc. How are you?" Nathan asked him.

"I'm ok. I know you've been through a terribly traumatic experience, losing your wife and daughter like that. I was just wondering how you were making out?"

"I'm fine, although, you just woke me up out of a sound sleep, just to see how I was doing."

"I'm sorry, I didn't think you were still sleeping at eleven thirty in the morning."

"Well, I was," Nathan said with a yawn.

"Ok, Nathan, I'll let you go, but if you ever need anyone to talk to, I'm only a phone call away."

"All right, doc, thanks for calling," Nathan said as he hung up the phone.

Nathan thought about going down to the lab, but decided against it. The scientist was feeling depressed. Nathan knew there wasn't much he could do in the lab without the parts he ordered. *I suppose I should have tried to see who killed my wife and daughter, instead of going back further in time to see my mother; now I'm gonna have to wait till I get those parts,* Nathan sadly thought. Loneliness had grabbed a hold on the good scientist.

*
**

Back at the police station, Detective Gonzalez was reporting his findings with Captain Martinelli. Gonzalez had explained to the captain that Hector Delgado had not been home, again. Gonzalez also told the captain that the building superintendent wasn't able to locate him either.

"So, you say that his super was looking for him too?" Captain Martinelli asked him.

"That's right, Captain. He said he was a week late on his rent," Gonzalez replied.

"Something's not right about this. Did you ask the super if he could let you in?"

"He doesn't have the key, Captain. The super claims that everyone has their own lock on their apartment door. The tenants are supposed to give him a key, but not everyone does."

"Well, shit, do some more digging and if push comes to shove, we'll have to get a warrant for probable cause to bust into his apartment and search it. Find out if Mr. Delgado has any family members. I want some DNA samples from this guy to see if he's our man."

"Sure, anything that would exonerate Nathan Harris of murder, right?"

"Well, yeah!"

"Yeah, right. I know where you're coming from, Captain," Gonzalez said sarcastically.

"Now don't get all bent out of shape here, Gonzalez. Remember, I am your superior, you know," the captain shot right back at him.

"Yeah, I know, and you won't ever let me forget that, will you?"

"That's right. Now go, get the hell out of here, and bring me some leads," Martinelli added.

Detective Gonzalez left the captain's office. He didn't know what to do at this moment. The detective was hoping he would find an easier way to get the groundskeeper's DNA samples for the captain. He went back to his office to think.

*
**

Three days later, on Friday afternoon, Detective Gonzalez was receiving a phone call from the building superintendent he just met, Jose Garcia. Jose told Gonzalez that the landlord wanted the apartment open to see if Mr. Hector Delgado was all right. The super went on to say that no one has seen Mr. Delgado in almost a month. Garcia thought that Delgado may have passed away in his apartment, since there was a bad odor coming from under the front door. The detective decided to bring a uniformed officer with him to go check it out just in case he needed assistance.

*
**

Later that afternoon, Detective Gonzalez and Officer Cheng had arrived at the old apartment house where Hector Delgado resided. Gonzalez and Cheng both went toward the green elevator door.

"Go ahead, Cheng, press the call button; maybe you'll have better luck than me," Gonzalez said with a chuckle.

"What do you mean by that shit? Is this a gag or something?" Cheng asked him.

"I mean that every damn time my ass comes here, this piece of shit elevator doesn't work and I got to go hoofing it, all the way upstairs to the sixth floor."

"Are you serious? Climb up six fucking flights of stairs, oh, *hell* no."

Officer Cheng pressed the elevator call button several times and waited. Detective Gonzalez told Cheng to stop wasting time and start walking. The two of them started walking away when suddenly, the elevator arrived and opened its door for them.

"You see; aren't you glad we waited?" Officer Cheng asked while walking into the elevator.

"*Sonofabitch,* I can't believe it," Gonzalez said before getting on board the elevator.

"You see; I must be good luck, you *need* my ass," Cheng retorted.

*
**

A few minutes later, Detective Gonzalez and Officer Cheng had arrived at apartment 6I, the apartment that Hector Delgado was living in. Superintendent Jose Garcia was there waiting for them.

"Ok, my boss, *Señor* Gomez, say you can break down the door, but try not to do too much damage, please," Superintendent Garcia told them both.

"We'll try not to do too much damage," Detective Gonzalez replied.

Officer Cheng yelled at the door one more time for Hector Delgado to open up. Cheng noticed the bad odor coming from the gap underneath the door. Officer Cheng slammed his right shoulder a few times up against the door before it finally busted open, with part of the lock hanging down from the door. The three of them walked right into Delgado's apartment, holding their noses to block out the stench. The first thing they all noticed was a small black dog that was lying there on the floor in the hall, surrounded by its own feces and urine. Gonzalez cautiously walked over to where the dog was laying down.

"This dog is stone cold dead; that's messed up," Gonzalez sadly said.

"What killed him, Gonzalez?" Cheng asked with a concerned look on his face.

"He literally starved to death," Gonzalez stated, noticing how thin the animal looked.

"*Oh, shit,* he looks emaciated. I can't look at this shit, I love dogs," Cheng said while turning away.

"He look like he no have any water, too," the super added.

The three men looked around the three-room apartment, looking

86

for Hector Delgado. Gonzalez noticed a small brown bag precariously sticking out from one of the sofa cushions in the living room. He grabbed the bag and opened it.

"Well, well, well, what do we have here?" Gonzalez asked as he looked at the clear plastic bags full of white powder, hidden in the brown bag.

"I bet you it isn't sugar," Officer Cheng said as he came over toward the detective.

Detective Gonzalez opened up one of the bags, stuck his finger in, and tasted a sample of the powder.

"No, it's not. We'll bring this shit down to the lab and have it analyzed; dollars to doughnuts, it's probably cocaine," Gonzalez stated.

"*Mira*, I didn't know that he was into that shit, *¡Coño!*" Garcia stated.

Detective Gonzalez and Officer Cheng did a clean sweep of the three-room apartment to see if they could find any more drugs. Gonzalez went over toward the bathroom; he looked at the sink and found Delgado's hairbrush on it.

"Bingo," Gonzalez happily said, noticing that there was hair on the brush.

"Well, I guess we got our DNA sample for the captain," Cheng said while looking in the medicine cabinet.

"You bet, and then some," replied the detective as he placed the brush into a plastic bag that he had on him.

"Mira, it look like Hector no here for a long time," Garcia stated.

"You are absolutely right, *Señor* Garcia, absolutely right," Gonzalez replied.

The three of them left the apartment. Garcia closed the door, knowing he was going to have to come back and clean up later. Detective

Gonzalez and Officer Cheng headed on back to the police station.

*
**

A half-hour later, Detective Gonzalez and Officer Cheng had arrived back at the police station with the brown bag of white powder and the hairbrush containing Hector Delgado's hair. They both went into the captain's office to give him the good news.

"Here you go, Captain, I'm sure the hair on this brush belongs to our elusive groundskeeper, Hector Delgado. I'm also sure this bag contains cocaine," Gonzalez said, while handing the bags over to the captain.

"I'm deeply proud of you men. I'll just send this off to the lab for a DNA analysis and then I'll have them check this white powder. We'll know soon enough if Mr. Hector Delgado was Mrs. Harris's lover and what he was up to," Captain Martinelli said to them both.

Detective Gonzalez shook his head in acceptance and walked out of the captain's office. Officer Cheng followed right after him, thinking that Gonzalez was receiving all the credit for getting the sample. *What did I get for all of this shit, nothing but pain in my right shoulder for busting down that door,* Cheng thought to himself. Officer Cheng decided to go out for lunch. *I think I'll go get me a slice of peperoni pizza and a soda,* he thought while walking out the door.

*
**

On the other side of town, Nathan Harris was back down in his laboratory. The scientist was checking out his time transportation equipment to see if there was any more damage he may have overlooked. Nathan knew his machine had an overheating problem that he had to address. *Man, I can't wait three to four weeks to get my parts; this is ridiculous,* Nathan thought.

Nathan turned and looked at the dark corner of his lab. *I could have sworn I saw someone or something there,* the scientist nervously thought. The left corner of his lab was dark, due to the fact that his fluorescent

88

ceiling light fixture had a problem of burning out the light tubes prematurely, sometimes within a week. Nathan knew it had to be a ballast problem, but he never got around to replacing it.

"*Shit,* there it is again," the scientist and inventor said to himself.

Within seconds, Nathan saw an image of his late daughter, Alice, wearing the same pink pajamas she died in. Alice was waving to him in the dark corner of the room.

"Alice, is that you?" Nathan nervously asked.

Nathan slowly started walking over toward the dark corner. He kept looking at the image of his daughter, but as he got close enough to touch her, she disappeared right before his eyes. Perhaps, it was his own imagination getting the best of him. *Maybe I ought to cut back on coffee,* he thought to himself. Nathan decided to leave his lab and take a nap upstairs in the bedroom.

*
**

After waiting close to two weeks, Captain Paul Martinelli finally got the DNA report back from the lab. He took a sip from his morning cup of coffee, then the captain started to open up the manila envelope containing the report. *Just as I suspected,* he thought. Martinelli reached for his desk intercom.

"Hey, Gonzalez, get in here now, please!" Martinelli called out.

"I'll be right in, Captain," Gonzalez replied.

Within seconds, Detective Gonzalez was in the captain's office. Martinelli handed the report over to him.

"It looks like both of our hunches were right. Nathan's groundskeeper, Hector Delgado, was indeed Mrs. Harris's lover. The DNA confirms it. Also, that white powder was six ounces of pure cocaine," Captain Martinelli said to Detective Gonzalez.

"Yep, I figured it was him and I figured it was cocaine, but that *still* doesn't mean he killed her, Captain. If Mr. Harris caught them red-handed in the act, it would have given him probable cause; a motive to kill them both," Gonzalez responded.

"Aw, come on now, will you? If that were true, where's Delgado's body? What evidence are you basing your theory on? Just because you didn't find him home, doesn't mean he's dead, you know."

"Never mind, Captain, I know where this is going and I don't feel like arguing right now."

"Fine by me. Hey, why don't you go on over to the Harris residence and ask Nathan if he knows where Mr. Delgado could be," the captain suggested.

"All right, Captain, sounds like a plan," Gonzalez replied to him.

Detective Gonzalez walked out of the captain's office and grabbed his coat. *That's the smartest suggestion he's made. Martinelli's up Harris's ass so deep, he can't see that this guy could still be our killer, shit,"* Gonzalez angrily thought to himself. He knew it would take a lot to convince the captain that Harris may be guilty of murder. *I just need some proof; some good, hard evidence,* he thought.

*
**

Later that morning, Detective Gonzalez had arrived at the Harris residence again. Gonzalez got out of his white car and admired the bright sun and the perfectly blue sky above him. It was nice out and the detective thought he may have overdressed, especially since he was wearing a heavy black winter coat. Gonzalez listened to the sounds of the birds for a moment. He distinctively heard the melodic sounds of robins; their song sounded like a cry. Gonzalez was an avid bird watcher, but the man didn't expect to hear robins in late February. *This is way too early for robins,* he thought. Gonzalez walked up the brick pathway toward the front door, rang the bell, and waited.

"Who is it?!" Nathan shouted over the intercom.

"It's Detective Gonzalez!" he yelled at the door looking at the camera above him.

Nathan jumped out of bed, came down the stairs, and opened up the front door. Gonzalez had a surprised look on his face. Nathan looked a little disheveled standing there.

"You look like you just woke up," Gonzalez stated.

"Yeah, I was just taking a nap," Nathan replied.

"Sorry I woke you, but I've got to ask you some questions about your groundskeeper. May I come in?"

"Sure, come on in, Detective."

"You know what? I'm really surprised at you, Mr. Harris," Gonzalez said while walking into Nathan's home.

"Surprised?"

"Yeah, you got all this fancy security equipment and you still asked me who I was at the door."

"The camera's down," Nathan said while pointing to the camera at the doorway.

"Oh, just wondering."

Nathan led the detective into the kitchen. He turned on the coffee pot and faced Gonzalez.

"Would you like some coffee, Detective?" Nathan politely asked him.

"No thanks; I just want to ask you about your former groundskeeper, Hector Delgado," Gonzalez replied.

"What about him?"

"Did you know he was into drugs?"

"Drugs?! No, I didn't."

"We found some cocaine in his apartment."

"I wouldn't know anything about that. I don't do drugs; drugs are for losers."

"Do you know where he could be?"

"I gave you his address, Detective. Other than that, I haven't the slightest idea where he could be."

"He wasn't home, hadn't been there for a while. You see, Mr. Harris, I went over to his apartment several times and each time I came up empty handed. Even the building superintendent was looking for him; he said he's been late on his rent."

"Wow, well I can't help you out there, Detective. I've paid him for his services, what he did with the money was his business."

"Do you know if Delgado had any friends or relatives, especially anyone nearby?"

"Not that I know of, Detective. Delgado pretty much kept to himself."

"Oh, I wouldn't say that, Mr. Harris. Delgado was pretty close to your wife."

"What do you mean by that, Detective?"

"I mean that Delgado was your wife's lover."

"What?!"

"That's right, Mr. Harris. We took a sample of Mr. Delgado's hair from his hairbrush, then we matched it with the semen sample that was in your wife's reproductive tract, also the blood on her fingernails. The DNA results came up as a positive match."

"What?! You expect me to believe that my wife had a tawdry little affair with our groundskeeper? Why, that's preposterous!" Nathan angrily shouted.

"Believe what you want, Mr. Harris, but DNA tests don't lie. Who knows what else she may have kept from you," Gonzalez logically stated.

"This is outrageous! I think you'd better leave now, Detective."

"I can find my way out."

Detective Gonzales walked out of the mansion and headed for his car. Nathan watched him leave through the window. *He was way out of line. To think that my wife had an affair with our groundskeeper; why, that's just ludicrous,* Nathan angrily thought. Nathan knew that Hector Delgado was a young and handsome man. He also recalled the two of them occasionally flirting with one another, although Nathan didn't think too much about it at the time, but now he wondered. *What if it's true? If the DNA tests show that it is..."* Nathan's thoughts trailed off.

The telephone started ringing but Nathan didn't feel like talking to anyone right now. He let the answering machine pick up the call.

"Nathan? Nathan it's me, Nancy, I know you're home, please pick up the phone. I need to talk to you," she said, sounding extremely worried.

Nathan refused to pick up the phone. He waited for her to hang up. The scientist and inventor needed time to think. *I can't talk to her now, not now,* he thought before going back upstairs, but not to the master bedroom suite. *Tomorrow I'll call the painters to repaint the room, then I'll order new carpeting and drapes,* Nathan thought. He knew it was time to get rid of the constant reminder of his wife's murder. He knew it was time to move on.

CHAPTER 8

BACK IN TIME AGAIN

𝕱riday afternoon, the tenth day of March, Nathan Harris heard his doorbell ring. Nathan came down the stairs wondering who it was. *I hope it's not that damn detective again; I've had it with him,* he thought to himself.

"Who is it?!" Nathan yelled out.

Nathan called out again, but there was no answer. He cautiously opened up the front door, wishing his security camera was functioning.

"There's no one here," he said to himself.

Nathan saw a delivery truck leave his driveway. The scientist looked down in front of his door and noticed a small package, waiting there for him.

"My parts! It's about time; it's only been about a month since I ordered them," he happily said to himself.

Nathan bent down, picked up the small brown box, went back inside, and closed the door. He brought the box down to his laboratory and opened it up. Nathan carefully examined the electronic components in the package. *Looks like everything I ordered is here,* the scientist and inventor thought. Nathan knew he had a lot of work ahead of him. He took out his soldering iron and plugged it in to heat up. The scientist went through his schematics to see how he could utilize the improved parts.

"I've got to make this machine run as efficiently as possible," Nathan said to himself.

Nathan knew that heat was the downfall and the enemy in any electronic circuit; heat destroys semiconductors and integrated circuit chips. *If this machine overloads and overheats while I'm in another time and place, I could be stuck there forever,* he nervously thought to himself. The scientist wasn't leaving anything to chance; everything had to be just right. *I got lucky last time, next time I might not be so lucky,* he thought. Nathan methodically laid out all the new electronic parts on his workbench, in the order he would use them for his equipment. Nathan started the tedious job of replacing the old, damaged parts with the newer, high-efficiency components, one by one.

Photo courtesy of RF Studio

*
**

After four grueling hours, Nathan had completed updating and upgrading his time transportation machine. He performed some final tests to make sure his invention wouldn't overheat again. The inventor replaced all of the protective covers on the machine, then he made sure all the fasteners were on tight.

Photo courtesy of Pexels

"Well, I guess I'm ready to go back in time again," Nathan said to himself.

Nathan donned his navy-blue suit with its retractable hood. Next, the scientist strapped on his electronic belt and started to walk back toward the transporter chamber, until he spotted his late daughter, Alice, again. Alice was in the dark corner of the room again, dressed in the last thing she had worn when she was alive—her pink pajamas.

"Alice? Sweetheart, is that really you?" Nathan hesitantly asked.

The figure never said a word. Alice just stood there in her pajamas and waved. Nathan cautiously walked over to her and then she disappeared.

"No! Come back to me, my little one, I miss you!" Nathan said with a cry in his voice.

Nathan was close enough to see something else on his daughter before she disappeared; the bloody gash on the back of her head when she turned around. The scientist was beginning to feel distraught.

"I think I'm going mad; I'm seeing things," Nathan said to the empty corner of the room.

Nathan decided to take a seat by the workbench. He placed his head in his hands and started to cry. The poor man really missed his family, especially his little daughter. Nathan wondered why he was seeing vivid visions of his late daughter, but not of his wife. Nathan literally cried himself to sleep by his workbench.

⁎

An hour had passed and Nathan Harris finally woke up from his tearful nap at his workbench. *I have got to pull myself together and get back to work,* he thought to himself. Nathan got up from his chair and slowly walked back toward the transporter chamber. He fired up all of his equipment and set the date dials to Tuesday morning, January seventeen; the day he left for his trip to Oregon. Nathan set the location to be outside, in front of his mansion, at five o'clock in the morning. He also set the return time for 4:49 p.m., the time the grandfather clock had stopped; assuming it was in the evening. The scientist wanted to get back before his family was actually murdered, hoping he could have time enough to prevent it from ever happening.

Nathan walked into the transporter chamber and waited for the retractable cylindered doors to close on him. He powered up his controller belt, reached behind his collar, and pulled up on his retractable hood to cover his head. Nathan placed his hand onto the touchscreen that was mounted on the back wall of the machine.

"Hello Mr. Harris, and welcome aboard," the machine announced in its female robotic voice.

"Hello Alice, commence time travel sequence," Nathan replied to the computer, as he put on his dark glasses to protect his eyes from the powerful lasers in the machine.

"Affirmative, Mr. Harris, initiating time travel sequence in ten seconds."

The Time Transporter began its countdown.

"Ten, nine, eight, seven, six, five, four, three, two, one, zero," the computer stated while displaying the numbers on its LCD screen.

The overhead electrodes began to energize, followed by the halo laser that was circulating powerful light rays around him in the tubular chamber. The transporter started back up with its powerful whirring sound. Nathan Harris felt strange as his body began to demolecularize within the chamber. Within seconds, Nathan's molecules were being transported back in time again.

When all of his molecules arrived in the past, they began to remolecularize back in the same order. What Nathan didn't realize was that the new CPU chip he installed in his machine was not of the same quality as the previous one, making his Time Transporter highly inaccurate. Nathan had gone much further back in time.

✲
✲✲

Nathan Harris had arrived back in the past, in front of his mansion. He looked around the property and noticed it looked different. *Where's the snow?* Nathan mentally asked himself; he also noticed it was bitterly cold. *I'm sure glad this suit has a thermal liner,* he thought. Nathan's swimming pool was still there, but covered. He remembered having the pool back-filled years ago, when his little daughter Alice fell in and almost drowned. Alice was only five years old at the time and highly curious. Nathan and his wife, Heather, thought filling it in would be the safest thing to do.

"My Bentley, where's my Bentley?" Nathan quietly asked himself.

Nathan always left his Flying Spur Hybrid Bentley in the driveway, since his five-car detached garage was full with his two Mercedes Benz's, his black Lincoln Navigator, the wife's Corvette, and other paraphernalia; besides, he enjoyed looking at the Bentley's flawless emerald color, shining in the sunlight through his window. All of a sudden, a big German Shepherd came out of nowhere and started charging at him. Nathan franticly tried his key in the front door lock, but it didn't fit. He thought for sure he'd become the next meal in the vicious dog's tummy. Then, the front door opened with a middle-aged man standing there in a black suit. Nathan had never seen this person before in his life. The man was tall and thin with salt-and-pepper hair.

"Jonathan, sit and stay!" the man yelled out to his dog.

The big German Shepherd stopped in his tracks and sat down. Nathan was relived, but still he was stunned, to say the least. The man turned and looked at Nathan, analyzing him.

Photo courtesy of Ave Calvar Martinez

"Excuse me, sir, but who are you and what are you doing in my home?" Nathan asked in bewilderment.

"I beg your pardon, sir, but did you say, *your* home?" the man asked with a confused look upon his face.

"That's correct, sir, my home."

"Indeed, and who might you be, sir?"

"My name is Nathan Harris and I own this property."

"Really? Well, that's certainly news to me since my family and I have been living here for over ten years now."

"There must be some mistake. Isn't this 1 Imperial Road in Solville?"

"Indeed it is, sir."

"Then, who are you?"

"My name is Reginald Carrington, surely you heard of me."

"Not really, are you related to Edgar Carrington?"

"I should hope so; Edgar is my son."

"Well, I think that explains some of this. You see, Edgar Carrington was the one that sold me this mansion, about fifteen years ago."

"Really? Well, that would certainly be a neat trick, sir. My son Edgar just turned five yesterday. If I may be so bold, you haven't been, shall we say, dabbling into the spirits, have you?"

"No, I haven't been drinking at all," Nathan angrily replied to him.

Nathan was starting to go into shock. The scientist was beginning to have palpitations.

"Excuse me, did you say your son just turned five yesterday?" Nathan nervously asked.

"That's correct, my son just turned five years old," Mr. Carrington replied.

It was all Nathan could bear. Nathan Harris collapsed right there in front of Reginald Carrington, by his front door.

"Sir, sir! Are you all right?" Mr. Carrington asked in horror, wondering what to do.

Mr. Carrington called his maid and butler over to help Nathan. Carrington's maid placed some smelling salts under Nathan's nose to restore his consciousness. When Nathan finally woke up, Carrington's butler helped him back up onto his feet.

"Are you all right, sir?" Mr. Carrington asked him again.

"Yes, yes I'm fine," Nathan replied.

"Would you care for something to drink?"

"No thank you. Please, can you just tell me today's date?"

"The date? Sure, it's Monday the seventeenth."

"January seventeen?"

"That's correct, sir."

"Something's wrong, did you say Monday?"

"That's correct, Monday."

"That's impossible, it should be Tuesday. I need to know the year; what year is it, sir?"

"Good heavens, are you sure you're feeling all right?"

"Yes, yes I am, now will you *please* tell me what year this is?"

"Very well, sir, it's nineteen-seventy-seven."

"Oh, no, the transporter must have malfunctioned," Nathan said as the color faded from his face.

"Good heavens, what are you talking about? Sir, you look like you've seen a ghost. Shall I call you a doctor?"

"No, no I'm fine."

"You're not going to pass out on me again, are you?"

"No, I just need some time to digest this."

"Tell me something, what's that contraption you have on your belt?"

"It's my experiment; you wouldn't understand."

"Experiment? Are you an inventor?"

"Yes I am."

"Have you created anything that I might know of?"

"No, none that you would know."

Nathan looked at the time on his gold Rolex watch; it was seven fifteen in the morning. Nathan knew his machine would transport him back to the present at 4:49 p.m., if all goes well, since he was supposed to arrive at five o'clock in the morning and in the year 2023. The scientist and inventor figured that he had nine and a half hours to be back at this very same spot if he were to leave temporarily. Nathan wanted to visit his mother once more, since he had time. He asked Mr. Carrington to call him a cab.

✱✱

Two hours later, Nathan had arrived in New York City, uptown in front of his mother's old apartment house. When he got out of the yellow cab, Nathan noticed some people were wearing bell-bottom pants with Afro hairdos. A teenager came out of the building with a huge boom box on his shoulder, blaring out disco music. Nathan recognized the tune from the oldies station; it was, "You Make Me Feel Like Dancing" by British singer Leo Sayer. *Oh, the sights and sounds of the seventies that I've read about and seen on television,* Nathan thought.

Everyone had donned their heavy winter coats to combat the brutal cold weather. It seems that the bright sun had no effect on the frigid air that surrounded it. Some people were talking about the latest horror flick, *Hitch Hike to Hell*, as they were passing by. Nathan walked into the old apartment building marked 605 on 183rd Street and took the elevator up to the fourth floor. Nathan remembered her apartment number, it was 4A. Nathan was about to ring the bell until he caught himself. *It's 1977, forty-six years ago; I was born in 1978. She'll never know who the hell I am*, he sadly thought to himself. *I still want to see her while I'm here.* He decided to ring the bell after all.

"Who is it?!" a woman yelled from behind the apartment door.

"It's Mr. Harris from building management," he replied.

The woman opened up the red-colored steel door and gazed upon him. Nathan was stunned by her beauty. The young woman had long red hair with a smile that would brighten anyone's day. Alice was very slim and looked great in her rose-colored house dress. Nathan remembered seeing pictures of his mother when she was young, but seeing her in person was quite different.

"May I help you, sir?" Alice asked him.

"Hello Mom, excuse me, miss, my name is Mr. Harris from building management. I just wanted to make sure everything is all right in the building. Um, do you have any complaints?" Nathan asked her.

"Well, a little more heat would be appreciated, Mr. Harris. Sometimes it gets rather cold here, you know."

"I'll certainly see that it's taken care of, miss."

"I'm sorry, did you say your name was Mr. Harris?"

"That's correct."

"You look a little familiar, as a matter of fact, you remind me of my husband, strange isn't it?"

"I guess I have that kind of face, miss."

"Well, you must be new, I've never heard of a Mr. Harris working here. What happened to Mr. Robinson?"

"Oh, well, he's still here, I'm assisting him."

"Ok, Mr. Harris, I must be going, so if there's anything else…"

"No, no I guess I've taken up enough of your precious time already."

"Very well then, have a good day," Alice Harris said as she closed her front door on him.

Nathan slowly walked away from her apartment door, feeling warm inside. He grabbed the elevator and went downstairs to the lobby. Nathan instinctively turned on his smartphone and tried to call a cab, until he realized his smartphone was totally useless in 1977. Cellular phones and their associated service infrastructure weren't commercially available in North America until 1983. *I guess that explains why I have no service here,* Nathan thought while looking at his phone.

The scientist and inventor had another problem; the early satellites in space in the seventies were primitive by today's standards, and might be incompatible with his remote controller belt. *Well, I got here, didn't I? I should be able to get back to my time,* Nathan thought. Nathan knew he needed to get a cab ride back to his mansion and be back by 4:49 p.m., or he'll miss the return window and be stuck in 1977. Nathan looked at his watch again and noticed it was only ten o'clock in the morning. *I have plenty of time, but how am I going to call for a cab?* Nathan nervously thought. He decided to walk down the street to look for a payphone.

*
**

Later in the morning, Nathan finally found a working phone booth with a complete phonebook. *Wow, it's almost eleven o'clock, I've got to hurry,* he thought. Nathan searched the phonebook for a local car service. After looking at a few promising ads, he settled on one. Nathan dug in his pocket for change. *Man, only ten cents for a local call? I don't remember it being less than a quarter for the first three minutes,* he thought while calling the car service.

✳✳

About three hours later, Nathan had arrived back at his mansion. The cab driver had to deal with a lot of northbound traffic due to a car accident on the parkway. Nathan looked at his watch and noticed it was already two o'clock in the afternoon. *That leaves me with two hours and forty-nine minutes to get back, if all goes well,* Nathan thought. Nathan paid the driver and got out of the cab. As the driver backed out of the driveway, Mr. Carrington opened up his front door to greet Nathan.

"Back so soon, young man?" Mr. Carrington asked.

"Yes, I need to stay here for a bit before I can go back home," Nathan replied.

"I thought you had gone back, that's why you wanted the cab, correct?"

"No, I just wanted to visit someone, that's all."

"Well, I'm afraid I don't understand. Why have you returned back here? Shall I call you another cab, sir?"

"That won't be necessary, a taxi cab can't bring me back home. Like I said before, I just need to wait here for a little while so I can get transported, I mean, so I can get my ride back home."

"Well then, how long is a little while, if you don't mind me asking, sir?"

"Until 4:49 this afternoon, Mr. Carrington."

Mr. Carrington looked at his pocket watch, then he gave Nathan an inquisitive look.

"Why, that's almost three hours from now. If you're short on funds, I can have my chauffeur give you a ride into town," Mr. Carrington offered.

105

"Thank you but no, that won't be necessary. I'm afraid that even your chauffeur cannot bring me back to *my* home," Nathan sadly replied while looking at his former home.

"I suppose you must live very far away, correct?"

"Oh, yes, I live very far, indeed," Nathan replied with a chuckle.

"Well, sir, it's quite cold out here, much too cold to be waiting. You're quite welcome to wait for your ride inside my home; it's much warmer inside, you know."

Nathan accepted Mr. Carrington's gracious offer and went inside the man's mansion. Mr. Carrington offered Nathan a cup of coffee and a pastry while they talked some more. Nathan kept looking at his timepiece, waiting for 4:49 to arrive.

*
**

Later that afternoon, Nathan noticed it was 4:45 p.m. *It's almost time for my transport,* he thought to himself. Nathan excused himself from Mr. Carrington's home and waited outside, at the very same spot he arrived at. Nathan looked at the countdown timer on his remote controller belt. The Time Transporter was set to send him back to the present in less than four minutes. The countdown timer started up on the remote controller belt. Nathan pulled up on his collar and covered his head with the retractable hood. He stood there, listening to the machine's electronic female voice counting down over the remote controller belt's built-in speaker.

"Ten, nine, eight, seven, six, five, four, three, two, one, zero," the computer stated while displaying the numbers on the belt's LCD screen.

After the countdown was completed, Nathan Harris was still in the past. Nathan waited a couple of minutes, standing there in the cold, but nothing happened.

"Oh, Lord, please don't tell me my machine malfunctioned again," he softly said to himself.

"Sir, are you just going to stand out there in the cold? You'll catch your death," Mr. Carrington asked him.

Nathan didn't notice him standing right there in front of his doorway. Nathan looked up at the sky and prayed.

"Mr., come on back inside, you'll freeze to death out here," Mr. Carrington said as he began to approach Nathan.

Suddenly, a flash of lightning lit up the sky. Mr. Carrington watched in awe as Nathan slowly started to disappear, right before his very own eyes. Within seconds, Nathan Harris had completely dematerialized and was sent back to his time and place, in the future.

*
**

Scientist and inventor Nathan Harris had finally arrived back to his present time and place in his laboratory. Nathan was standing in the transporter chamber. He waited for the retractable cylindered doors to reopen. Nathan powered off his controller belt, retracted his hood, and walked out of the transporter chamber.

"Well, I'm back, but I've got to find out what the hell went wrong in the first place," he said to himself.

Nathan started tearing down his equipment, mainly the new circuits he employed. The scientist finally narrowed it down to the inferior CPU chip he previously installed. Nathan quickly realized that the new chip had a much slower clock speed than the original that was in there.

Photo courtesy of Cottonbro Studio

"Cheap foreign junk. What a waste of time and money. Why the hell can't they manufacture anything here in the United States anymore?" Nathan asked himself aloud.

Nathan knew it was time to go back to the drawing board again. The scientist powered up his computer and started to surf the internet again for electronic parts. *Well, at least everything else held up without overheating,* he thought. Nathan made sure to stay away from the previous site that he ordered from. This time, the man was going for a more well-respected brand name and was willing to pay extra for it. *You get what you pay for, at least that's what I was always taught,* he thought.

Nathan heard an alert tone on one of his monitors. The scientist turned around toward the viewing screen; he noticed it was Nancy Stevens ringing his front doorbell again. Nathan turned up the audio feed so he could hear what she had to say.

"Nathan! We need to talk! Why are you avoiding me! You can't hide in your fortress forever! Let me in!" Nancy screamed.

CHAPTER 9

GLADYS DELGADO

etective Juan Gonzalez was sitting in his office on a beautiful Monday morning, March thirteen, drinking his cup of coffee. Gonzalez, like a lot of other people, was happy that most of the snow had finally melted away and there wasn't any in the immediate forecast. The beautiful spring-like weather had brightened up almost everyone's spirits. Gonzalez picked up the morning paper and then his phone began to ring.

"Detective Gonzalez, homicide," he answered.

"Hello, I want to report a missing person," the woman on the phone nervously said.

"Ok ma'am, who's the missing person and how long as he or she been missing?" Gonzalez asked her.

"It's, it's my, my bro-ther," she managed to say before breaking down and crying on the line.

"Ok ma'am, calm down and get yourself together, please. I need a name."

"His, his name is Hector, Hector Delgado," the woman struggled to tell him.

"Excuse me, did you say Hector Delgado?"

"Yes, Hector Delgado."

The name struck a chord with the good detective. Gonzalez

remembered him. *Hector Delgado was the Harris's groundskeeper and apparently Mrs. Harris's lover,* he thought. The whole police force had been looking for Delgado for well over a month now.

"Miss, you said you're Mr. Delgado's sister, what's your full name, please?" Gonzalez asked her.

"My name is Gladys, Gladys Delgado," she replied.

"Ok Miss Delgado, when was the last time you made contact with your brother?"

"I think it was sometime in the middle of January, *Señor* Detective, at least that's what I remember."

"Are you telling me that you haven't made any contact with your brother in two months, and just now you're reporting him missing?"

"My brother was always too busy for me. I think he may be mad at me. I call and I call and most of the time I just get his voice mail, but two days ago I get a recording saying that his number is no longer in service. I knew something was wrong, so, yesterday I went over to his apartment to find the super cleaning out the place and changing the locks. He told me that the police were there looking for him. I'm scared, *Señor* Detective, it's not like him to just disappear like that. I think, I think, maybe, something bad happened to him," Gladys barely finished before crying again.

"Miss Delgado, you need to come down here and file a missing person's report. Please bring a recent photo of your brother. Don't forget to ask for me, Detective Gonzalez."

"Ok, I'll see you soon, Detective Gonzalez," Gladys said before hanging up the telephone.

Detective Gonzalez hung up the phone and took some notes. *We're gonna have to put out an APB on Mr. Hector Delgado,* he thought. The detective got up from his desk and went over to tell the captain what just transpired.

⁕
⁑

An hour later, Gladys Delgado was at the front counter of the Solville Police Department, looking for Detective Gonzalez. The young female police officer working the counter called Gonzalez to greet her. Gladys didn't have to wait too long at all; within a couple of minutes, the good detective had come to greet her. Gonzalez was stunned by the young woman's beauty. Gladys had long, wavy, jet-black hair, which he found very intriguing. Gonzalez took note of her sweet, innocent-looking face. She had bright green eyes with long eyelashes. The detective also noticed how her floral print dress helped to accentuate her slim, but womanly figure. *This girl's a complete knockout; she looks like a living doll,* he thought to himself.

Photo courtesy of OG Productionz

"Miss Delgado?" Gonzalez asked her.

"Sí, Señor, Detective Gonzalez?" Gladys asked.

"Sí, come into my office, please."

Miss Delgado followed the detective toward his office. Gladys knew Gonzalez liked her; her woman's intuition had kicked into high alert. Gladys noticed Gonzalez was blushing when he stared at her for that brief moment. The detective led her into his office and then he closed the door behind her.

"Have a seat, Miss Delgado," Gonzalez said with a smile.

Gladys sat down on the chair directly in front of the detective's desk. Gonzalez pulled out some forms from his desk drawer.

"Did you know that your brother had a cocaine habit?" Gonzalez asked her.

"No, but I guess that explains why he was always hitting me up for some money," Gladys angrily replied.

"We found several ounces of cocaine in his apartment. Your brother also had an affair with his employer's wife, Mrs. Harris."

"What?! Are you sure?!"

"Yes, I'm sure. He's also a prime suspect in the murder of Mrs. Harris and her daughter. I'm sorry to have to tell you that."

"Oh, my God, what are you saying, *Señor* Detective?! It can't be true, not *my* brother."

"I'm sorry, but it's true. Your brother's semen was found in the body of Mrs. Harris and his blood was found under her fingernails. Now, that still doesn't mean he killer her, but *he is* one of our prime suspects, Miss Delgado."

"So, you think he's running away from the scene of a crime? My brother wouldn't hurt anyone, Detective," Gladys replied with tears in her eyes.

"Your brother disappeared in a hurry, so much so that he left his own dog to starve to death in his apartment."

"What? Bruno's dead? He loved that dog. He was still a puppy."

"Yeah, well, the dog had no food or water and was lying there in his own feces and urine. Tell me something, Miss Delgado, is there somewhere that you know your brother would go to? Somewhere that he would go to if he wanted to hide?"

"No, not that I know of," she replied.

"What about his friends? Maybe he might be hanging out with someone he knows."

"His only friend was Joey; he grew up with him."

"And where is this Joey?"

"He died in a hit-and-run car accident last year."

"So, it appears we're back to square one. Here's the forms I told you about over the phone to file for a missing person," Gonzalez said as he handed her the papers.

"*Gracias, Señor* Detective," Gladys replied.

"Did you bring a recent photo of your brother?"

"The only pictures I have are on my phone."

"Well, with your permission, we can hook up your phone to our computer and print out a recent photo."

"I have a better idea; can I email you the picture?"

"Sure, here's our email address," Gonzalez said while handing her a card.

Gladys took out her smartphone and selected a recent photo of her brother, then she emailed it to the police station. The disheartened young woman remained in the chair. Gladys brushed her hair away from her face and filled out the missing person forms that Gonzalez had given her. The attractive young woman could tell the detective was checking out her assets. Gladys finally handed the completed forms back to Gonzalez, while a lonely teardrop fell from her eye.

"Listen, we're gonna do everything we can to locate your brother. If we find anything, we'll call you, but also, if *you* make any contact with your brother, please call us right away, all right?" Gonzalez aske as he handed her his card.

"*Sí,* I will let you know. Please find him, he's the only relative I have left, and he's not a murderer."

Gladys Delgado left the police station heartbroken; she realized that the detective didn't have a clue as to where her brother was. Detective Gonzalez felt genuinely concerned about her, but he really didn't know where else to look. Gonzalez wondered if Hector Delgado was even still alive.

*
**

Back at the Harris residence, Nathan was in his home theater, sitting in the front row watching an exclusive movie, a movie that no one has ever seen before, and never will. The sadness and sorrow had caught up with the scientist again and for the umpteenth time, Nathan was watching his favorite Blu-ray disk, a home movie of him and his family last Christmas. *We were all so happy back then, opening up our presents,* Nathan sadly reminisced. Nathan watched his daughter being magnified up on his twenty-five-foot-wide screen, in 4K ultra hi-def resolution, opening up her gifts. *I wish I could go back in time to that very same day,* he thought. Then, the scientist and inventor realized that he could.

"I *could* go back in time; I have a time machine!" Nathan said out loud, nearly overriding the surround sound system in his home theater.

However, Nathan quickly realized the sad truth; the Time Transporter had become totally unreliable and unpredictable. *God only knows when and where it'll take me next time,* he miserably thought. *Maybe William could help me.* Nathan got up from his seat and shut down all of his professional audio-visual equipment, then he went back downstairs to the lab.

*
**

On the other side of town, Gladys Delgado had just returned back to her home. Gladys was living in an old ranch house that she rented on Williams Road in the town of Carney; it was all she could afford on her salary. Gladys was working as an administrator for Solville College. The twenty-six-year-old woman was still upset about her older brother, Hector. *What the hell was he thinking? Hector may be my older brother, but he sure isn't as mature as I am,* she thought.

"I can't believe my brother had an affair with his boss's wife, and into cocaine, too?! Shit!" Gladys said out loud in anger in the empty room.

Gladys knew her brother did stupid things sometimes, but this was the icing on the cake. She tried to contemplate what her brother was thinking.

"Did he love her, or was he just thinking with his dick?" Gladys said in disgust.

Nevertheless, the young woman was still worried about her brother. *I wonder where the hell he could be? I hope he's all right,* she thought. Gladys had tried several times to contact her brother, but he never answered her calls or text messages. One important thing that Gladys kept from the police was the last time she met her brother in mid-January, they had a heated argument about money. Hector was always borrowing money from his sister. Hector needed a cash infusion of $1,500 to buy a used car, supposedly, but Gladys refused to lend him the money. She had told him, "If your boss ain't paying you enough to survive, ask for a raise, or quit and get a better job. I'm tired of being your sugar momma." Gladys now regretted saying that to him. Unfortunately, Gladys never knew about her brother's addiction to cocaine, up until now. If his sister knew about his habit, maybe she could have helped him quit; Gladys was very persuasive and Hector always valued her opinion. The distressed young woman sat down on the living room sofa and started to think. *I hope I can see him again. I need to tell him how sorry I am and that I love him very much,* she sincerely thought.

"I don't believe he killed Mrs. Harris and her daughter. Oh, Lord, please let him be all right. If anything's happened to him, I'll…"

Gladys couldn't finish her own sentence; she broke down and cried like a child. The poor woman was so distraught that she was heaving with every wail. Gladys Delgado cried herself to sleep on her own sofa. The young woman never got a chance to get out of her dress and get comfortable.

*
**

Later in the afternoon, Detective Gonzalez was trying to piece together all of the evidence for a case against Hector Delgado. Gonzalez believed since Delgado was missing, he was now the number one prime suspect, although the detective was not ready to exonerate Nathan Harris of murdering his wife and daughter just yet.

Gonzalez looked at the picture that Gladys emailed the station. It was a selfie of her and her brother Hector together. Gonzalez took the picture and hung it up on the big white board they called "the murder board," which hung up on the back wall of the main office. Gonzalez placed the picture near the pictures of Nathan, his wife, and his daughter, then he printed Hector's name under it with a marker. Captain Paul Martinelli walked into the room full of workers at their desks, holding a cup of black coffee.

"I see you still have Mr. Harris's picture up on the murder board," Martinelli stated.

"That's right, Captain, I do," Gonzalez replied.

"Why? It's clear to me who the *real* culprit is, Gonzalez, Mr. Hector Delgado."

"Why, because he's a Latino? Or you just can't stand the fact that your precious Nathan Harris could be our cold-blooded killer after all?"

"Hey, watch it Gonzalez, you're treading *mighty* dangerous waters here. You can't go on accusing a multimillionaire, a philanthropist, and a longtime supporter of this town of being a cold-blooded murderer," Martinelli angrily replied.

"If we find Delgado's body, then what, Captain?"

"We'll cross that bridge when we come to it. In the meantime, we've got an APB out on Mr. Delgado. Find him."

After that, Captain Martinelli stormed out of the office. Detective Gonzalez kept looking at the murder board. He stared in disgust at the bludgeoned pictures of the victims, mainly the ones of Mrs. Harris. *Don't worry, ladies, I'll find your killer and bring his ass to justice, even if it is your husband, or your father,* he thought while looking at the dreadful pictures.

**
***

Nathan Harris was down in his lab working on some modifications to the Time Transporter. He had ordered two high-quality, high-speed central processor chips to replace the slow, inferior one he previously ordered. Nathan looked up from his computer screen and saw an image of his late daughter Alice. She was wearing the same pink pajamas that the young teenager died in. Alice was waving at him from the dark corner of the room.

"*Daddy, you let me and Mommy die,*" his daughter cried out to him in a ghostly voice.

"Honey, is that you again?" Nathan asked while almost falling off of his chair.

Nathan stood up and bolted to the dark corner of the room where he spotted his late daughter Alice. Unfortunately, by the time the scientist and inventor got to the dark corner, Alice had simply faded away.

"This is fucking ridiculous! Where the hell are you, Alice?!" Nathan shouted out loud.

Nathan went over toward the cabinet and located a bottle of whiskey. The distraught scientist decided to have himself a good stiff drink, right out of the bottle.

"She can't be alive, I saw her lifeless body when she was stuffed in the grandfather clock," he softly said to himself.

Nathan took another big swig out of the bottle, then he placed the half-empty bottle back into the cabinet. He could almost hear his wife telling him to lay off the sauce as he closed the cabinet door.

"I need William. Where the hell is William?!" Nathan asked out loud.

"Nooo yooou don't, Daddy," Alice answered him in a spooky voice.

Nathan looked around for his dead daughter, but he could not find her. *It's in my mind. My mind's playing tricks on me, I know that now,* Nathan logically thought to himself. The scientist chalked it up to stress. Nathan's brain could no longer function properly. Nathan wavered around a little, until he finally collapsed right onto the cold, hard, tiled floor.

*
**

The next morning, Gladys Delgado woke up on her living room sofa with dried tears on her face. She tried to look at the time on her watch, but it stopped; the battery had died. The young woman realized that she was still in her floral print dress.

"Shit, I never changed? Look at my dress, it's all wrinkled," she said to herself.

Gladys started thinking about everything that Detective Gonzalez had told her about her brother. "Your brother's semen was found in the body of Mrs. Harris and his blood was found under her fingernails. Now, that still doesn't mean he killer her, but he is one of our prime suspects," she vividly remembered the detective saying to her. Gladys couldn't stomach the fact that her brother Hector was being accused of murdering a mother and her child. *It's just not like him,* she thought. Hector Delgado *was* being accused of murder, drug possession, and now, he was on the run. Gladys was going back down to the police station to plead with Detective Gonzalez, but first she was going to take a long, hot shower and change her clothes.

*
**

Back at the Solville Police Department, Detective Gonzalez was staring at the murder board while holding a cup of coffee. *Something's not right here,* he thought. *Why would Hector Delgado kill her and her daughter? What's his motive?* Gonzalez asked himself. *Maybe, just maybe they weren't lovers at all. Maybe Hector got carried away and just raped her, but things may have gotten well out of hand. Mrs. Harris could have even enticed him, then after they had sex, she threatened to tell her husband. Hector couldn't have that. Mr. Harris would have fired him for sure, maybe even have him arrested for raping his wife. It could have all been a ploy devised by Mrs. Harris to get her husband jealous, craving his attention,* Gonzalez figured.

I remember how sexy she used to dress, wearing those low-cut blouses that accentuated her large breasts. Mrs. Harris even wore tight-fitted jeans to show off her hips and butt; she did all that, but still, Mr. Harris was always too busy for her. Nathan was always working on some new invention down in the lab, Gonzalez recalled. *What about their daughter, Alice Harris? Why would Delgado kill her and stuff her body in an old grandfather clock? Did she see something she shouldn't have? Obviously, whoever the killer was, he, or maybe even she, had plenty of time to conceal the bodies: one in the sofa and one in the antique clock. Now, Nathan Harris would have had plenty of motive to kill his wife, especially if he caught her in bed with Hector Delgado, but he didn't have the time, and why would he kill his only child, his daughter? Did Alice see something that she wasn't supposed to see and had to be eliminated? Then there's the other two questions, where the hell is Mr. Hector Delgado and is he still alive?* Detective Gonzalez asked himself, while searching his mind for answers.

"Any new leads yet?" Captain Martinelli asked as he walked into the room holding his cup of coffee.

"No, not yet, Captain. There are too many variables," Gonzalez replied.

"You *still* suspect Mr. Harris?"

"Hey, I never really stopped, but clearly, Mr. Hector Delgado's my *numero uno* prime suspect."

"You *still* don't know where he is?"

"No, I don't; none of us do, Captain."

"Well Christ, we've got an APB on his ass, he's bound to turn up sooner or later, keep looking."

"We will, Captain, we will. You know I'm not a quitter; I won't stop till I find him," Gonzales said as Captain Martinelli left the office.

Detective Gonzalez stared at the murder board again, hoping that it would generate some more ideas in his head. *What a way to go; to be brutally stabbed to death sixteen times and then stuck into a sofa. The poor young girl, stuffed inside an antique clock. Shit, they didn't deserve that, no one does,* he sadly thought. Gonzalez finished his coffee and went back to his office to contemplate the case some more.

CHAPTER 10

THE BODY

Two weeks later, Tuesday morning, March twenty-eight, Gladys Delgado had arrived in Detective Gonzalez's office holding two large cups of coffee. Gladys was wearing a light-blue dress, shiny black shoes, and a warm smile on her face. The young lady came early enough so she wouldn't feel rushed to get to her job.

"Well, well, well, good morning to you, Miss Delgado. What brings you here this morning?" Detective Gonzalez said with a big smile on his face.

"I just came by to bring you some coffee; I didn't know how you like it, so I got you regular," Gladys replied.

"Coffee, for *me?*"

"*Sí,* I thought you could use it to help you stay awake on the job."

"Really? What's the occasion, or better yet, what's the catch?"

"Well, I just wanted to know if you found out anything about my brother, that's all," she said while still smiling.

"Oh, that's it. Miss Delgado, I really do appreciate the coffee but I'm afraid I don't have any news for you, yet, I'm sorry."

"No, no that's ok, please let me know when—"

"You'll be the first person I call; I promise. Look, we've got an APB out on him, we'll find him," Gonzalez said sincerely.

"What's an APB?"

"It's an 'all-points bulletin,' it means everyone's looking for him."

"Ok, if you don't need me, I'll see you next time, Detective, chow," Gladys said while slowly turning around and walking out of the detective's office.

Captain Martinelli waited right by the doorway for her to leave.

"What was all that about?" Martinelli said while entering the detective's office.

"She's been coming around here practically every two days for the past two weeks, wondering if we found out anything about her missing brother, Hector Delgado," Gonzalez replied.

"Our prime suspect in the Harris murders?"

"That's right."

"I see she brought you coffee, it's getting serious," he said with a chuckle.

"Stop it, will you? My interest in her right now is to help solve this case."

"Your key words were, *right now.*"

"There you go again, dissecting everything I say."

"I'm merely saying, don't be so hard on her, or yourself, for that matter."

"Excuse me, Captain," Officer Ramsey said as he came through the open door.

"Yeah, what is it Ramsey?" Martinelli responded.

"Well, I was just wondering if you approved my time off for tomorrow?"

"Sorry, Ramsey, I had to deny it."

"Captain I really needed that day off, it's my daughter's birthday and my ex is being a pain, she's gonna take her out of town after tomorrow to her mother's, please sir!"

"Oh, Jesus, you're breaking my heart; we're gonna be shorthanded as it is tomorrow. I need you here!"

"What if I could switch with someone?" the distraught young man asked.

"If you can find someone to cover your job, you've got it, all right?"

"Thanks, Captain," Officer Ramsey said as he headed out the door.

"Unbelievable. I feel like I have a bunch of children around here, always crying and complaining about something or someone," Martinelli said while throwing his hands up in the air.

"Captain!" Officer Cheng shouted by the open doorway.

"Now what!" Martinelli barked back.

"Someone's found a body up on a roof of an apartment house!" Cheng replied.

"What? Where?" Martinelli asked him.

"It was a satellite service tech working on the roof of that old apartment house we went to recently," Officer Cheng said while looking at Detective Gonzalez.

"You talking about where Hector Delgado lives?" Gonzalez asked.

"Yeah, the one we found the dead dog in," Cheng replied.

"Let's go!" Gonzalez said as he started to leave with Officer Cheng.

"Keep me updated!" Martinelli shouted at them as they walked out.

Captain Martinelli stood there in Detective Gonzalez's office, thinking. *I wonder if it's Hector Delgado's body? That would solve one mystery,* Martinelli thought. The captain decided to go back to his office and finish up his coffee.

*
**

Later that morning, Detective Gonzalez and Officer Cheng had arrived back at the old apartment house located at 610 Maiden Street in Oakwood; the home of their prime suspect in the Harris murders, Hector Delgado. The two men started walking into the building and were immediately greeted by Superintendent Garcia; the satellite service technician was also there in the lobby with him.

"*Señor* Detective, come I take you to the roof," Garcia told them.

"Are you the man that found the body?" Gonzalez asked while looking at the young African American repairman holding a toolbox.

"Yes, sir. I went up on the roof to replace a malfunctioning dish for one of our customers, then I found what was left of a male body, leaning up against the elevator extension structure," the technician replied.

"I need your name and ID number please."

"My name is Paul, Paul Langford," the technician nervously replied to the detective while handing him his ID card.

"All right, Mr. Langford and Mr. Garcia, let's all go up to the roof."

The four men took the elevator up to the top floor and then they walked up the steps to the roof. Gonzalez and Cheng were both relieved that the elevator was functioning; they didn't feel like taking the stairs all the way up. Langford, the satellite technician, really didn't want to go back up there to see the body, but he knew it was his civic duty to show the police officers.

*
**

A couple of minutes later, the four men were up on the roof. The sun was out, but it was still cool outside. Langford and Garcia took the detective and the officer to where the body was.

"There it is," Langford said as he turned his head, not wanting to see it again.

The three men gazed upon the hideous site. Leaning up against the elevator extension structure were the remains of a young man in a dark brown leather jacket with a pair of blue jeans on him. The man's face and most of his head had been eaten up by rodents, hawks, and other hungry animals that dared to come up there, leaving not much to be recognized. Bird droppings were all over the body. The corpse was also surrounded by rodent droppings. Some rats were *still* hanging around nearby as flies and other insects were buzzing around it.

Officer Cheng had succumbed to his body's reaction from the sight and stench; he ran over to the other side of the roof and then spewed his morning breakfast all over the tar-covered rooftop.

Detective Gonzalez noticed dried blood on the man's neck and the front of his jacket. The detective also noticed a bloodied hunting knife in what was left of the victim's right hand.

"*¡Ay Dios Mío!* Cheng! Are you all right over there?!" Gonzalez asked.

"Yes, I'm ok now, Gonzalez," Officer Cheng responded while walking back to the crime scene.

"*Mierda.* One thing's for sure, he's been here a while. It looks like suicide to me. You see the knife in his hand? He slit his own throat."

"What hand? Both of his hands were eaten up by those little monsters. I *hate* rats!"

"It's gonna be hard to identify him without a face and no fingerprints. I guess they'll have to do a dental on him, it'll take time though."

"Do you think he's our man, Hector Delgado?"

"He might be. He fits Hector's height and build. The medical examiner will have to take a DNA sample from him and send it off to the lab."

"Excuse me, officers, but may I go now?" Langford asked.

"We need you to come downtown to the station and give us a statement," Detective Gonzalez replied.

"What about *me?*" Garcia asked.

"Were you here when Langford discovered the body?" Gonzalez asked him.

"No, he came down to me after he called you."

"Ok, then we just need you, Mr. Langford," Gonzalez replied while facing the satellite technician.

"I guess I'll call the captain on the radio," Cheng said.

"Yeah, tell him to get forensics over here."

"*Señor* Detective, how soon we can get him off our roof?" Superintendent Garcia asked.

"Don't worry, boss, it'll be done in a timely manner," the detective replied.

Officer Cheng radioed the captain to tell him what they found. Detective Gonzalez explained to the super that this was now officially a crime scene, no one was to be allowed up on the roof, except for police officials. Gonzalez took some photos of the body with his smartphone. After that, the four men left the roof. Gonzalez told the super to lock it up, while Officer Cheng was busy placing yellow "CRIME SCENE DO NOT CROSS" tape around the stairwell leading up to the roof.

*
**

Photo courtesy of kat Wilcox

Later on, Detective Gonzalez, Officer Cheng, and the satellite technician had arrived back at the Solville Police Department. Captain Paul Martinelli came out of his office holding another cup of coffee.

"Is this the man that found the body?" Martinelli asked them.

"Yup, he's the satellite repairman that found him on the roof, Captain," Gonzalez replied to him.

"I can see that he's a little shook up."

"Wouldn't *you* be if you discovered a body while doing your job?" Langford shot back at him.

"Make sure you get a statement from him before you let him go, Gonzalez," Martinelli stated while facing the detective.

"That's what we brought him back for, Captain," Gonzalez told him.

"After the ME is done with the body, contact Miss Delgado to see if it's her brother."

"I'm right on it, Captain."

Detective Gonzalez brought Paul Langford, the satellite technician, into his office to get a statement from him. Langford told the detective that he didn't have much time and he had to get back to work. Gonzalez had assured Langford that he wouldn't keep him too long.

*
**

Three days later on Friday morning, March thirty-first, Detective Gonzalez had called Gladys Delgado in to ID the body. Gonzalez strongly believed that the male corpse up on the roof was that of her brother, Hector Delgado. Gonzalez waited impatiently for her to arrive at the station, but at the same time, he regretted to have to give her the bad news. Suddenly, Gladys Delgado was standing in front of his open office door, wearing a light-blue dress with a black sweater.

"Good morning, Detective. May I come in?" Gladys asked while holding two large cups of coffee in her hands.

"Sure, sure come on in and have a seat, will you?" Gonzalez nervously replied.

"I brought you some coffee."

"I see, please, have a seat, Miss Delgado."

"Over the phone you said you had some important information to tell me. Is it about my brother? Have you found him?" Gladys asked with a smile as she sat down in the chair in front of his desk, while placing the coffee cups on it.

"We found a body up on the roof of the building your brother lived in; we think it's your brother. I'm sorry," Gonzalez empathetically told her.

Gladys lost her smile. She sat there, not knowing what to do or say. The young woman gazed at the detective in complete shock. Her defense mechanism went into a complete denial mode.

"You're lying to me; it cannot be true. It must be someone else," she said firmly, wanting to believe in her own words, while she nervously twirled her long black hair in her right hand.

Gladys noticed something about Detective Gonzalez; it was his face. Gonzalez had a serious but sorrowful look on him. It was a look that genuinely expressed concern and regret, regret from having to inform her of the bad news.

"It can't be my brother. Show me the body. I'll tell you it's not him," she said emotionally.

"I can take you down to the morgue to ID the body, but let me give you a heads up, his face is almost completely gone from the ravages of rodents feeding on him," Gonzalez told her solemnly.

"Oh, my God," Gladys said in an emotional tone.

"Does he have any identifying marks on his body that you know of?"

"Yes, yes he does; he has a tattoo of an eagle on his right shoulder."

Gladys had agreed to go down to the morgue to identify the body. Detective Gonzalez didn't get a chance to read the report from the medical examiner; he didn't know anything about a tattoo on the body. Gladys was *still* in complete denial, not wanting to believe the body she was about to see would be that of her brother, Hector.

*
**

A half-hour later, Detective Gonzalez and Gladys Delgado had arrived at the county morgue. Gladys had left her sweater back at the police station and was now shivering from the cool breeze. Gonzalez, being the gentleman that he was, gave her his jacket to keep her warm. They took the elevator up to the second floor and walked toward a locked steel-gray door. Gonzalez pressed the intercom button and waited for a reply.

"Who's there?" the man on the intercom asked.

"It's Detective Gonzalez with Miss Delgado," Gonzalez replied.

The door buzzed and Gonzalez was able to pull it open. The two of them were greeted by a young African American male wearing a white lab coat.

"Hey Gonzalez, how've you been? Long time no see," the man said.

"Hey Brown, I guess I'm surviving. Listen, I brought Miss Delgado over here to ID the faceless body you just got."

"Ok, follow me," Mr. Brown said as he led them to where the body was stored.

Detective Gonzalez and Gladys Delgado followed Mr. Brown to the last freezer door on the top. The medical examiner turned the cold, stainless-steel handle to open the door. Then, he pulled open the drawer to expose what was left of the man's body. Tears started to well up in Gladys's eyes as she looked at the pale body of the male victim. There was a Y-shaped incision measuring the length of the torso that was held together by staples. Gladys got all choked up.

"I need to see his right shoulder; he has a tattoo of an eagle on his right shoulder," Gladys apprehensively said, hoping it was not on that body.

The medical examiner agreed to the woman's wishes. He slowly pulled down the cover on the body enough to reveal its right shoulder. A tattoo of a dark brown eagle with its white head and yellow beak, having a very intimidating, but proud look about him, was on the shoulder of the victim's body.

"Oh, my God, it's him, it's my brother!" Gladys said as she noticed the tattoo on the body.

Gladys was on the verge of fainting but Gonzalez grabbed her just in time. The poor woman wailed uncontrollably in the detective's arms. She soaked his white shirt with tears of sorrow; tears that expressed her love for her only sibling. Tears that showed everyone there the pain of knowing that she'd never ever see her brother alive again. The detective thanked the medical examiner for his time and then he took the distraught young woman back to the police station.

*
**

About an hour later, Gonzalez and Delgado had arrived back at the police station. Gonzalez decided to stop at the corner coffee shop and pick up some breakfast for the two of them. The detective brought the young woman back into his office and asked her to sit down.

"You really should eat," Gonzalez told her.

"I'm not hungry, but thank you for the food anyway," Gladys said with tears still in her eyes.

"I'm really sorry for your loss."

"Are you really, Detective? I mean, he was your prime suspect, isn't that what you told me?"

"Yes, he was."

"How did it happen? How did he die?" Gladys asked, still with tears in her eyes.

Gonzalez pulled out a bloodied hunting knife in a plastic bag from his desk drawer. It was the same knife that was found at the crime scene.

"What's that?!" Gladys shrieked.

"That knife was found in your brother's hand at the crime scene. Does it look familiar to you?" Gonzalez asked her.

"No, I've never seen it before in my life."

"We've checked it for fingerprints, but there were none on it. Hector Delgado's death was ruled as a suicide. I'm sorry," Gonzalez solemnly stated.

"Wait! You're telling me that my brother stabbed himself to death?"

"Yes, he slit his throat from ear to ear."

"It can't be, *that knife* killed my brother?"

"No, Miss Delgado. That knife is just a piece of metal, a tool, an instrument. Your brother killed himself with it."

"I don't understand. Why? Why would my own brother commit suicide?"

"Oh, I don't know, maybe he felt guilty about killing Mrs. Harris and her daughter."

"You know, that's a cheap shot, Detective," Gladys angrily told him. Gladys got up and left the detective's office, without her coffee and breakfast sandwich.

Gonzalez finally decided to read the medical examiner's report on the body. The victim was being described as a male, approximately twenty-seven to twenty-nine years of age. The report stated that the tissue samples taken from the body showed he was dead eight to nine weeks. Cause of death was a deep laceration of the throat by a right-handed person from behind, while the head was restrained firmly. The incision measured from ear to ear, severing the victim's trachea and major blood vessels. Lividity showed that the victim may have been killed somewhere else, before being brought to the roof where he was found. There were traces of cocaine in the body. The victim also had dried blood scratch marks on his back that appeared to have been caused by human fingernails.

"Shit! He was murdered, but by who and why?" Gonzalez said to himself.

Detective Gonzalez sat at his desk, drinking his now cold cup of coffee, looking at the photos and thinking. He reread the report, focusing on the last few lines that read, *Cause of death was a deep laceration of the throat by a right-handed person from behind, while the head was restrained firmly. The incision measured from ear to ear, severing the victim's trachea and major blood vessels. Lividity showed the victim may have been killed somewhere else, before being brought to the roof where he was found.*

"I'm gonna have to inform the captain about this shit," Gonzalez said to himself.

The detective also knew he was going to have to tell Gladys that her brother didn't commit suicide after all. He would have to inform the woman that her brother was murdered. *This shit keeps getting worse,* he thought while getting up from his desk.

CHAPTER 11

BACK TO THE CRIME SCENE

Thursday afternoon, the thirtieth day of April, Nathan Harris had just received his express delivery of the parts he had ordered. *Maybe now I can get my Time Transporter working and find out who really killed my wife and daughter,* the scientist and inventor thought. The multimillionaire scientist no longer thought very highly of the Solville Police Department; he decided to take matters into his own hands to solve the murders. Nathan grew weary of the police, especially Detective Juan Gonzalez, who was constantly trying to pin the murders on him. *I guess they'll appreciate me more when it comes to donation time; they're not getting shit out of me anymore,* he spitefully thought. Nathan happily brought his electronic parts down to his lab.

***

Detective Gonzalez was back at the murder board again, holding a cup of coffee and trying to piece things together. Gonzalez knew he had to share this new piece of evidence with Delgado's sister, Gladys. The detective was hoping that he could shine some light on the case by staring at the board. Captain Martinelli had just walked into the office wearing a big coffee stain on his powder-blue shirt.

"You still staring at that board?" Martinelli asked.

"Yup, what else can I do, Captain?" Gonzalez replied.

"Have you got any leads yet?"

"Nope, but did you fully read that ME's report on Hector Delgado, especially the part that said, 'The victim also had bloodied scratch marks on his back that appeared to have been caused by human fingernails?"'"

"Yes, I did see that."

"You know what I'm thinking?" Gonzalez asked.

"That it was Mrs. Harris that did it."

"Bingo! I'm glad to see we're on the same page, Captain. Remember, Mrs. Harris had Delgado's blood and tissue samples under her fingernails. That was probably done in the heat of passion."

"She could have also done that to try and defend herself from rape," Martinelli sternly added.

"I suppose it's possible, but not probable. I believe Mrs. Harris and Hector Delgado both had consensual sex, *and* judging by the marks on his back from the photos, she enjoyed it."

"You have your beliefs and I have mine."

"I guess this is another time where we don't see eye to eye, Captain."

"Have you told Delgado's sister that her brother was murdered?" Martinelli asked while changing the subject.

"Not yet, Captain, not yet."

"Well stop procrastinating and do it. She has a right to know that her brother didn't commit suicide."

"I'll go call her now, Captain."

Gonzalez left the murder board and headed for his office. He sat down at his desk and looked through his black notebook for Gladys Delgado's number. Gonzalez begrudgingly picked up the phone and called her.

*

A couple of hours later at the Harris residence, Nathan had

135

completed the repairs on the Time Transporter. *This new CPU is much faster than that reject I had. It should function much better, with more accuracy,* he thought. The scientist and inventor knew there was no margin for error if he were to solve the mystery of his wife and daughter's murder.

Nathan donned his navy-blue suit with its retractable hood. Next, the scientist put on his electronic belt and walked back toward the transporter chamber.

"Here we go again, back to the cold and snow," the scientist said to himself.

Nathan activated all of his equipment and set the date dials to Tuesday morning, January seventeen; the day he left for his trip to Oregon. Nathan set the location to be outside, in front of his mansion, at five o'clock in the morning. Nathan also set the return time for 4:49 p.m., the time the grandfather clock had stopped; assuming it was in the evening. *Let's hope I arrive at the right place and time, this time,* he thought. The scientist had to get back before his family was murdered, hoping he could have time enough to prevent it from ever happening.

Nathan walked into the transporter chamber and waited for the retractable cylindered doors to close on him. He powered up his remote controller belt, reached behind his collar, and pulled up on his retractable hood to cover his head. Nathan placed his hand onto the touchscreen that was mounted on the back wall of the time machine. Then he waited for the machine's response.

"Hello Mr. Harris, and welcome aboard," the machine announced in its electronic female voice.

"Hello Alice, commence time travel sequence," Nathan replied to the computer, as he put on his dark glasses to protect his eyes from the prevailing lasers in the machine.

"Affirmative, Mr. Harris, initiating time travel sequence in ten seconds."

The Time Transporter began its countdown.

"Ten, nine, eight, seven, six, five, four, three, two, one, zero," the computer stated while displaying the numbers on the LCD screen.

The overhead electrodes began to energize, followed by the halo laser that was circulating powerful light rays around him in the tubular chamber. The transporter started up with its powerful whirring sound again. Nathan Harris felt strange as his body began to demolecularize within the chamber. Within seconds, Nathan's molecules were being transported back in time again. When all of his molecules had arrived in the past, they began to remolecularize back in the same order.

*
**

Nathan Harris had arrived back in the past, over two months ago, in the snow and right in front of his mansion. He turned around to see his past self drive off to the airport for his trip to Oregon. *I made it back at the right time. There I go for my seminar in Oregon,* Nathan happily thought.

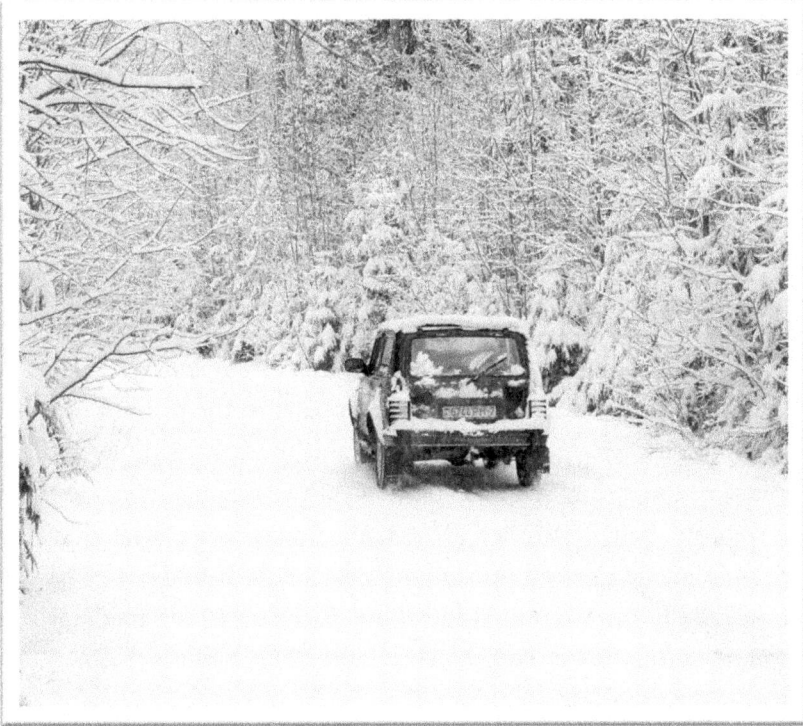

Photo courtesy of Artem Podrez

"Now I just need to get inside and wait for the killer to arrive," he said to himself.

Nathan reached into his right front pants pocket and searched for his house keys, and then he searched his left pants pocket, but they were both empty. Nathan frantically searched his jacket pockets, but still he came up empty.

"Shit! Of all the damn…" Nathan was so disgusted, he couldn't finish what he wanted to say.

The scientist didn't want to wake anyone up at five o'clock in the morning, so ringing the doorbell was completely out of the question. Nathan decided to try the back door, but it was locked. He then checked the side door; it was also locked. Nathan thought about the garage doors, but the keypad needed batteries. Both of the remotes were in the vehicles; one was in the garage and the other one just drove away. Clearly the scientist and inventor was running out of options. *I'm gonna have to ring the bell and wake them up; their lives depend upon it,* he thought. Nathan rang the doorbell and waited to see if any lights went on in the room windows upstairs. When there was no response, he rang it again and again. After the fourth ring, Nathan simply just gave up.

"Boy, they must be dead to the world, oblivious to anything and everything," Nathan softly said to himself.

Had Nathan tried to open the front door originally, he would have been pleasantly surprised to find that it was indeed unlocked. The Time Transporter was set to send him back to the present at 4:49 p.m., but Nathan wasn't going to hang around there, outside in the cold, for almost twelve hours. Nathan flipped on the manual override switch on his remote belt controller. The countdown timer started up on the remote unit. He pulled up on his collar and covered his head with the retractable hood. Nathan stood there, listening to the machine's female voice counting down over the controller belt's built-in speaker.

"Ten, nine, eight, seven, six, five, four, three, two, one, zero," the computer stated while displaying the numbers on the belt's LCD screen.

After the countdown was completed, Nathan slowly started to disappear. Within seconds, Nathan had completely dematerialized and was sent back to his time and place, in the future. The scientist had wasted a trip back in time for nothing.

*
**

Scientist and inventor Nathan Harris had finally arrived back to his present time and place, in his laboratory. Nathan was standing in the transporter chamber. He waited for the retractable cylindered doors to reopen. Nathan powered off his controller belt, retracted his hood, and walked out of the transporter chamber. *That takes a lot out of me,* he thought. Nathan decided to take a nap before going back again.

*
**

At the Solville Police Department, Gladys Delgado had just arrived at Detective Gonzalez's office wearing a light green dress and a black jacket. She wondered what the detective wanted from her now. Gladys sat down in the same chair, right in front of the detective's desk.

"Ok *Señor* Detective, what happened now?" Gladys asked him in an annoyed tone.

"*Señora* Delgado, I just wanted to share some important information about your brother," Gonzalez calmly told her.

"Who else did he kill, or did you find some more drugs in his apartment or car?"

"*Mira, señora,* it was none of the above. It appears that your brother Hector did not kill himself after all; your brother was murdered."

"What?! Are you sure, Detective?!"

"Yes, the examination results prove, beyond a shadow of a doubt, that Hector Delgado was indeed murdered."

"Oh, my God!" Gladys cried out.

"Someone overtook him from behind and slashed his throat in

cold blood."

"No, no, oh, God please, no; I can't believe it," she said on the verge of tears.

"Miss Delgado, did your brother have any enemies? Any that you can think of?"

"I don't know, I really don't know, but I figured he, he, didn't kill, himself; Hector wouldn't do that."

Gladys started to cry on the detective's desk. Gonzalez got up and went over to comfort her. The detective hated giving people bad news, especially women and children.

*
**

The next day, Friday morning, April fourteen, at the Harris lab, Nathan was getting ready for his trip back in time. This time he remembered to bring his house keys with him and a set of AA batteries for the garage keypad. Nathan donned his navy-blue suit with its hood. Next, the scientist put on his electronic belt and walked back toward the transporter chamber. Nathan activated all of his gear and again, set the date dials to Tuesday morning, January seventeen; the day he left for his trip to Oregon. Nathan set the location to be outside, in front of his mansion, at five o'clock in the morning. He also set the return time for 4:49 p.m. Nathan walked into the transporter chamber and waited for the retractable cylindered doors to close on him. He powered up his remote controller belt again, reached behind his collar, and pulled up on his retractable hood to cover his head. Nathan placed his hand onto the touchscreen on the back wall of the machine, so it could identify his handprint.

"Hello Mr. Harris, and welcome aboard," the computer announced in its artificial female voice.

"Hello Alice, commence time travel sequence," Nathan replied to the computer, as he put on his dark glasses to protect his eyes from the predominant lasers in the machine.

"Affirmative, Mr. Harris, initiating time travel sequence in ten seconds."

The Time Transporter began its countdown.

"Ten, nine, eight, seven, six, five, four, three, two, one, zero," the computer stated while displaying the numbers on its LCD screen.

The overhead electrodes began to energize, followed by the halo laser that was circulating powerful light rays around him in the tubular chamber. The transporter started with its powerful whirring sound again. Nathan Harris felt that strange feeling again as his body began to demolecularize within the chamber. Within seconds, Nathan's molecules were being transported back in time again. When all of his molecules had arrived in the past, they had begun to reassemble back in the same order as before.

*
**

Nathan Harris had arrived back in the past, over two months ago, right in front of his mansion, again. He turned around and observed himself drive off in the past, to the airport for his trip to Oregon. This time, Nathan had his hands on the house keys in his pocket. He inserted the key into the door lock, turned it, but it didn't click, it turned freely with no resistance at all.

"Sonofabitch, it was open all along, shit," he softly said to himself.

Then, Nathan remembered what Detective Juan Gonzalez had told him over the phone when he called from Oregon: "He claims the door was unlocked, sir." Gonzalez was referring to Jonathan Mitchel, the insurance agent that had walked into his home when he was away. *So, it must have been me who forgot to lock the door in the first place, not Heather. No one ever locked it later on. That's my family for you, not very security minded,* the man thought.

Nathan turned the doorknob, opened up the door, and closed it right behind him. The scientist walked into the hall of his home and then he sat down on the plush green chair that was near the antique grandfather clock and the staircase. *I'll wait here all day if I have to,* the scientist thought to himself. Nathan was willing to stand guard there for almost twelve hours, if needed, before the machine would send him back to his time. *Well, at least I'll be near the bathroom,* he thought.

Nathan realized he probably wouldn't be there too long, knowing that his daughter would be getting ready for school in just a few hours. Nathan wasn't sure if his wife had anything planned for the day. The scientist turned his head to look at the majestic clock that stood near him, but he couldn't see the time on its face from his angle. *It's probably a little after five,* Nathan thought, not wanting to look at his gold Rolex watch for the time. The scientist was growing tired; he slowly fell asleep in the comfortable chair.

*
**

Six hours later at about eleven o'clock in the morning, Nathan had gotten up to relive himself in the downstairs bathroom. The scientist was still tired; he went right back to sleep again in the chair. *I never realized how comfortable this chair really is,* he thought. Nathan hadn't been sleeping well since the murder of his wife and daughter, plus, him being accused of the murders had really taken a toll on his mental wellbeing. The scientist and inventor never looked at the majestic clock or his watch to see what time it really was. So far, no one had gotten up. The house was dead quiet, while Nathan slept soundly in his chair.

*
**

A few hours later, Nathan was rudely awakened by his computerized belt.

"Commencing return countdown in T-minus thirty seconds," the remote belt unit recited.

"Huh? Oh, shit, it's time for me to go," Nathan said as he bolted out the door without even locking it.

Nathan stood outside of his mansion, listening to the

countdown, as he pulled up on his collar and covered his head with the retractable hood.

"Ten, nine, eight, seven, six, five, four, three, two, one, zero," the computer stated while displaying the numbers on the belt's LCD screen.

After the countdown was completed, Nathan slowly started to disappear. Within seconds, Nathan had completely dematerialized and was sent back to his time and place, in the future. The scientist had wasted another trip back in time for absolutely nothing. Nathan *still* wasn't any closer to solving, or even preventing, the murders of his wife and daughter.

*
**

Scientist and inventor Nathan Harris had finally arrived back to his present time and place in his laboratory. Nathan was standing in his transporter chamber. He waited for the retractable cylindered doors to reopen. Nathan powered off his controller belt, retracted his hood, and walked out of the transporter chamber feeling extremely disappointed and frustrated.

"Jesus H. Christ, I can't believe I fell asleep while my family was getting murdered! I never heard anything, sonofabitch!" Nathan shouted to himself.

"They had to have been killed while I was there sleeping. It was 4:49 in the evening when I got sent back," he logically said.

Nathan Harris knew he was a heavy sleeper. If there was an earthquake, Nathan probably wouldn't even know about it. *This is taking a toll on me and my equipment. All of this back and forth in time, for absolutely nothing,* he sadly thought. *Before I go back to the crime scene again, I better get a good night's sleep,* he logically thought to himself. Nathan heard the phone ring, then the telephone answering machine picked up the call.

"Hello Nathan, it's Doctor Berlin again. Please call me at your earliest convenience, it's imperative," he said before hanging up.

Nathan wasn't ready to talk to him yet. The scientist just wasn't

143

ready to open up to anyone about his problems. He was going to try and handle everything *his* way, at least for now.

✳
✳✳

Monday morning, April seventeen, at the Solville Police Department, Detective Juan Gonzalez had just walked in from the pouring rain with his broken umbrella. He had just spilled his morning cup of coffee on his tan-colored raincoat, struggling to close his umbrella.

"Mierda!" Gonzalez shouted loud enough to be heard by everyone there.

"Are you having a bad morning?" Officer Cheng said to him with a chuckle.

"Oh, shut up. Don't you have someplace to be and something to do?" Gonzalez angrily asked him.

The now disheveled detective walked into his office shaking out his umbrella. Gonzalez looked like a wet rat. *Well, it is April, April showers, mierda,* he angrily thought. Gonzalez opened up his umbrella and placed it in the corner of his office, near his desk. When he turned around, the detective was surprised to see he had a visitor, a female visitor.

"Buenos dias, Señor Detective," Gladys Delgado softly said to him.

"Buenos dias señora, I didn't expect to see you standing there behind me," Gonzalez said while feeling startled.

"I didn't mean to surprise you like that. *¡Perdon!"*

"It's ok."

Gladys looked like a sight for sore eyes to him. She had her long, wavy, jet-black hair all the way down to her buttocks, with a nice flowery print dress on. The woman had a black shoulder bag on her right shoulder and she was holding two large cups of coffee in her hands.

"I brought you some coffee, you look like you really need it," Gladys told him as she handed him one of the coffees.

144

"*Oh*, I do, *muchas gracias*. I spilled all my coffee fighting with this umbrella and the rain," he replied.

"*De nada,*" Gladys responded as she sat down in front of his desk.

"So, what brings you here, Miss Delgado?"

"Oh, right to the point, ok. You asked me if my brother had any enemies, remember?"

"*Sí,* I remember. Did he?"

"I'm not sure, but I heard him argue over the phone one time when we were having breakfast at a diner."

"Did he tell you who he was talking to, or what the argument was about?"

"Hector said it was nothing, but I heard him mention something about money; yeah that's what it was. He said he'd have the money soon. *¡Ay Dios Mío!* I should have known he was into drugs," Gladys said with a cry in her voice.

"Did he mention a name? Do you remember him calling the person something over the phone?"

"I think he said Darius; he said, 'Don't worry about it, Darius, you know I'm good for it.'"

Gonzalez knew he had another lead, another suspect. The two of them finished their coffees and then Gladys left for her job at the college. The good detective started looking through all of the criminal files on anyone named Darius. *He's obviously a drug dealer,* the detective thought.

CHAPTER 12

ANOTHER SUSPECT

𝕿uesday morning, April eighteen, Detective Juan Gonzalez was still looking for another suspect in the Delgado murder case. It had been over a week since Gladys Delgado had given him a clue. She had mentioned to him that her brother had a quarrel with a person named Darius over the phone. So far, the detective came up with blanks on all leads.

"Hey Gonzalez, get on over to 610 Maiden Street in Oakwood, on the double!" Captain Martinelli shouted through the detective's open doorway.

"Are you sure it's 610 Maiden Street in Oakwood? That's the building that Hector Delgado lived in," Gonzalez stated.

"Brilliant deduction, Watson. The superintendent called here saying some young African American male was pounding on Delgado's old apartment. So, go and check it out, bring Officer Cheng with you."

"I'm on it, Captain; I'll get Cheng," Gonzalez said as he left his office.

Detective Gonzalez went and grabbed Officer Cheng. He filled Cheng in on what was happening at where Delgado lived, saying it would probably be a big break in the Delgado murder case. Cheng was almost ready to leave; he just had to make a pit stop in the men's room first. Gonzalez had told him to hurry up and that he'd be waiting in the car for him.

*
**

About a half-hour later, Detective Gonzalez and Officer Cheng had arrived back at 610 Maiden Street in Oakwood. Cheng parked the police cruiser on the corner near the building. The two men walked toward the tenement, just in time to see Superintendent Jose Garcia get assaulted by a young African American male wearing a black leather jacket and blue jeans, right in front of the building. The perpetrator was now behind Garcia, holding a knife at his neck.

"Solville PD, drop the knife and freeze!" Officer Cheng shouted while pointing his service revolver at the perpetrator.

The young man released Garcia and bolted down the street with Officer Cheng hot on his heels. Gonzalez started running after them also. Cheng couldn't believe how stupid the man was; running away while he was pointing a gun at him.

"Shoot him in the leg!" Gonzalez shouted.

When the culprit heard that, he immediately stopped in his tracks and put his hands up.

"Don't shoot, please don't shoot! I give up!" the perpetrator shouted as he stopped dead in his tracks and raised his hands up, while still holding the knife in his right hand.

Officer Cheng caught up to him, told him to drop the knife, and to put his hands behind his back. Detective Gonzalez finally caught up to them, huffing and puffing with every step he took. Gonzalez got in front of the perpetrator and trained his gun on him, while Cheng handcuffed him.

"You thought you could give us the slip, huh? That was a very *stupid* thing to do, mister. You could have gotten your ass killed. Do you know that? You're under arrest! Read him his rights, Cheng!" Gonzalez barked.

"You have the right to remain silent. Anything you say can and will be used against you in a court of law. You have the right to an attorney before we ask you any questions. If you cannot afford an attorney, one will be appointed to you before a court of law. If you decide to answer questions now without an attorney present, you have the right to stop answering at any time. Do you understand these rights?" Cheng asked while he searched him.

"Yeah, I do," the man solemnly stated.

"Now, who the hell are you and why were you attacking that man?"

"He started it."

"No, I, I didn't. You tried to kill me," Garcia struggled to say while finally catching up to all of them, looking all ruffled up, trying to catch his breath.

"The officer asked you a question, state your same, sir," Gonzalez sternly told him.

"My name is Darius," the perpetrator replied.

Gonzalez thought in an instant that this was probably the man he was looking for. The detective wondered how many men named Darius there were in the area, *if* he was from around here.

"Darius, what?" Gonzalez asked him.

"His name is Darius White, he lives at 122 Clayton Street right here in Oakwood," Officer Cheng replied after reading the man's driver's license.

"Mr. Garcia, are you all right?" Gonzalez asked while facing him.

"Si, señor, I'm ok," Garcia replied.

"Do you want to press charges, Mr. Garcia?"

"No, just take his ass away."

Then Garcia turned around and faced his attacker.

"Mira, If I see your ass here again, I call the police and *this time,* I press charges," Garcia sternly told him.

"Why did you attack Mr. Garcia?" Officer Cheng asked.

"He came up and told me to stop banging on my friend's door," Darius replied.

"You were making a lot of noise; the tenants called me and complained. They say you were screaming and cursing, 'Where's my fuckin money!?' The way you were banging and kicking the door, look like you were trying to break it down," Garcia replied.

"Well, he owes me a lot of money, shit," Darius said in a nasty tone.

"Who owes you money?" Gonzalez asked him.

"My friend," Darius replied.

"Your friend huh; what apartment was he trying to get into, Mr. Garcia?"

"The same one you two were at the last time you were here, apartment 6I."

"And what happened after that, Mr. Garcia?" Gonzalez asked him.

"This *moreno* took out a knife and chased my ass down the stairs saying that I know where he is."

"If you're looking for your friend, Hector Delgado, he's dead," Gonzalez told Darius.

"What?!"

"Did you kill him because he owed you money?" Gonzalez asked him.

"Shit no! I didn't kill anyone!"

"I guess you were his drug dealer, right?"

"I ain't saying *shit* without my lawyer."

"So, how much did he owe you?" Officer Cheng asked.

"I done told you, I ain't saying *shit* without my lawyer," Darius firmly stated.

"Well, you gonna need one because I found *this* in your pocket!" Officer Cheng said while holding up a small, clear, plastic bag full of white powder.

"Well, well, well, we can all guess that *this* shit ain't sugar!" Gonzalez said while looking at the bag.

"You know it," Cheng added.

"All right, throw his ass in the car, Cheng. I'm getting too old for this shit," Gonzalez stated.

"Yeah, I saw the way you were running, man, you look like you were gonna have a heart attack or some shit," Cheng replied with a snicker.

Photo courtesy of Cottonbro Studio

"Oh, shut the hell up and let's get going," Gonzalez angrily replied back to him.

Officer Cheng stuck Darius in the back of the cruiser and he got in on the passenger side. Detective Gonzalez got in on the driver's side and started up the car. Gonzalez knew he was out of shape, but the man was leery about joining a gym now with COVID-19 cases still on the rise. *Maybe I'll just get me a treadmill, like one of those that Harris has,* Gonzalez thought as he drove off.

⁎
⁎⁎

Later that morning, Gonzalez and Cheng were pulling in to the police station parking lot with their prisoner, Darius White. Gonzalez and Cheng brought the prisoner into the police station. Captain Martinelli came out of his office with his white shirt hanging out of his pants, holding a cup of coffee in his right hand and looking directly at their new prisoner.

"Well, is this the infamous Darius that you were looking for, Gonzalez?" Martinelli asked him.

"Yeah, Captain, he tried to give us the slip, but we got him," Gonzalez happily reported.

"Y'all ain't got nothing on me. I want my lawyer," Darius retorted.

"He had *this* on him," Gonzalez said while holding up the plastic bag full of white powder.

"Oh, so you gonna lawyer up, eh? Listen here, punk, we got places for lowlife people like you and I'd be glad to bring your ass there," Martinelli shot back at him.

Buenos Dias, Señor Detective," Gladys Delgado said as she entered the station wearing a light-blue blouse and a brand-new pair of tight-fitting blue jeans, while holding two large cups of coffee.

Darius White turned around to see her. Gladys nearly dropped

151

the coffees as she stared at Darius in shock, trying to remember where she had seen this man before. The young woman stood there, trying to place his face in her mind. *Where have I seen this man?* she wondered. Then, it became all too clear to her. It was as if someone had just flipped on a recall switch in her brain, activating all of her memory cells at once.

"I, I saw this man before, I saw him giving my brother something," Gladys nervously stated.

Detective Gonzalez looked at her; he saw a sense of urgency and fear in her facial expression. It was something in her face that commanded his attention, fast.

"Do you know this man, Miss Delgado?" Gonzalez asked her with a curious expression on his face.

"I've seen him give my brother something, something recently," Gladys said.

"What was it, Miss Delgado?"

"He, he gave my brother a brown paper bag, then, then he grabbed my brother and stuck his finger right in my brother's face, Detective," Gladys struggled to say with tears now emerging from her eyes.

"Cheng, why don't you bring Darius into the interrogation room? I'll be there in a few minutes," Gonzalez told him.

Gonzalez brought Miss Delgado into his office and closed the door behind them.

"Now, you said you know this man?" Gonzalez asked Miss Delgado.

"I've seen him maybe once or twice, but the last time I remember him giving a brown paper bag to my brother. He looked like he wanted to hurt Hector. Is he the one that killed my brother?" Gladys asked emotionally with tears in her eyes.

"We don't know that for sure, yet. Do you remember when all of that happened?"

"It was sometime in January, I don't remember exactly when, Detective. Is this guy, Darius, the one my brother was talking to over the phone?"

"Well, that's his name and he *was* looking for your brother at his apartment."

"Then he's got to be Hector's killer."

"Let's not go jumping to conclusions here, Miss Delgado. I'm not a hundred percent sure if this guy's got anything to do with your brother's death, so I need time to interrogate him, you understand?"

"*Sí, Señor* Detective, I go now. You do your job and catch my brother's killer."

"I promise I'll let you know what we find," Gonzalez reassuringly told her.

Gladys Delgado sadly walked out of Detective Gonzalez's office. Gonzalez noticed that she left him both cups of coffee on his desk. He wondered if she did that purposely, or was the woman so distraught that she completely forgot all about it? He tried to go and catch up to her with one of the coffee cups, but Gladys was already gone. *Man, she's fast,* Gonzalez thought while scanning the area.

*
**

A few minutes later, Detective Gonzalez was in the interrogation room with the prisoner, Darius White. The interrogation room resembled a small recording studio, with large soundproofing materials that were glued up on the walls to deaden the sound. There was a small table and two chairs in the room. A video camera on the wall and two microphones were also present there on the table. Captain Paul Martinelli and two other officers were watching and listening in the other room, while the interview was being conducted and recorded.

153

"For the record, state your full name," Gonzalez asked in a matter-of-fact tone of voice.

"My name's Darius White," he replied.

"What were you doing banging on Hector Delgado's door this morning?"

"He owes me a lot of money."

"How much money?"

"Three thousand dollars."

"And was this drug money for the cocaine that you sold him?"

"*Yo* man, that's it. I ain't saying anymore shit without ma damn lawyer."

"So, where's your lawyer?"

"I ain't got one yet, but I'ma get me one."

"You know, Mr. White, you could make it a hell of a lot easier on yourself and us by cooperating. Now tell me, did you kill Hector Delgado?"

"*Yo man*, I done told you I ain't had *shit* to do with that. I didn't even know he was *dead*. If I did, *why* would my ass be bangin on his door early in the mornin'?"

Gonzalez knew he had a point there, but he wasn't ready to quit yet.

"When was the last time you saw Mr. Delgado alive?" the detective asked him.

"It was sometime in January," White replied.

"That's when you sold him the coke?"

"Yo man, we done. I want ma lawyer."

"You said you didn't have one! Quit playing games, White, stop wasting my damn time! Now, would you be willing to take a polygraph test?"

"What's that?"

"In layman's terms it's called a lie detector test."

"Yeah man, I'm down with that if it'll show y'all that I didn't kill Hector."

Detective Gonzalez took Darius White to the room where the polygraph machine was. The technician hooked White up to the machine with all the wires and then he asked him some preliminary questions, before turning the interrogation over to the detective. Gonzalez grilled him all over again, asking, pretty much, the same questions.

*
**

An hour later, Gonzalez was in the captain's office giving him the report.

"Well, what have you got? Is he lying or what?" Captain Martinelli asked.

"You're not gonna like this, Captain, but it appears White's telling us the truth," Gonzalez said sounding disappointed.

"Well then, we got to let him go."

"But Captain, we can't just let him go like *that*."

"Have you got anything on him, any kind of proof that says he killed Hector Delgado, or anything that connects him to the Harris murders?!"

"White had a few ounces of cocaine on him, which proves he was Delgado's drug supplier."

"That's all it proves. Look, Gonzalez, we deal with homicide, not drugs. Turn him over to narcotics. If and when you come up with something that connects him to any of the murders, then will deal with him," Martinelli told him.

Detective Gonzalez walked out of the captain's office feeling like a dog with his tail stuck between his legs. He knew the captain was right, but it didn't feel right to him, not at all. Gonzalez went over to where White was being detained; he was going to have him set free, begrudgingly. *Shit, another bullshit lead, this sucks,* he thought while feeling disgusted.

*
**

Nathan was home in his bead; he went to sleep late and was still sleeping late in the morning. The scientist was having an unnerving dream, but in reality, it was sort of a flashback. In his dream, Nathan was very young and was witnessing his parents having the biggest fight he could ever remember; it was all about William. However, Nathan saw something different this time. His mother had picked up a big kitchen knife and was just about to stab his father in the stomach with it.

"No, Momma, don't! Don't kill my daddy!" Nathan screamed as he woke up.

Nathan looked around and found that he was in his own bed in his mansion, all alone, with the smell of new paint in the room. The bright sun had been shining through his new curtains and drapery. Nathan was hyperventilating with sweat dripping down from his face, even though it was cool in his room.

"It was just a dream, but it seemed so damn real," he said to himself.

Nathan never saw his mother raise a knife to his father, but there was a very heated argument. He tried to remember it as vividly as he could; it was about his friend, William. Nathan remembered his mother throwing dishes at his father, he even remembered his mother pushing him up against the wall, screaming at him from the very top of her lungs, but there was never a knife involved. That was all he could remember.

Nathan looked at the antique clock up on the wall, it was almost twelve noon. *I guess I'm not going to make that fundraiser at the school today,* he thought. The scientist and inventor had missed quite a few social events ever since his family had been murdered. He was on a downward trend, still depressed, trying to get over it and move on with his life, but it was going to take time, plenty of time. *Why, Lord? Why did you let someone take them away from me? Why did you let this happen?* Nathan miserably asked himself.

CHAPTER 13

TIME TO CATCH THE KILLER

Wednesday afternoon, on the nineteenth day of April, Nathan Harris had been working in his laboratory all morning, tweaking his Time Transporter. The scientist and inventor was getting ready for yet another trip back in time to three months ago when he had last seen his wife and his daughter alive. This time, Nathan was going to bring a deck of cards with him to entertain himself while he waited for the murderer to arrive. Nathan thought about bringing his pocket game console or smartphone, but he figured there would be electronic interference between the devices and his remote belt controller. After all, his invention *did* contain built-in navigational equipment to facilitate time travel.

Nathan put on his navy-blue suit with its protective hood. Then, the scientist strapped on the electronic belt and walked back toward the transporter chamber in the room. Nathan activated all of his equipment and set the date dials to Tuesday morning, January seventeen; the day he had left for his trip to Oregon. Nathan set the location to be outside, in front of his mansion, at five o'clock in the morning. He then set the return time for 4:49 p.m. Nathan walked into the transporter chamber and waited for the retractable cylindered doors to close up on him. He powered up the controller belt, reached behind his collar, and pulled up on the retractable hood to cover his head. Nathan placed his hand onto the touchscreen on the back wall of the machine and then he waited for the apparatus to respond.

"Hello Mr. Harris, and welcome aboard," the computer announced in its synthetic female voice.

"Hello Alice, commence time travel sequence, please," Nathan replied to the computer, as he put on his dark glasses to protect his eyes from the powerful lasers in the machine.

"Affirmative, Mr. Harris, initiating time travel sequence in ten seconds."

The Time Transporter began its countdown.

"Ten, nine, eight, seven, six, five, four, three, two, one, zero," the computer stated while displaying the numbers on its LCD screen.

The overhead electrodes began to energize, followed by the halo laser that was circulating powerful light beams around him in the tubular chamber. The transporter started with a loud whirring sound. Nathan Harris began to feel strange as his body began to demolecularize within the chamber. Within seconds, Nathan's molecules were being transported backward in time. When all of the scientist's molecules had arrived in the past, they began to reassemble back in the same exact order.

*
**

Nathan Harris had gone back into the past, exactly three months ago, standing right in front of his mansion. He turned around and witnessed himself drive off in the past, to the airport for his seminar in Oregon. Nathan remembered that he originally forgot to lock the door. He turned the doorknob and walked right in, closing it behind him.

The scientist walked into the hall of his home and then he sat down on the plush green chair that was near the grandfather clock and the staircase. Nathan turned his head around to look at the majestic clock that stood near him, but he couldn't see the time on its face from his angle. This time, though, he decided to get up to look at the clock and compare the time with his wristwatch. Nathan looked up at the clock's face and noticed it was 4:49.

"That can't be right, this clock must be slow," he said to himself.

Nathan pulled up his left sleeve to look at his watch; it was 5:05 in the morning. Nathan carefully placed his left ear up close to the clock to listen for its tick-tock sound, but the clock was dead silent. Suddenly,

159

a deep chill came from within him. Nathan knew something was wrong, terribly wrong. The scientist started having palpitations, and he broke out in a cold sweat. Nathan could literally hear and feel his own heart pounding inside his chest.

"No, it can't be," he fearfully said to himself.

Nathan begrudgingly took a slow walk up the stairs toward the master bedroom suite, worrying what he might find in the room. Nathan slowly walked over toward the doorway, while his heart was pounding a mile a minute. The door was closed. He already knew deep down inside how this was going to turn out.

The scientist slowly opened up the bedroom door and was completely horrified. The room looked like a crime scene of a horrific murder. There was blood splattered everywhere. The king-sized bed, which included its sheets and pillows, were all saturated in blood. The white carpeting surrounding the bed had large blood stains on it. The walls were also sprayed with blood, and so was the lamp shade that was on the nearby nightstand. Some blood had also sprayed onto the tan-colored curtains that were hanging on the ornate windows. It was enough to make anyone cringe with fear.

There was no trace of his wife, Heather; he knew she had to be dead and tucked into the sofa downstairs in the parlor. Nathan screamed and ran out of the room so fast that he caused a breeze strong enough to shut the bedroom door behind him. Nathan ran right into the downstairs bathroom to vomit in the toilet. He slowly stood back up, cleaned himself off, and flushed the toilet.

Nathan Harris now realized that the murders did indeed occur in the morning and not in the evening. *The clock had stopped at 4:49, because my daughter was stuffed inside of it, preventing the mechanism from running. Obviously, none of them left here alive that day. The killer must have come late at night, hid somewhere, and waited for just the right moment, probably while I was still in the lab*, Nathan thought. *That's right because Alice's schoolteachers claimed my daughter was never there that day*, he remembered.

"I've got to go back and try again, only this time, I have to get here earlier, much earlier, if I'm going to catch this killer," he said to himself.

Nathan hit the manual override button on his computerized belt to return him back to the present.

"Commencing return countdown in T-minus thirty seconds," the remote belt unit recited.

Nathan walked out the door without locking it. The scientist stood outside of his mansion, listening to the countdown, as he pulled up on his collar and covered his head with the retractable hood.

"Ten, nine, eight, seven, six, five, four, three, two, one, zero," the computer stated while displaying the numbers on the belt's LCD screen.

After the countdown was completed, Nathan slowly started to disappear. Within seconds, the scientist had completely dematerialized with his invention and was sent back to his time and place, back in the future. The disheartened scientist had wasted yet another trip back in time, all for nothing.

*
**

Scientist and inventor Nathan Harris had finally arrived back to his present time and place in his laboratory. Nathan was standing in the transporter chamber. He waited for the retractable cylindered doors to reopen. Nathan powered off his controller belt, retracted his hood, and walked out of the transporter chamber, feeling quite distressed.

"The killer was right there in my own home while I slept," he tensely said to himself.

Nathan Harris was very unnerved by this new revelation; the man didn't have a clue as to how he was going to handle it.

"Shit! He could have *still* been in the house, while I was there," he said, feeling very tense.

Nathan knew he was playing with fire. *Next time I'll bring my gun with me, just in case,* he thought. *To think, my wife and daughter were killed in my bedroom while I slept downstairs in the lab,* Nathan somberly thought to himself. *I should have stayed upstairs with her; maybe I could have prevented it, or maybe I would have been killed too,* he pondered while feeling extremely guilty. The scientist decided to go out for dinner, hoping it would help take his mind off of his troubles.

*
**

The next morning at the Solville Police Department, Gladys Delgado had arrived and was bringing coffee to Detective Gonzalez. Gladys has made this a ritual ever since she discovered her brother, Hector, was missing. The young lady was growing very fond of the detective, but she wasn't ready to admit it. Gladys had been hurt too many times in the past by men that cheated on her.

The young Latina waltzed into the detective's office wearing a light-blue blouse, a pair of blue jeans, and a black shoulder bag; the young lady was also wearing a black sweater to help keep her warm. This time, Gladys decided to wear her hair in a ponytail.

"Buenos dias Señor Detective," Gladys said with a smile.

"Buenos dias señora. What brings you here this morning?" Detective Gonzalez responded.

"I brought you some coffee and a blueberry muffin," she said while handing him the coffee and a small brown bag from her shoulder bag.

"Wow, breakfast, *gracias, señora.*"

"I was wondering if that man you brought in that day was my brother's killer," she asked while sitting down in the chair that was near his desk.

"Well, I told you I would let you know if—"

"I know, I know, but I have to know, please."

"It doesn't look like Mr. White is our killer. There's no physical evidence to link him to your brother's murder, and he passed a lie detector test. Mr. White is guilty of selling your brother cocaine, but that's about it."

Gladys looked disappointed. The young woman looked like she was ready to cry as she lowered her head. Gonzalez felt saddened, seeing the happy, enthusiastic smile simply vanish from her sweet face, but he knew there was nothing he could do to ease her pain and sorrow, nothing that would make this beautiful creature smile again.

Detective Juan Gonzalez was never good with women; he never considered himself a lady's man at all. Gonzalez always had his nose up in the grindstone of any case he was working on, trying his best to solve it in a timely manner. The good detective never made time for women. He was still highly upset and hurt from seeing his ex-wife in their bed with another woman. If Gonzalez hadn't come home early from work that day, he wouldn't have seen it. *Three years with the same woman and I never knew she was bisexual,* the man sadly remembered. Even though it's been five years since their divorce, it still pains him.

Gladys sadly left the police station to go back home. The young woman never told the detective that she was on vacation for two weeks. Gonzalez wondered why she even took the time out to come down there, without ever calling first.

*
**

Nathan had just finished his breakfast and was ready to go back down to the laboratory. This time, Nathan knew he had to go back a little further in time in order to catch the killer. The scientist also remembered to pack his revolver with him. *I've got to be prepared for danger,* he thought.

Nathan put on his navy-blue suit with its hood. Then the scientist put his electronic belt on and walked back toward the transporter chamber. Nathan activated all of his equipment again but this time, he set the date dials a little bit earlier to Tuesday morning, January seventeen, at four o'clock in the morning, an hour earlier than last time. Nathan had also set the location to be outside, in front of his mansion. He brought his house keys, figuring the door would be locked at that time, since it was before he left for Oregon. Then the scientist set his return time for five a.m., one hour later. Nathan walked into the transporter chamber and waited for the retractable cylindered doors to close up on him. He powered up the controller belt, reached behind his collar, and pulled up on the retractable hood to cover his head. Nathan placed his hand onto the touchscreen on the back wall of the machine.

"Hello Mr. Harris, and welcome aboard," the computer announced in its artificial female voice.

"Hello Alice, commence time travel sequence, please," Nathan replied to the computer, as he put on his dark glasses to protect his eyes from the lasers in the machine.

"Affirmative, Mr. Harris, initiating time travel sequence in ten seconds."

The Time Transporter began its countdown.

"Ten, nine, eight, seven, six, five, four, three, two, one, zero," the computer stated while displaying the numbers on its LCD screen.

The overhead electrodes began to energize, followed by the halo laser that was circulating powerful light rays around him in the tubular chamber. The transporter started with a loud whirring sound. Nathan Harris felt strange as his body began to demolecularize within the chamber. Within seconds, Nathan's molecules were being transported back in time. When all of the scientist's molecules had arrived in the past, they began to reassemble back in the same precise order as before.

*
**

Nathan Harris was back in the past, over three months ago, standing there in the snow, right in front of his mansion again. Nathan inserted his key in the front door lock, but it didn't click, indicating that it was never locked. He turned the doorknob and walked right in.

"There's something terribly wrong here. How could any of us leave the front door unlocked all night long?" Nathan softly but tensely said to himself as he closed the door behind him.

The scientist walked into the hall of his home and then he sat down on the plush green chair near the grandfather clock and the staircase. The scientist turned his head to look at the majestic clock that stood near him, but he couldn't see the time on its face from his angle. This time, he got back up to look at the clock and compare the time with his wristwatch. Nathan looked up at the clock's face and then at his watch; he noticed it was two minutes after four.

"That's right on the money," he said to himself.

Nathan placed his left ear close to the clock to listen for its tick-tock sound.

"It's ticking. They're still alive," he quietly said to himself, feeling very relieved.

All of a sudden, there was a noise coming from the parlor; it was the sound of a sofa bed being closed. Nathan briskly walked over toward the parlor. He looked at the torn family portrait that was hanging above the fireplace. The painting was slowly moving from side to side on the wall, as if it were being pushed. Cold chills began to come over Nathan's body. The hairs on his neck were now standing at complete attention as Nathan's heart began to beat faster. The scientist and inventor, who was never really fearful of his life, simply just froze there in complete terror, knowing he was now in the room with a coldblooded killer. A killer that would stop at nothing to complete its mission. Nathan reached his trembling right hand into his jacket pocket to grab his gun, but it was too late. The assassin struck Nathan from behind with a fire stoker, knocking him out cold. Nathan Harris collapsed onto the dark green carpeted floor, right in front of the slaughterer.

*
**

Less than an hour later, Nathan was awakened by his electronic controller belt.

"Commencing return countdown in T-minus thirty seconds,"

the remote controller unit recited.

Nathan slowly stood up while scratching his head, feeling the new bump that was prevalent there. He walked out of the room and over toward the grandfather clock, noticing it had stopped at 4:49 again. Nathan walked out the front door without ever locking it. The scientist stood outside of his mansion, listening to the countdown, as he pulled up on his collar and covered his now aching head with the retractable hood.

"Ten, nine, eight, seven, six, five, four, three, two, one, zero," the computer stated while displaying the numbers on the belt's built-in LCD screen.

After the countdown was completed, Nathan slowly started to disappear. Within a few seconds, the injured scientist had completely dematerialized. His complete molecular structure was now sent back to his present time and place, back to where he belonged in the future.

*
**

Scientist and inventor Nathan Harris had finally arrived back to his present time and place in his laboratory. Nathan was standing inside the transporter chamber. He had waited for the retractable cylindered doors to reopen. Nathan powered off his remote controller belt, retracted his protective hood, and walked out of the transporter chamber. The scientist was deeply disappointed and frustrated, to say the least. *So close and yet so, so far. I never got to see what the hell he looked like. He must have snuck up behind me and knocked me out. Again, I didn't get to save them,* Nathan sadly thought while rubbing his head from the pain.

"Again, I failed. I guess I'm lucky he didn't kill me too," he said to himself.

Nathan realized he was going to have to be a little more ingenious next time. He reached into his pocket for the revolver. *Oh, no, it's gone. I must have dropped it on the floor in the parlor,* Nathan thought. The two AA batteries were still in his pocket from last time; the batteries he brought for the garage keypad that he never got a chance to install. He quickly ran back upstairs to the parlor. Nathan searched the entire floor, looking for the gun, but it was not there.

"It's gone! The killer must have taken it, shit!" Nathan shouted.

The scientist and inventor knew the murderer would be even more dangerous. *Now, I've inadvertently armed him with a gun; if he didn't have one already, he's got one now,* he sadly thought. Nathan knew he was going to have to be more careful now.

*
**

Gladys Delgado had just finished her bowl of cereal and coffee as she sat down at her table. Gladys stared at the wall in front of her in the kitchen, as if she were looking right through it, feeling very lonely while twirling her long black hair between her fingers. The young woman didn't enjoy living all by herself, but now she had no one to talk to at all. Her brother was gone, and even though they had a strained relationship, they still kept in contact, to a degree, except after their last fight. *All this time I thought he was mad at me. All this time I thought he was ignoring my calls and texts. He was dead, dead for two whole months and I didn't even know it,* she sadly thought. Gladys couldn't even turn to her parents; they both died over two years ago while flying in a small private plane that had crashed. The woman didn't even have a man in her life.

"Some vacation I'm having. I got no place to go and no one to spend my free time with, damn," she miserably said to herself in the empty room.

Gladys thought about Detective Gonzalez, but she figured he was damaged goods, at least that was the impression she got from him. The woman often thought that she herself was damaged goods. *He is handsome, though, I'll give him that,* she thought with a positive attitude. Gladys got up from her kitchen chair and put the empty bowl and cup in the sink.

*
**

Back at the police station, Detective Juan Gonzalez was staring at the pictures hanging up on the murder board, while holding a cup of coffee. Gonzalez knew he was back at square one. His new prime suspect in the Delgado murder had gone dry; the guy appeared to be innocent. Gonzalez stared at the board, looking at the pictures of Heather and Alice Harris, again, thinking that he let *them* down, too. *I still believe Nathan Harris is behind this shit. Maybe he killed Hector Delgado too. Harris could have caught them in bed together and killed them both; but why his daughter? Did she just get in his way? Was his daughter's death an accident?* Gonzalez wondered.

The good detective had one card left up his sleeve. Gonzalez knew that although Mr. Harris gave a DNA sample, he never submitted himself to a polygraph examination. Of course, Gonzalez knew deep down that it wasn't going to be easy to convince the captain that his friend, Nathan Harris, should take a lie detector test. Gonzalez knew he had his hands full with that. *I'm running out of options here; what else is there?* Gonzalez mentally asked himself. However, Detective Gonzalez knew that polygraphs were not infallible, but it was worth a shot. He took a red grease marker and put a question mark on the board under Nathan's picture.

*
**

Back at her home in Oakwood, Nancy Stevens was frantically searching her dresser drawers for something. *I know they're in here somewhere, I've got to find them,* she said to herself. Nancy kept thinking about Nathan, wondering what he was going through. She wondered why Nathan was avoiding her. *Nathan needs me, I know he does, but he won't admit it,* she thought. Nancy didn't know that Nathan Harris wasn't ready yet; he just wasn't ready to have any kind of a confrontation with his sister-in-law. Nancy went back to search her drawers. For what? Only time would tell.

CHAPTER 14

I'M INNOCENT

Wednesday morning, April twenty-six, almost a week had passed since Nathan Harris had his brush with death, going back in time. Nathan was almost killed by the man who assassinated his wife and daughter back in January. Nathan was worried that the man would kill even more innocent people now that he had Nathan's gun. *Obviously, he would have used a gun if he had one. It would have been much easier and less messy to shoot my family, or anyone else, instead of stabbing them. As for the noise, he could have used a poor man's silencer, a pillow. Now thanks to my own stupidity, he's armed and dangerous. It just keeps getting worse*, Nathan sadly thought.

Nathan was just about to have his morning cup of coffee and a bagel, until the front doorbell rang. The scientist and inventor turned to look at the security monitor on the wall; it was Detective Juan Gonzalez, again. Nathan walked over toward the door and begrudgingly opened it.

"Good morning, Juan, what can I do for you?" Nathan asked while gritting his teeth.

"Good morning, Mr. Harris. We need you to come down to the station again," Gonzalez stated.

"What is it this time? Let me guess; you found some incriminating evidence to pin on me, right?"

"No, Mr. Harris, not yet. We *would* like you to come down and take a polygraph test."

"A lie detector test? *Sure*, if it'll prove my innocence. Let me just grab my coffee and jacket before we go."

Nathan returned to the kitchen and left the detective standing in the doorway. He poured coffee from the pot into a thermos, then Nathan quickly buttered a bagel and wrapped it in aluminum foil. The scientist grabbed his jacket from the hall closet and left with the detective.

*
**

Shortly after, Detective Gonzalez was pulling up to the Solville Police Department with his suspect, Nathan Harris. Gonzalez marveled at the beautiful blue sky and the nice weather, but his comments fell directly on Nathan's deaf ears. The scientist deliberately ignored him, wanting only to get this inconvenience over with, clear his name, and then move on with his life. The two of them walked into the police station and were greeted by Captain Paul Martinelli.

"Good morning, Mr. Harris, sorry to bring you down for this but—" Martinelli tried to say.

"Don't worry about it, Paul. I'm sure the test will prove I'm innocent," Nathan interrupted.

Gonzalez took Nathan over to where the polygraph machine was stationed. Mark Lalo, the technician, hooked Mr. Harris up to the machine and asked him some preliminary questions, before turning the interrogation over to the detective.

"State your full name, sir," Gonzalez said.

"My name is Nathan Montague Harris," he replied, while Gonzalez looked at the technician and his machine.

"Did you kill your wife?"

"Why would I kill my wife?"

"Just answer yes or no, please," Gonzalez warned.

"No, I did not kill my wife."

"Did you kill your daughter?"

"No."

170

Photo courtesy of Pexels

"Did you hire anyone to murder them?"

"Really?"

"Just answer yes or no, Mr. Harris," Gonzalez scolded him again.

"No, absolutely not," Nathan retorted.

"Did you murder your groundskeeper, Hector Delgado?"

"No! I didn't even know he was dead!" Nathan said shockingly.

"Do you know who killed your wife and daughter?"

"No, I do not. I wish I did," Nathan sadly responded.

Gonzalez saw the technician shake his head no and asked the question again.

"Again, Mr. Harris. *Do you know* who killed your wife and daughter?"

"No, I don't," Nathan said again, hating to have to repeat himself.

Detective Gonzalez looked at the technician again. Gonzalez viewed the printout from the machine. He told Nathan to stay there a minute, while he stepped outside with the technician for a bit. Nathan was wondering what the hell was going on while he looked at his watch. Before Nathan got too comfortable, Gonzalez returned back into the room with the technician.

"No further questions, Mr. Harris," Gonzalez stated.

"Now what? Am I free to go?" Nathan asked.

"Not yet, Mr. Harris, let's just step into the captain's office for a minute, please."

The three men marched into the captain's office. Captain Martinelli asked Nathan to have a seat. Gonzalez and the technician stood by the doorway. Martinelli asked Gonzalez to close the door and give him the results of the polygraph.

"Well, Captain, it appears that Mr. Nathan Harris passed the polygraph with—" Gonzalez started to say.

"You see, I told you I was innocent," Nathan interrupted.

"Mr. Harris, you didn't let me finish," Gonzalez angrily stated.

"I'm sorry, Detective. Please go on."

"Yes, please continue, Gonzalez," the captain ordered.

"As I was saying, sir, Mr. Harris passed the polygraph with one exception," Gonzalez stated.

"What exception, Gonzalez?" Martinelli asked him.

"It appears there was a hiccup when Mr. Harris was asked if he knew who murdered his wife and daughter," Mark Lalo, the technician reported.

"Is that right, Gonzalez?" Martinelli asked.

"Yes sir," Gonzalez replied.

"Well, is it possible that the machine could have malfunctioned, or Mark here could have read something wrong?"

At that point, Mark Lalo was defensive. *Is he questioning my ability to conduct a polygraph? I've been doing this shit for over five years here,* the young African American technician thought.

"No disrespect, but I have been conducting these exams for well over five years now, right here in this police station, and I've always calibrated my machine before each and every use, sir," Mark proudly replied.

"Nathan, is there something you're not telling us?" Martinelli asked with a concerned look on his face.

"Paul, if I told you, you just wouldn't believe it," Nathan replied.

"Try me, please, I'm trying to help you out here."

"Let's just say I've encountered my wife *and* my daughter's killer, but he overtook me from behind."

"So, you're saying, you *know* who killed your family?"

"Not exactly, Paul. I was in the room with him, but he snuck up from behind me and struck me with a fire stoker. I was knocked out cold before I saw what he even looked like."

"Let me get this straight, you were there when this guy killed your wife *and* your daughter, and you didn't do anything to prevent it? I thought you were away in Oregon."

"I was."

"Listen, Nathan, I'm trying to help you out here, but you can't be in two places at the same time."

"I was away, but I went back to try and prevent it from ever happening."

"Well excuse me, Nathan, for being confused here, but how the *hell* did you go back to the scene of the crime while it was happening?" Martinelli asked him while scratching his head.

Nathan thought for a moment, thinking about how he was going to present this. *If I tell him I went back in time with my Time Transporter, he'll think I'm a fruitcake,* he seriously thought. However, Nathan knew there really was no way around the truth; he decided to go for it and hope for the best.

"I went back in time, Paul, that's the truth," the scientist sincerely said.

"Come again, Nathan?"

"You see? I knew you wouldn't believe me! I built a time machine and went back to that day in January."

"Nathan, you're my friend and I respect you, but I think you're overworked and maybe grief-stricken."

"I'm telling you the truth, Paul."

"And I'm sincerely asking you, are you feeling all right?"

"Yes sir, I'm fine. Why don't you ask Juan here, he was there, he saw my equipment," Nathan defensively responded.

"For the record, Captain, Mr. Harris showed me and Officer Cheng his lab and it was full of some futuristic shit, I mean, stuff that I've never seen before, except maybe in a science fiction movie," Gonzalez answered.

"Yeah, I remember you telling me that. You also said that Mr. Harris claimed that he had a time machine, and then you told me not to tell anyone about it. Now Nathan, I know you're a very gifted scientist and inventor, but *really*, a *time machine* that could take you back to the scene of a *crime*? Go home, get some rest, take it easy, and don't say anything about this shit to anyone, it could only hurt your reputation, especially if the media got ahold of it. When you can prove beyond a shadow of a doubt that it's true, then and only then, bring it back up to me again."

"All right, Paul, you win."

"Good, I'm glad you're seeing it my way. Gonzalez, bring in Officer Cheng."

Detective Gonzalez stepped out to summon Officer Cheng. Martinelli dismissed the polygraph technician; he thought the investigation of Nathan Harris was concluded. Within seconds, Gonzalez returned with Officer Cheng.

"You wanted me, Captain?" Cheng asked.

"Yes, take Mr. Harris back home. We're done here," the captain commanded while pointing to Nathan.

"Right this way, Mr. Harris," the officer said while escorting Nathan out the door.

Nathan knew it was futile to argue with the captain of the police force, even if he was his friend. The scientist didn't feel like he had to prove himself *or* his invention to anyone, at least not yet anyway. *Somehow, I've got to find this damn killer and stop him before he kills my family*, Nathan thought.

"You need me for anything else, sir?" Detective Gonzalez asked.

"As a matter of fact, yes, I do. Close the door please and sit down, Gonzalez," Martinelli asked.

"What's up, Captain?"

"I don't want to hear any more *shit* about Mr. Nathan Harris being accused of murdering his own family. *Unless* you can bring me any concrete evidence, this ends now! Do you understand what I'm telling you here?" Martinelli angrily stated.

"Yes sir," Gonzalez somberly replied.

"Good. Nathan Harris is a well-respected scientist and a great asset to this community. He's going through a *lot* of shit right now, suffering the loss of his family *and* being accused of murdering them on top of that, mainly by you, Gonzalez. As far as I'm concerned, Nathan Harris passed the polygraph with flying colors. I strongly do believe that Mr. Harris is starting to suffer a mental breakdown and he's gonna need therapy, but it's not my place to tell him that. A *time machine, really?* Jesus H. Christ. You're dismissed here, Gonzalez. And take Nathan's picture off of that murder board!" Captain Martinelli commanded.

"Yes sir."

Gonzalez walked out of the captain's office as if he were a dog with his tail caught between his legs. *He's got his head so far up Harris's ass that he can't possibly be objective,* Gonzalez angrily thought to himself. The good detective walked by the murder board and removed Nathan's picture from it, for now. So far, all of his trails and suspects came up dry, *really* dry. Gonzalez then strolled into his office to have a cup of coffee and to think.

Gladys Delgado was walking into the police station holding two large cups of coffee. The young woman asked Officer Ryan at the front desk if she could see Detective Gonzalez. Ryan made a quick call over the phone and asked her to wait. Within a minute, Gonzalez was there to greet her.

"Well, aren't *you* a sight for sore eyes. What brings you down here this morning, *Señora* Delgado," Gonzalez said with a big smile on his face.

"I brought you some coffee, and a doughnut," Gladys said while returning the smile.

Gonzalez admired her, coming out of her way just to bring him coffee and a doughnut. Surely, he didn't have any new information about her late brother and he was sure she knew that. Gonzalez looked at this sweet young woman, dressed up in a spring floral print dress. He marveled at her delightful young face, wearing just enough makeup to accentuate her sweet expression, without taking away the gentleness she possessed. Gladys had a very delicate perfume on that had a fresh natural scent, but it wasn't overpowering. The lovely young woman had her hair down, long and straight and parted in the middle, just the way Gonzalez liked it, but he never told her that. Somehow, she either knew that or the lady was taking a wild guess. The young Latina was the perfect pick-me-up that the detective needed right now, especially after having his ass chewed out by the captain. Gonzalez happily escorted Gladys into his office and closed the door behind her.

"Have a seat, *Señora* Delgado," Gonzalez said while sitting down behind his desk.

"You can call me Gladys," she said while sitting down next to his desk, still smiling.

Gladys handed him his coffee and put her coffee down on the desk also. She reached into her black shoulder bag and handed him a small brown bag.

"Here's your doughnut; oh, I see you already have coffee," Gladys said while noticing his coffee cup on the desk.

"Oh, I finished it; I could use another cup. Where's *your* doughnut?" Gonzalez asked her.

"I'm good."

"You ate already?"

"I had a small bowl of cereal."

"Watching your girlish figure, right?"

"You know it," Gladys said with a giggle.

177

"I'm sorry, but I don't have anything new on your brother's case right now."

"I know, but you'll keep trying, right?"

"Of course, I will. Now, what can I do for you?"

"I'm on vacation, so, I just thought I'd do something nice for my favorite detective."

"I'm flattered, but you're on vacation and you come down *here*? Don't you have anywhere else to go?"

"No, and I can't very well visit by brother, can I?"

"No, you can't. I'm so, so sorry this had to happen to you."

"I know you are, but it's not your fault. You're a good detective, I'm sure you'll find out who killed my brother."

"How do you know that?"

"I just do," Gladys said reassuringly.

At that moment, Gonzalez felt really regretful and concerned for her, wishing that there were something he could do to make her pain go away. Gonzalez felt helpless and he didn't like feeling like that at all. The good detective was going to work really hard at finding her brother's killer. He knew nothing could ever bring him back, but it would sure bring Gladys some closure. Gonzalez got called in by the captain and he had to say goodbye to her. He wondered what Martinelli wanted this time.

*
**

Officer Cheng had just dropped Nathan Harris off at his mansion. Nathan searched his pocket for the house keys and unlocked the door. He walked inside and slammed the door closed behind him, without turning around. Nathan tried to disarm the alarm and realized it was already off. Then, he walked a few feet before being interrupted.

"Hello Mr. Harris, don't turn around. Get your hands up. I've got a gun pointing right at your back," a deep, gruff voice said from behind him.

Nathan felt the gun pressing right up against his back. His heart began working overtime, pumping fast and hard as the beads of sweat began to form on his face. Nathan complied and put his hands up. He wondered who the hell this intruder was and what the interloper wanted from him.

"Who are you and what do want from me?" Nathan nervously asked.

"Who I am is irrelevant. What I want, well, *everything*, everything you own, Mr. Harris," the intruder said with a snicker.

Nathan tried really hard to identify the intruder's voice, but he couldn't place it. *Maybe it's some disgruntled employee I once had,* he thought.

"How did you get in? I know I locked the door. I don't see any broken windows and the alarm wasn't set," Nathan said while trying to look around.

"I said don't turn around! Don't sweat the small stuff, Harris, I have my ways. What I want to know is how you did it?" the intruder asked.

"Did *what?*"

"How the hell did you get back here so fast that night? I thought you were gone. Oh, I get it, you were hiding somewhere, somewhere in the house, weren't you?"

"I'm afraid I don't understand what you're talking about. What night?"

"The night I took your gun away from you, the one I'm pointing at you right now."

Suddenly, Nathan knew exactly who this intruder was. The one he was looking for all along had come to him. Nathan's anger began to grow inside of him.

"*You!* You're the one that killed my wife and daughter. You sonofabitch," Nathan hissed.

"Very good, Sherlock. Now, why the hell aren't you in jail yet? I tried my best to frame you," the killer said.

"None of your damn business. Why don't you get the fuck out of here before I kill you?" Nathan jeered while slowly turning around and putting his hands back down.

"Stop! Stop or I'll shoot!"

Nathan tried to see the invader's face, but the intruder wore a black mask, dark aviator type sunglasses, and a black ski hat. The trespasser also wore black leather gloves to match a black leather jacket. Nathan also noticed that the trespasser had on a pair of very worn blue jeans. Nathan couldn't see the intruder's face, but he *did* notice the person had bloodstains on their white sneakers, probably from when the murderer was killing his wife.

"I said stop and get your hands back up or I'll shoot, I mean it!" the murderer shouted.

"Go ahead, I dare you!" Nathan shouted.

The killer squeezed the trigger several times, but nothing happened. The gun was completely empty.

"You said that was my gun. I neglected to tell you something; I forgot to load it," Nathan said with a devious smile.

Nathan took a very big gamble. What if the killer reloaded the gun? He would have been shit out of luck. Nathan would have been dead. The scientist was being way too reckless and way too sure of himself.

The killer looked at the gun and threw it at Nathan, hitting him in the chest. Nathan started to approach the assassin. Then, the murderer pulled out a large hunter's knife from their right jacket pocket and pointed it at Nathan.

"Stop right there, Mr. Harris. I'm gonna leave now, don't try to stop me and don't do anything stupid," the intruder said.

The murderer dressed in black slowly reached for the door behind and opened it, all while keeping the knife *still* pointed at Nathan. The killer quickly turned around and bolted out the door, counting on the fact that they were in better shape than Nathan.

The murderer ran to a small, dark green car that was hidden behind the bushes, beyond the driveway and gate. Nathan watched the assassin run and drive off, knowing he was in no shape to capture the culprit. *It's been a while since I worked out in my gym, I guess it's time to go back to my health regimen,* he thought. Nathan walked back inside and closed the door behind him. *He's got to have keys to this place. The gate was unlocked and I know for a fact that I locked the front door,* he thought. Nathan was disappointed in himself. If he were in shape, he could have caught the perpetrator. The scientist thought about calling the police, but how could he explain the fact that the killer stole his own gun from him, while he was right there at the time of the murders? *Well, one thing good, at least I got my gun back,* he thought to himself.

CHAPTER 15

NANCY STEVENS

𝕿he sun was shining brightly on Monday morning with a warm breeze. Nathan Harris was still trying to get all of the locks around the mansion and the entry gate changed. *It's May first, almost a week has passed since that murderer was back here in my own home,* Nathan thought. *I still can't get a locksmith out here to change the damn locks.*

"This is bullshit," he angrily said to himself.

Nathan found out that the only locksmith in town had passed away. He had called two other locksmiths in nearby towns, but they were all backed up from the extra load. Nathan had become so paranoid that he was sleeping with a fully loaded gun under his pillow. Nathan wanted to catch the killer himself, before the killer decided to return to his mansion and threaten him again. Nathan looked at his watch and noticed it was now nine o'clock in the morning. The scientist and inventor was getting ready for a fundraiser at the Harris Foundation. Nathan knew he had to be there at ten, so he was trying his very best to be out and on the road in fifteen minutes.

⁎⁎⁎

Detective Juan Gonzalez was at the murder board, again, trying to piece things together. Gonzalez had come full circle and was now fresh out of leads in solving the Harris murders and Hector Delgado's murder. *Is there a connection? If so, where the hell is it?* he thought. *If the killer was the same one that committed all of the murders, then what we have now on our hands is a serial killer, shit,* Gonzalez grimly thought, knowing that the killer would probably strike again.

"Hey Gonzalez, you've got a visitor again," the officer at the front desk shouted.

"I hope I'm not disturbing you, *Señor* Detective," Gladys Delgado softly said from behind him with two cups of large coffee in her hands.

"You, señora? You could never disturb me," Gonzalez replied in a flirtatious way.

Gonzalez looked at her starry eyed. Gladys wore a light pink dress and she had her hair up.

"You changed the way you wear your hair," he said, sounding disappointed.

"You don't like it?" Gladys questioned.

"It's, nice," he said somberly.

"You don't like it; ok I'll fix it."

Gladys put down the coffees on a nearby desk. She took out the hairpins and ties from her hair, shook it out, and let it all hang down.

"You like?" Gladys asked.

"Ah, much better," he said with a smile.

The two of them headed off to his office. As usual, Gonzalez closed the door behind them. He sat down behind his desk, while the young lady sat down beside him.

*
**

Later in the afternoon, Nathan was finally returning home from his fundraiser at the Harris Foundation. He walked into his home and disarmed the alarm. This time, Nathan turned around and closed the door, fearing someone was behind him.

"Hello Nathan," a voice from inside called out.

"Shit!" Nathan cried in shock while dropping his black briefcase

183

on the floor.

Nathan's heart began pounding all over again, thinking the intruder made good on his threat and returned to finish his job. However, he realized that the voice sounded different this time, very different; it sounded feminine. Nathan then heard the sound of a woman giggling, coming from the green chair that was near the grandfather clock. Nathan cautiously walked over to where the sound was coming from. He saw a pair of very sexy legs dangling from the chair that was partially blocked by the massive, old-fashioned clock. Suddenly, the woman rose from the chair and faced him, smiling.

"*Nancy?* What the hell are you doing here?" Nathan asked in a mix of confusion and anger.

"Aren't you going to wish me happy birthday, Nathan? I just hit the big three-0," Nancy said.

"Happy birthday, now, what the *hell* are you doing here in my home?" Nathan angrily asked her.

"Well, you wouldn't answer any of my calls, hell, you didn't even answer the door when I came over last time. So, I decided to come over and visit you," Nancy said with a devious smile on her pretty face.

Nathan was trying to contemplate this *very* unauthorized visit. *I need a locksmith, dammit, NOW,* he angrily thought. However, the scientist was very impressed with the way his sister-in-law presented herself. Nancy was wearing a *very* sexy, low-cut red dress with a string of pearls swathed around her neck. She reminded him of the actress Sharon Stone in the 1990s, except Nancy had longer blonde hair, hair that was all the way down to her waist.

"I want to know how the *hell* you got in here and disabled the alarm?" Nathan asked her.

"Easy, my sister had given me a copy of the house key and the combination to the alarm, just in case something happened. By the way, Nathan, I saw you at the funeral three months ago. I tried to come over and talk to you, but you cut out in a hurry," Nancy replied.

"I was trying to avoid another confrontation."

"Confrontation? Oh, you mean like my father threatening to kill you if he ever found out that you killed his daughter and granddaughter? You see, Nathan, I know *all* about that. I *know* you'd never, ever kill little Alice, but did you kill my sister?" Nancy said while getting in his face.

"No! I would never even think about killing Heather; I loved her."

"Whoa there, big boy, don't get so damn defensive. I couldn't care less about that bitch. As far as I'm concerned, she stole *you* from *me*. We had *our* little history, *remember, honey?*"

Nancy softly touched his face with her right hand. Then she slowly put her arms around him. Nancy tried to kiss him, but Nathan turned away from her inviting red lips.

"That was a long time ago," Nathan wretchedly said.

"I know, I was sixteen. If Mom and Dad ever found out, that would have been your ass, you know that, don't you?"

"It was wrong and I know it, but you *did* come on to me, remember, Miss Hot Pants?"

"I loved you, but you went for my older sister instead. You and her started a life together and left me for shit," Nancy said while being on the verge of tears.

"I'm so sorry, but you were *way* too young. I could have gone to jail. It never should have happened."

"Well, it *did* happen, Mr. Harris and *I* got pregnant with *your* child, a child that *you* let get murdered. How could you?! You were supposed to protect her, instead, you went gallivanting around to your stupid little seminar, the same way you missed your mother dying in that hospital," she said while getting emotional.

"Wait a minute, what are you saying, Nancy?" Nathan asked with a surprised look on his face.

"That's right, Nathan. Alice was *my* daughter; she was *our* daughter."

Nathan Harris nearly collapsed right there on the spot, wondering how this could be true.

"It *can't* be, Alice belonged to Heather and I. Heather was pregnant with my child."

"She lost the baby, Nathan. The doctor said she could never carry a child to term after that, but she never told *you* that, did *she*? Alice was *our* child."

"But that's impossible. How?"

"Don't you remember that Heather and I were both pregnant at the same time?"

"You claimed you were raped coming home from school. You said you never got a good look at the guy because he got you from behind in the park, I remember. Your parents wanted you to get an abortion, but you refused."

"Well, I wasn't raped; I made up that story to protect you from going to jail. I loved you, but you couldn't keep it in your pants, could you? You knocked us both up, me and my sister. The only difference was that *I* brought our baby to term," Nancy cried out with tears streaming down from her blue eyes.

"I still can't believe all this shit," Nathan said with doubt in his mind.

"You were away for over two months when Heather and I were both in the hospital, remember?"

"I remember. I was trying to sell the military my newest invention that would make soldiers appear to be invisible."

"It didn't work, did it?"

"No, it became very unstable after only five minutes of use. I called Heather up several times while she was at the hospital. She told me everything was fine with the baby."

"Well, she lied. Heather had a minor breakdown when she lost the baby. Mom and Dad convinced me to give her *my* baby, since I was underage and I couldn't really take care of it. They thought it would be best being that you were already engaged to her. We all agreed to never tell you, so that you would raise her up as your own child."

"This is all so hard to digest. I need to sit down," Nathan barely said.

Nathan slowly walked into the parlor with Nancy right behind him. They both sat down on the tan-colored sofa; it was a new sofa, but the same color as the old one. Nathan recently acquired it to replace the one his wife's body was stuffed into, just four months ago. Nancy pulled a tissue out of her red handbag and blew her nose.

"Do you know how hard it was for me to see our child growing up with you and my sister? For over thirteen years I kept it a secret from Alice and you. I, I never got to hold her like a mother holds her own child. I never got to tell her how much I really loved her, how I was sorry for giving her up. Heather and my parents swore me to secrecy; I resented them all for that shit. Alice was our baby, Nathan, and she never got to find out. Curse you for letting her get killed, right here in her own home where she was supposed to feel safe." Nancy couldn't talk anymore; she just broke down and cried on Nathan's shoulder, lightly punching him in the chest.

"I, I still find it so hard to believe," Nathan softly said.

"Well, Mr. Scientist, if you don't believe me, why don't you just run a sample of her hair for a DNA analysis. You've got her hair sample. I'll even give you some of mine, if it'll help," Nancy told him while twirling her hair.

"How did you know that?"

"The funeral director said you were so upset that you asked him to cut off a lock of Alice's hair to keep for yourself. You didn't want Heather's hair, just Alice's."

"Your sister was cheating on me."

"I know, she told me. Heather said you were always in the lab, busy with your experiments. She said you never spent enough time with her. As far as I'm concerned, she got what she deserved. I'll never forgive her or my mother and father for what the hell they made me do."

"I figured Heather was cheating on me, but I didn't want to believe it. When the police found Hector Delgado's semen in her, it proved my suspicions."

"Did you say Hector Delgado?"

"Yeah, that's who she was sleeping with."

"Wow, way to go, the hired help? I didn't know that. To think she said *I* was desperate, *shit.*"

The two of them cuddled and consoled one another on the couch. Nathan felt even more betrayed. His late wife had lied to him; she was never really the mother of their only child. *The real mother of my child is right here, still alive,* Nathan thought while Nancy was still crying on his shoulder.

"I'm sorry, I'm sorry this had to happen," Nathan sincerely told her in a soft voice, while brushing the hair away from her face with his hand.

"Nathan, there's something I never told you," Nancy said while looking up at him, sniffling.

"Shit! There's more?!"

"I've never slept with anyone else after you. You don't know how much I loved you. I never stopped. You were my first true love; my only true love, even though I probably didn't mean all that much to you," Nancy said while looking up at him with tears streaming down from her eyes, ruining her makeup.

"You did mean something to me, but I knew it could never be. You were too young. You had your whole life ahead of you. I didn't want to hold you back. Things might have turned out differently if I knew you were pregnant with my child. You said you were raped; I guess I was stupid enough to not put two and two together at that time. I'm sorry for that."

"Oh, stop apologizing already and kiss me, please?" Nancy begged him.

Nathan gave in this time and lightly kissed Nancy on her cheek, but she wanted more. Nancy put her left arm around his neck, pulled him closer to her lips, and then she tried to give him a long, sensual kiss, but Nathan pulled away from her.

"No, this isn't right. I'm still in mourning. Christ, I just lost my entire family!" Nathan cried out.

"Now, *I'm* sorry. I'm just a little, oh, I don't know," Nancy tried to say.

"I believe the word you're looking for is, *lonely?* Can't we just enjoy each other's company without—"

"Ok, how about if you just pour me a drink then?"

"That sounds like a great idea, what'll it be?"

"Scotch on the rocks."

"Two scotch on the rocks coming up," Nathan said while he got up from the sofa.

When Nathan walked out of the room, Nancy looked around at her surroundings. She noticed the family portrait hanging above the fireplace. Nancy got up and walked over toward the painting. She saw that her sister's face had been visibly slashed up. *Why would Nathan keep something so revolting as that around?* Nancy questioned in her mind. Nathan returned with the two drinks and noticed her gazing up at the painting.

"Here's your drink, Nancy," Nathan said with a concerned look upon his face.

"Thank you. Why do have a torn-up picture like that hanging above your fireplace?" Nancy asked.

"It's a remembrance of what the murderer left me when he killed my family."

"The killer left you that?"

"That's correct."

"Wow, why don't you see if you can get it repaired somewhere?"

"I want it left exactly the way it is, to remind me just how precious and fragile life really is."

"You still love her, don't you?"

"Heather? After you spend over thirteen years with someone, it's hard not to, but I'm still hurt and very angry at what she did to me. As for my daughter, I'll always love and cherish her. Nothing can ever take that away from me."

"I'll admit, when I first saw this picture, I thought you cut it up in a fit of rage."

"Well now, it seems that *you* and the good Detective Gonzalez have something in common; he thought *I* did it. Just like he thought that I killed them both."

"My goodness will you look at the time? It's six thirty, I didn't know it was *that* late," Nancy said while looking at her watch.

"Is there someplace you've got to be?" Nathan asked.

"I've got to get back home and walk Sandy."

"Sandy?"

"Yeah, my ten-year-old golden retriever. She has to get fed, too."

"Your dog? You don't have a man in your life?" Nathan asked, completely befuddled.

"No, I don't," she said while lowering her head.

"Why? An attractive young woman like you and you just go home to a dog? I mean, look at you, you're drop-dead gorgeous. You could have any man you want."

"I don't want just any man, Nathan, I want you. I've always wanted you. When my sister told me you two were having marital problems, I thought the two of you were finally going to split up. I thought I would finally have you all to myself. Silly of me, isn't it? I didn't expect her to be murdered. I didn't want you *that* way," Nancy said with tears streaming down her pretty face again, ruining more of her makeup.

Nathan felt really bad. There, standing right in front of him, was the *real* mother of his child, a woman that always loved him. *I should have waited for her to get a little older. She wouldn't have cheated on me; I know that now. If only I'd known she was carrying my baby, things would have turned out differently,* he somberly thought. Nathan took his fingers and gently wiped the tears away from her face.

"Are you all right, I mean, to drive back home?" Nathan asked her.

"Oh, how sweet, you're concerned about my wellbeing. Don't worry, Nathan, I didn't finish the drink and I'm only five miles away from you on Shirley Drive," Nancy responded.

"I know where that is. You own a home over there?"

"Yes, it's a small ranch house, not anything like *this*. Maybe next time you could come over and visit *me*."

"I'd like that, or you can stop by here again, if you'd like. Only next time, please don't sneak in here. You almost gave me a damn heart attack."

"I'd love to come by here again, and I promise I won't break in again, but please, Nathan, answer the phone," Nancy stated to him while giggling.

"I will, I promise. You always did have a nice smile, it's nice to see it again."

Nancy gave Nathan a goodbye kiss on the cheek and then he escorted her out toward the front door. He watched her walk down the driveway, through the open gate, and get into her small, dark green car that was hidden behind the bushes, beyond the gate. *That's the same exact place the killer parked his getaway car,* Nathan mentally thought while watching her.

"Her dark green car blended right in with the bushes; I'm gonna have to trim them," he said to himself.

Nathan grew weary of waiting for a locksmith to come over. He needed to change all the locks around the mansion ASAP. *The hell with it, I'll just have to change all the locks myself, except for the gate, I don't know how to do that one, don't even know if they'll have it in the store,* he thought. Nathan was going to go down to the hardware store to pick up some door locks, then he would deal with the alarm people to change the code. Nathan tried to change the code himself, but it was too complicated and he ran out of patience. *For what I'm paying them every month for their service, they should help me for free,* Nathan thought while getting ready to leave again.

CHAPTER 16

SAVING ALICE AND HEATHER

Scientist and inventor Nathan Harris was up early Tuesday morning on May second. The scientist was on a mission; he was going to replace every door lock in his mansion—every lock with the exception of the entry gate. Nathan had his coffee and a cordless screwdriver by his side.

Photo courtesy of Karolina Kaboompics

193

The man also made sure to pack his gun with him, just in case he got surprised from behind while being outside. Nathan had just completed the last door; it was the back entrance of the mansion. He went back inside to call the alarm company so they could walk him through the process of changing the alarm code, since he didn't have the patience to do it himself.

*
**

An hour later, Nathan was back in his lab contemplating saving Alice and Heather from being murdered. Although he wasn't too sure about saving his wife after finding out that she not only cheated on him, but also lied to him about their own daughter. *How could they? How could they steel Nancy's child and act like it's all right?* he thought. However, Nathan *still* had feelings for his wife and he was going to try and save them both, regardless of what Heather did to him and the laws of time travel.

"Damn them, damn them all, Heather and her parents," he said with an angry tone in his voice.

Nathan knew the rules about time travel. He knew you shouldn't change things to alter the past; that would upset the space and time continuum. However, the scientist was willing to take a chance if it would bring them back to him. Nathan checked his pocket for his revolver and made sure it was loaded.

The scientist and inventor put on his navy-blue suit with its hood. Then he put on his electronic belt and walked back toward the transporter chamber. Nathan activated all of his equipment again but this time, he set the date dials even earlier to Tuesday morning, January seventeen, at 3:30 in the morning, an hour and a half earlier than the last time he went. The scientist planned on sneaking upstairs before the killer had arrived. Nathan had also set the location to be outside, in front of his mansion. He brought his house keys, just in case, and then the man made sure the two AA batteries were still in his pocket. Nathan set his return time for 4:30 a.m., one hour later.

Nathan walked into the transporter chamber and waited for the retractable cylindered doors to close up on him. He powered up his controller belt, reached behind his collar, and pulled up on the retractable hood to cover his head. Nathan placed his hand onto the touchscreen on the back wall of the machine and waited for its response.

"Hello Mr. Harris, and welcome aboard," the computer announced in its mock female voice.

"Hello Alice, commence time travel sequence, please," Nathan replied to the computer, as he put on his dark glasses to protect his eyes from the lasers in the machine.

"Affirmative, Mr. Harris, initiating time travel sequence in ten seconds."

The Time Transporter started its countdown.

"Ten, nine, eight, seven, six, five, four, three, two, one, zero," the computer stated while displaying the numbers on its LCD screen.

The overhead electrodes began to energize, followed by the halo laser that was circulating powerful light rays around him in the tubular chamber. The transporter started up with a loud whirring sound. Nathan Harris felt strange as his body began to demolecularize in the chamber. Within seconds, Nathan's molecules were being transported back in time. When all of the scientist's molecules had arrived back in the past, they began to reassemble again in the same precise order as before.

*
**

Nathan Harris was back in the past, almost four months ago, standing in the snow right in front of his mansion again. Nathan turned the doorknob, assuming it was open, then he walked in and closed the door behind him. The scientist strolled into the hall of his home and listened for any activity before proceeding any further. Nathan quietly went up the stairs to the master bedroom suite and was about to open the door when he heard some moaning. *It's Heather, she's in trouble,* he thought. Nathan grabbed the doorknob, turned it, and opened the door.

"Nathan?!" Heather shrieked.

Nathan Harris was both shocked and completely appalled. His wife, Heather, was lying there on her back in bed with the groundskeeper, Hector Delgado, right on top of her. The two of them were completely naked. Nathan was so angry and disgusted that he slammed the door shut and walked away. *I had to see that shit with my own two eyes. What a bitch,* he thought. The scientist went over to his daughter's bedroom and opened up the door. Alice was lying there awake in the bed wearing her pink pajamas, partially covered by her blanket that had pictures of horses printed on it.

"Daddy? What happened? What was that noise?" Alice innocently asked.

"Nothing. Listen, we've got to get out of here, now!" Nathan urgently said to his daughter.

"Where are we going, Daddy?"

"Out of this house."

"What about Mommy? Is she coming too?"

"Don't worry about Mommy, she'll be all right," Nathan said, thinking of what he just witnessed.

"In my pajamas? I have to get dressed, Daddy; it's cold outside."

"There's no time for that! Put your sneakers and coat on, we have to leave, *now!*"

Nathan waited for Alice to put her sneakers and winter coat on and then he grabbed his daughter and quickly went down the stairs with her, telling Alice to be absolutely quiet. Nathan took his daughter over to the garage to get the Lincoln Navigator out. He replaced the batteries in the keypad with the ones that were in his pocket. Nathan typed the code into the keypad to open the garage door. Nathan reached into his pocket for the car keys, realizing that he didn't have them on him.

"Shit!" Nathan said.

The scientist and inventor was desperate to save his daughter from being murdered. Nathan knew the killer was on the way there and he was clearly running out of options. *There's no way I could take her into the future with me,* Nathan thought. He knew that even if he tried to wrap her up close to him with the suit and transporter belt, her molecules could get mixed up with his. The scientist wanted to drive his daughter over to her *real* mother, but Nathan didn't think he had enough time to go back inside and get the car keys. *I can't believe this shit! There's always something to derail my plans,* Nathan angrily thought to himself, while trying to figure out a solution.

All of a sudden, the two of them heard a blood-curdling scream coming from within the mansion, a scream that Nathan never heard back in January when it originally happened, simply because he was asleep in his soundproof laboratory. Nathan knew what it was; it was the sound of his wife, Heather, being stabbed to death by her killer.

He's in the house already? Where's his car? How the hell did he get here? Nathan asked himself.

"It sounds like Mommy!" Alice shrieked.

"The killer is already here; we have to leave!" Nathan said with urgency.

"What killer? I'm not leaving without Mommy!" Alice cried out.

"There's nothing we can do for her now! It's too late!"

Alice broke away from her father's grasp and ran back inside the mansion. Nathan remembered how viciously his wife was murdered. He knew that she didn't stand a chance against the killer. Nathan knew she was probably dead already.

"Wait! Come back here, Alice!" Nathan screamed out to his daughter.

Nathan started to chase her until he heard his transporter belt starting its countdown.

"No! It's time to go back already?!" he shouted as Alice was entering the house.

Nathan closed the garage door. He pulled up on his collar and covered his head with the retractable hood, knowing that he couldn't abort the countdown after it had started.

"Five, four, three, two, one, zero," the computer stated, while displaying the numbers on the belt's illuminated digital screen.

After the countdown was completed, Nathan slowly began to disappear. Within a few seconds, Nathan Harris had completely dematerialized. His complete molecular structure was sent back to his present time and place, in the future.

*
**

Scientist and inventor Nathan Harris had arrived back to his present time and place in his laboratory. Nathan was standing in the transporter chamber. He waited for the retractable cylindered doors to reopen. Nathan powered off his controller belt, retracted his hood, and walked out of the transporter chamber, disappointed again. The scientist was deeply saddened. *I was so damn close*, Nathan miserably thought. *I'm sure the killer must have killed Alice and stuffed her into the clock.*

"Was Hector Delgado the one that murdered my wife after having sex with her? No, I don't think so; it couldn't be him," he said to himself.

Nathan remembered Detective Gonzalez asking him if *he* had killed Hector Delgado. *Hector was murdered too*, Nathan thought. He also realized that somehow, the killer was hiding out in his home, but he didn't know where the killer was hiding, or for how long. *Shit, the killer must have overpowered Hector and killed him too, but what did he do with Hector's body?* Nathan asked himself. The scientist knew his body was never found in his home. *Gonzalez must have found his body somewhere else*, he thought. All of a sudden, an image of Alice in her pink pajamas was standing in the dark corner of his lab again, except this time Alice had blood all over her pajamas.

"Daddy, you didn't save us. We're dead," Alice said before fading away.

Nathan started to cry, until the black phone on the counter began to ring and startled him. Nathan gazed at the phone for a moment, wondering if he should pick it up. Then Nathan remembered the promise he had made. *What if it's Nancy? I promised her I would answer her calls, I'm sure it's her,* he thought. Nathan had decided to pick it up before it stopped ringing.

"Hello?" Nathan asked the caller.

"Nathan? It's me, Nancy," she replied.

"Hello Nancy, how are you?"

"I'm doing ok. Hey, I'm off the rest of the week and was wondering if you'd like some company, at least for *today*."

"I take it you want to come over."

"Or you could just come over here if you'd like."

"You can come over here if you want to, but I must warn you, I'm not going to be much company."

"That's why it might be better if you came over here, Nathan. You need to get away from that house with all its memories for a while."

"Yeah, maybe you're right," Nathan somberly added.

"I know I'm right. It can't be easy for you, staying in the same house that your wife and daughter were both stabbed to death in. That's just too many bad memories."

"I know but, wait a minute; what did you just say?" Nathan asked her questionably.

"I said, it can't be easy for you, staying in the same house that your wife and daughter were stabbed to death in."

"Heather was stabbed, not Alice," Nathan said while feeling confused.

"Nathan, are you feeling all right?"

"I'm fine, why do you ask?"

"Well, don't you remember? They were both found stabbed to death and stuck inside the sofa in your parlor."

Nathan nearly dropped the phone and collapsed into the seat by the counter. The scientist realized that he really *did* change history. His daughter Alice was still dead, but instead of her being stuffed into the grandfather clock with a gash to her head, she was now stabbed to death, just like Heather was, and then both of them were squeezed into the sofa.

"Nathan, are you still there?" Nancy asked over the phone.

"Yes, yes I'm still here."

"Listen, how about if I come pick you up and bring you here? I'll cook you a nice home-cooked meal and maybe we could watch a movie."

"Ok, that sounds good. I just don't feel like driving right now."

"Great! I'll pick you up in about an hour, ok?"

"Sounds like a plan. See you then, bye," Nathan said while hanging up the phone.

Nathan wasn't really in the mood for company; he felt like he let his family down again. *I let them both get killed again by that psychotic killer,* the scientist thought. *Maybe some company is what I really need right now.* Nathan removed his remote time controller belt from his waist. Then he took off his navy-blue suit with its hood and hung it up in the closet in the lab. The scientist decided to go upstairs and take a quick shower before Nancy came over to pick him up.

*
**

A few miles away at the Solville Police Department, Detective

Juan Gonzalez was in his office enjoying the company of Gladys Delgado. Gladys had brought the good detective coffee and a doughnut again. Gonzalez was asking her again whether or not her brother had any enemies.

"I'm sorry, *Señor* Detective, but like I told you last time, I don't know if he had any enemies. I thought it would be that black guy that sold him the drugs, but I guess I was wrong," Gladys sadly told him.

"*Mira,* we're gonna find out who's responsible for killing your brother, but we need help. If you ever remember anything else about his acquaintances, please feel free to call me here," Gonzalez told her while giving her his card again.

"*Gracias Señor* Detective, you're a good detective and a good man. I want to ask you something," she said while getting up from her chair.

"Sure, what is it?"

"Well, I was wondering if, I mean, are you married, or seeing anyone?" Gladys nervously asked him, wondering what he would say to her.

Gonzalez gazed at the young woman standing right before him, wearing a pink dress. *Is she trying to ask me out? I've never had a woman ask me out before in my life,* he thought.

"I guess I could ask you the same thing," Gonzalez said.

"Well, I wouldn't have asked you if I was in a relationship with someone, Detective," she said jokingly.

"You're absolutely right," he added while laughing.

The two of them were now laughing together. Then Gladys looked at him, admiring the man that he was. She was relieved to find that the good detective had a sense of humor to him.

"I was wondering if you would like to go out to dinner someday, nothing serious, just dinner," she said to him while shaking from embarrassment.

"I would love to," Gonzalez replied.

"Good," she said with great relief.

"Listen, I'm working late tonight, but I'll be free tomorrow night after six."

"Ok, let me give you my address and I'll be ready by six tomorrow night."

Gladys Delgado happily wrote down her address and phone number on a piece of paper for the detective. She handed Gonzalez the paper with a smile and said goodbye to him. Gonzalez watched her leave his office; he liked the way she walked. *What's a beautiful young woman like her want with me?* Gonzalez asked himself, knowing he was obviously older than her.

Detective Gonzalez decided to get out of his office and head on over to the murder board, over in the main office. The good detective stared at the pictures of Heather and Alice Harris. Then, he gazed at the other murder victim, Hector Delgado, Gladys's brother. *Wouldn't it be something if they were all killed by the same person? That would make it a serial killer,* Gonzalez thought.

"If it's not Nathan Harris or Darius White, then who the hell is it?" Gonzalez asked himself in a low voice.

"Did you say something, Detective?" a young female officer sitting at her desk near the murder board asked him.

"No, I'm just talking to myself," Gonzalez replied.

*
**

Later that afternoon, Nathan was all dressed up waiting for Nancy to come and pick him up. He wore a dark gray suit with pinstripes. The scientist was also sporting a light pink shirt with a bowtie. Nathan wanted to look nice for her. The phone rang and he decided to pick it up, thinking it was Nancy.

"Hello, Nancy, are you running late?" Nathan asked.

"Hello, Nathan, this is Doctor Berlin. I've been trying to reach you," he replied over the phone.

"Oh, I'm sorry, Doctor, I was expecting someone else. What can I do for you?" Nathan asked him.

"You mean, what can *I* do for *you*, Nathan? First of all, I'd like to express my deepest sympathy for your family; you must be feeling quite lonely now."

"Yes, I am, Doctor, but I'm slowly managing."

"Good, glad to hear it. Listen, Nathan, I have an opening here at nine a.m. tomorrow. If you'd like to come over and talk to me, I could get you in."

"Well, yeah. I'd like to talk to you about an apparition I've been seeing."

"Don't say anything more, Nathan; I'll see you tomorrow at nine."

"Ok, Doctor, I'll be there. Goodbye," Nathan said before hanging up the phone.

The doorbell rang; Nathan went over to answer it, knowing who it was.

"Well, well, *well*, look at *you*, Mr. Nathan Harris! You look positively handsome!" Nancy exclaimed.

"And you, well, you look absolutely gorgeous, Nancy," he struggled to say.

Nancy was dressed in a lovely new lavender dress with a white sweater over it. She had a string of pearls wrapped around her neck. Nancy had her long blonde hair up in a new hairdo, which made her look a bit older than she really was. The woman was also wearing a new pair of red Prada shoes with high heels that made her look even taller than she already was. Nathan, on the other hand, wasn't completely thrilled about her new look, but he wouldn't dare tell her that. Nathan liked Nancy better with her hair all the way down and a little less makeup; she looked younger that way and less harsh to him.

The two of them walked out of the mansion, while Nathan locked the door behind him. They walked down the brick pathway and into Nancy's dark green sports car that was waiting in the driveway. Nathan buckled up his seatbelt and hoped she wasn't going to drive foolishly and fast, especially when Nancy had told him to hang on. *Well here goes nothing,* he thought as they sped away.

CHAPTER 17

DOCTOR BERLIN

On Wednesday, May third, Nathan Harris was at Doctor Berlin's downtown office. The office was small and was inside an old building, on the second floor, but Nathan thought it was quaint. The young female receptionist told him to go on inside. Nathan walked into the psychologist's office and was greeted by his doctor.

Doctor Paul Berlin had been practicing psychology for well over fifty years. Berlin had just turned seventy-five and was finally considering retiring and going back to his home in Germany. The doctor's hair had turned completely gray. He was also having his share of health problems, mainly with his heart. The doctor was also slightly overweight, but since he was on the short side, his body mass index showed he had a problem. Berlin had been treating his patient, Nathan Harris, for depression and guilt for about twenty-two years. He put on his thick lens, wire-framed glasses and asked Nathan to lie down on the cream-colored couch in his office, but Nathan had some questions first.

"I see you've got a new friend," Nathan said while pointing at the white, mid-sized birdcage that stood in the left corner of the room.

"Yes, I have. That's Maggie, she's my new baby; a yellow-naped Amazon parrot and *quite* a companion," the doctor said.

Nathan looked at the green parrot with its yellow patch of feathers on the back of her neck. He watched as the bird wiped her beak along the bars of the cage. Nathan thought it reminded him of a prisoner dragging his tin cup along the prison bars, looking for the guard.

"Does she talk?" Nathan asked inquisitively.

Photo courtesy of Manuel Rose

"No, not as of yet, she's only six months old," Doctor Berlin said reassuringly.

"Oh, I just wondered because I know those birds can repeat what you say and—"

"I know where you're getting at with this, Nathan. Well, if you're really uncomfortable being here with her, we can just go into another office."

"No, no, that's all right, as long she can't repeat what we say here, it's fine with me," Nathan said while feeling relieved.

"Good, because I didn't bring you in here to discuss my new companion animal. Now, please make yourself comfortable on the couch."

Nathan walked to the sofa and laid down. Doctor Berlin started up his microcassette tape recorder; he wasn't a fan of digital recorders. The doctor trusted tangible items, like tapes and paper. He grabbed his notebook and sat right down next to Nathan in his black leather chair.

"All right now, today is Wednesday, the third of May, and the time is now nine o'clock in the morning. I am here with Mr. Nathan Harris in my downtown New York office. Now, Nathan, you spoke to me over the telephone about a recent apparition you've been seeing; can you please elaborate on that for me?" Doctor Berlin asked him.

"Yes, Doctor. I've seen my late daughter, Alice. Alice comes to me in the very same pink pajamas that she was wearing when she was mur-dered," Nathan struggled to say.

"Where exactly have you seen her, Nathan?"

"I have seen her a few times in my laboratory. She seems to materialize only in a dark corner of the room."

"Now, tell me, Nathan, have you seen Alice anywhere else in your home?"

"Yes, Doctor, I've seen her in my dreams."

"Does Alice say anything to you at all when you've seen her?"

"Yes, the last time I saw her in the lab, she said to me, '*Daddy, you didn't save us. We're dead.*'"

"Now, where exactly were you when your wife and daughter were both brutally murdered, Nathan?"

"I was away, again, on a seminar in Oregon," Nathan gravely said.

"Well, to me, this sounds like you feel guilty for leaving them alone in the first place, the same way you've felt guilty all these years about not being there for your mother when she passed away in the hospital."

Nathan had to think about what he was going to say next. He no longer felt guilty about his mother, since he was able to go back in time to finally rectify *that* situation. *I can't tell him that, though, he may have my ass committed for sure,* Nathan thought. The scientist decided to choose his words more carefully.

"You know something, that does sound logical, Doc," Nathan told him.

"I know it does, that's why I'm the doctor and you're the patient. This is all about guilt. You've simply got a guilt complex, Nathan. I personally think you're being a bit too hard on yourself. You need to relax and take it easy. You also need time to allow yourself to grieve, especially before jumping into another relationship," the doctor said while feeling genuinely concerned about him.

"I *am* grieving, Doctor. There's not a day that goes by that I don't think about them, especially while I stay in that lonely ole mansion with all of its memories of them."

"Nathan, who's Nancy?"

"Nancy?"

"Yes, when I called you at home yesterday you thought I was Nancy. As a matter-of-fact, your exact words, if my memory doesn't fail me, were, 'Hello, Nancy, are you running late?' At least that's what I recall."

"Nancy Stevens is my sister-in-law."

"I see. So, Nathan, tell me, are you dating your sister-in-law?"

"Right now, we're just friends, although, she has made a few advances toward me."

"I see. Tell me, just how did you respond to her advances toward you, Nathan?"

"I pushed her away and told her it wasn't right; I said I was still grieving."

"I see. Forgive me for asking, but do you feel uncomfortable at all being with your sister-in-law in that manner?"

"No, Doc, not at all; besides, since my wife was murdered, Nancy is no longer my sister-in-law. However, right now we're just friends, Doc," Nathan said defensively.

"I see," the doctor responded and took some notes.

"Nancy did come by yesterday after I spoke with you over the phone. She brought me over to her home and cooked me dinner. Then we talked a little and had a few drinks before watching a movie on TV."

"What happened then?" Doctor Berlin asked with great interest.

"After that, she brought me back home."

"That was it, Nathan?"

"Yeah, it was kind of late and I was tired."

"So, the two of you didn't have sex?"

"No, Doctor, although the thought had crossed my mind. I

didn't and I couldn't, not now anyway."

"Did your sister-in-law want to have sex with you?"

"Oh, yes, Doctor, she did. Nancy was indeed quite frustrated with me for turning her away, but in the end, I think she really understood."

Nathan noticed the disappointment in his doctor's eyes. He thought that Doctor Berlin was hoping for a juicy story. The scientist wasn't about to divulge the fact that Nancy had always loved him. Nathan wouldn't dare mention the fact that he had sex with a minor years ago and made that girl pregnant. He was not about to tell the good doctor that Alice, his late daughter, *was* that child.

"Ok, Nathan, let's move on, shall we? What about William? Do you still see William anymore?" Doctor Berlin asked him.

"No, I haven't, but I have thought about him, Doc," Nathan replied to him.

"Good, like I've been trying to convey to you all of these years, William is just a figment of your imagination, a fabrication. You've created him when you very young and lonely from being an only child."

"I'm not so sure about that, Doc," Nathan said in defense.

"If he really does exist, then where is he, Nathan?" Doctor Berlin said as if trying to discount Nathan's beliefs.

"When I was young, I overheard my parents talking about William. As I recall, my mother was very upset at my father and I truly believe it was all about William," Nathan barely said while trying his very best to hold back the tears that were starting to emerge from his eyes.

"Did you ever confront your parents about it, Nathan?"

"No, I didn't dare too; besides, it would have been an admission to eavesdropping on them."

Nathan still believed that William was indeed real. Nathan

remembered bringing him up to his mother in the hospital when he went back in time. Alice became livid at the very mention of his name. Nathan remembered what she had said to him while lying in the hospital bed, dying. *"William? Don't you ever mention his name to me again!"* Alice had told him.

"Nathan, I know you must be feeling depressed lately. It's perfectly normal, but how have you been handling your depression?" Doctor Berlin asked him.

"I try not to think about it. I'm trying to move on, Doc," Nathan replied.

"You mean with Nancy?"

"If it came to that, yes. I would be open to having a relationship with my ex-sister-in-law, but not right now. Like I said before, we're just friends, Doc, enjoying each other's company."

"Ok, Nathan. This concludes our session for today; it appears our time is up. I would like to see you again, maybe next week?"

"I'll have to let you know about that, Doc. I've got a lot on my plate right now."

"Ok, that's fine. Call me when you're ready for another session, Nathan."

Photo courtesy of Manuel Rose

211

Nathan rose from the couch and walked toward the parrot in the cage before leaving the doctor's office. He stared at the bird for a moment, then the bird told him, "Goodbye." Doctor Berlin was so excited. The doctor claimed that was the first time he had ever heard the bird speak. Nathan wondered if he was being deceived about the ability of the bird not being able to talk. He wondered what other words the bird could say. The scientist walked out of the office with an uncomfortable feeling inside him. Nathan went toward the front desk to pay for his visit before leaving the building.

*
**

That evening at the Solville Police Department, Detective Gonzalez was wrapping things up, getting ready for his big date with Gladys Delgado. The detective pulled a piece of paper out of his pocket and began to read it; it was Gladys's address. *It's 15 Williams Road in Carney; that's not too far from here,* Gonzalez thought. He went to relieve himself in the men's room and then Gonzalez clocked out of the station. The detective thought he could save some time by going straight there, instead of going home first. Gonzalez was extremely nervous; it was the first time he was going to be alone with a woman since his ex-wife, even though he pretty much knew Gladys. *I hope everything goes ok,* Gonzalez thought.

*
**

A half-hour later, Detective Gonzalez was standing in front of the green-colored front door of Gladys Delgado's home, wearing his dark gray work suit. He looked at the old ranch house with its cedar wood siding and its surroundings, admiring how picturesque it was. Gonzalez straightened his tie, sprayed his mouth with breath freshener, and then he rang her doorbell.

"Who is it?!" Gladys yelled from beyond the door.

"It's me, Detective Gonzalez!" he nervously shouted back to the door.

Within seconds, Gladys opened up her door. Gonzalez looked at the beautiful young Latina standing their all dolled up. She had her hair down just the way he liked it, with just enough makeup on. Gladys had donned a beautiful wine-colored evening gown and a pair of matching shoes. Gonzalez was flabbergasted, to say the least.

"Hello, *Señor* Detective. You look like your eyes are going to pop out," she said with a giggle.

"*Eres muy bonita,*" Gonzalez said, approving of her beauty.

"*Gracias,* come in," Gladys replied while blushing in front of him.

The young woman ushered Gonzalez into her home and closed the door behind him.

"You're early," she said with a smile.

"I tried to call you, but I just wanted to get out of the station before the captain gave me something else to do," he replied.

"That's ok. I just have to go to the bathroom really quick before we leave."

"Take your time," Gonzalez said while standing in the hallway. He looked at his watch and noticed it was almost six o'clock.

"Where would you like to go eat," Gonzalez shouted out.

"We can go to that new Mexican place, *El Toro,* if that's ok with you?" Gladys yelled back.

"Fine by me."

Gonzalez felt his smartphone vibrating in his right front pants pocket. He took it out and noticed there was a text from Captain Martinelli that read; *If you want to work some overtime tonight, give me a call.* Gonzalez ignored the text and put the phone back into his pocket. Gladys came back out to him.

"Why didn't you come in and sit down?" Gladys asked him inquisitively.

"I'm good. Are you ready?" Gonzalez asked her.

"*Sí*, I'm ready and I'm treating tonight."

"No, no, no, I'm treating."

"No papa, I want to treat."

"Ok let's settle this. You know that Chinese hand game Rock Paper Scissors?"

"Yes, I do. Come on let's do it."

The two of them played Rock Paper Scissors. Gladys got paper, while Gonzalez got scissors.

"I win, I'm treating," Gonzalez happily stated.

"No, no, no, let's go another round," Gladys said with a disappointed look on her face.

"No, let's just go, *please?*"

"Ok, but you know something? I don't even know your first name. I'm sure you don't want me to keep calling you *Señor* Detective, do you?"

"It's Juan. My name is Juan Gonzalez."

They both left her house and walked toward his white four-door sedan, while admiring the beautiful moonlit sky. Gonzalez was the perfect gentleman; he opened up the passenger door first to let her in, then he closed the door for her. After that, the detective went around to the driver's side of the car and got in. Gonzalez buckled up, started the car, and drove off.

*
**

Over at Doctor Berlin's office in downtown New York, the doctor was going over the recording of Nathan Harris's last session in his office. The doctor didn't trust his new secretary with sensitive information; besides, she had already gone home for the day. He decided to transcribe the recording himself. While he listened to Nathan's voice, the doctor suddenly remembered something else that was in Nathan's file. Something that would explain a great deal about Nathan's fictitious friend William.

"Yes, there was something about William; I remember it now," he said to himself.

"Hello," the green parrot replied.

"My goodness, you are a fast learner, my fine feathered friend," the doctor told his bird.

Doctor Berlin was going to go home since it was almost seven o'clock in the evening, but he decided to do some research on Nathan Harris and his parents first. Berlin decided to go to his own personal filing cabinets that were hidden behind the wall unit, toward the back of his office. He took the key out of his pocket and inserted it into the walnut-colored wood cabinetry. Berlin turned the key and pulled the wall unit open. Hidden behind the wall unit were a group of file cabinets. The commercial file cabinets were made of heavy gauge steel; each one housed five file drawers and were all painted black, complete with individual locking keys. Berlin looked at the six file cabinets and decided to search the second one for Nathan's personal files.

Doctor Berlin was very meticulous about his filing system. He not only sorted everything and everyone by name, but also chronologically by years. The doctor finally found what he was looking for—the earliest folder on Nathan Harris. Berlin took the folder with him. He closed the file drawer and the wall unit. Then the doctor sat down at his desk and began to read about Nathan's childhood. Doctor Paul Berlin also had information on the scientist's parents. He particularly looked at the data he had collected on Nathan's father, Kevin William Harris.

"I wonder…" Paul said to himself.

"Hello," the parrot said as if answering him.

"My, my, it appears you really *are* trying to talk to me, Maggie. Hello to you too," he answered her back.

Doctor Berlin turned his computer back on and started searching through his paid online sources that he subscribed to, for even more information on Nathan and his parents. Doctor Berlin went through the online databases, looking for what he believed would hold the key to Nathan's imaginary friend. Paul knew he was grasping at straws, but the doctor wanted so desperately to solve this mystery. Finally, after extensive online searching, the doctor found what he was looking for.

"My word, I was right!" Paul said in complete disbelief.

Suddenly, the pure excitement of it all got the best of him. Doctor Paul Berlin began to suffer extreme pain in the left side of his chest. *Oh no,* he thought, knowing there was no one there to help him. Paul frantically searched his pockets, looking for his nitroglycerin pills, but they weren't there. Paul knew damn well what he was experiencing; he knew that his heart was failing him.

The doctor was now in agonizing pain. Paul Berlin was clenching his chest, while trying to reach the black phone on his desk. He kept reaching for the desk phone, trying to grab the handset and almost had it, but the pain was just too great for him. Doctor Berlin inadvertently knocked the phone onto the carpeted wood floor below him. *I'm dying and there's nothing I can do about it,* he miserably thought. Doctor Paul Berlin finally succumbed to his massive heart attack and collapsed right there on the floor, knocking over and unplugging his computer in the process. He laid helplessly clinging to whatever life he had left, right near the telephone that was sounding the off-the-hook warning tones.

Poor Doctor Berlin; he never got his chance to retire. Paul Berlin was never able to enjoy the fruits of his dedicated labor. The good doctor died alone in his office on the verge of a major breakthrough in his patient's case, Nathan Harris's case. No one should ever have to pass away like that, no one at all.

CHAPTER 18

CHANGING THE PAST

Thursday morning, May fourth, Nathan Harris was back in his lab booting up his time travel equipment. He was going to try and save his family from death, again. Nathan checked his pocket for his revolver and made sure it was loaded. He also made sure he had his car keys and Nancy's home address with him. The scientist and inventor put on his navy-blue suit with its protective hood. Then, he strapped on his electronic belt and walked back toward the transporter chamber. Nathan activated all of his equipment again but this time, he set the date dials earlier to Tuesday morning, January seventeen, at two thirty in the morning, an hour earlier than the last time he went. Nathan wanted to sneak upstairs before the killer had arrived. He had also set the location to be outside, in front of his mansion. Nathan made sure to bring his house keys with him, just in case. Then, the scientist set his return time for four thirty a.m., the same as last time. Nathan walked into the transporter chamber and waited for the retractable cylindered doors to close up on him. He powered up his controller belt, reached behind his collar and pulled up on the retractable hood to cover his head. Nathan placed his hand onto the touchscreen on the back wall of the machine and waited for the computer to respond to him.

"Hello Mr. Harris, and welcome aboard," the computer announced in its simulated female voice.

"Hello Alice, commence time travel sequence, please," Nathan replied to the computer, as he put on his dark glasses to protect his eyes from the powerful laser beams in the machine.

"Affirmative, Mr. Harris, initiating time travel sequence in ten seconds."

The Time Transporter started its countdown.

"Ten, nine, eight, seven, six, five, four, three, two, one, zero," the computer stated while presenting the numbers on its LCD screen.

The overhead electrodes began to energize, followed by the halo laser that was now circulating powerful light rays around him in the tubular chamber. The transporter began operating with a loud humming sound. Nathan Harris began to feel strange as his body began to demolecularize from within the chamber. Within seconds, Nathan's molecules were being transported back in time. When all of the scientist's molecules had arrived back in the past, they started to reassemble in the same exact order as before.

*
**

Nathan Harris was sent back to the past, almost four months ago, right in front of his mansion again, standing in the cold snow. Nathan turned the doorknob, assuming it was open, then he walked right inside and closed the door behind him. The scientist walked into the vestibule of his home and listened for any type of activity in the house, before continuing any further. Nathan silently crept up the stairs to his master bedroom suite and was ready to open the door, until he heard his wife moaning in gratification. *That conniving, deceitful bitch. How long was she screwing him?* Nathan angrily wondered. He grabbed the doorknob and opened the door, with unmistakable hatred in his eyes.

"Nathan?!" Heather shrieked.

"*Señor* Harris?!" Hector shouted in disbelief.

Nathan Harris was completely disgusted. His wife, Heather, was laying there on her back, in the king-sized bed, entirely naked with their groundskeeper, Hector Delgado, on top of her, the same exact way he'd seen them there before, only this time, she was clawing at his back in ecstasy. Nathan was both angry and disgusted.

"How long has this *shit* been going on?!" Nathan angrily shouted at the two of them.

"You never had time for me, so I had to find someone that did!" Heather said in defense, as if it was all right.

Nathan stared at her in complete disbelief. *Wow, Heather actually believes that she did no wrong? Ain't this a bitch,* Nathan angrily thought. Then, he looked at her lover, how pitiful the young man looked, now trying to hide his face in complete shame. However, Nathan still loved this woman, not really knowing why. He wanted to do the right thing. Nathan was going to warn them of the imminent danger of staying there any longer.

"You have to leave, now!" Nathan said with great urgency in his voice.

"He's not going anywhere. Hector's a better lover than you ever were," Heather hissed.

"How dare you. It's bad enough that you've lied to me all this time about our own daughter, but cheating on me with the groundskeeper, *shit!*"

"What about our daughter?"

"I know for a fact that she's *not* yours!"

"How the *hell* did you know that?!"

"Oh, so you admit it?"

"I didn't say that; I merely asked you—"

"Don't worry about how I found out, Heather; I have my ways. The charade is over, sweetie," Nathan said sarcastically.

Nathan now firmly believed that Nancy was telling him the truth. If there was ever any shred of doubt in his mind, Heather's reaction clarified that.

"I'm *still* not leaving here at this ungodly hour of the night, *screw you!*" Heather cried out while *still* clinging to her lover.

"You know, I don't give a shit what the hell the two of you do together; as far as *I'm concerned*, you two deserve each other. I'm just trying to save your assess from being killed. There's a killer coming and it's not safe here.

"And how the *hell* would you know that? You're full of shit, Nathan. Get out! Get out of here, *now!*" Heather shouted at him while holding on to Hector.

The scientist slammed the door on them in complete anger and bewilderment. *I tried to save them,* he thought. Nathan went over to his daughter's bedroom and opened up the door. Alice was wide awake in bed wearing her pink pajamas, partially covered by her blanket that had pictures of horses printed on it. Alice was upset, knowing that her parents were fighting next door.

"Daddy? What happened? What was all that yelling about?" Alice innocently asked.

"Listen, we've got to get out of here, now!" Nathan urgently told his daughter.

"Where are we going, Daddy?"

"Out of this house."

"This late at night? What about Mommy? Is she coming too?"

"Don't worry about Mommy, she'll be all right. Let's go, honey," Nathan said, not really caring about Heather anymore.

"In my pajamas? I can't go out like this; it's cold outside. I have to get dressed, Daddy."

"There's no time for that! Listen, put your sneakers and coat on, we have to leave right now!"

Nathan grabbed his daughter and quickly went down the stairs with her, telling Alice to be absolutely quiet. He picked up the kitchen phone to call the police, but the line was still dead from the snow storm.

I forgot about that, Nathan thought. He took Alice over to the garage to get his Lincoln SUV out. Nathan entered the code on the keypad to open the garage door. He reached into his pocket for the car keys, and then Nathan opened up the doors with the key remote. Nathan looked at his daughter shivering from the cold and knew he had to act fast.

"Come on, Boo-Boo. Get in the car, please," he urgently said to her.

"Where are we going, Daddy?" Alice asked while folding her arms around her to keep warm.

"Mommy has to go somewhere; she asked me to bring you over to Aunt Nancy's house, before I go out to Oregon for my seminar."

Alice begrudgingly got into the SUV. Nathan went around to the driver's side and got in. He was lucky the man he hired to clean up the driveway from the snow had already come by. Nathan buckled himself up and made sure that Alice was buckled up, too. He dug into his pocket for Nancy's address; Nathan read it to refresh his memory before starting the car and driving off. The scientist and inventor was desperate to save his daughter from being murdered. Nathan knew the killer was coming. *There's just no way I could take her into the future with me; I know that now,* Nathan thought. The scientist was driving his daughter over to her *real* mother's home on Shirley Drive, that's why he got there earlier this time. Nathan was going to drop her off at Nancy's and then return the vehicle back in time, so that his past self could take it to the airport for his seminar in Oregon.

**

Nathan Harris had just arrived at 16 Shirley Drive in Solville, NY, the home of his sister-in-law, Nancy Stevens. The five-mile trip took him over fifteen minutes. He remembered the small ranch house from his last visit with Nancy, back in the future. Nathan looked at his dashboard clock and noticed it was now three o'clock. He parked the car in Nancy's driveway and got out. Nathan then went around and let his daughter out. *It's dark and cold out; I've got to get Alice inside the house before she freezes,* he thought while watching his child shiver. Nathan was thankful that his suit was insulated, it had to be, to protect the internal wiring and antenna system it contained.

"Come on little one, let's go see Aunt Nancy," Nathan said while grabbing his daughter's hand.

"Daddy, I'm cold," Alice said while shivering.

"I know you are, let's go inside."

Nathan cuddled his daughter while they walked toward the front door of the small white ranch house. He rang the bell and waited for Nancy to answer. After a few minutes, the outside lights came on as his sister-in-law approached the front door, startled and half-asleep.

"Who is it?" Nancy asked from inside.

"It's me, Nathan," he replied.

Nancy unlocked and opened the front door. She stood there in her light green nightgown, in disbelief.

"Nathan, Alice, what brings you two here at three o'clock in the morning? Come in, come in it's cold outside," she told them while yawning.

Nathan brought his daughter inside while Nancy closed the door behind them.

"I need a big favor, Nancy," Nathan told her while he too was now shivering from the cold.

"Oh, you know I'd do just about anything for you, Nathan, what is it?" Nancy asked him.

"Can I please go to the bathroom, Aunt Nancy?" Alice asked while rocking back and forth.

"Sure, let me show you where it is, honey. I'll be right back, Nathan," she told him while bringing Alice to the bathroom.

Nathan watched her take his daughter down the hall. He picked up the phone on the wall and tried to call the police again, but Nancy's phone was also dead from the storm. Nancy was now returning back toward him.

"Ok, now what's this all about, Nathan?" Nancy asked him with a concerned look on her face.

"Listen, I need you to take care of Alice while I'm away in Oregon," he replied.

"What? What's wrong with Heather?"

"She's with her lover. Look, I don't have time for details right now. Please just trust me on this. I know you still love me; I also know that you're *really* her mother."

Nancy lost all the color in her face. The woman was now completely shocked. She glared at Nathan, not knowing what to say or do.

"Are you all right? You look like you've seen a ghost," Nathan asked her.

"How did you know?" Nancy asked him.

Nathan realized that the conversation he had with Nancy hadn't happened yet, it was in the future.

"I have my ways," Nathan said without giving away any information.

"Does Heather know you two are here?"

"I told you, Heather's with her boyfriend. I just caught her in bed with our groundskeeper," he said with both a disgusted and hurt look on his face."

"Oh, Nathan, I'm so sorry," she said with a concerned look on her face.

"Yeah, so am I, Nancy. I didn't want my daughter to see that shit and I can't take her with me where I'm going. Please, just look after her for a while, all right?"

"All right, I can see you're visibly upset, but—"

"I'll explain everything later when I get back. Whatever you do, keep her far away from my home, it's imperative that you do."

"What have you told Alice?"

"I only told her that Mommy had to go somewhere and she needed me to bring her here. One more thing, is your cellphone working?" Nathan asked in a last-ditch effort to try and save Heather from being slaughtered.

"No, the blizzard knocked out everything, including cell service," Nancy replied.

"Right, ok, I've got to go or I'll miss my flight to Oregon."

"The airports resumed service again?"

"Yeah, I heard on the radio that the runways were cleared and they're flying again, probably with some delays, though."

"What's in Oregon?"

"My seminar. Look, remember what I told you, please keep her *away* from that mansion until I call you, all right?"

"All right, Nathan, have a safe trip."

Nancy gave Nathan a tender hug and kissed him on his left cheek. He looked at her with such admiration, knowing that this woman gave up her only child; a child that she created with him. Nathan could see all the pain and hurt in her face, wishing he could do something to alleviate it. Alice had finally returned back from the bathroom with a worried look on her face.

"Are you leaving me, Daddy?" Alice asked with a cry in her voice.

"Only for a little while, Boo-Boo. Kiss and hug?" Nathan asked her with open arms.

Alice gave her father a big hug and kissed him on the cheek. Nathan told her that he loved her, and then the scientist said goodbye to both of them as he left the house. Nathan got back in his SUV, started it back up, and drove off, with tears dripping down his face.

*
**

A few minutes later, Nathan Harris had just returned back to his mansion. He parked the Lincoln back in the garage and closed the door. Nathan looked at his watch, it was almost four o'clock. *I'm early, that's ok, better early than late,* he thought. Nathan walked up to the mansion and pressed the override button on his belt. He pulled up on his collar and covered his head with the retractable hood, while listening to the countdown.

"Five, four, three, two, one, zero," the computer stated, while displaying the numbers on the belt's illuminated digital screen.

After the countdown was completed, Nathan slowly started to disappear. Within a few seconds, Nathan Harris had completely dematerialized. His complete molecular structure was sent back to his present time and place, in the future.

*
**

Nathan Harris had arrived back to his present time, close to four months later in his laboratory. Nathan was standing in the transporter chamber. He waited for the retractable cylindered doors to reopen. The scientist powered off his controller belt, retracted his hood, and walked out of the transporter chamber.

Nathan knew he had to contact his daughter and sister-in-law. *What the hell am I going to say to them? It's been nearly four months since I left them,* Nathan thought. *Clearly, I didn't think this one out thoroughly.* He decided to pick up the phone and call Nancy Stevens, not knowing what his past self may have said or done. Nathan waited impatiently for Nancy to

225

answer and after the fifth ring, Nancy finally picked up her phone.

"Hello, who is it?" Nancy asked over the telephone.

"Nancy? It's me, Nathan," he replied.

"Who?!"

"Nathan, Nathan Harris."

"I heard you the first time. Where the *fuck* have you been? Did you become a recluse for the past few months?!" Nancy angrily asked him.

"I don't understand, what do you mean?" Nathan asked feeling so confused.

"Oh, don't play stupid with me, hon, you know *exactly* what I mean."

"I'm afraid I don't."

"Well maybe I need to refresh your damn memory a little. May I come over?"

"Sure, anytime."

"Good, because there's something I want to give you. I'll see you in an hour."

"That'll be fine," he replied, but Nancy had already hung up her phone.

Nathan wondered what had happened since he dropped off his daughter with her, almost four months ago. He wondered what his past self had done or said during that time. *She sounded extremely angry with me,* the scientist thought. *She never once mentioned Alice. I hope she's all right.* Nathan went upstairs to relieve himself and change his clothes. After that, he was going to wait patiently for Nancy's arrival, wondering if she was bringing Alice with her.

CHAPTER 19

THE AFTERMATH

Thursday afternoon, May fourth, scientist and inventor Nathan Harris had been waiting patiently for his sister-in-law, Nancy Stevens, to arrive. He had decided to take a quick shower and put on some casual cloths before she arrived. Nathan heard a car coming up his driveway and went to open the front door for her. Nancy parked her car, got out, and closed the door while taking in a deep breath. She marched right up to him, with anger on her face that was redder than the dress she was wearing.

"Hello Nancy," Nathan said with a smile.

"Well, well, well, if it isn't the hermit himself. I have something for you, Nathan," Nancy said in anger.

Nancy raised her right hand and slapped him so hard in the face that she left her hand print on him.

"What the hell was that all about?!" Nathan asked while rubbing the left side of his face in pain.

"That's for all the *shit* you did to me!" Nancy angrily replied.

"I wish I knew what the hell you were talking about. Hey, where's Alice?"

"What?! Are you serious?"

Nancy started to get choked up. She couldn't believe what just came out of his mouth. Nathan saw she was becoming unglued. He reached over and tried to give her a hug.

"Don't touch me!" Nancy retorted while pulling away from him.

"Please, come on inside, sit down, and let's talk," he told her.

Nancy finally agreed and followed him inside his mansion. The two of them walked into the parlor and sat down on the tan-colored sofa. Nancy looked up and noticed that he *still* had that torn-up family portrait hanging above the fireplace.

"Must you keep that horrid-looking thing hanging up there as a constant reminder of what happened?" Nancy asked him with a cry in her voice.

"Would you like me to take it down right now?" Nathan softly asked her.

"No, that's all right. I want to ask you something, something very important and I need an honest answer from you, Nathan, no bullshit, please."

"Anything; what is it?"

"Nathan, I need to know the truth. Did you kill my sister?" Nancy asked him with a worried look upon her face, hoping his answer would be no.

"No, of course not. How could you even *think* I would do something like that? I loved Heather a lot."

"Well, because when you dropped off Alice to me that night in January, you said it was all because Heather was with her lover. As a matter-of-fact, your exact words to me were, 'I caught her in bed with our groundskeeper.' Now, I *knew* you were hurt when you told me that, but—"

"Nancy, listen to me, will ya? Yes, it's true; I caught her in bed with our groundskeeper, Hector Delgado, but I would *never, ever* even *think* about killing her, *or* her lover. I need you to believe me, please?" Nathan asked her while reaching for her hand.

"Then where did you really go off to that night?" Nancy asked while looking him straight in the eyes.

"I told you; I had a seminar in Oregon. After I left you, I headed straight on over to the airport. You've got to believe me on this, Nancy!"

"I do, but I'm afraid that detective doesn't."

"What detective?"

"I can't remember his name, Spanish guy, average height with curly black hair and a mustache," she said while still sniffling.

"That would be Detective Gonzalez. He still accuses me of killing my wife and daughter."

"Wha-what? Alice? I know for a fact you didn't kill her, Nathan, but he came around asking questions about you. I covered for you. I told him you had dropped Alice off in the evening because of your trip. I also told him that Heather had to go out of town and she couldn't take Alice with her. He wanted to question Alice to get her side of the story, but when I went to the guest room where I had her staying, that's when I found the note she had left on the bed."

"What note? Where is she? Please tell me she's all right!"

"Nathan, are you feeling all right?"

"What do you mean?"

"Alice has been dead now for over three months," she said while the tears started to fall from her eyes again.

"No! It can't be! I did everything in my power to save her, to save our little daughter," Nathan barely said as the tears began to well up in his eyes.

"Nathan, I can't believe you; you're acting as if you just found out about it. What happened to you in the past three months?" Nancy asked him with great concern.

"Oh, God, Nancy, If I told you, you wouldn't believe me," he weakly said with tears now streaming down his face.

Nathan now knew that his elaborate attempt to save his loving daughter and the wife that cheated on him, had failed miserably, again.

"How, how did it happen? How did she die this time?" Nathan asked her.

"*This* time? What do you mean, *this* time?"

"Oh, please, Nancy, tell me, how did she die?"

"Alice was hit by a car, walking down the road; she was running away and heading back home, don't you remember? You buried her and my sister both on the same day and then, you disappeared into hibernation. You became a recluse. I tried calling you several times; I even came over a couple of times, but you wouldn't answer the door or the phone. I really needed to talk to you and you weren't there for me, Nathan. There was that one time I actually came by and unlocked your door with Heather's spare key, but you weren't home and I got tired of waiting for you, so I left, feeling upset and lonely."

"Why? Why did she run away?"

"We were watching the news together on TV; the news reporter was covering my sister's murder. He said the police found Heather stabbed to death and stuffed into a sofa in her own mansion. Alice got so upset that she ran into her room, locked the door, and cried herself to sleep. I-I kept begging her to open the door for me, but she wouldn't, Nathan. I just wanted to hold her. The next morning, she asked me to bring her back home, when I told her we had to wait for your call, she told me she hated me and locked herself back up again." Nancy stopped to blow her nose with a tissue from her bag.

"Then what happened?" Nathan urgently asked her.

"I told her I was going to the supermarket to pick up a few things and we'll discuss this later. When I returned about an hour later, that detective was there already waiting for me. I let him in and then he questioned me about you. After that, he wanted to question Alice. That's when I found her, her note," she struggled to say before crying again.

"Wha-what did her note say?" Nathan asked with a curious look on his face.

"It said, she, she was going back home to see her mommy. Then, the detective got on his radio and called for assistance. One of the cops spotted her sprawled out on the road about a mile away from my house," Nancy couldn't talk anymore; she just wept on Nathan's shoulder.

"After all I did to try and save her and *still*, she dies. She was meant to die," Nathan sadly said.

"Oh, Nathan, what the hell are you talking about? It was a hit-and-run. After all this time, those stupid cops never found the driver—that's bullshit!"

They hugged each other on the couch, trying to comfort one another. Nathan miserably realized the truth about time travel; you cannot change history, and if you try to, one of two things will happen. One, serious repercussions will happen down the line, and the second thing that *could* happen is, the future will try to balance itself out. This is what happened in this scenario. Nathan found out the hard way that his wife and daughter were both destined to die. When Nathan tried to save Alice last time, she ran back into the house and was murdered along with Heather. This time, his daughter was run over and killed by a car while walking back home. *I can't win. No matter how many times I try to save them, it will always be the same aftermath—Alice and Heather were destined to die,* Nathan sadly thought with tears in his eyes. *I couldn't have even saved Heather; she wouldn't listen to me.*

Nancy finally broke away from Nathan. She grabbed another tissue from her bag and blew her nose again. By now, the two of them were looking disheveled. Nancy took out another tissue and wiped Nathan's tears off of his face. She looked at him with bewilderment.

"I'm having a hard time believing that you don't remember any of this at all. Did you suffer from amnesia or some kind of memory loss? You're not going senile on me, are you?" Nancy asked with great concern.

Nathan looked at her for a moment, not quite knowing what to say to her. The scientist knew damn well he couldn't divulge anything about time travel to her, remembering what happened the last time he did that with the police. Nathan decided to agree with *her* conclusions.

"Yes, that's what the hell it was all right, temporary amnesia brought on from a fall I had in the lab," Nathan answered, trying to be as convincing as ever.

"How did it happen? Did you hit your head or something?" Nancy curiously asked him.

"Yes, I slipped on some papers that were on the floor and I fell," he said with a chuckle.

"When did it happen?"

"I don't remember when, but it was a while ago."

"Well, you seem all right now, but you should have yourself checked out. You never know, you may have a concussion or something."

Nancy started feeling his head for any bumps. Nathan looked at her inquisitively.

"What are you doing, trying to massage my head?" Nathan asked her.

"Well, if you must know, I'm checking your head for any bumps," Nancy said.

"Did you find any?"

"No, there's nothing there. I *am* sorry for slapping your face though."

"Does it look bad?"

"*Well,* I kind of left my hand print on your face. I didn't realize I slapped you *that* hard."

"Yeah, you did."

"I'm sorry, Nathan."

"It's all right, I'll get over it and it'll go away," he said reassuringly.

Nancy went into her purse for her makeup, but she dropped her lipstick on the floor. Nancy bent down to get it and noticed the bloodstains on the lower part of the sofa. Suddenly, a big chill nestled over her body. Nancy looked Nathan square in his eyes with a worried look on her face.

"What's the matter, Nancy? You look like you've seen a ghost," Nathan asked.

"Is that blood on your sofa?" she nervously asked him.

"Where?"

"Down there," Nancy said while pointing to the stains on the couch.

Nathan bent down to look at what Nancy was pointing to on the couch.

"That must be from when I scraped my ankle outside. I guess I was still bleeding when I sat down on it," he softly replied.

"Oh, for a moment I thought this was the sofa that my sister's body was stuffed in by the killer."

"No, that's gone, but she *was* killed in this room, Nancy. I won't deny it."

"Nathan, I'm not comfortable knowing that. Can we please just go to another room?" Nancy stated while now standing up in front of him.

"We can go into the family room, there's two more sofas and chairs in there."

"Anywhere else but here."

Nathan got up and brought Nancy over toward the family room. Nancy noticed the décor was all winter green, with the exception of the dark oak wood flooring and the marble fireplace. The two of them sat down on the green sofa and resumed their conversation.

"Nathan, I meant to ask you something, something that's been gnawing at me?" Nancy questioned.

"What is it?" Nathan asked.

"That night in January when you brought Alice over, did you suspect that Heather's lover was going to kill her? Is that the *real* reason you brought Alice over?"

"No, I knew Hector wasn't the killer."

"I heard on the news that the police originally suspected *you*, Nathan, until they found evidence of Heather having an affair with someone else, which later turned out to be Hector Delgado."

"Detective Gonzalez still believes I had something to do with her murder."

"Well, yeah, after Hector turned up dead on the roof of his building, they're now suspecting you of not only killing Heather, but also her boyfriend. Heck, my own parents even believe you did it, especially my father. Daddy thinks you're one hundred percent guilty of killing his daughter."

"That sure is comforting," he replied.

Nathan wanted to tell her that he did everything in his power to save her sister. Alice *was* his priority, but he *did* try to save Heather, too. Nathan felt that he had to warn Nancy of the killer, but he had to be tactful about it.

"Nancy, there's something that I have to warn you about; it's not safe here," Nathan told her in a serious tone.

"What? Your fortress is not safe?"

Nancy had to think about what she was going to say next, knowing that the killer was still out there. Nancy was also ignoring the fact that her own sister was killed here. She began to realize that until the murderer was caught, no one was safe anywhere, not even here in Harris Manor.

"All right, Nathan, I'm all ears. Let me hear what you have to say," she said to him.

"The killer, he was here again," Nathan told her.

"What?! When?!" Nancy asked on the verge of hysteria.

"About two weeks ago."

"Did you tell the police?"

"Not the second time, since they didn't believe me the first time, especially since Detective Gonzalez *still* believes that I killed them."

"Second time? How many times was he here?" Nancy nervously asked him.

"Twice, so far," Nathan grimly replied.

"Nathan, you need to tell the police before they convict you on some trumped-up charges, or they come up with enough incriminating evidence to lock you up. I mean, if there's even the slightest chance of finding the real killer, you'd be off the hook. Do you understand what I'm saying?"

"Yes, I do, but—"

"No buts. Did you get a good look at him?"

"No, the man was wearing a black mask, dark glasses, and a black ski hat that was pulled down to the top of his eyes. I did see blood stains on his white sneakers though; it probably was Heather's blood."

"Oh, God, Nathan, what did he want from you?"

"He said he wanted everything, everything I had."

"Is there anything else you remember about him, like maybe the sound of his voice?"

"He had a deep, gruff voice, but I didn't recognize it. I *did* see him drive off in a small, dark green car. He had kept it hidden behind the bushes by the gate, and no, I couldn't see his plate number; it was too far away. The man obviously had keys to the mansion. I changed the locks after that, even the alarm code."

"I know you did. I came over again a few days ago and my keys wouldn't fit. Nathan, I want you to know that I never really did believe you killed my sister, but I wanted to hear it from you."

"Well, now you have."

"I still would like to know one thing, Nathan?"

"What's that?"

"How the hell did you know that Alice was our daughter? You never told me that."

"*You* told me. You also told me that you still love me," Nathan softly replied while looking into her blue eyes.

"No, Nathan, you told *me* that night when you brought Alice over. You also said you knew that I still love you. When I asked you how you knew that, you told me you had your ways. Now, it's true, I've never stopped loving you. After all these years, I've only wanted one man, and that's you. You were my first and only love, Nathan. I still want to know who the hell told you?" Nancy asked while feeling utterly confused.

Nathan had to think fast. He obviously changed other elements of the future when he went back in time again. Nathan now realized that the day he spent with Nancy while she poured her heart out to him never happened. *Who knows what else I inadvertently changed while going back in time,*

Nathan thought.

"Well, it was a lot of little things. Things that Heather would say. I've also noticed the way you've reacted toward Alice *and* me when you came to visit. I kind of just put two and two together, that's all," Nathan said while trying to weasel his way out of another interrogation.

"Oh, Nathan, I do still love you, I always have and I always will," Nancy said while putting her arms around him.

Nathan looked deep into her soft blue eyes and could see nothing but love in them. She pulled him closer to her. Nathan could almost taste her warm, sweet, inviting lips. He was finally getting ready to kiss her when they heard the front doorbell ring. Their love trance had been broken. *Maybe it's for the best,* he thought.

"I, I have to go see who it is," Nathan barely said.

"No! What if it's the killer again?!" Nancy exclaimed.

"Do you *really think* the killer is going to ring the bell? What if it's Gonzalez, again? I'll go and check the monitor first."

Nathan got up and went over toward the wall monitor near the front door. His suspicions were correct; Detective Gonzalez was at the front door, wearing a dark gray suit and a light-blue shirt, with his badge prominently hanging down from his neck. Nathan opened up the door and greeted him.

"Detective Gonzalez, what can I do for you?" Nathan asked.

"Mr. Harris, I need you to come down to the station with me to answer some more questions, please," Gonzalez stated.

"Nathan! You've got to tell him about the killer!" Nancy shouted while walking over toward them.

"*Well,* I didn't know you had company. What's this about the killer, Miss Stevens?" Gonzalez asked her, wondering how close they really were to each other.

"He came around again, about two weeks ago," Nathan told him.

"Why didn't you call us then? This is withholding important information."

"You didn't believe me the first time, Juan, neither did your captain. The both of you thought I was crazy."

"Well, let's face it, Mr. Harris, you were talking a lot of nonsense about time travel. Now, let's be clear, did you really see the killer two weeks ago and can you identify him?"

"I *did* see him, but I'm afraid I can't give you much of a description, he was pretty covered up, but I'll go downtown with you and do my best," Nathan said to him.

The three of them left the mansion. Nathan locked up and said goodbye to Nancy, and she told him to call or text her when he got back home. Nathan got into the car with Detective Gonzalez and they drove off. Hiding behind the bushes near the gate, the murderer was watching and waiting for just the right time to strike, again…

Photo courtesy of Sefa Tekin

CHAPTER 20

INTERROGATED AGAIN

Detective Gonzalez had just pulled into the police station parking lot with Nathan Harris. It was still fairly bright out, even though it was almost six o'clock in the evening. Gonzalez was putting in some overtime, knowing that he wouldn't have to tomorrow. The detective wanted to keep Fridays open from now on in case he scored another date with Gladys. *I don't think she likes me anymore though. Gladys wouldn't let me kiss her at all, not even on her cheek,* he thought. Gladys had told him that she never kissed anyone on a first date. Gonzalez wondered if it was true, or maybe he just didn't click with her.

It was warm out, much too warm for Gonzalez. *Shit, it's only May fourth and it's eighty fricking degrees already; it's gonna be a long, hot summer, ¡Ay Dios Mío!* he thought. Gonzalez got out of his car and escorted Nathan into the police station. Then, he brought Nathan to the captain's office.

"Thank you for coming down here again, Nathan," Captain Martinelli said.

"Did I have a choice, Paul? Why am I being interrogated again? This is getting monotonous. I've got better things to do with my time than to keep coming down here, to be interrogated over and over again for the same damn thing," Nathan complained to him.

"Now wait a minute, Nathan. You're not really being interrogated. We're not even in the interrogation room. I just want to ask you some more questions, that's all. Now please, have a seat."

"Yes, Captain."

"Close the door, will ya, Detective?"

"Sure," Gonzalez replied.

Nathan sat down in the black chair in front of the captain's desk. Detective Gonzalez closed the office door and stood guard, right behind Nathan. Martinelli took some papers out of his desk drawer and looked up at Nathan.

"Ok, Nathan, first of all, I just wanted to tell you that we've finally caught the hit-and-run driver that killed your daughter. He actually turned himself in, claims he was guilt-stricken. Again, I just wanted to say that I'm very sorry for your loss," the captain said in a somber tone.

"I see. Was he drunk, or was he impaired in any way?" Nathan asked him.

"Yes, yes, he was. He claims that by the time he saw your daughter, it was just way too late for him to stop his car. Secondly, you *do* know that your groundskeeper, Hector Delgado, was murdered, right?"

"Yeah, I gathered that."

"But what you *don't know* was that Delgado was *killed* somewhere else *before* he was brought up to the roof of his apartment house. We believe he was murdered in your home, Nathan. The medical examiner had determined that both Delgado's body and your wife's body were both killed around the same time. I'm still trying to figure out why the killer would hide your wife's body in your home, in the sofa, and then drag Delgado's body back to his place of residence to make it look like a suicide. I mean, he obviously had plenty of time to do all this shit."

"It seems that way, Paul."

"You know what I think, Nathan?"

"What's that, Paul?"

"I think that someone's trying to frame you," the captain told him.

240

"Oh, I know that, he told me," Nathan added.

"What? What are you talking about, Nathan? *Who* told you?"

"The murderer. He told me that he wanted everything, everything I owned."

"Well, when the *hell* did you speak to him?!"

"About two weeks ago; he was in my home, waiting for me to arrive."

"Did you know about this shit, Gonzalez?!"

"I tried to tell you, Captain, but you and him were on a roll and I didn't want to interrupt," Gonzalez added.

"Well just kiss my Italian ass here! Why the *hell* am I always the last person to know about any shit around here? I'm only the fricking captain of the police force for Christ's sake! What the hell else are you two not telling me?!" Martinelli angrily asked them while slamming his desk drawer shut.

"That's about it, Captain. Mr. Harris claims that he'd seen his wife's killer in his home. I told him he was withholding critical information," Gonzalez said.

"Damn straight he is!"

"I'm sorry about that, Paul, but after the way the two of you practically accused me of going insane last time, what the *hell* was I supposed to do?" Nathan asked both of them.

"Well, what did you expect, Nathan? The last time you were here, you were talking all this mumbo jumbo crap about time travel. Until you can prove to me beyond a shadow of a doubt that your equipment can actually take my ass, or anyone else's ass for that matter, back in time, then it's just nothing but pure science fiction. Do you understand what I'm saying?"

"Yes, Paul, I do," Nathan somberly replied.

"Good, now tell me, can you describe our killer?"

"Not really. I didn't get a good look at his face. However, I *can* tell you that he was of average height and build, he wore a black ski cap, a black mask, and dark sunglasses."

"Oh, Christ, that could be anybody! Anything else you wanna add to that description, Nathan?"

"Yeah, he was wearing black leather gloves to match his black leather jacket. He also had on a pair of worn blue jeans."

"Anything else?"

"Yeah, his sneakers."

"What about them?"

"They were white with bloodstains on them. I think it could have been my wife's blood," Nathan sadly said.

"You said he spoke to you. Can you recognize his voice if you heard it again?"

"I think I could, it was deep and gruff, kind of like a smoker's voice."

"And you have no idea who it could be?"

"No sir, I really don't. At first, I thought it might have been a disgruntled employee of mine, but his voice just didn't ring a bell to me."

"Now, what exactly did he say to you, Nathan?" Martinelli inquisitively asked him.

"Well, after he surprised me from hiding behind my door, he told me to put my hands up and that he had a gun pointing at my back. I asked him who he was and what he wanted. He told me that who he is was irrelevant, what he wanted was everything, everything I own."

"And then what?"

"He asked me why the hell I wasn't in jail yet. He said he tried his best to frame me. There's something else I have to tell you, Paul," Nathan admits.

"And what's that, Nathan?"

"This guy had to have had keys for my home, even the gate. He also must have had the alarm code. There was no sign of forced entry that I could find anywhere—no broken windows or anything like that. I checked everywhere and everything."

"It has to be someone you know, Nathan. I suggest you change all your locks and the alarm code."

"I've already done that, Paul."

"All right, Nathan, I'm gonna set you up with the police artist."

"Sounds good to me."

"Gonzalez!"

"Yes, Captain?"

"Take Mr. Harris over to our artist," Martinelli ordered.

"Ok, Captain. Mr. Harris, follow me, please," Gonzalez said while motioning Nathan to come with him.

Detective Gonzalez brought Nathan Harris over to the police artist. Nathan gave the artist the best description he could from recalling his encounter with the killer. By the time the artist was finished, he had a fairly detailed sketch of the murderer, according to the information Nathan had furnished him. A copy of the drawing was hung up on the murder board and more copies were made into wanted posters. Captain Paul Martinelli ordered an APB out for the suspected killer.

*
**

Detective Gonzalez was finally bringing Nathan back home. Nathan got out of the car and walked up the redbrick pathway to his front door. Gonzalez waited for him to go inside. *I wonder if he's really telling the truth, or is he just trying to cover his ass up,* the detective thought. Unlike Captain Paul Martinelli, Detective Juan Gonzalez *still* believed that Nathan Harris was perfectly capable of not only murdering his wife, but also her lover, Hector Delgado.

"I guess I'll have to watch his sister-in-law, Nancy Stevens, too. I think she may be more than just a sister-in-law to him," he said to himself.

Gonzalez looked at his watch and noticed it was almost eight o'clock. *Shit, time to go home,* he thought. Gonzalez finally decided to leave. He backed out of the long driveway, turned his car around, and went home.

*
**

The next morning, Nathan was in his lab trying to overcome a malfunction in his biometric security system. He could not get any of the motorized doors in the basement to close up. *Shit, just what I need, now anybody could get in here,* the man thought with a worried look upon his face. Nathan removed the picture of his mom off the wall that was concealing his wall safe. He opened up the safe and removed all the blueprints of the basement from it. Nathan also grabbed his plans for the Time Transporter. The scientist took all the papers and placed them on his workbench.

"I've got to get to the bottom of this. I need my security system functioning again," he said to himself.

Nathan started going over all of the blueprints for the basement first. He paid careful attention to the biometric security system that controlled all the entry doors down there. Then, his phone began to ring.

"Hello, Harris residence," Nathan answered.

"Nathan, when did you get back? You never called or texted me, I was worried sick about you," Nancy said over the phone.

"I'm sorry, Nancy. I got home late. I was tired and just wanted to go to bed."

"Are you all right? You sound kind of weird."

"I'm fine, just a little tired that's all."

"Do want any company? I could come over if you'd like. Maybe I can make us some breakfast?"

"I have a better idea, how about if I come over and pick you up, we can go out for breakfast, my treat, how's that?"

"I like that idea even better. How soon can you get here?" Nancy asked.

"Give me about twenty minutes."

"Sounds great! I'll see you then," she said before hanging up the phone.

Nathan hung up and left the lab the way it was, knowing he couldn't secure it. The scientist went back upstairs to brush his teeth and change his clothes. Nathan grabbed his black dinner jacket and left the mansion. He got into his emerald Bentley, started up the engine, and left, admiring the deep-blue sky above him. After Nathan left, Doctor Berlin's secretary had called and left a message on his machine.

"Hello Mr. Harris, this is Doctor Berlin's secretary. I'm sorry to inform you of his passing. I don't know if you were planning on making an appointment with him. If you need a referral for another doctor, please call the office at (212) 555-3979," she said before hanging up the phone.

✳
✶✶

Later on that morning, Detective Gonzalez was staring at the murder board again for the umpteenth time, hoping something would pop. The detective was so deep in his own thoughts that he didn't notice Captain Martinelli observing him. *I wonder, I really wonder if he did it? I still believe he did, but he's slick, that's for sure,* Gonzalez thought.

"I see you're analyzing that board again, Gonzalez," the captain stated.

"Good morning, Captain," Gonzalez said back to him.

"You still suspect Nathan Harris, don't you? I see you put his picture back up there after I told you to take it down."

"Well, when our number one suspect Hector Delgado turned up dead, Harris seemed to be the most logical choice again, Captain."

"We've been down this road before, Gonzalez."

"Captain, suppose, just suppose that the contraption Harris built in his lab really works."

"Oh, Jesus H. Christ, now you're starting to sound as nutty as he is," Martinelli said while scratching his head.

"Think about it, Captain. If Harris was *really* able to go back in time, he would have had time, time enough for murder. Harris would have been able to kill them all. He could have had time to hide his wife's body in the sofa to throw us off. Then, Harris could have brought Delgado's body back to his apartment house, placed him up on the roof, and made it look like suicide. Harris still would have had plenty of time to make his trip to Oregon, all without anyone suspecting him of murder. I mean, the story just writes itself. The perfect murder, indeed."

"Interesting theory, Gonzalez, except for one thing."

"What's that, Captain?"

"There's no such thing as time travel, as we know it. It just doesn't *exist.*"

"But Captain, you didn't see that big machine he had down in his laboratory."

"I don't need to see it to know that it doesn't work, *Gonzalez.* Nathan Harris *could* be experimenting with time travel for all we know, but I seriously doubt he succeeded. Harris could have been playing you like a harp. He could be laughing at your ass right now. Like I said before, there's no such thing as time travel, except in the movies and on television. Do I make myself clear?"

"All right, Captain, but it *still* doesn't clear Harris of my list," Gonzalez added while writing "Prime Suspect" with a red marker under Nathan's picture on the board.

"Listen, just be careful about accusing him of murder again. We don't want to get sued, all right?"

"All right, Captain."

"You're a good detective, Gonzalez, I'd hate to lose you to some dumb shit like this," the captain said before going back to his office.

✳
✳✳

That evening at Harris Manor, Nathan was just returning back home from his date with Nancy. He parked his car in the driveway and looked at the moon-lit sky. *It was a really nice day,* Nathan thought. The two of them had gone out for breakfast at his favorite restaurant, enjoying each other's company. After breakfast, they took in a matinee at the local cinema. Nathan loved horror movies even though they were so unrealistic, especially the ones where the killer keeps coming back after being shot multiple times, or even burned to death. However, Nancy would have preferred a cozy mystery or crime thriller, instead.

Nancy had dragged Nathan to the mall to shop around for some new clothes after the movie. He decided to look in the electronics stores for the latest gadgets. The two of them finally met up at the main entrance of the mall and then Nathan dropped her off at her home. She had asked him to come in for a bit, but he was tired and didn't want to be pressured into anything. Nathan *did* have strong feelings for Nancy, but deep down inside, he still loved Heather, even after she cheated on him with their groundskeeper. *I wonder if I should even try to save them again. It's probably futile, destiny is destiny,* he thought. Nathan looked at the clock on his dashboard before turning the car off.

"Nine thirty? I can't believe it's that late already," he said to himself.

The scientist left his vehicle, walked up the brick pathway, and entered his mansion. Nathan was greeted by an alarm that was coming from downstairs. He ran down to the basement, past the gymnasium, and right into the laboratory. Nathan's computers were screaming in agony while they started to burn from being short circuited.

"Intruder alert! Malfunction, overload! Intruder alert! Mal..." the computer said in its synthesized female voice before the final explosion.

Nathan tried to duck from the flying debris but it was too late. A large piece of metal flew and struck him right in his chest, embedding itself in the process. Nathan was out cold—on his back and on the floor in an instant. The Time Transporter was completely destroyed. Nathan Harris's lab was burning with him in it.

"I guess I don't have to worry about *your* ass anymore. Sucks for you, Harris, sucks for you!" the intruder said with a smile while leaving the premises.

Nathan never saw the intruder that was hiding in the corner waiting for him to return. Poor Nathan was unconscious, laying there on the floor, and dying with his own creation. The overhead sprinkler system had finally kicked in, but it was no match for the growing electrical fire that was now devouring everything in its path, getting closer and closer to Nathan's cataleptic body, as the smoke alarm screamed in agony.

Photo courtesy of Marina Leonova

CHAPTER 21

POOR NATHAN

ancy Stevens was thinking about how thoughtful Nathan was. *He was a perfect gentleman, lending me his credit card to shop for clothes in the mall,* the woman thought. Nathan had told her if she had any problems with a store not taking his card, she should call or text him on his cell. Nancy rang up over five hundred dollars on his card with no problems and now, she felt guilty. The woman was going through her shopping bags and found Nathan's VISA card tucked in between her garments. She had inadvertently tossed it in the bag while leaving the store. *I've got to give him back his card ASAP; it's the least I can do,* she thought. Nancy could have brought his card back in the morning, but she really wanted to see him again. Now, Nancy was driving over to Nathan's mansion, in the late evening, to return his credit card.

A car had sped by Nancy going in the opposite direction. The car was moving so fast that it made her look as if she was standing still. *What the hell was his problem? Where's the fire?* Nancy thought.

Nancy was finally pulling into Nathan's driveway when she noticed the front door was left wide open. *That's not like him to leave the door open like that,* the woman thought. Nancy knew Nathan would never leave his doors or windows open without screens; he hated bugs. She got out of her car and started walking toward the open front door. Nancy heard the smoke alarm coming from within, not knowing what it was. Then, she smelled the smoke.

"Oh, my God! Nathan?!" Nancy screamed.

Nancy followed the sound and smell to an opened door with stairs that led down to the basement. She briskly walked down the stairs, calling for her brother-in-law.

"Nathan! Nathan where are you?! Are you all right?!" Nancy kept shouting while walking quickly.

Nancy walked through the gymnasium, admiring the exercise equipment. She had never been down there before. The alarm was getting louder as the woman got closer toward the source. Now, Nancy was not only smelling the smoke, but seeing it, along with the flames that were consuming the lab. She covered her mouth with a napkin from her bag. Nancy's heart almost stopped when she found Nathan lying on the floor, helplessly unconscious with a piece of metal protruding from his chest.

"Nathan!" Nancy shrieked.

Nancy's adrenalin kicked into high gear. She held her breath, grabbed Nathan by his shoulders, and dragged him out of the lab, just before the flames roasted him. Nancy kept dragging him through the basement, up the stairs, and through the mansion, never once stopping until the two of them were finally outside in the cool, fresh air. Nancy started to give Nathan mouth-to-mouth resuscitation, until the fire department showed up, responding to Nathan's alarm system. The men gave him oxygen.

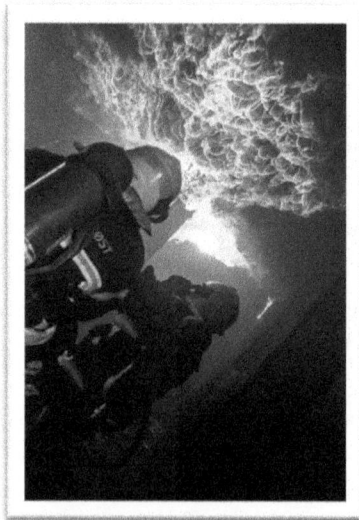

Photo courtesy of Bjørn Nielsen

"Is there anyone else inside?!" the fireman asked Nancy.

"I don't think so, he was living alone since his wife and daughter were killed a while ago," she replied.

Photo courtesy of Pixabay

The rest of the firemen went into the mansion with their hoses, trying to salvage what was left of Harris Manor. The entire laboratory was completely destroyed. Most of the gymnasium was spared, with the exception of one very expensive treadmill. An ambulance showed up and took Nathan and Nancy over to Solville Medical Center. Nancy was also given oxygen as a precautionary measure. The two fire engines and their crew remained on-scene until the fire was completely extinguished.

✻
✻✻

The paramedics and EMTs brought Nathan into the emergency room. Nancy declined medical attention and just focused on Nathan. The medical team brought Nathan into the operating room for emergency surgery, with the doctor that was on call. The doctor was concerned that the piece of metal protruding from Nathan's chest may have severed a major artery. Nancy waited in the hospital waiting room, extremely concerned about Nathan.

*
**

Over three hours later, a thin, young doctor named Mark Winters was looking for Nancy in the waiting room.

"Nancy Stevens? Is there a Nancy Stevens here?" Doctor Winters asked.

"Yes, that's me!" Nancy replied to the man dressed in the white lab coat wearing glasses.

"Hello Miss Stevens, I'm Doctor Winters. Did you bring in Mr. Nathan Harris?"

"Yes, I did, is he going to be all right?"

"Yes, he is. Mr. Harris survived the surgery, but he's not out of the woods yet. He's a lucky man, though. The piece of metal that impaled him is his chest was only three millimeters away from his heart's right ventricle."

"Where is he now, Doctor?"

"He's in the intensive care unit. The next few hours are crucial to his survival. I understand you pulled him out of a fire in his home," he said when brushing his brown hair away from his face with his right hand.

"I only did what any human being would have done."

"You're being way too modest. You saved his life, Miss Stevens. I understand you're related to him?"

"I'm his sister-in-law. When can I see him?" Nancy asked the doctor.

"I'm sorry, Miss Stevens, but due to COVID-19 restrictions and

252

his condition, no one can visit Mr. Harris until he's moved to a private or semiprivate room," Doctor Winters firmly stated.

"When will that be, Doctor?" Nancy asked with a concerned look on her face.

"In about two days, I'm sorry."

Nancy walked away feeling helpless. She desperately wanted to see Nathan. *I guess I might as well go back home,* she thought. *Poor Nathan, in there struggling to stay alive and there's not a damn thing I can do to help him,* Nancy thought with a worried look on her face.

*
**

Monday morning, May eighth, it had been over two days since Nathan Harris was brought into the hospital. Nancy had been calling the hospital twice a day for the whole weekend of his stay and finally, she heard he was being moved to a private room. *Thank God, I can finally go and see him,* she thought. Nancy packed up the latest thriller novel, *Avalina* by Manuel Rose, to read to him. she knew that Nathan loved horror and thriller stories.

*
**

Detective Juan Gonzalez was in his office enjoying a morning cup of coffee, especially with the company that had brought it for him, Gladys Delgado.

"I heard about what happened to my brother's former boss, Mr. Harris," she said while sipping on her coffee.

"Yes, Harris was very lucky that his sister-in-law was there to save him. She pulled him out of the fire in his home," Gonzalez told her.

"How did it happen?"

"We don't know for sure yet. It could have been electrical, with all the shit he had down there, it's possible. The fire marshal stated that the fire looked like it was set intentionally, which means it was arson."

253

"Is he gonna be all right?" Gladys asked with a look of concern on her face.

"Well, they moved him out of intensive care, so that's a good sign. I can't interview him yet, though," Gonzalez said disappointedly.

"Why not?"

"Because he's still unconscious, probably from smoke inhalation."

"They said on the news that he had some piece of metal sticking out of his chest; did someone try to stab him?"

"No, the fire chief thinks it came from an explosion in his basement. Well, so much for his time machine; now we'll never know if it really works."

"He built a time machine?" Gladys asked.

"That's what Harris claimed."

"Wow!"

"So, what are you doing tonight?" Gonzalez asked, changing the subject, with a hopeful look in his eyes.

"Nothing. You want to come over again, *Señor* Detective?" Gladys said coyly.

"*Si señora,* how's seven o'clock look?"

"Fine by me, papa. I'll see you at seven. Don't be late," she said while giving him a quick kiss on his cheek.

Gladys left his office and went straight to work. Gonzalez watched her as she left; he loved her gait. *That woman's gonna drive me crazy, but in a nice way, I hope,* he said to himself. Gonzalez was so happy to see her again. *She kissed me, wow,* he thought. Then Gonzalez's phone began to ring.

"Detective Gonzalez, homicide," he answered.

"*Señor* Detective, this is Consuelo Hernandez, do you remember me?" Consuelo asked.

"Yes, you used to be the maid for the Harris's. What can I do for you, Miss Hernandez?"

"I, I just heard about Hector, Hector Delgado. I was away," she said while choking back the tears.

"It sounds like you two were kind of close, am I right?"

"Well, you could say that I was closer to him than he was to me."

"How close?"

"I won't lie, *Señor* Detective. I liked Hector, I liked him a lot."

"I see."

"I liked him, but he no really liked me, he love *Señora* Harris, I think. I cover for him many times, even to you. Remember I told you a few months ago that *Señora* Harris have boyfriend with blond hair and blue eyes?"

"Well, you said she was *talking* to someone that fits that description a few times."

"I sorry, I make him up to cover for Hector. Am I in trouble, *Señor* Detective?"

"You lied to the police, mainly to me, but I can't see arresting you now for that, especially since it wouldn't help in any way. But in the future, please don't ever lie to the police again, you could be in big trouble. Do you understand, *Señora*?"

"*Si, si, muchas gracias, Señor* Detective, *chow*," she happily said while hanging up the phone.

Gonzalez hung up the phone and thought about it for a moment.

255

All this time I was looking for someone that didn't even exist, he angrily thought. The detective knew it still didn't explain who killed Hector Delgado or Mrs. Harris. *I don't care what the captain believes, as far as I'm concerned, Mr. Nathan Harris is my prime suspect. If Harris caught them in bed together, then that would have been his motive for murdering them,* Gonzalez thought.

*
**

A few miles away at Solville Medical Center, Nancy Stevens had just arrived. She parked her car in the hospital parking lot and walked into the facility. Nancy went over to the information counter to find out where Nathan was. She seemed intimidated by the heavyset, African American woman that was yelling at someone over the phone. *My God, this woman's like a bulldog, I'm almost afraid to ask her anything,* Nancy thought.

"Yeah well, the same to you, don't ever call here again. I ain't got time for this shit! Man, some people," the receptionist said while slamming the phone down.

The woman took one look at Nancy and complained before she even said a word.

"Miss you can't be comin' in here like that! Where's your mask?! Ain't you heard about COVID-19?!" the receptionist bawled at her.

"I'm sorry, I don't have one. I thought we were through that," Nancy innocently replied.

"Well, you thought wrong. This is a hospital and you *always* have to wear a mask in a hospital. Lucky for you, I got some," she said while handing Nancy a mask.

"Thank you. I need to know what room Mr. Nathan Harris is in, please," Nancy said while putting on the mask.

"Are you a relative, miss?"

"Yes, I'm his sister-in-law."

"Oh, I thought you were his wife, my mistake."

"His wife passed away. Now what room is he in please?"

"Mr. Harris is in room 300. His doctor right now is Doctor Winters. You can take the elevator over there, miss," the receptionist said while pointing to the right.

Nancy walked over to where the elevators were and pressed the call button. She waited for the door to open, and then Nancy got onboard. She took the elevator to the third floor and started searching for Nathan's room. "There it is, room 300," Nancy said to herself after finding his room. When Nancy walked into the room, she was greeted by a slim, young, Asian nurse that had short black hair.

"Oh, hello, you here to see Mr. Harris?" the nurse asked.

"Yes, I am. How is he doing?" Nancy asked with a cry in her voice.

"He's doing better, but still not awake yet. Are you his wife?"

"No, I'm his sister-in-law."

"Oh, ok. His wife come soon?"

"No, his wife passed away."

"Oh, I see. You can still talk to him. He may be able to hear you. I know Doctor Winters was worried about him, not knowing how long he no have oxygen."

"Has he woken up at all?"

"No, I sorry. Doctor Winters say Mr. Harris like that ever since he been here, at least he can breathe on his own and doesn't have to be intubated. I'm sorry I don't have better news for you. Doctor Winters tell you more later when he come back. Bye, nice to see you," the young nurse said as she left the room.

Nancy looked at poor Nathan lying there on the bed looking so frail. He was hooked up to a heart monitor machine and an IV was connected to his left arm. Nancy pulled down her mask to kiss his right cheek, and then she sat down in the chair next to him on his right side.

"Oh, my love, if you only knew how much it pains me to see you like this. At least you've got a private room. I brought you a new book from one of your favorite authors, I'll read it to you, honey," she said to him with tears forming in her eyes.

Nancy took out the paperback novel she had brought him from her black shoulder bag. Nancy poured some water from the pitcher into a plastic cup and drank it. Then, she grabbed a tissue from the box and blew her nose. Nancy brushed her blonde hair away from her eyes, opened up the book, and began reading to Nathan as he laid unconscious in bed.

"It was a moderately cold Monday afternoon, February third, 1969. The sun was trying to shine through some dreary clouds, making it look overcast. Some folks were even saying that it looked like a snow sky, and they were right. A winter storm was coming into a small suburban town called "Merryville," just outside of New York City. The storm was expected to dump up to twenty-five inches of snow with blizzard-like conditions," Nancy read before drinking some more water.

"What happened then?" Nathan barely said in a feeble and groggy voice.

"Nathan?! You're awake?!"

"May I have some water, please?"

"Sure, honey."

Nancy poured him some water, put a straw in the cup, and gave it to him. Nathan tried to drink, but he kept spilling most of it on himself. Nancy pressed the button on his remote to raise his back on the bed, making it easier for him to drink his water.

"Well, well, well, I see you've finally come back to us, Mr. Harris," Doctor Winters said while entering the room.

"He just woke up, Doctor," Nancy told him while pulling up her mask.

"Mr. Harris, you're a very lucky man. Your sister-in-law here saved your life. She pulled you out of the fire," the doctor reported to him.

"You did?" Nathan weakly asked while turning his head to her.

"Yes Nathan, I did. You were lucky I came back to give you your credit card that I found in my bag," Nancy replied.

"I guess I owe you one," Nathan said.

"You don't owe me anything, sweetie, just get better."

"My chest hurts," he said while touching his chest.

"Oh, don't touch that, those are your stiches from your operation," Doctor Winters said.

"Operation? What operation?" Nathan asked his doctor.

"Mr. Harris, when you were brought in here, you had a metal shard protruding from your chest that had to be removed. You were lucky, it just barely missed your heart. You're gonna have to remain here in the hospital for about seven to ten days to recuperate. After that, you'll need about four to six weeks of recovery time at home. Do you have anyone at home that can care for you, Mr. Harris?"

"He does now. I can take care of him, Doctor. That is if you'll let me, honey?" Nancy said while facing Nathan.

"You'd do that for me?" Nathan asked her.

"I wouldn't give it a second thought," she said with a loving smile on her pretty face.

"Well then, it's settled. Do you need anything else before I go, Mr. Harris?" Doctor Winters asked.

"Yes, Doctor, some food would be greatly appreciated."

"All right, I see you're certainly getting better. I'll go tell the nurse to bring you some food," Doctor Winters said as he exited the room.

"What was that you were reading to me before?" Nathan asked Nancy.

"Oh, it's a book I just got you, *Avalina,* by one of your favorite authors," Nancy said while holding up the book for him to see.

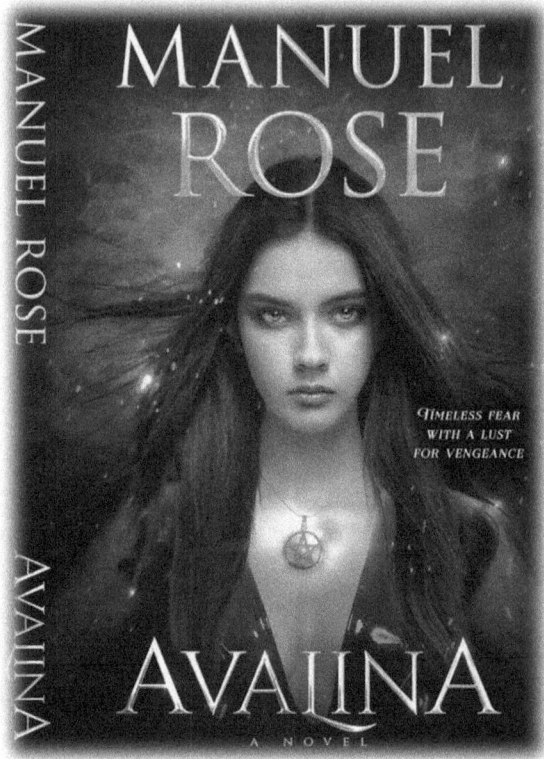

Photo courtesy of Robynne Alexander of Damonza

"Beautiful girl, as a matter-of-fact, she's hot," Nathan said with a sexy smirk on his face.

"Well, I know *you're* feeling better, mister," she said in an annoyed tone.

"I don't recognize the author's name, Manuel Rose?"

"I noticed that you had a couple of his books on the table in the parlor along with Stephen King. You had plenty of his books there."

"I love Stephen King, but those are Heather's novels. I mostly read technical books. But thank you anyway."

"I'm sorry, I thought you liked horror."

"I do, horror movies; you're in and out of the theater in about two hours."

"When did my sister get into horror?" Nancy asked with an inquisitive look upon her face.

"Oh, quite a while ago, maybe about five years or more. I won't lie to you; I still miss her, even after what she did to me," Nathan said with tears emerging from his face.

Nancy knew Nathan was still in pain, both emotionally and physically. *Damn her for hurting the only man I ever loved,* she thought. Nancy *did* miss her sister, but she knew what Heather did was wrong. *Heather stole my man and my daughter, it's hard for me to forgive her after all that,* Nancy miserably thought.

"Will you read to me some more?" Nathan asked her.

"Sure I can, but before I do, I just want you to know that I'm not trying to replace my sister, even though I still feel like she stole you from me. I loved you first," Nancy told him.

"You still do, and I'm forever grateful to you for saving my life," he said sincerely.

Nancy opened up the book again and began reading from where she left off. Nathan looked at her with admiration and love in his eyes. He *did* love her, but Nathan knew she was right, Nancy could never replace Heather, no one could. There would always be a special part in his heart for his wife, even after everything she did to him *and* her sister. Nathan still had trouble understanding why Heather and her parents stole Nancy's baby and kept it from him. He thought that was a really shitty thing to do to someone, especially a close relative.

All of a sudden, Nathan's heart monitor sounded its alarm; Nathan's vitals were dropping fast. Doctor Winters ran into the room with two nurses. Nancy began to panic, screaming, "Save him please, oh, Lord! Don't let him die! Don't let him die!" while the medical team tried their best to stabilize poor Nathan's failing heart.

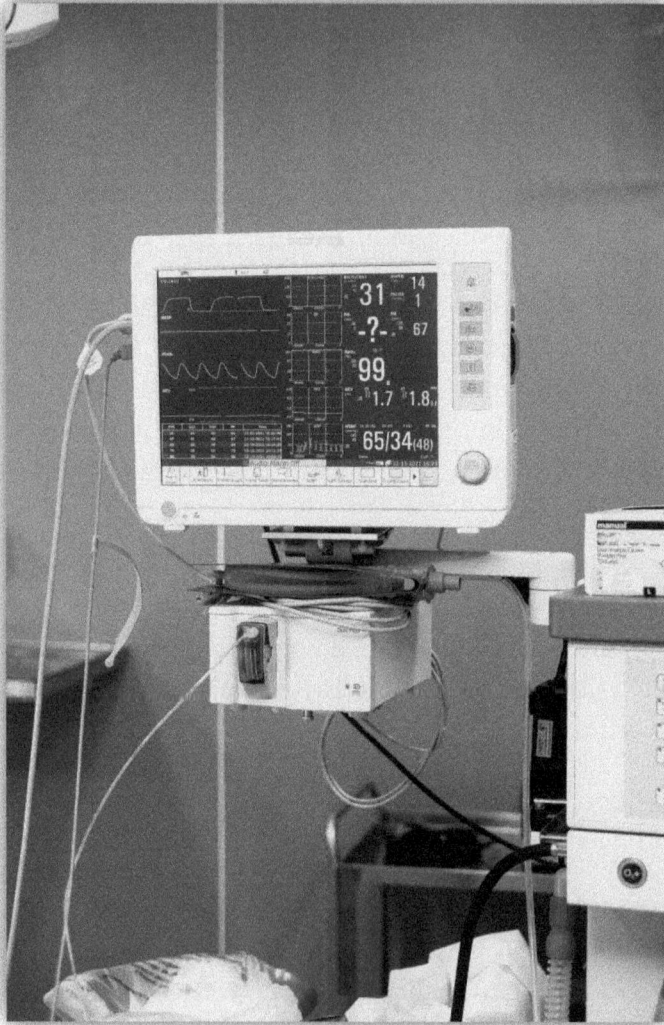

Photo courtesy of Anna Shvets

CHAPTER 22

FIRST KISS

etective Juan Gonzalez was getting ready for his dinner date with Gladys Delgado. *Who knows, maybe I might even get lucky this time, not that I'm rushing it,* he thought. *At least she wants to see me again; that's a good sign.* Gonzalez was both happy and frightened about being in a relationship again. He hadn't been with another woman ever since his marriage went south.

Gonzalez promised Gladys that he'd pick her up at seven o'clock. It was almost six and he wasn't even dressed yet. The good detective looked at his smartphone for her address again for the umpteenth time. Clearly, he was nervous about seeing her again. It was the second time Gonzalez had taken her out. He'd seen her at the police station several times before, but going out and being alone together was quite different. Juan Gonzalez was acting like an anxious teenager going out on a hot date for the first time in his life, even though it was his second date with Gladys Delgado.

"*¡Ay Dios Mío!* She's so young and beautiful; what the hell does she see in me?" Gonzalez said to himself.

Gonzalez left his bathroom and went to the bedroom of his three-room apartment. He thought about the nice, two-story colonial home that he had shared with his ex-wife back in the day, but unfortunately it had to get sold as part of the divorce settlement. The two of them agreed to split everything in half. Gonzalez picked out a dark blue suit and a white shirt from his wardrobe. He wanted to look nice for Gladys, especially since he'd planned on taking her out to a nice Italian restaurant.

"This woman is driving me crazy, but she's making me feel young and alive again. I haven't felt like this in a very long time," he said while looking at his reflection in the mirror that was hanging on the wall.

The detective splashed some cologne on his face and then screamed from the burning pain.

"Sonofabitch! You'd think I know better by now not to put that damn shit on my face after shaving," he angrily said to himself.

Gonzalez made sure to pack his personal gun with him just in case something bad went down. *You can't be too careful these days,* the man thought. He finally left his apartment and went out to his car.

*
**

Back at Solville Medical Center, Nathan Harris was brought back into the operating room again for emergency surgery. Nancy was in the waiting room weeping, while the doctor and his assistants were frantically trying to save Nathan's life again. *I don't know how much more of this shit I can take. He was doing so well. What the hell happened to him?* Nancy asked herself. She wondered what could have gone wrong, since Nathan was doing so well. Nancy could still hear the doctor shouting, "He's crashing, we've got to bring him back into the OR quick." Nancy loved Nathan with all her heart. *Oh, God, I almost lost him before, I can't lose him again. We've shared a child together, for Christ's sake. I lost Alice, I can't lose Nathan too.* Nancy couldn't think anymore. The distraught young woman went into the lady's room, locked herself in one of the stalls, and cried her eyes out.

*
**

About three hours later, Doctor Mark Winters came into the waiting room, looking for Nancy Stevens. She picked her head up almost anticipating bad news from the doctor. Nancy tried to read the expression on his face to determine the outcome, but the doctor had an almost emotionless look upon him. The young doctor noticed she had been crying. Nancy's makeup was running all over her face.

"Miss Stevens, are you all right?" Doctor Winters asked her in a concerned tone of voice.

264

"Yes, I'm fine, Doctor, but what about Nathan?" Nancy asked in anticipation of bad news.

"Mr. Harris is stabilized. It appears he had a nicked artery caused by the metal shard that was lodged into his chest. It was initially hidden and probably wasn't that bad to begin with, but in time, well…"

"So, he's going to be all right?"

"Yes, we expect him to have a full recovery."

"Oh, thank you, Doctor. You don't know what that means to me," Nancy joyfully said while hugging the doctor.

"Miss Stevens, please…"

"Oh, I'm so sorry, Doctor. I'm afraid I got a little carried away," she said while releasing the doctor.

"We're going to keep him in intensive care for about forty-eight hours."

"When may I see him. Doctor?"

"When we send him back to his room, sorry."

Nancy knew she was back at square one. *I have to wait two more days before I can see him again? Shit!* Nancy thought. She went back to the ladies' room to freshen up before going back home.

✳
✳✳

Later that night, Detective Gonzalez was bringing his date back to her home. Gonzalez parked his car in Gladys's driveway and looked at the dashboard clock before turning off his car. The evening went by so fast that he couldn't believe it was so late.

"My God, eleven thirty already?" Gonzalez questioned.

"Really? Wow, the time just flew by like a bird," Gladys said with a smile.

"*Mira,* I don't know about you, but I had a great time. The food, the atmosphere, and mainly the company was perfect," he said while smiling back at her.

"I feel the same way, especially about the company."

The two of them stared at each other in the car for a moment, not saying a word. Gonzalez decided to be brazen and try to steal a kiss from her, but Gladys beat him to it. She turned to him, put her arms around him, and gave him a long and sensual kiss. Their hearts were beating fast and strong. Beads of sweat were now forming on Gonzalez's face. Gladys finally pulled away from him in slow motion, gazing at him, leaving him wanting more. It had been their first real kiss.

"Wow, we should have done this long ago," Gonzalez said breathlessly.

"I cannot remember the last time I felt this way," Gladys softly said.

"Let's do it again," he said while pulling her back close to him.

They kissed again, only this time it was longer, much longer. This time, Gonzalez slowly pulled away. He enjoyed watching her breasts rise and fall with every breath she took, but he tried not to look so obvious.

"You think maybe I could come in for a while?" Gonzalez asked with a hopeful look in his eyes.

"No, not yet. I don't want to spoil what we have right now by having sex. Let's just take it slow, papa, ok?" Gladys gently asked.

"Ok, mama, whatever you say. Besides, it's getting late, we both have to work tomorrow."

"*Si,* it's almost midnight. I see you tomorrow morning with coffee again."

"Ok mama, it's a date!"

She gave Gonzalez a quick kiss on his lips and left the car.

266

Gonzalez took out a napkin from the glovebox and cleaned his windows from the fog. *Boy, I guess it was hot and steamy in here,* he thought. Gonzalez watched her go into her home. She turned and waved goodbye before closing the door. Then, he left.

**

Tuesday morning, May ninth, Nancy had returned back to the hospital, knowing that Nathan was returned back to his room. She got off the elevator and headed straight for room 300. Nancy walked into Nathan's room and found him struggling to drink his water.

"Here, let me help you with that," Nancy said while raising his bed with the remote and holding the straw for him to drink.

"Thank you, Nancy," Nathan said after drinking some water.

"You're quite welcome."

"It's so nice to see you again. I thought I was a goner."

"I guess it wasn't your time yet."

"That's all right because I'm not ready to go yet. I've got a lot of living to do."

"I should hope so. I spoke to the doctor and he said you're gonna be just fine."

"Really? Did he say when I'll be discharged?"

"He said in about ten days. After that, I'll be your nurse at home."

"I really appreciate all that you've done for me, Nancy, really," Nathan sincerely told her.

"Nathan, I suppose you know that there isn't anything I wouldn't do for you. I love you. I just want you to know that, even if you don't exactly feel the same way for me."

"I don't know what to say."

267

"You don't have to say anything, just get better," Nancy said while holding his hand.

"Well, well Mr. Harris, I see you're doing ok," Detective Gonzalez stated while entering the room.

"What are *you* doing here?!" Nancy snapped back at him.

"I could ask you the same thing, Miss Stevens."

"I'm here visiting my brother-in-law."

"Is that all?"

"Yes, that's all, Detective. What's *your* excuse?"

"I'm here to interview Mr. Harris, if he's up to it."

"Nathan, you don't have to talk to him if you don't want to."

"It's all right, Nancy. I'll talk to him," Nathan softly told her.

"I suppose you need me to leave?" Nancy asked the detective.

"No, Miss Stevens, I want to talk to *you too*."

Gonzalez noticed the worried look upon Nancy's face, as if she had something to hide.

"Now Mr. Harris, can you explain to me what happened on Friday, May fifth?" Gonzalez asked him while pulling out his notebook.

"Well, I was out all day until I came home in the evening," Nathan told him.

"Where were you, Mr. Harris?"

"I had gone out for breakfast and then I decided to take in a movie."

"Were you alone, Mr. Harris?"

"No, I wasn't."

"Who were you with?"

Nathan didn't want to get Nancy implicated in anything, but he knew where this was going. Nathan gave his sister-in-law a look that said, *I'm sorry but I can't lie.* He then faced the detective and told him the truth.

"I spent the whole day with my sister-in-law," Nathan struggled to say while now looking at her.

"Miss Stevens? You spent the whole day with Miss Stevens, like on a date?" Gonzalez asked in an accusatory tone while he looked at her.

"Yes, that's correct."

"I see."

"No, you don't see! We were just out enjoying each other's company. That's all there is to it," Nancy shot back in defense to the detective.

"Calm down, Miss Stevens, before you say something you'll regret later," Gonzalez said while giving her a stern look.

Nathan gave her a look that said, *take it easy.*

"Now, where else did the two of you go to, Mr. Harris?" Gonzalez asked while he looked at Nathan sitting up in the bed.

"After that, we went shopping in the mall," Nathan replied to him.

"And then what?"

"After that, I brought Nancy back home."

"Did you stay there for a while?"

"No, Detective. I went straight home."

"About what time did you get back home?"

"It was nine thirty when I got out of my car."

"So, you got home and saw that the place was burning?"

"Not exactly. When I walked inside, I heard an alarm that was coming from downstairs. I went down to the lab and the computer was screaming, "Intruder alert! Malfunction, overload!" Then there was an explosion and a fire. Things were flying all over the place. That's when I got struck by something that landed my ass on the floor."

"You claim that the computer said there was an intruder; did you actually see anyone there?"

"No, I didn't, and that's all I can recall," Nathan solemnly replied.

"Miss Stevens, how did you discover Mr. Harris at his home?" Detective Gonzalez asked while turning his attention over to her.

"I was going through my packages and found Nathan's credit card. I knew I had to return it to him," Nancy replied.

"What were you doing with Mr. Harris's credit card?"

"Nathan had graciously lent me his credit card to go shopping."

"I see. What did you do after that, Miss Stevens?"

"Like I said before, Detective, I knew I had to return Nathan's credit card to him, so I got in my car and drove to his home. When I got there, I noticed his front door was wide open. I knew something was wrong. Nathan wouldn't intentionally leave his door open like that. He wouldn't want bugs or critters coming inside his home."

"Then what did you do?"

"Well, I went inside. I started to smell smoke and I heard what sounded like a smoke alarm, so I followed the sound to the basement. That's when I saw the fire and him on the floor with this, this thing coming out of his chest. The fire was coming close, closer to him. I'm sorry," Nancy started to cry again.

"Please Miss Stevens, please go on," Gonzalez anxiously stated.

"I, I knew I had to act fast. I held my breath and dragged Nathan out of there, up the stairs, and out of the house as, as fast as I could. If I hadn't been there, Nathan would have…" Nancy trailed off and cried again.

"It's all right, honey, it's over now," Nathan said to her in a soothing voice.

"Miss Stevens, I see that this is hard for you, but I must know, did you see anyone else there?" Gonzalez calmly asked her.

"No, no I did not," Nancy said while blowing her nose.

"So, none of you actually saw anyone there that could have started the fire?"

"No, Detective, but I have a feeling it was sabotage and I think it's probably the same one that killed my wife," Nathan told him.

"Well, I'm afraid that's purely speculation, Mr. Harris, unless you have proof," Gonzalez stated.

"Wait a minute, Detective, there is one more thing I remember," Nancy added.

"I'm all ears, Miss Stevens."

"Well, when I was approaching Nathan's mansion, I saw a car speeding in the opposite direction."

"Can you describe the car, Miss Stevens?"

"Um, it was small, but it was kind of a blur. Like I said, it was moving so fast."

"What about the style or the color of the car."

"I would say it was green, or dark green. Yes, a small, dark green car, that's what it was," Nancy said with uncertainty.

"Did you say a small, dark green car?" Nathan interjected,

271

remembering what the killer was driving.

"Yes, a small, dark green car. He was going so fast I thought he was going to hit me. Now, I'm not a hundred percent sure, but it looked like the car was coming from your home, Nathan," she continued.

"You didn't get his plate number, did you, Miss Stevens?" Gonzalez asked.

"No, I didn't. Like I said before, he was moving way too fast, almost like a blur."

"Ok, I'm gonna have uniforms look for this car. If you two remember anything else, please, don't hesitate to call my office," Gonzalez said.

Detective Gonzalez handed them both his card and he left. Nathan turned and faced Nancy. The scientist knew he had to ask her a most dreadful question, a question he'd been putting off until now.

"Nancy, I have to ask you a very important question and I want you to be totally honest with me, don't sugar coat it, ok?" Nathan asked.

"Oh, boy, this sounds deep. What is it, Nathan?" Nancy asked him back.

"Since you were the last one there before the fire department got there, you should pretty much know its condition. My lab, Nancy, is it completely destroyed?" Nathan reluctantly asked, afraid of the answer.

"Yes, Nathan, it was, I'm sorry," she sadly said, knowing it would hurt him.

"Oh, God, all my work, destroyed?"

"Oh, Nathan, the main thing is that you're alive and that's all that really matters. God sent me there to save you and only you. Oh, darling, can't you see that you're all that matters to me, you're all that I've ever wanted? You can always rebuild. I can help you."

"You'd play lab assistant for me?" Nathan asked.

"Sure! I'll admit I don't know shit about science, but I *do know* a thing or two about electronics," she reported.

Nathan looked at her with loving eyes. He knew she was right. Nancy had saved his life from a horrible fire. Right there and then at that very moment in time, the scientist knew that this woman would do absolutely anything for him, even jeopardize her very own existence to save his. He leaned over toward her and grabbed her hand as she sat in the chair.

"Come here to me," Nathan softly requested.

Nancy got up from her chair and looked at him with such adoring eyes. She pulled down her mask and leaned over to him as close as she could without disturbing the wires and tubes that were hooked up to him. This time, Nathan made the initiation. He tenderly kissed her; a long and sensual kiss that had them both wanting even more...

CHAPTER 23

BETRAYAL

Monday morning, May twenty-second, Nancy Stevens was finally bringing scientist and inventor Nathan Harris back to his mansion. Nancy had agreed to stay at the mansion for at least four to six weeks to nurse Nathan back to health. The scientist was given a cane to help him get around the house without straining himself. Doctor Winters had told Nathan to take it easy and not to put any unnecessary stress or strain on his heart. Winters also told him he needed time to heal, but Nathan was being stubborn and practically demanded Nancy take him down to the laboratory to examine its condition.

"Nancy, please, I've just got to see the devastation in my lab. I have to access the damage in order to see what's salvageable and what's not," Nathan begged.

"Don't you remember what Doctor Winters told you?!" Nancy cried out.

"Oh, please, baby," he pleaded.

"*Baby?* Wow, all right, but we're gonna take it slow going down there. You hold on to me and the moment you feel any pain, we'll stop, is that clear, dear?"

"Yes, very, now please, let's go."

The two of them slowly walked toward the basement door and started their descent down into the lab. Nathan had one arm around Nancy and the other on the banister since the stairway was wide enough to accommodate the two of them walking side by side. When they got to the bottom of the stairs, Nathan had to stop walking to catch his breath.

"I'm getting too old for this shit," he said.

They made their way through the gymnasium. Nathan noticed minimal damage in the gym area; only one out of the four treadmills was completely destroyed, the one that was closest to the laboratory entrance.

"It's a good thing you left all these doors open, Nathan, or I probably wouldn't have been able to save you," Nancy said.

"The doors were unlocked and opened because of a malfunction in the security system. I had absolutely nothing to do with it, Nancy," Nathan replied as he had to stop again for a moment since he felt a little winded.

After a minute, they started walking once more. Nathan slowly entered what was left of his laboratory with Nancy. He scanned the room with depression. All of his experimental work had been destroyed by the explosion and the fire. The room reeked of smoke from the electrical fire. The Time Transporter was nothing more than just a memory. Tears began to flow down from Nathan's eyes as he witnessed the overhead electrodes from the apparatus, simply just dangling from its control cables. The LCD screens were all shattered into a spider web-like fashion. Nathan turned around to Nancy and simply cried like a child on her shoulder. Nancy placed her loving arms around poor Nathan to comfort and support him as he wept.

"It's, it's all gone. The whole damn lab is completely destroyed," Nathan sobbed.

"I'm so sorry, honey. I wish there was something I could do," she said in sympathy.

Nathan peeled himself away from Nancy and turned his attention over toward the burned workbench. He walked over to it and quickly scanned the bench. Nathan noticed something. He looked again to make sure before saying anything. Then, the scientist turned around to face Nancy.

"It's gone!" Nathan cried out in anguish.

"What's gone, hon?" Nancy asked with sympathy in her blue eyes.

"All my work, my research, the plans to this whole damn laboratory, and everything else. I remember taking out all of the papers from my safe and placing them on this bench before I was struck down."

Nathan walked over toward the wall safe; it was open. He looked inside of it, noticing it was completely bare.

"Shit! He knows! He knows everything! Sonofabitch!" Nathan screamed out in pain.

"Who knows, Nathan? What the hell are you talking about?" Nancy asked with concern.

"Now I know for sure, Nancy, that this was sabotage. Sabotage from the one who murdered my Heather and probably Hector Delgado, too," Nathan said in an accusatory tone.

"But how do you know for sure?"

"By putting two and two together, babe. You told the detective you spotted a small, dark green car speeding away from here. I'm willing to wager it was the same green car that I saw him leaving in when I first encountered him."

"But the detective is going to want some proof or evidence, honey."

"Right. I think I may have something for our detective. Let's go back upstairs, Nancy," Nathan suggested.

*
**

Back at the Solville Police Department, Gonzalez was placing a picture of Nancy Stevens up on the white murder board that by now was full of pictures of victims and suspects to the crimes he was trying to solve. Captain Martinelli walked into the office holding a cup of coffee in his right hand. Martinelli looked inquisitively at the photo of the attractive young blonde before asking Gonzalez who she was.

"Who's the blonde?" Martinelli asked.

"Beautiful, isn't she?" Gonzalez said.

"Yeah, but who is she and why is she up on our murder board?"

"Her name is Nancy Stevens, she's Harris's sister-in-law," he said while writing her name on the board underneath the picture with a red grease marker.

"All right. That answers the first question, but why is she on our murder board, Gonzalez?"

"It appears they seem to be more than just brother and sister-in-law, Captain. I caught her holding his hand in the hospital."

"That still doesn't mean they're lovers, Gonzalez."

"Really? I just found out that they had spent the whole day together, having breakfast, taking in a movie, and even shopping in the mall together."

"When was this?"

"The day that Mr. Harris was discovered in his home while it was burning, Friday May fifth, over two weeks ago."

"And you know this for certain?"

"Yes, Captain, she told me so herself. Do you remember who discovered and saved Mr. Harris from the fire?"

"Yeah, Nancy Stevens."

"Bingo! Miss Stevens claims that she found Mr. Harris's credit card in one of her shopping bags. It seems that Harris lent her his card to go shopping. You get the picture, Captain?"

"Yeah, I do," Martinelli said with a sigh.

"Miss Stevens also claimed that she decided to return Harris's credit card that night, and that's when she found him in the basement, lying on the floor."

"I see," the captain said while scratching his head.

"You know what I think, Captain? I think that Mr. Harris killed his wife and her lover, just to be together with Miss Nancy Stevens. Maybe, just maybe, Miss Stevens was in on it too."

"You're speculating again, Gonzalez. Remember, Nathan claims that he saw the killer and spoke to him, he even gave us a description of him, for Christ's sake."

"The key word that you just said was 'claims.' Harris claims he saw the killer. I mean, look at that description he gave us, Captain. It could be anybody. You said so yourself that you didn't really believe him."

"Now wait a minute, Gonzalez. Don't put words in my mouth. I was referring to that cockamamie story about him going back in time. But in light of these new findings, I think you should bring them both in for questioning."

"I'm glad you're finally seeing things my way, Captain," Detective Gonzalez said with a snicker.

Captain Martinelli left Gonzalez and returned back to his office. He didn't want to believe that his friend, Nathan Harris, was guilty of murder, but Gonzalez was making perfectly good sense. *What if it were true? If Nathan and his sister-in-law were indeed having an affair, Nathan could have wanted his wife out of the way,* the captain thought. Martinelli sat down behind his desk, drank his now cold coffee, and thought some more about his friend.

*
**

An hour later, Nathan Harris was back upstairs in the master bedroom suite with Nancy. Nathan was in the walk-in closet looking for something while Nancy was lying on the bed, watching him, intently. She noticed the telephone answering machine flashing its red light.

"Nathan, I think you've got a message on your machine," Nancy said.

"Press the play button, babe," Nathan replied.

Nancy pressed the play button on the machine and the message played.

"Hello Mr. Harris, this is Doctor Berlin's secretary. I'm sorry to inform you of his passing. I don't know if you were planning on making an appointment with him. If you need a referral for another doctor, please call the office at (212) 555-3979," the recording played before the machine announced, "end of messages," in its robotic voice.

"Oh, shit! Well, he *was* old, probably died of a heart attack," Nathan sadly said.

Then the two of them heard the main doorbell chime.

"I wonder who that could be," Nathan said.

"Do you want me to see who it is?" Nancy asked him.

"No, I'll go see who it is, you stay here."

Nathan grabbed his cane and gingerly went down the stairs, still thinking about the news of his therapist. Nancy got up from the bed and watched him to make sure he was ok, before returning back to the room. Nathan took a quick view at the wall monitor before answering the door, already knowing who it was.

"Good morning, Juan, what can I do for you?" Nathan asked as he opened up the front door.

"Hello Mr. Harris, this is not a social visit. I need you and Miss Stevens to come downtown to the police station with me."

"And what makes you think she's here?"

"Come on now, Harris, we both know she's here," the detective said in an accusatory tone.

"It's all right, Nathan, I can defend myself," Nancy said as she came down the stairs after hearing the detective.

"let's go you two," Gonzalez said.

"Now just a darn minute, Juan. Before we go downtown with you, there's something you need to see first, before you go and accuse me of murder again, assuming that's what you came here for. Am I right?" Nathan asked him while sounding like a defense attorney.

"That's correct, Mr. Harris. Whatever you have to show me, make it quick," Gonzalez said impatiently.

"Would you please follow me upstairs, Detective?"

"What's upstairs that I need to see, Harris?"

"You'll see."

Nathan escorted the diligent detective to the master bedroom suite. He brought him into the walk-in closet. Nathan pressed a hidden button and a retractable shelf came down from the ceiling with audiovisual equipment on it. Nathan turned on the twelve-inch color LCD monitor and pressed the rewind button on the recorder. Detective Gonzalez started to laugh.

"You have got to be kidding me, a VCR in this day and age? That shit is old fashioned. What are you trying to prove here, Harris?" Gonzalez said jokingly.

"Well, since you've confiscated my old DVR and never returned it, I hooked up what I could find, Juan. I can assure you that the VCR is fully functional. I took the liberty of hooking it up wirelessly to a camera down in the lab with a motion sensor and infrared lighting. Now, let's all see what's on the tape, shall we?" Nathan insisted.

Nathan pressed the play button on the old video cassette

recorder and the monitor sprung to life. A low-resolution image of the lab before it was destroyed was now being displayed on the screen. After a minute, a subject appeared upon the screen. Both Gonzalez and Nathan tried to analyze the person to see if they could recognize who it was. The perpetrator was wearing the same exact outfit that it had on when Nathan first had the encounter with the intruder.

"Yeah, that's him all right, wearing the same black leather jacket, jeans, and the black ski hat he had on last time he was here," Nathan said.

"Yup, just like you said, Harris, he's even wearing a black mask, dark sunglasses, and gloves," Gonzalez added.

"It's too bad I can't zoom in on his face."

"Maybe *you* can't, Harris, but our tech guy down at the station probably can, after they digitize this recording and enhance it."

They then watched the suspect on the screen pull off its hat and shake out its long blonde hair. Nathan and Gonzalez realized that the suspect wasn't a man after all; it appeared to be a woman. Suddenly, both men turned their attention over to the only woman with long blonde hair in the room, Nancy Stevens, who was now sitting up on the bed in her red dress, watching them attentively. Nathan was going to confront her, but through the corner of his eye, he watched the woman on the screen go over to a family picture that hung on the lab wall. The woman smashed the glass in the frame, took out a pocket knife, and cut Heather's face out of the picture.

"Look Gonzalez!" Nathan shouted.

The woman was now seen packing up all the papers that were on the workbench into a black shoulder bag. Then the perpetrator picked up something else that could not be seen on camera. After that, the wicked intruder started smashing all the lab equipment with a baby sledgehammer she had in her bag. The two men *still* couldn't see the woman's face because of her mask and dark glasses, but they figured out who it was. Finally, the woman pulled off her mask and some apparatus that was under it, then, she left it on the end of the workbench before leaving the scene of the crime, never once picking her head up for the camera to see her face.

"Two guesses who this looks like," Gonzalez said.

Phot courtesy of Alina Matveycheva

"But it *can't* be. The killer had a deep voice. Why would Nancy do this to me?"

"Miss Stevens, stand up please," Gonzalez said as he approached her.

"Huh? What is it, Detective?" Nancy said in a worried voice.

"Get off the bed and stand up please," Gonzalez commanded.

"Wh-what's this all about?"

"Miss Stevens, I'm not asking you again. Stand up!"

Nancy slowly got off the bed and looked at Nathan. The scientist could not make eye contact with her at all. Nathan looked down toward the floor with a disappointed look on his face.

"Miss Stevens, turn around please. You're under arrest for vandalism, theft, and possibly the murder of your own sister, Heather Harris," Gonzalez stated while placing handcuffs on her.

"What?! You have *got* to be kidding! Nathan help!" Nancy cried out.

Gonzalez read Nancy her rights. Nancy kept crying out to Nathan. Nathan kept looking down to the floor as if he were in shock, not knowing what to do or say. He felt so betrayed.

"Why'd you do it, Nancy? I trusted you. I thought you loved me," Nathan solemnly said to her after finally picking his head up from looking down.

"Oh, Nathan, darling, I do love you with all my heart. I've loved you from the start," Nancy tearfully confessed.

"You're on my surveillance tape destroying everything in my lab, everything that I've worked so hard on for years. Why, Nancy, why?"

"Perhaps, I could explain why she did it, Mr. Harris. Miss Stevens, you've just admitted that you've loved Mr. Harris from the beginning, correct?" Gonzalez questioned.

"That's true, I've always loved him, but I would never—"

"You love him. In fact, you love him so much that you would remove all obstacles that stood in your way, just to have him all to yourself."

"That's not true!"

"Really? I think it is. Your sister was your biggest obstacle, followed by the lab," Gonzalez concluded.

"I'm being framed here. I demand to see that tape!"

"Bring her over here, Gonzalez. She deserves to see the evidence against her," Nathan said.

Detective Gonzalez brought Nancy over to the closet where Nathan was standing while she was handcuffed. Nathan rewound the tape back to the beginning and played it for her. Nancy watched the incriminating evidence that was being shown to her on the screen.

"That's not me. I don't wear a mask or a hat. Why don't you go check that mask? See if you can find DNA from saliva or something and compare it with mine," Nancy suggested while trying to sound like her own attorney in a court of law.

"That's if the fire didn't destroy it," Gonzalez said.

Nathan grabbed his cane again. He escorted Gonzalez and Nancy down to the lab. Nancy felt as if the walls of justice were wrongfully closing in on her. Gonzalez still wondered if Nathan was involved in everything.

*
**

A few minutes later, the three of them arrived at the basement lab. Gonzalez had donned his latex gloves and frantically searched for the black mask. The detective finally found the charred remains of the mask under some debris on the end of the workbench, along with something else.

"I don't know if they can get anything useful from this in the lab, but look what else I found under the mask," Gonzalez happily stated.

"It looks like some kind of electronic device. I can't believe I missed that before," Nathan said.

"It is. It's got a label on it that reads, 'Rose Electronic Voice Changer, makes any man sound like a woman, or makes any woman sound like a man. Made In China.' Mr. Harris, didn't you say that the killer had a deep voice?"

"Yes, I did."

"Well, that explains it. Miss Stevens had used this voice changer under her mask to disguise her own voice. This way, you wouldn't recognize her voice, Mr. Harris."

"I can't believe you went through such an elaborate scheme like that just to have me all to yourself. You killed your own sister and destroyed my lab. To think I was falling in love with you all over again," Nathan sadly said to Nancy.

"But I didn't do it! Nathan, can't you see this is all just a setup? I've been framed," Nancy cried out, desperately trying to clear herself.

"Who would want to frame you, Miss Stevens?" Gonzalez asked her.

"I don't know! This is all just a bad dream!"

"Where are my research papers, Nancy? What have you done with them?" Nathan asked her.

"I don't know. I didn't take them, Nathan. I love you way too much to ever want to hurt you."

"Well, you have. I don't know if I could ever forgive you for what you've done to me and my daughter. She would probably still be alive today if…"

Nathan stopped short for a moment of thought before saying anymore. He knew that Alice was originally murdered and stuffed into the old grandfather clock. *Nancy wouldn't intentionally kill her own daughter, would she? I just can't see her doing that,* he thought. However, the scientist knew he couldn't reveal the way Alice was originally killed, because Nathan had altered history by going back in time. Alice had now been killed by a drunk driver. Nathan looked at Nancy's womanly figure. *Nancy has fairly large breasts; the killer I saw was flat chested, like a man,* he thought. However, Nathan had figured that Nancy could have been wearing some kind of a binder to flatten out her breasts.

Gonzalez decided to bring them both down to the police station along with the VCR, its tape recording, the black face mask, and the voice changer. Nathan had complained that Gonzalez could have just taken the tape and not the machine, but the detective wasn't sure if they had a functioning VCR down at the police station. Gonzalez was also going to request for a search warrant for the home of Nancy Stevens. *If Harris's research papers are in her home, then that's all the evidence I need to put her ass away, at least for vandalism and theft,* he thought while taking them to his vehicle.

CHAPTER 24

I DIDN'T DO IT

Monday afternoon, the twenty-second day of May, Detective

Juan Gonzalez had just arrived at the police station with both Nathan Harris and his prisoner, Nancy Stevens. Gonzalez also brought Nathan's VCR with him under his arm, along with the voice changer and mask he found in Nathan's laboratory. The detective proudly brought them all into the captain's office, like a cat that's captured a mouse for its owner.

"Hey Captain, I think we finally have our killer!" Gonzalez happily reported.

"Oh, Jesus H. Christ, not Nathan Harris again?" Captain Martinelli asked in a disappointed tone while looking at them.

"No sir, Nancy Stevens, his sister-in-law, or should I say, girlfriend?"

"Girlfriend? We're back with that again, eh?"

"That's correct, sir, and we have proof, at least of her vandalizing and stealing from Mr. Harris's home," Gonzalez said while holding up Nathan's VCR, the voice changer, and the mask in his hands.

"Really? What the hell have you got there, Gonzalez?"

"This is a VCR with a tape recording of Miss Stevens breaking in and vandalizing Harris's home. The tape also shows her stealing from him."

"I see, and what the hell is that other thing in your hand?"

"This is the electronic voice changer she had under her mask to disguise her voice, Captain."

"And you're sure it belongs to Miss Stevens?"

"The tape will show her taking it off, sir."

"That's not mine and I didn't do it!" Nancy shrieked.

"Well, we'll just send it on over to the lab, check it for prints, and then have a DNA done on it to see if it's really hers," Captain Martinelli said.

"We should also get a search warrant for her home. I'm sure we'll find plenty of evidence there to put Miss Stevens away for a *long time*, Captain."

"What exactly are we looking for, Gonzalez?"

"Well for one thing, my research papers, Paul, that's if it's there," Nathan told him.

"I tell you I didn't take them, Nathan! Don't you believe me?" Nancy pleaded.

"We'll just see about that, Miss Stevens," Gonzalez said to her with an accusatory tone in his voice.

"All right, Gonzalez, have Officer Winston put her in one of the holding cells. I'll take the VCR over to our media room where I can see what the hell's on that tape. Nathan, I'm gonna need a statement from you on this."

"You've got it, Paul," Nathan sadly said.

Captain Paul Martinelli gave Nathan a disappointed look before he walked him out of his office. Martinelli felt that Nathan's love relationship with his own sister-in-law was highly irregular. *I guess I gave that man a little too much credit. God help him if he was indeed responsible for his own wife's murder,* he sadly thought.

⁑

The next morning, Captain Martinelli received the search warrant for Nancy Stevens's home. The captain was unimpressed with the video tape recording from Nathan's home. Martinelli couldn't really tell if that was Nancy or someone else destroying the scientist's lab. He went over to Detective Gonzalez's office, looking for him. *Where the hell is he?* Martinelli asked himself in the empty office. He decided to go over to the murder board to see if Gonzalez was there.

"I figured you'd be here, Gonzalez," Martinelli said while walking up to the murder board.

"I still think Harris is involved in this shit, somehow, Captain," Gonzalez speculated.

"You wanna peel yourself away from that board and go on over to Nancy Stevens's home?"

"You got the search warrant?"

"It just came in."

"Good, I'll get right over there."

"Take Detective Cheng with you."

"You mean, Officer Cheng, don't you?"

"No, Detective, he just got promoted."

"Well, good for him, but you know I usually work alone, except when I need some uniforms to assist me, Captain."

"When you have my job, you can make that call, Gonzalez, but for now, I'm paring you up with our new detective. That's not going to be a problem now, is it?"

"No sir, no problem," Gonzalez answered while gritting his teeth, like a junkyard dog that was ready to attack its prey.

"I thought so, now the two of you head on over there, pronto," the captain ordered before walking away from him, knowing that Gonzalez wasn't thrilled with his decision.

Detective Gonzalez was not happy being paired up with a rookie detective, even if it was former Officer Cheng. Gonzalez liked Cheng, but he would rather work alone than babysit a new detective and show him the ropes.

"Hey Gonzalez! I heard we're gonna team up!" Detective Cheng said with a smile while entering the office.

"It's gonna be a long ass day, I feel it already," Gonzalez mumbled under his lips while shaking his head.

*
**

Shortly after, Detective Gonzalez and Detective Cheng were arriving at the home of Nancy Stevens. They got out of the police cruiser and walked right up to the small ranch house at 16 Shirley Drive in Solville. The two detectives put on purple latex gloves before touching anything. Gonzalez took out the house keys the captain had handed him and unlocked the front door. The two men walked inside the house to commence their investigation. Gonzalez was hoping to find Nathan's research papers, or anything else that would incriminate Nancy Stevens.

"At least you look the part; where did you get that suit?" Gonzalez asked Cheng while pointing to his navy-blue jacket.

"You like it?" Cheng asked back.

"Yeah, it's all right."

"I just got it on sale at Manny's Men's Wear."

"I'll go and see what else they have; it's time for a new suit."

"Yeah, I know."

"Watch it, rookie," Gonzalez angrily shot back while feeling highly offended.

"Nothing for nothing but, I always see you wearing the same old gray suit, shit. It's time for a change. That suit looks so stiff it could walk on its own," Cheng said with a chuckle.

"Look, you worry about your ass and I'll worry about mine, all right?"

"Yeah, yeah, I get it. Now, what are we supposed to be looking for, Gonzalez?" Cheng asked him.

"Basically, anything that ties Miss Stevens to the murders, but also, Harris's research papers that she stole from him," Gonzalez replied.

The detectives split up and started searching the house. Detective Cheng was searching the living room, while Detective Gonzalez took the master bedroom. Gonzalez went through all of the dresser drawers and the closet, but he came up empty handed. Then, something popped. Detective Cheng found a large manila envelope full of papers, underneath a newspaper, on an end table located right near the sofa. He quickly went through the papers before calling his partner over.

"Hey Gonzalez!" Cheng shouted.

"What?!" Gonzalez asked.

"I think I found something, come here!"

Gonzalez went to the living room to see what Cheng wanted. Cheng started showing him the papers that were in the large envelope.

"Hey, what is this shit?" Gonzalez asked him.

"It looks like Harris's research papers," Cheng responded.

"Oh, shit, you're right, it doesn't look good for Miss Stevens. I knew it," Gonzalez said while putting the papers back in the manila envelope and handing it back to Cheng.

"Let's see what else we can find, partner."

"*Partner?* Hey watch that shit, man! Let's be clear here, I work alone, comprende?" Gonzalez angrily asked.

"Yeah, I get it," Cheng somberly replied.

Detective Gonzalez left Cheng and went to relieve himself in the bathroom; that's when he saw the broken window. Gonzalez flushed the toilet with his gloved hand. Then, he thoroughly examined the window, without touching it, before calling Detective Cheng over.

"Hey Cheng, come here!" Gonzalez yelled out.

"What, you need help going to the bathroom now?!" Cheng yelled back.

"Come here, will ya?! Never mind the bullshit!"

Detective Cheng briskly walked into the bathroom to see what Gonzalez wanted.

"Oh, shit, we got a broken window here!" Cheng said.

Photo courtesy of Lisa Fotios

"We got to dust it for prints; I think someone may have broken in here," Gonzalez stated.

Gonzalez and Cheng dusted the whole bathroom and the front door for fingerprints. Cheng was being extremely careful with Harris's research papers. He put them into a plastic bag he had with him. The two men finished checking out the rest of the house, before finally leaving the premises.

*
**

Later on that afternoon, Detectives Gonzalez and Cheng had both arrived back at the police station. They walked into Captain Martinelli's office and found Nathan Harris there, talking to the captain. Gonzalez handed Martinelli a plastic bag containing Nathan's research papers.

"Is that my research papers, Juan?" Nathan asked him.

"Yes, Mr. Harris, we found them in your sister-in-law's home."

Nathan became dismayed again. The scientist had come to tell the captain that he couldn't believe Nancy would be the killer. Nathan didn't believe that Nancy would steal anything from him, but now, there was evidence. *I still can't believe she'd kill her only daughter, our daughter; where's the logic in that?* Nathan asked himself.

"Well, Nathan, I know you didn't want to believe it, but this *does* shine a different light on things, you know," the captain said.

"There was something else there, Captain," Detective Cheng interjected.

"What's that, Cheng?" Martinelli asked him.

"We found evidence of a break-in."

"Really?"

"Yes, Captain. It appears that someone broke in through the bathroom window. We dusted the whole area for prints," Gonzalez added.

"Was the place torn apart?" Martinelli asked him while pulling up on his belt.

"No, sir. It didn't appear that anything was taken. The whole place looked neat and cleaned, except for the broken glass that was on the bathroom floor."

"Well then, why would someone break into a home and not take anything?"

"Unless of course, they weren't trying to steal anything, but rather, bring something in," Nathan added.

"Maybe someone planted your research papers there to frame Miss Stevens," Detective Cheng said.

"You know, for a new detective, I like you already," Nathan happily stated.

"You know, it's quite possible. Gonzalez, run all the prints you two collected and we'll compare them with Miss Stevens's," the captain ordered.

Nathan had a spark of hope. He found it really difficult trying to digest the fact that Nancy, his own sister-in-law, was a murderer and a thief *I really hope it's not her; if it is, then I really won't have anyone,* the scientist sadly thought. Nathan asked the captain if he was needed there anymore. Captain Martinelli told him to go home and get some rest, and Nathan did just that.

*
**

The next morning, Nathan got a phone call from Captain Martinelli. The captain wanted him down at the station to discuss their new findings. Nathan hoped it was news that would exonerate Nancy Stevens. He got dressed, then Nathan made himself a cup of coffee and a bowl of cereal. *It can't be Nancy; it just can't be. That was a man that confronted me, I know it,* he thought, trying to reassure himself. Nathan finished his breakfast. He put the dirty dishes in the sink, grabbed his jacket, and left.

*
**

Over an hour later, Nathan had finally arrived back at the police station; he thought he'd never get there. They had closed a main road off due to a serious car accident and everyone had to get rerouted. Nathan grabbed his cane and got out of his car. He walked into the police station and went right up to the reception counter to announce his arrival.

"Good morning, my name is Nathan Harris, I'm here to see Captain Martinelli," he said to the young female officer with bright red hair at the front counter.

"He's been expecting you, Mr. Harris. I'll tell him you're here," she said before calling the captain on her phone.

Nathan kept wondering what the captain had to say about the case. He nervously stood there and waited until he spotted Captain Martinelli walking toward him.

"Well, good morning, Nathan, would you like a cup of coffee before we go into my office?" Captain Martinelli asked him while pulling up on his belt again to cover his belly.

"No, I'm fine, Paul. I'm just curious about your findings," Nathan responded.

"Well in that case, we'll just go into my office now."

Nathan followed Martinelli into his office and sat down in the chair near the captain's desk. The captain reached into his desk drawer and pulled out some papers. He took a sip of his coffee and then Martinelli looked up at Nathan with an apologetic look in his eyes.

"The partial prints that my detectives got from your sister-in-law's bathroom window, and your research papers, were not hers, in fact, they're not even in our system," Martinelli stated.

"Oh, thank God," Nathan said with enormous relief.

"Also, the strands of blonde hair that were found on her mask and that voice changer gadget were not human. They were synthetic, like from a cheap wig."

"I knew it! Nancy was being framed!" Nathan happily said.

"Don't be too thrilled just yet, Nathan. We still have to wait a week for the DNA results on that mask, but by now, I'm pretty damn sure it's not from Miss Nancy Stevens."

"So, in light of these findings, I guess the question is, are you going to release her?"

"Yes Nathan, I'll release her in your care, but she's not to leave town, at least until the DNA results get back here with a negative on her match."

"Thanks, Paul. When can I see her?"

"Give me a few minutes. You can wait for her out front," the captain told him.

Captain Paul Martinelli escorted Nathan back to the front desk and told him to wait there for Nancy. Martinelli left him and went toward the back of the station. Nathan was happy he was going to be with Nancy again. *She may be pissed off at me, who knows?* he thought.

✲
✲✲

About a half-hour later, Detective Cheng was bringing Nancy Stevens to where Nathan was waiting for her. Nancy looked disheveled and tired. Nathan greeted her with a warm smile.

"Hi Nancy, I'm here to take you home," Nathan told her.

"Really? I have something for you, Nathan," Nancy angrily said.

Nancy raised her right hand to slap Nathan, but he ducked just in time.

"Oh, no you don't, not that again," Nathan said with a smirk on his face.

"You learn fast, sweetie," she replied.

"Maybe this wasn't such a good idea, Mr. Harris. I could take her back if you'd like," Detective Cheng said.

"No, that won't be necessary, Detective. I guess I had that coming to me," Nathan replied.

"You sure did, honey," Nancy hissed.

"Look, I'm sorry, Nancy, but what the hell was I supposed to do? All the evidence pointed to you."

"You could have believed in me, shit! After all these years and all we've been through, you *still* don't trust me?! Shit! Really?! I've got a good mind to club you with your own cane!" Nancy shrieked.

"You're absolutely right, babe. I'm sorry, I'll make it up to you. Anyway, I'm here to give you a ride home, if that's what you'd like," Nathan sincerely told her.

"I'm supposed to be taking care of you while you heal, remember?"

"Yeah, I do. I could bring you back home with me, providing you don't hit me again."

"I'll try not to, but it won't be easy," Nancy said with a chuckle.

"I'll take her from here, Detective."

"Are you sure, Mr. Harris?" Cheng asked him.

"Yes, I wouldn't have it any other way. Come on, Nancy, your chariot awaits," Nathan happily said.

"Hey Nathan, wait up!" Captain Martinelli shouted while briskly walking toward them with another coffee stain on his white shirt, holding a large manila envelope.

"What's up, Paul?" Nathan asked him.

"I think you'd want your research papers back; we don't need them anymore," Martinelli said while handing Nathan back the envelope with his papers.

"Thanks, Paul, I really appreciate that," Nathan told him, wondering how many people have gone through all of his papers by now.

Nathan took Nancy out of the police station and into his car. Nancy noticed Nathan struggle a little getting into his car, so she offered to drive, but he declined her offer. Nathan drove into a fast-food drive-thru to pick up some coffee and breakfast for them on the way home. He knew Nancy was starving and there wasn't much food left in the mansion. Nancy told him she'd do food shopping for him tomorrow.

*
**

A week later on Wednesday morning, May thirty-first, Captain Martinelli called Nathan to tell him the DNA results of the face mask were negative, Nancy Stevens was completely exonerated. Both Nancy and Nathan were happy. The two of them decided to go out for a celebration breakfast. This time, Nancy wouldn't take no for an answer; she was going to drive them in his Bentley.

Photo courtesy of Aleksey Kuprikov

"You drive my Bentley?" Nathan asked her.

"What's wrong with that? It's just a car," Nancy replied.

"Just a car? A Bentley is not just a car; it's a driving machine; a very expensive driving machine, I might add. Let's just say, I'm not too thrilled about the way you drive, Nancy, that's all."

"Gee thanks. Look, I promise not to drive too fast, all right?"

"All right, but remember, you'll have precious cargo with you— *me*," Nathan told her as he handed her the car keys before they left.

Outside by the front gate, the murderer was sitting in his dark green car. He had been watching and listening to Nathan and Nancy on his smartphone. The last time the killer was at Harris Manor, he had hacked into Nathan's audio and video security system. Everything that Nathan's cameras and microphones were capturing, were being broadcasted over to his smartphone. *Enjoy yourselves, you too. When the time is right, I'll get you. You can be sure of that,* he hissed to himself.

CHAPTER 25

PLEASE DON'T DIE

etective Juan Gonzalez was bringing his date, Gladys Delgado, back home. They didn't want to stay out late, since it was only Wednesday and the two of them had to work tomorrow. Gonzalez couldn't believe it was the end of May already. *Another month gone and I'm still not any closer to finding our killer or killers yet,* he sadly thought.

"*Mira* Papa, you look like you are a million miles away," Gladys said to him.

Gladys was sitting next to him in his car, wearing a light-blue blouse and a pair of blue jeans. She couldn't understand what was bothering her boyfriend. Clearly, Gladys cared enough about him to want to help.

"I'm sorry, honey, but these cases are getting to me, and I think they're related," Gonzalez told her with a worried look upon his face.

"Really? You think that the one who killed my brother is also the same one that killed Miss Harris?"

"Yup, I really think so."

"Wow, I can't believe that. Well, anyway, I *did* have a nice time tonight, Juan."

"Yeah, me too. It's too bad that we have to go to work tomorrow, right?"

"*Sí.* I'd invite you in, but it's almost eleven o'clock and I have to get up early tomorrow," she told him while looking into his eyes and lightly stroking his face with her hand.

"We could do this again on Friday, if that's all right by you?" Gonzalez asked, hoping she'd say yes to his invitation.

"Of course, I see you then," Gladys said while giving him a quick kiss on his lips.

"Cool, will I see you tomorrow morning at the police station?"

"No papa, I'm sorry. I have to be in early tomorrow to train someone. I see you Friday, ok?"

"All right."

"Ok, Juan, see you Friday, chow."

Gladys opened up his car door, got out, and closed it back up while blowing a kiss to him. Then, she walked onto the pathway toward her front door. Gonzalez waited for Gladys to get inside her home before he backed out of her driveway, knowing he was going to have to get his own coffee and doughnut tomorrow morning. The detective was still wondering who the killer was. *Every time I find me a suspect, it always turns out to be a bullshit lead,* he thought while feeling disgusted. *I got shit for luck.*

*
**

In another town only a few miles away, Nathan Harris was finally returning back to his home with Nancy Stevens. The two of them were out all day long, celebrating Nancy's exoneration. Nathan was just about ready to turn the car off, when the local oldies station they were listening to played a familiar song for them, "When a Man Loves a Woman" by Percy Sledge. It was a song that had great meaning to Nancy, bringing back memories of her youth, innocence, and the budding relationship that she had with Nathan, before he went for her older sister, Heather. She looked at Nathan, story eyed and emotionally.

"Wait, Nathan, don't turn it off yet, please!" Nancy begged him.

"Wow, I haven't heard that one in years," Nathan said while

feeling melancholy.

"Do you remember that song, Nathan?"

"Oh, yeah."

"You used to sing that to me when we were together, remember?" Nancy asked while looking at him as if she were going to cry.

"Yeah, but I can't sing for shit."

"I don't care, sing it to me, please?"

Nancy wished that he'd never left her for her older sister. *If I were only a few years older back then, I could have made him mine right from the start,* she thought. *The only thing that really tied us together was Alice, and now she's gone,* Nancy painfully thought while reminiscing about the past.

Nathan began singing the old song to her while the radio played it. When it was over, Nancy threw her arms around him and kissed him tenderly on his lips, while the tears fell from her eyes. Tears of hope, hoping that the love he once had for her could be rekindled and they would be together again as one. The car windows were getting fogged up with the loving heat that the couple had just generated.

"I, I think we should go on inside and continue this," Nathan softly said to her.

"I don't know, honey. Do you really think your heart can take me right now? Remember, you're still recuperating from your operation, you know," Nancy asked him with a concerned look on her face.

"My heart's fine and I know what it wants—you, Nancy. I want you, now," Nathan said in a sensual tone.

Nathan turned and looked at his dashboard clock, noticing it was eleven fifteen. *No wonder it's so damn dark outside,* he thought. Nathan turned off the car engine, grabbed his cane, and the two of them got out of the car. They walked up the brick pathway together holding hands, until the couple reached the front door of his mansion. Nathan unlocked the door and the two of them walked inside. He closed the door behind them and tried to disable the alarm; however, Nathan quickly noticed it was already disabled. Then, he reached over to turn on the light, but it didn't work. A cold chill came over him, knowing that something was deadly wrong in the mansion.

"Hello Harris," a voice hiding in the dark said.

Nancy screamed.

"Shit! It's you again!" Nathan roared.

"That's right, your old friend, ha, ha, ha."

"Nathan, I can't see, is it the—"

"Shut the hell up, bitch! There *is* no light, I disabled it, and why the *fuck* is your ass out of jail, bitch?!"

"You destroyed my lab, what the *fuck* do you want now, money?!" Nathan angrily shouted.

"I told you what the hell I wanted, *everything*, everything you own, including this place!"

Nathan and Nancy were trying their best to see the invader, while standing in the large foyer near the old clock, but the only light that was available to them was the moonlight shining in through the windows. The intruder had smashed all the nearby lightbulbs in the area. Nancy was terrified as she slowly moved closer toward Nathan for support. All they could see was a dark figure, standing at the end of the entrance hall. It appeared to them that the intruder was holding something up with its right hand, possibly a gun. Then, Nathan saw some very familiar-looking lights emanating from the intruder's waist.

"You've got my time travel belt. I thought it was destroyed!" Nathan exclaimed.

"You thought wrong, asshole. I've got it now, and I know what it's capable of doing. Shit, I originally took it because I thought it was a cool-looking belt. Then when I got home and read some of your research papers, knowing what it could do for me, I was glad I took it."

"Nathan, what the hell is he talking about?" Nancy asked while feeling very confused.

"Bitch! Shut the fuck up, or I'll shut you up, permanently!"

"You can't talk to her like that!" Nathan shouted back in Nancy's defense.

"I can and I will! I'm the one who's holding a gun on you, and *this time,* it's mine *and* it's loaded, so don't you try anything stupid, Harris, you understand?!"

"Nathan, that voice, I think I know who he is," Nancy said while trying to remember.

"Not for long, you stuck-up bitch!"

With that, the intruder shot Nancy right in the chest.

"Noooo!" Nathan shouted while Nancy Stevens collapsed onto the hardwood floor, while blood began to spill out of her new wound.

Nathan went over to Nancy to check on her wound. He took a handkerchief out of his pocket, placed it over her bullet wound, and told her to hold it there as tight as she could to stop the bleeding.

"You will *never* be happy, Harris, *never!* Not as long as I breath!" the intruder shouted.

"You sonofabitch! I'll get you for this!" Nathan screamed as he began to charge at him with his cane.

"Stop or I'll shoot you too!"

Nathan came to a screeching halt, like a freight train that slammed on its emergency brakes. He looked at the perpetrator in complete rage, wanting to destroy him. However, the scientist didn't want to land his ass back into the hospital again, or even worse, wind up in the morgue.

"This is how this is going to play out, Harris. My ass is going back in time and your ass will remain here with your dying sister-in-law, or should I say, girlfriend, understand?"

"Completely," Nathan hissed.

"Good, now goodbye, Harris, may you rot in hell with your bitch here."

The killer set the date dials to go back in time ten years earlier, in front of the Solville Medical Center. He figured it would buy him time enough to save himself, armed with the information he had under his jacket. He pressed the manual override button on the belt and the countdown began.

"Ten, nine, eight, seven, six, five, four, three, two, one, zero," the computerized belt stated while displaying the numbers on its little LCD screen.

After the countdown was completed, the electronic belt verbally reported an error and shut itself down. The intruder noticed he was still there. This time, there were no laser lights, and his body didn't demolecularize and go back in time. The machine failed miserably. The killer was highly upset, to say the least.

"What the fuck happened?! Why am I still here?! Shit!" the perpetrator shouted.

"Now who's the asshole? Apparently, you didn't read enough of my research to know that the belt you are wearing is just a remote-control device for the *real* time machine. The one you so viciously destroyed downstairs, *asshole*. You ain't going anywhere in time, you're stuck here with me," Nathan said with a sneer.

The killer was so pissed off that he tore off the remote-control belt and threw it at Nathan, like a spoiled child that didn't get his way. Then he bolted toward the front door. This time, Nathan tried to chase him, but he was no match for the criminal's stamina and speed, especially in Nathan's present condition. Nathan stopped while feeling his heart struggle and pound in his chest like a jackhammer. He was also worried about popping his stitches. The scientist watched in anger from the end of his pathway while the killer disappeared down the driveway. Nathan then saw headlights come on, while the murderer drove off into the night. The scientist waited to regain his composure and then went back inside the mansion as quickly as possible to check on Nancy.

"Nancy! Are you all right?!" Nathan asked while trying to get a pulse from her wrist.

Nancy was now totally unconscious. Nathan took over applying pressure on her wound with his handkerchief that was now full of blood. He pulled out his smartphone with his free hand and called 911.

"911 what's your emergency?" the female operator asked.

"Hello, my name in Nathan Harris, I'm in my home at 1 Imperial Road in Solville. My sister-in-law's been shot by an intruder!" Nathan nervously said.

"Ok, where was she shot, Mr. Harris?"

"In her chest, near her heart!"

"Is she breathing? Does she have a pulse?"

"Her pulse is very weak. She's unconscious and she's bleeding a lot!"

"Sir, put pressure on her wound to stop the bleeding. We're sending the medics right over," the operator stated.

"Please tell them to hurry!" Nathan said desperately.

Nathan stayed on the line with the operator, but he turned on the smartphone's flashlight to see Nancy better. He placed both of his hands over Nancy's wound in an attempt to stop anymore bleeding. The blood was blending in with her red blouse and already starting to cover her jeans. The scientist looked at her face in horror as Nancy's color slowly faded away. Tears slowly dripped out from Nathan's eyes, wondering if she'd survive.

"Nancy, please, please don't die on me. Please Lord, not her, don't take her away from me too, I love her, I love her with all my heart and soul," he pleaded and begged while looking up at the ceiling, feeling as helpless as an infant.

*
**

A few minutes later, the ambulance arrived along with the police. Nathan yelled at them to come in through the front door that was still opened. He didn't want to release the pressure on Nancy's wound.

"Ok, sir, well take it from here," the young male paramedic said while going over to Nancy.

Nathan got up from the floor and moved out of their way. The team of two men shined their flashlights on Nancy, gave her oxygen, and began working on her, trying to control the bleeding. They placed Nancy on the stretcher and proceeded to take her out to the ambulance, while Detective Gonzalez and Detective Cheng came in with a young female police officer, with their flashlights on, to question Nathan.

"Ok, Harris, tell us what happened," Detective Gonzalez stated while taking out his book.

"We, we had just gotten back from celebrating Nancy's…" Nathan trailed of and began to cry.

"Mr. Harris, I know it's hard, but please pull yourself together so we can get all the facts," Detective Cheng said in a calm tone to him.

"We walked inside and heard his voice. The lights didn't work and—"

"Who's voice?" Gonzalez interrupted.

"The-the killer; he was here again," Nathan struggled to say in between his tears.

"I suppose you didn't get a better look at him this time, did you?" Gonzalez asked.

"No, he busted all the lights, but Nancy, Nancy claims that she recognized his voice. That's when he shot her. I've got to know if she's all right," Nathan said while he started to leave.

"Mr. Harris, hold up, we're not done here yet!" Detective Cheng told him.

"Officer Martin, follow that ambulance to the hospital. The victim is a possible witness!" Gonzalez shouted to the female officer.

"Ok, Detective," the officer replied while leaving.

"Mr. Harris, did you happen to see where the perpetrator was heading to?" Gonzalez asked him.

"Apparently, he was parked behind the bushes, near the front gate. He made a right turn from there onto Imperial Road. I tried to chase him, but I obviously wasn't in any kind of shape to catch him," Nathan solemnly said.

"I understand, Mr. Harris," Gonzalez replied.

Nathan stayed and answered the rest of their questions. He tried to give them as much information as possible, under the circumstances. The medical team loaded Nancy into the ambulance and drove away, as the police car followed closely behind them. Detective Gonzalez informed Nathan that they were taking Nancy to Solville Medical Center.

*
**

Later, Nathan had finally arrived at the emergency room of the medical center. He looked at his watch and noticed it was twelve thirty. *Wow, it's way after midnight and I'm back here again, only this time, it isn't for me, it's for Nancy,* Nathan miserably thought. The distraught scientist walked into the hospital and went over to the reception counter. There was a young African American woman at the counter that motioned him to come over.

"Sir, you have to wear this while you're here," she said while handing Nathan a mask.

"Yes, of course," Nathan said while putting on the mask she gave him.

"Now, may I help you, sir?" she asked him.

"Yes, miss, I'm trying to find some information on my sister-in-law. The ambulance brought her in here about an hour ago. Her name is Nancy, Nancy Stevens," Nathan impatiently said while trying to remain calm.

"Ok, sir, your name, please?"

"It's Nathan, Nathan Harris."

"Ok, Mr. Harris, and you said that she's your sister-in-law, is that correct?"

"That's correct. She was shot in the chest in my home by an intruder."

"Oh, my, let me see…"

The young woman started typing the information on her computer keyboard and looked up at Nathan after viewing her screen.

"Yes, Mr. Harris, Miss Stevens is in the operating room right now with Doctor Green. She was just brought in here in critical condition with a gunshot wound to her chest. I also see that she's under police protection."

"May I wait here, please?"

"I'm sorry, sir, but due to COVID-19 restrictions, you cannot wait for anyone here. If you give me your number, I can have someone call you when she's out of surgery."

Nathan gave the woman his contact information. *I guess I might as well go home,* he thought. However, Nathan knew he couldn't relax, knowing Nancy's life was hanging by a thread. The scientist and inventor was getting tired. He decided to go to the all-night diner down the road. Nathan wanted to get some coffee to help him stay awake. He figured on also getting a bagel with cream cheese. *It's been a long day and a long and terrifying night,* he thought. *It could have been a very nice evening. That sonofabitch! He ruined it for us. If anything happens to Nancy, you're dead meat.*

*
**

Two hours later, Nathan was awakened by his smartphone ringing. It was a call from the doctor that worked on Nancy Stevens. Nathan had taken a nap in his car back in the hospital parking lot, after he left the diner.

"Hello, is this Mr. Nathan Harris?" Doctor Green asked over the phone.

"Yes, yes, this is he," Nathan replied.

"This is Doctor Green from Solville Medical. I understand you're related to the patient, Miss Nancy Stevens?"

"Yes, Doctor, I'm her brother-in-law. How is she?" Nathan nervously asked him.

"She's in intensive care right now. Miss Stevens had emergency surgery to remove a bullet that was lodged near the right ventricle of her heart. It's a good thing it was a .38 caliber and not a .45 or larger, otherwise she wouldn't have made it this far. I was notified by the paramedic that her heart did indeed stop for two and a half minutes on the way here, and because of that, I don't know if she sustained any brain damage as of yet. Miss Stevens has lost a lot of blood, which she's receiving right now, but she's still unconscious. We've done all that we can for her. All we can do now is pray and hope for her recovery. I'm sorry, I wish I had better news for you, Mr. Harris," the doctor gravely stated.

Nathan dropped his smartphone on the carpeted floor of his car. The scientist completely broke down and cried like a child that's lost his favorite friend.

"Why, Lord, why? What did she do to deserve this shit? Why couldn't it be me instead, why?" Nathan wailed alone in the front seat of his car.

Nathan continued to cry until he finally fell asleep in his vehicle. The scientist had thought about going back into the past and reversing the whole incident, but he quickly realized that his Time Transporter was completely destroyed by Nancy's attacker. Nathan also remembered what had happened the last time he tried to prevent his family's murder from ever happening. The future somehow balanced itself out and his family *still died*, only a little bit differently this time, especially his daughter. However, unlike his wife, Heather, and his daughter, Alice, Nancy wasn't dead, as of yet. There was *still hope* for Nancy Stevens.

*
**

The morning sun came around and woke Nathan. He had spent the entire night sleeping in his car. Nathan looked at his watch and noticed it was nine o'clock.

"Wow, it's that fricking late already? I can't believe it," Nathan said to himself.

He decided to put his mask on and go back into the hospital emergency room to check on Nancy's condition. The receptionist informed him that Nancy was still in critical condition in the intensive care unit, and she was still unconscious. The scientist decided to go back home, knowing there wasn't anything else he could do there, especially since the receptionist told him that he couldn't wait in the area.

*
**

Later on that morning, Nathan Harris was back in what was left of his laboratory. *I've got to try, try to rebuild it, for Nancy's sake,* the scientist thought. He opened up the large manila envelope that Captain Martinelli had given him. Nathan pulled out his research papers and went through them in horror. The stack of papers were just copies of the first three pages, over and over again.

"Sonofabitch! I've been duped! He's got my research papers, shit!" Nathan screamed out loud in the empty, damaged room, wishing he had made copies of his plans.

The distraught scientist and inventor buried his head on the burnt-up workbench and wailed. Nathan wondered what he was going to do now. Nathan knew that he couldn't rebuild another time machine now, not without his plans and not in time to save Nancy if she passed on. *Even if I could, would it even make a difference? Or would Nancy still die, but in another way, like Alice did?* Nathan sadly asked himself in sorrow.

CHAPTER 26

MOUNTING EVIDENCE

Saturday afternoon, June third, the sun was beaming down bright and hot, letting everyone know that summer was here, even though officially it was still spring. It had been about two days since Nancy Stevens was brought into the hospital emergency room for that near fatal gunshot wound to her chest. Nathan Harris was calling the hospital two to three times every day checking on her progress. The scientist felt like a little helpless puppy, knowing that there was absolutely nothing he could do to help her. *I can't even attempt to go back in time to try and save her from being shot,* he thought while standing in the remains of his lab. *I need to know who the hell this bastard is, where is he hiding, and what he's done with my plans,* Nathan thought. Then he remembered something; something that may help the police find this heartless criminal.

✷✷

An hour later, Nathan Harris was back at the Solville Police Department. Nathan wore a gray sweat suit, thinking he would go out and do some light jogging, but the scientist decided to go look for Detective Juan Gonzalez instead. Detective Cheng was standing near the reception counter talking to the young female officer there. Cheng looked at Nathan inquisitively before speaking to him.

"Mr. Harris, what can I do for you?" Detective Cheng asked.

"Hello, I remember you, but I'm looking for Detective Gonzalez, is he around?" Nathan asked.

"No, I'm sorry Mr. Harris, Detective Gonzalez stepped out for lunch, is there something I can help you with?"

"I'd rather speak to him if you don't mind. When's he returning?"

"He'll be back in about a half-hour," Cheng replied while looking at his watch.

"May I wait here for him? I promise I won't get in anyone's way," Nathan pleaded.

"Ok, Mr. Harris, you can hang out here by the reception counter, if that's all right by you, Officer Robinson," he said while turning toward the young female officer at the counter.

The young officer shook her head in agreement. Officer Cheng told Nathan he'd let him know when Gonzalez arrives. Nathan decided to check his email on his smartphone.

*
**

Almost an hour had passed when Detective Gonzalez came out to greet Nathan. The detective came in through the back entrance with a gray jacket in his arm, so Nathan never saw him come in. Nathan reached into his pocket for a pair of blue rubber gloves he had with him, then he put them on while holding a brown paper bag.

"So, Mr. Harris, I understand you want to see me," Gonzalez said.

"Yes, Juan, I do. Can we go into your office, please?" Nathan asked.

"What's in the bag?"

"I believe this may be evidence to help you locate our infamous killer," Nathan said while pulling out the item in his bag.

"Really? Ok, let's go," Gonzalez said with a smile on his face.

Nathan put the item back in the bag and followed the detective toward his office. Gonzalez sat down at his desk while Nathan took the seat that was next to the desk. Nathan pulled out the item from his bag again and placed it on the detective's desk.

"Ok, Mr. Harris, what *is* that thing?" Gonzalez asked him.

"It's part of my invention that was destroyed in the fire, Juan," Nathan solemnly answered.

"Your time machine?"

"That's right, Juan, this is all that's left of it. It's the remote-controller belt."

"You're not trying to tell me that this *thing* is going to take you back in time, are you?"

"Oh, no, but the *killer* thought so. In fact, he not only *stole* it from me, but he was wearing it when he shot Nancy, thinking he could leave the scene of the crime. There may be fingerprints on it, so don't touch it without gloves," Nathan said while holding up his gloved hands.

"Well, the problem is, if it's the same prints that we found before, it's gonna be hard to find out who it is. The prints we got from your sister-in-law's home and your papers don't exist in our database, unless, of course, this device of yours can tell us some kind of a story."

"Oh, but it can, Juan. You see, the unit records the operator's information, such as voice and video in high definition. This micro-SD card recorded the user, or in this case, the intruder's vocal commands and his face, from the bottom up, of course. It also has a secondary, forward-facing camera. The recorded images are shown side by side in a split-screen fashion. I must warn you that since the cameras recorded everything, including Nancy getting shot, the images are *quite graphic*, although you're probably used to that," Nathan said while extracting the memory card from the electronic belt and giving it to the detective.

"Very interesting, Mr. Harris, especially since he never spoke a word on that videotape you had of him."

"Precisely! Unfortunately, our criminal wore a mask again; however, it *did* record his voice, up until he destroyed it by throwing it at me."

"You didn't catch it?" Gonzalez asked with a smirk on his face.

"No, I did not. It hit the wall and smashed onto the floor. The device was a precision instrument, Juan. It wasn't meant to be thrown or dropped."

"So, how do you know it recorded anything, Harris?"

"Oh, it did. I played the recording on my laptop. I also took the liberty of making a copy of it on my laptop, just in case," Nathan stated.

"So, we'll have some more mounting evidence on this perpetrator."

"There you go, Juan."

"The recordings on that card, are they a standard file type that we can play on our computers?"

"Yes, they are. The belt records all audio-visual material in standard mp4 format. You won't have any problems playing mp4 files on your computer."

Just then, the detective's phone began to ring. Gonzalez put up his hand to let Nathan know he had to answer the call.

"Detective Gonzalez, homicide," he answered, then Gonzalez listened to what the caller wanted.

"I see, is she conscious? Oh, ok, all right. Thanks for the heads-up," Gonzalez said before hanging up the phone.

"That was our officer at the hospital. It appears that your sister-in-law, Miss Stevens, was transferred to a private room, but she's *still unconscious*," he reported to Nathan.

"Oh, thank God, that's definitely a step in the right direction," Nathan said with a sigh of relief.

Detective Gonzalez thanked Nathan again for bringing him some evidence for his case. Nathan left the police station and headed straight for the hospital. The scientist knew there wasn't much he could do if Nancy wasn't conscious, but Nathan wanted to see her; he had to see her.

*
**

Not too far away, in a garden apartment complex on Cranberry Drive in Cortland, Nathan's ex-maid Consuelo Hernandez was talking to her boyfriend on her couch.

"I still no see why you had to kill him, I liked him," Consuelo said.

"More than me?" the man asked her.

"No, of course not, I love you and I know you love me, too, right?"

"Of course, I do. You shouldn't even have to even ask me that shit, girl."

"So, why you killed my friend? Were you jealous or something?"

"Me? Jealous of Hector? Hell no. He just got in the way, that's all. Hector Delgado had nothing to offer you that I do. Besides, he was in love with Heather Harris, your ex-boss's wife, remember? Hector wasn't interested in you, not like *I am*. I love you, everything about you," he said while petting her long black hair and gazing into her soft brown eyes.

"Really?"

"Yes, really; there isn't anything that I wouldn't do for you, my sweet, petite Latina."

"I glad you said that, because I really need to know something."

"What is it, baby?"

"I, I saw on the TV that *Señor* Harris's sister-in-law was shot in his house," she said nervously to him.

"What else did they say?"

"They say she alive, but in a coma."

"Alive? I thought she died, shit!"

Consuelo looked into his black, ice-cold eyes and knew he was responsible for that.

"You shot her, didn't you?"

"It was an accident. Sh-she charged at me when I was there," he said while acting as innocent as a top-notch actor playing an angel.

"What were you doing there in the first place? You said you were going to leave Mr. Harris alone. You lie to me. I sorry, but I no cover for you no more," Consuelo said while standing up from her sofa.

"Oh, come on now, honey. You can't mean that. I love you!"

"*Mira,* I sorry, but you have to go, now!"

"No, Consuelo, look at me… I love you. I need you. Let's go in the bedroom and I'll give you a nice massage, please, baby," he pleaded with her.

"No! Go now before I call police! I no lie for you anymore!" Consuelo commanded.

"Ok, honey, I'll go. It was nice while it lasted. Can I at least get a goodbye kiss?" he begged.

"Ok, last kiss."

"That's right, the last kiss."

The killer got up from the sofa, put his arms around Consuelo Hernandez, and gave her a sensual kiss that left her wanting more. He pulled away and looked deep into her soft brown eyes, as a tear slowly started to fall down from his own eye. The coldblooded and coldhearted killer that he was reached down into his jacket pocket to grab something.

Consuelo was totally unaware of what her former lover was about to do to her. The slaughterer quickly turned the young woman around and slashed her throat with a sharp, serrated knife, then he dropped Consuelo back down onto the sofa. The poor woman sat there slouched, bleeding profusely all over her yellow housedress and the couch, while her killer just watched her life slowly drain away.

"I'm so, so sorry it had to end this way. I really didn't want to kill you, baby, but you left me no choice. I *can't* and I *won't* go to jail. You were the only one I trusted, but you were also the only one who could identify me. For what it's worth, I really *did* love you," he said to the dying woman that was gasping for air.

Consuelo was literally drowning in her own blood. Soon, the once young and beautiful Latina breathed no more. The killer dropped his knife, collapsed right down onto her lap, and cried. Consuelo was his third victim, so far, branding him now officially a serial killer.

*
**

Officer Martin was at the Solville Medical Center, standing guard outside of the room that Nancy Stevens occupied. Detective Juan Gonzalez walked over to her with Nathan Harris trailing close behind him.

"Hey, is she still in a coma, Martin?" Gonzalez asked the young female officer that was twirling her short, black hair from boredom.

"Yes, Gonzalez, Stevens is still comatose," Officer Martin replied.

The two men walked into the patient's room and closed the door behind them. Nancy was hooked up to heart monitoring equipment, along with a blood pressure monitor on her arm. She had an intravenous drip for fluids and was given oxygen via an intubation tube.

"My poor baby. At least she's in a private room," Nathan said to her.

"You can thank us for that, Harris," Gonzalez stated.

Nathan walked over toward Nancy, pulled his mask down, and lovingly kissed her on her forehead. Then he pulled his mask back up before anyone else walked in.

"That woman really means a lot to you, doesn't she?" Gonzalez asked.

"Well, she's my sister-in-law, Juan," Nathan replied.

"More than that, right?"

"Jesus, Juan, she saved my life, for Christ's sake."

"Come on now, it's more than that. Admit it, you love her, don't you?"

"Yes, I won't lie or try to deny it, I love her and I want to be with her. It absolutely kills me to have to see her…"

Nathan couldn't speak anymore. He started to cry in front of Nancy and the detective. Gonzalez felt a little sorry for him and offered him a tissue. Nathan pulled his mask down, blew his nose with the tissue, and walked out of the room. Gonzalez walked out also, knowing that he couldn't possibly get any information out of Nancy in her present state of mind. Officer Martin had remained there, standing guard over Nancy Stevens in case the killer returned to finish the job.

*
**

Detective Gonzalez got back to his car and took off his gray suit jacket. He started up the vehicle and put the A/C on. *I can't stand this damn hot weather,* he thought while opening the windows a little to let the hot air out. Gonzalez was ready to leave the medical center, until he got a call from Captain Martinelli. The captain informed him that he just received a call about another murder. Martinelli wanted Gonzalez to go check it out.

"All right, Captain, where is it?" Gonzalez asked.

"It's at 15 Cranberry Drive in Cortland—a garden apartment

complex. I think you were there a few months ago, Gonzalez," Martinelli said.

"Yes, Captain, I was," he said to him while writing down the address.

"I'm gonna have the forensics team meet you over there."

"All right, Captain, I'm on my way."

Gonzalez hung up his phone, put his white, four-door sedan into drive, and left the hospital parking lot. A lonely teardrop slowly fell from his right eye as he recalled who lived at that address. *I was just there in February, shit,* he thought. Gonzalez drove his car to the address while sadly remembering who the victim was.

*
**

Detective Gonzalez had finally arrived at the victim's home located at 15 Cranberry Drive in Cortland. He looked at the dashboard clock before shutting off his car. Gonzalez couldn't believe it was already four thirty in the afternoon. *This day is going by so damn quick, but not in a good way,* he thought. An old woman with a small, brown-colored Chihuahua was standing right near the open apartment door. Gonzalez left his vehicle and approached the woman, making sure his badge was dangling from his neck over the white shirt.

"Are you the police?" the woman asked while her little dog barked at Gonzalez.

"Yes, ma'am, Detective Gonzalez, homicide, from the Solville Police," he replied.

"I'm the one who called it in. I was walking my dog and he started barking and pulling me toward my neighbor's open door, this one right here. I called out to her to let her know that she left her door wide open, and that's when I saw her slumped there on her sofa, full of, of, blood. God, she's such a nice girl. Who, who would do such a terrible thing to—" she struggled to say while getting all choked up.

"Ok now, miss, did you see anyone else come or go from here?"

"No, no I didn't."

Detective Gonzalez put on his purple latex gloves and a pair of booties to preserve the crime scene. He walked into the open apartment. The living room was in plain sight, there was no vestibule in between the room and the front door. Gonzalez remembered being there and talking to the young Latina in the wintertime. He went over to the woman slumped on the sofa, covered in her own blood from the big laceration in her neck. Gonzalez placed two fingers on the victim's neck to see if there was a pulse present.

"She's dead," Gonzalez sadly and quietly said.

"I knew it, I knew it," the old woman said hysterically while overhearing him.

"Ma'am, you're gonna have to leave here, this is now a crime scene investigation," Gonzalez told her at the doorway, preventing her from coming inside the apartment.

The woman walked away, tugging on her barking dog, while Gonzalez went back to look at the victim. The thirty-two-year-old Mexican immigrant, Consuelo Hernandez, was dead. *She was so sweet; she sure as shit didn't deserve this,* Gonzalez thought with remorse. Gonzalez noticed something else, something that might aid him in finding her assassin. The killer had left his murder weapon—the bloody knife that was at the foot of the female victim, taunting him, as if to say, "Do you *really* think I can help you solve this case?"

The forensics team of two had just walked into the apartment wearing booties and purple latex gloves. Gonzalez pointed to the murder weapon on the floor next to the victim. One of the men was taking pictures of the crime scene, before bagging the evidence. Gonzalez was also taking pictures on his smartphone. *Another victim picture for the murder board,* he thought. Gonzalez decided to call his captain on his smartphone.

"Solville Police, Captain Martinelli," he answered.

"Yeah, Captain, it's Gonzalez. Our victim was Consuelo Hernandez," he somberly stated.

"I had a feeling that's who it was, is she—"

"She's gone, Captain," Gonzalez interrupted.

"I see. Did forensics get there?"

"Yes, they're here, and so is the murder weapon. She was slashed in the throat with a serrated knife."

"Does her place look disheveled, like it was the scene of a robbery gone wrong?"

"From what I'm seeing, Captain, no. The place looks pretty clear to me. It looks like a murder, not a robbery. Someone wanted her dead. We have to find out who and why."

"We will, Gonzalez, we will," the captain said before hanging up his phone.

CHAPTER 27

THE PLOT THICKENS

Monday morning, June fifth, Detective Gonzalez was enjoying a cup of coffee with Gladys Delgado in his office. Gladys was wearing a white blouse with a pair of blue jeans. The young lady was a little shaken after hearing about the recent murder. Captain Paul Martinelli had just walked into Gonzalez's office holding a cup of coffee in his hand, at least what was left of it, since he spilled most of it on his shirt while answering the phone earlier. Martinelli looked a little sloppy today with his stained white shirt hanging out of his black trousers. Gonzalez thought the captain was trying to hide his belly, but he could also see that the man looked tired.

"Excuse me, I hate to break up your conversation here, but we've got work to do, Gonzalez," the captain told him.

"Oh, I'm sorry, I go now. See you tomorrow, Juan," Gladys said while giving Gonzalez a quick kiss on the cheek before she left the office.

"Whoa, she's on a first name basis with you. I guess it's getting serious," Martinelli said with a smile.

"Maybe, but none of us are in a rush. We're just enjoying each other's company right now."

"I'm happy for you, Gonzalez, she seems like a nice girl. Now let's go into my office, I wanna show you something."

Gonzalez followed the captain into his office. Martinelli handed him some papers from his desk.

"What you're looking at is the report from our forensics team, Gonzalez. As you can see, the prints they've pulled from the murder weapon, the bloodied knife at the home of Consuelo Hernandez on Saturday, matched the set of prints you and Cheng recently pulled from the home of Nancy Stevens," Martinelli stated.

"I knew it, it's the same killer. Now he's a serial killer, with three victims under his belt, shit," Gonzalez angrily said.

"There's something else on the next page. It turns out this killer's been there before. His prints, along with Consuelo's, were on a water bottle near the body, the refrigerator, and the TV remote."

"So, the plot thickens; they knew each other."

"Rather well, I might add. The medical examiner found semen in Consuelo's reproductive tract and we sent it out for DNA testing. If it matches the saliva from his water bottle, it will indeed confirm they were together. The only problem we have now is trying to find out who this sonofabitch is. His fingerprints are not in our database, which means the bastard doesn't have a criminal record, at least not yet."

"Sooner or later he's gonna slip up, and when he does, I'll get his ass, Captain," Gonzalez said while gritting his teeth.

"What gets me is, if Consuelo and him were lovers, why did he kill her?"

"Your guess is as good as mine, Captain. Maybe Consuelo knew too much and she didn't like what she knew about him. Maybe Consuelo wanted to break it off with him, and he didn't like that, not one bit."

"Yes, it's possible. Listen, I want you and Cheng to go back over there and question *all* of Consuelo's neighbors. If he was her lover, perhaps someone may have seen him coming in or out of her apartment. Maybe you guys can get some kind of a description of this sonofabitch so we can get his ass."

"All right, Captain, I'll go grab Cheng and head on over there," Gonzalez said before leaving the captain's office.

Gonzalez really wanted to go back there by himself, but deep down inside, he knew that Cheng would be of assistance to him. Cheng was a fast learner and that's why he got the promotion in the first place, Gonzalez had to admit that. Gonzalez went over toward the reception area, figuring he'd find Cheng over there, and he was right. Cheng was talking to the young female officer at the counter again. *I guess he likes her; he's always talking to her,* Gonzalez thought. He grabbed Detective Cheng and the two of them left the police station together.

*
**

A week later on Monday, early afternoon, June twelfth, Nathan Harris was back at the hospital, sitting in the chair next to Nancy Stevens's bed. Nathan had brought along a murder mystery novel to read to her. He looked at her hooked up to the life support equipment in the room, wishing she'd come out of her coma. Nathan got up and gently brushed some of her blonde hair away from her face with his hand.

"Nancy, please come back to me," he pleaded, hoping she would hear him.

Nathan sat back down and opened up the novel to the page where he left off. He poured some water from the pitcher into a clear plastic cup. Nathan pulled down his mask to take a sip of water from the cup, then he pulled his mask back up and began to read, until Nathan was interrupted.

"Hello, I'm Doctor Green," the young man with the white lab coat said, as he walked into the room.

Nathan looked at the young doctor, trying to analyze him. *My God, he looks like he's fresh out of med school. He's the one that operated on my Nancy?* the scientist thought, wondering just how experienced the doctor actually was. Doctor Green was in his early thirties, but he looked much younger than his real age. The doctor wore his short black hair in a spike-like fashion. Doctor Green was proud of his thin physique, making sure he had time enough for exercise.

"So, you're Doctor Green?" Nathan slowly asked while still scrutinizing him.

"Yes, I am," the doctor answered as if he were trying to defend himself in a court of law.

"I thought you were—"

"Older? Everyone thinks that. I can assure you I'm perfectly capable of—"

"Relax, Doctor, I'm not questioning your abilities to do your job," Nathan said reassuringly, not really believing what he just said to him.

"Good, now that we've cleared the air, I assume you're Mr. Nathan Harris?"

"That's correct, Doctor, we spoke over the phone."

"That's right, now about Miss Stevens, I'd like to point out that she's been in a comatose condition ever since she arrived here on Thursday morning. We may have to evaluate her brain activity," the doctor stated in a matter-of-fact tone.

"If you're suggesting that I let you pull her off life support, you're sadly mistaken," Nathan firmly snapped at him.

"Well, it's just that Miss Stevens has been in a coma for over eleven days without any sign of improvement, *and* she had an organ donor card with—"

"I'm very well aware of that, Doctor, thank you very much. Nancy will pull out of it. She just needs some more time, that's all, doc," Nathan firmly added, not wanting to hear anymore from Doctor Green.

"Ok, Mr. Harris," the doctor said while taking a hint and leaving the room.

✳︎
✳︎✳︎

At the Solville Police Department, Captain Paul Martinelli was in his office looking at the DNA report on the latest victim, Consuelo Hernandez, Nathan Harris's ex-maid. The report stated that the semen

327

found in her reproductive tract and the saliva that was in the bottled water in her apartment were indeed from the same man. *I was right all along, the killer was Consuelo's lover,* the captain happily thought. *That same water bottle had prints on it that matched the ones that were in Nancy Stevens's home, and on Nathan's papers.* The captain decided to inform both Detective Gonzalez *and* Detective Cheng of the new findings.

*
**

A few miles away from the police station in the small town of Sunnyside Falls, a middle-aged man was repairing the front door of his cottage. The old structure had seen better days and was never intended to be lived in year-round, but it was all he could afford. *That sonofabitch gets to live in perfect health, in his big ass, plush mansion, and all I get is this shit house shack that's falling apart. This shit ain't right,* he angrily thought. The man finished tightening up the screws on the shabby old wooden door, then he decided to sit down on the front steps and have a smoke. He pulled out his lighter from his black jacket and lit up his cigarette.

The man thought about Nathan Harris, but mostly, he was worried about Nancy Stevens. *That bitch recognized my voice; she could identify me, shit,* he thought. The man was worried, to say the least. He figured that Nancy probably had round-the-clock police protection outside of her hospital room. *Somehow, I've got to get to her and finish the job, then I'll handle Mr. Multimillionaire,* the angry man thought. He sat there smoking his cigarette, watching a young couple pushing their baby in its stroller, wishing he were the woman's husband. The man felt really alone. He didn't want to kill the love of his life, Consuelo Hernandez, but the man knew she was going to turn his ass in. Consuelo turned out to be a lose end and he didn't like lose ends. The man finished the cigarette and went inside his diminutive home. He had to take something for the pain in his head that was now growing.

*
**

Nathan Harris was on his way back home from the hospital when he got a call on his cell from Detective Gonzalez. The detective wanted him to stop by the police station. Gonzalez told Nathan he had something for him. *I wonder what it is this time,* he asked himself, not really wanting to know. Nathan turned his car back around and headed for the police station.

***

A few minutes later, Nathan was back in the police station parking lot. Nathan parked his Bentley and walked right in. He went to the reception counter and announced his arrival to the young female officer sitting there. Within seconds, Detective Gonzalez approached him holding a brown paper bag.

"Harris! I believe this belongs to you; we're finished with it," Gonzalez said as he handed the bag over to Nathan.

Nathan opened up the bag to inspect its contents.

"Oh, my remote controller belt. Did you get any useful information from it?" Nathan asked the detective.

"Well, at least we know what he sounds like, unfortunately, we don't have a useful image of him on there. I found it strange that there was only one short recording on that whole chip, the one of that last incident, especially when there was plenty of room for more," Gonzalez said with suspicion in his voice.

"I guess the killer erased the previous recordings on there to make room for more."

Nathan took the liberty of backing up the other recordings of him during his time travel escapades, then he simply deleted the original recordings from the memory card before handing it over to the detective. The scientist did not want to implicate himself in anything and in any way. Plus, as far as Nathan was concerned, that was top-secret information that he didn't care to share with the police, especially after the way they treated him the last time he brought up time travel.

"Were there any fingerprints of the killer on it?" Nathan asked.

"Yes, there was, but unfortunately, he's not in our system yet.

329

There were also prints from *you* on it," Gonzalez said in an accusatory manor.

"Well of course there were, Juan, after all, it *is my belt*," Nathan shot back.

Captain Paul Martinelli had just walked over to them.

"Hey Nathan, can I see you in my office for a bit? You too, Gonzalez," Martinelli asked.

The two men followed the captain into his office. Martinelli asked Gonzalez to close the door behind him, and then he asked Nathan to have a seat. The captain sat down behind his desk and pulled out the DNA report on Nathan's ex-maid, Consuelo Hernandez.

"Nathan, I just thought you'd like to know that your ex-maid, Consuelo Hernandez, and our killer were both lovers," Martinelli stated.

"What?! Are you sure?!" Nathan shouted.

"The DNA report on her confirms it. There was a water bottle at the scene with our killer's prints on it. The saliva that was inside the bottle was a perfect DNA match for the semen that was inside of Consuelo Hernandez's reproductive tract."

"Shit! I guess that explains a lot of things, like how he got into my home, how he disabled my security system, how he knew so much about me, and then some."

"In light of this, I'm having one of my men drive by and check on your surroundings from time to time. I won't lie to you, Nathan, you may be in danger," Martinelli said with great concern.

"The killer expressed to me that he wanted everything I owned, including my mansion. I see you still have police protection outside of Nancy's hospital room; I appreciate that," Nathan genuinely said.

"Well, I don't know how much longer we can afford to do that."

"What do you mean? Why?"

"It seems that Miss Stevens isn't doing too well. The doctor informed us that she has minimal to no brain activity and—"

"Stop, stop, I don't want to hear that, not from you too, Paul. I just heard that shit from her doctor. He was practically telling me to pull the plug on Nancy so they could have her organs. I'm not ready for that. I still have hope, hope that she'll come out of this shit and come back to me," Nathan cried out before walking out of the captain's office.

Captain Martinelli looked at Detective Gonzalez, while shaking his head.

"You were right, Gonzalez, you were right all along. He's in love with her. Nathan's in love with his sister-in-law," Martinelli said.

"I told you, but you didn't believe me," Gonzalez replied.

*
**

The next morning, Tuesday, June thirteenth, Nathan Harris assumed his usual spot at the hospital in room 205, sitting near Nancy's bed. He pulled down his mask, poured himself some water from the pitcher, drank it, and then pulled his mask back up. He grabbed the book he had placed on the bed. Nathan brought a romance novel with him and began to read it to Nancy, who was still in a coma.

"The man sat down on his bed, alone in his empty room, thinking of her; thinking about the only love he's ever had. He realized that when a man loves a woman, things change," Nathan read, before drinking some more water from his plastic cup.

All of a sudden, Nancy started thrashing in the bed. Nathan bolted out of the room to call for assistance.

"Nurse! Nurse! Please help, I think she's having seizures!" Nathan told the young, female, Asian nurse at the nurses' station.

Nathan brought the young nurse into Nancy's room. The nurse quickly went over to Nancy and started pulling out her intubation tube. Nancy started coughing and gagging and then, she asked for some water.

The nurse grabbed the bed remote to raise the head of the bed and handed her a cup of water, with a straw.

"Th-thank you," Nancy said in a very weak and croaky voice.

"She's awake, I go get the doctor," the young nurse said before she left the room.

"Sing it. Sing it too me, Na-than," Nancy barely got out.

"Na-Nancy? Oh, thank God you're awake!" Nathan said with great enthusiasm and surprise.

"Y-es, Na-than."

Nathan gave his best adoring eyes that welcomed her back, then he pulled his mask down and kissed her forehead.

"My prayers have been answered, you've come back to me, honey. Oh, Lord, you'll never know just how much I've missed you," Nathan said while holding her hand, being careful not to disturb the tubes and wires that were attached to her.

Doctor Green had just walked into the room.

"She's awake?" Doctor Green asked in amazement.

"Yes, Doctor, isn't it wonderful? To think you wanted to take her off life support," Nathan replied.

The doctor went over to check out her vitals.

"You're a very lucky woman, Miss Stevens, I'll admit it was a little scary there for you. Welcome back. Mr. Harris, please pull your mask up. I'll leave you two alone for a bit," Doctor Green said before exiting the room with a smile on his face.

"Na-than, sing it to me, please," Nancy barely asked him.

"Sing what, Nancy?" Nathan asked her with a puzzled look on his face.

"That song, our song, 'When a Man Loves a Woman.' I heard you mention it. I remember kissing you in your car after that song played."

"What else do you remember, honey?"

"Why, that's the last thing I can remember. Nathan, why am I here in this hospital?"

"You really don't remember?"

"No, I don't. What happened to me?" Nancy asked with confusion on her face.

**

Back at the Solville Police Department, Captain Martinelli had just received a phone call from Officer Martin, who was still stationed outside of Nancy Stevens's room. The officer informed her captain that Nancy Stevens had finally come out of her coma. Officer Martin also mentioned that Doctor Green said her prognosis was good, and he expected her to have a full recovery.

"Well, that's the best news I've heard all day. I'll send Detective Gonzalez over there to question her," Martinelli told her before hanging up his phone.

**

An hour later, Detective Gonzalez was parking his car in the hospital parking lot. He made sure to have his black book and recorder with him, before leaving his vehicle. Gonzalez decided to leave his gray suit jacket in the car, since it was sunny and warm outside. *It's gonna be hot today, I can tell it already,* he said to himself. Gonzalez put his mask on, knowing it was required at all times in the hospital. He walked into the medical center and headed straight for the elevators. Gonzalez took the elevator up to the second floor. When the detective got off the elevator, he spoke to Doctor Green and asked if it was ok to question Miss Stevens. The doctor replied yes, but told him to keep it brief. Gonzalez then went over to room 205. He acknowledged the female officer stationed outside the room and then the detective walked in to find Nathan Harris sitting there at Nancy's bedside.

"Mr. Harris, I didn't think you'd still be here," Gonzalez said to him.

"Hello, Juan. I was wondering when you'd show up," Nathan responded.

"What's *he* doing here?" Nancy asked in an annoyed tone.

"I'm here to interview you, Miss Stevens. Harris had said you knew who the killer was by the sound of his voice," Gonzalez stated.

"We have a problem with that, Gonzalez," Nathan stated.

"What kind of problem, Harris?"

"It appears that Nancy, here, is suffering from temporary amnesia, or at least we *hope* it's temporary. She doesn't appear to remember anything about that traumatic incident at my home."

"Oh, shit, is this true, Miss Stevens?"

"It's true, Detective. I don't even remember how the hell I wound up here in this hospital," Nancy answered.

"Well, what's the last thing you *do* remember, Miss Stevens?"

"Nathan sing-ing to me in his car," she barely said to him.

Detective Gonzalez looked at them both, dumbfounded. *Another bullshit lead and a damn waste of my time,* he miserably thought. The good detective turned himself around and walked out of the room. He knew this wasn't going to sit well with the captain. Gonzalez started to wonder if he was ever going to find the elusive serial killer. The detective took the elevator down to the ground floor and walked back to his vehicle, suppressing the urge to call Captain Martinelli on his smartphone. *I'll tell him the bad news in person when I get there,* Gonzalez thought as he started his vehicle.

CHAPTER 28

RELEASE ME

Wednesday morning, June fourteen, it had been fourteen days since Nancy Stevens was initially brought into the hospital with a life-threatening gunshot wound to her chest. Nancy wanted out of the hospital, but Nathan sided with the doctor's decision for her to stay there a little longer. Doctor Green wanted to keep her under observation for at least two more days, hoping that she would regain the rest of her memory. The other problem was that Nathan no longer had anyone at home to help him recover from his surgery, since Nancy was initially the one that was caring for him. Nathan had thought about hiring a stay-at-home nurse for himself, but the man was just too busy worrying about Nancy's condition to even *think* about himself. However, the doctor had insisted on checking Nathan's wound and removing his stiches, and Nathan had at least agreed on that.

Detective Gonzalez was in his office in front of the computer screen, watching the video of the killer from Nathan's electronic belt. He had a pair of headphones on, and for the umpteenth time he was trying to analyze the killer's voice and hoping he might see or hear anything that he might have missed. The video recording was, at best, an audio recording of the killer since the assassin was so well covered up. However, the recording *did* document Nancy Stevens getting shot at point-blank range. It also proved that Nathan Harris couldn't have done it, since it was quite clear in the recording that he was standing right next to her when she was shot. *You may be clear from this incident, Harris, but this doesn't exonerate you or her from the previous victims,* Gonzalez thought. The detective did find it quite disturbing to watch Nancy Stevens actually get shot on camera. Gonzalez took his headphones off, got up from his desk, and went over to the murder board. He looked at the pictures of all the victims, including the latest one, Consuelo Hernandez, and the pictures of the few suspects, including Nathan Harris, Nancy Stevens, Darius White, and Hector Delgado that were hanging up on the board.

"After all this time, I don't feel any closer to finding this damn killer, shit!" Gonzalez miserably said to only himself.

*
**

Two days later, on Friday morning, June sixteen, Nathan was at the hospital again with Nancy. The two of them were waiting patiently for one of the doctors to come by and give Nancy permission to be discharged. Nancy wanted out. She had had enough of being cooped up in the hospital, but Nathan was still being a bit more patient. He wanted what was best for Nancy, even if it meant that she'd have to stay there longer to recuperate.

Finally, a young doctor wearing glasses had arrived. Doctor Mark Winters came into the room holding a tablet, with a concerned look upon his face. Nathan and Nancy both remembered Doctor Winters as the one who recently operated on Nathan.

"Oh, Doctor, please release me. I want to go home," Nancy begged.

"Do you really think you're ready to go home, Miss Stevens?" Doctor Winters asked while looking at her chart on his tablet.

"Yes, yes, please Doctor, I'm ready."

"Do you have someone at home to help you recover? Someone that could help you with your household chores?"

"*Well,* I have *Nathan.*"

"You were supposed to be caring for *him,* during *his* recovery, *remember?*"

"Yes, yes, I remember."

"The fact is, you're getting excellent care right here in this hospital, but if you prefer to be home…"

"Oh, I do. I want to go home with Nathan," Nancy pleaded.

"How do you feel about this, Mr. Harris? Do you think you could care for Miss Stevens in your present condition, since you're not fully healed yet, yourself?" Doctor Winters asked him.

"I'll certainly give it my best, but maybe we *should* have a nurse come by for a few hours a day, for at least a few weeks," Nathan said.

"All right Mr. Harris, you've certainly twisted my arm. Let me just check out Miss Stevens's vitals and I'll put the paperwork through."

Doctor Winters checked Nancy's blood pressure and took her pulse. He took out his flashlight and examined both of her eyes. Then the doctor took note of the readings on the monitoring equipment that was hooked up to Nancy. Doctor Winters told them he'd be back and then he walked out of the room.

*
**

Two hours later, Nathan Harris was bringing Nancy Stevens back home to his mansion. Their new nurse, Cybill Templeton, was following close behind them in an old, beat-up, white Ford van. Nurse Templeton was in her mid-thirties, with shoulder length, light brown hair. Templeton was very attractive and very athletic. Nancy wasn't too thrilled when she met her. Nancy had thought that the new nurse could pose competition between her and Nathan. *I'll have to keep a close eye on those two*, Nancy had thought, especially since she noticed the way Nurse Templeton was smiling at Nathan. Nancy also knew that Nathan was a hot commodity, since he was rich, handsome, and now single.

Nathan pulled his emerald Bentley into the driveway and the nurse parked her van directly behind him. He turned off the car and got out with his cane. Nathan opened the back door and pulled out Nancy's cane. He opened the front passenger door to help Nancy out.

"Wait, wait, wait, that's what *I'm* here for, to help!" Nurse Templeton yelled while coming over to assist them.

"Thank you, Miss Templeton," Nathan said as he stepped aside to let her help Nancy.

"Oh, you can call me Cybill, Mr. Harris," the nurse said with a big smile on her face that made Nancy feel a little jealous.

Nurse Templeton helped Nancy out of the car and walked her toward the front door, while following Nathan. Templeton marveled at the nice weather and Nathan's mansion.

"It sure must be nice living here, Mr. Harris," the nurse said while walking on the brick pathway.

"It used to be, but now it's very lonely, ever since the death of my wife and daughter," Nathan told her.

"Oh, my, but I thought Miss Stevens here was your…"

"Wife? No, Nancy's my sister-in-law."

"Oh, I see," the nurse said while standing behind him and fixing her hair with her free hand.

Nancy shot back a disapproving look at her while waiting for Nathan to unlock the front door. The scientist was having difficulty unlocking his own door. It appeared that the lock was stuck.

"Here, why don't you let me get that for you, sometimes you just have to jiggle it," Templeton said while releasing Nancy's arm to help Nathan.

Nurse Templeton took over Nathan's keys that were stuck in the lock. She jiggled it back and forth a few times until the lock finally opened, and then the nurse turned the knob and pushed the door wide open.

"You see, that's all there is to it," Miss Templeton said with a smile.

"Thank you, Cybill, you're truly a gem," Nathan said with a smile of approval.

Nancy was beginning to turn as red as the blouse she wore. The blouse was similar to the one that Nancy was wearing when she got shot by her assailant at Nathan's mansion, over two weeks ago. *I'm watching you, bitch, keep your damn hands off of my man,* Nancy furiously thought while looking at Cybill.

*
**

In an old ranch house on Williams Road in the town of Carney, Gladys Delgado and Detective Juan Gonzalez had just completed a very steamy love session. The couple had taken some time off from work to be together. It was the first time in years that either Juan Gonzalez or Gladys Delgado had any kind of sexual relations with anyone in their lives. The two of them were completely exhausted and were now lying there on the bed, next to each other, recuperating under the sheet. Juan leaned over and kissed Gladys on her lips.

"You're something else, mama. I didn't know you were such a tiger in bed," Gonzalez told her with a surprised look on his face.

"You weren't so bad yourself, papa," Gladys said.

"We should have done this shit *long* ago."

"I had to get to know you, *you know*."

"Yeah, I know. *Man,* is that clock right?"

"*Si* papa, it's one o'clock in the afternoon. You want me to make you something to eat?"

"*Si,* I'm as hungry as a bear," Gonzalez said while giving her another kiss on the lips.

Gladys pulled the sheet off of her body and got out of bed, *still* completely naked. Gonzalez gave her an approving wolf whistle, while watching her ass wiggle as she walked out of the room. *Man, she's not only beautiful inside and out, but she's fine, too. That woman's gonna give me a heart attack for sure, but what a way to go,* he thought. Gonzalez loved everything about her. He marveled at how sweet and kind Gladys was. *She looks like*

339

the type of person that would literally give the shirt off her back to help anyone, Gonzalez thought.

*
**

A few miles away in Sunnyside Falls, the killer had just heard on his TV set that Nancy Stevens was finally released from the hospital. The murderer was worried, until he heard the news reporter mention that Nancy was suffering from memory loss and she couldn't identify the one who shot her. *I may be safe for now, but sooner or later that bitch is gonna remember me, shit,* the killer angrily thought, knowing he was going to have to eliminate her.

The man decided to grab a bottle of beer from the fridge and then, he pulled a cigarette out from his pack. He left his shack and sat on the front steps to enjoy the fresh air. *I'm not a very bright person. Harris had a time machine that could have sent me back in time. I could have had a second chance,* he thought while still looking up at the beautiful blue sky. *I fucked up big time. I destroyed the only chance I had for my own survival.* The killer felt imprudent. Had he read Harris's research papers from the beginning, instead of the middle, the man would have known that Nathan's time machine was indeed the contraption he destroyed in the basement, not the remote controller belt he saved. *I wonder how long it would take his ass to build another machine. I still have his damn plans here. Maybe I'll just make him an offer he can't refuse,* he thought with a smile forming on his face.

The killer finished his beer and cigarette. He stood up and admired the warm weather and bright blue sky. Then the man was struck with a sharp pain in his head, a pain that felt like a hot knife penetrating right through his skull. It was a pain that was all too familiar to him, making him drop his empty beer bottle onto the ground. The sound of the smashing glass bottle even intensified his pain. At that point, he literally felt like his head was going to explode. The killer collapsed on the ground, grabbing his head in agony. *It's getting worse. Shit, it's getting worse,* the man thought while he laid there on the ground in excruciating pain, until he simply went unconscious.

*
**

Back at the Harris residence, Nathan and Nancy were finally enjoying some quiet time together in the master bedroom suite. Nurse Templeton had left for the evening. Nancy had gingerly unbuttoned the lavender pajama top she had on, to inspect her wound in the full-length mirror that Nathan had in the corner of the room. *I hope it's not going to look too ugly; it's right in my cleavage area,* Nancy thought with a concerned look on her face.

"Don't take off your bandages, babe," Nathan sternly told her while sitting up in the king-size bed, watching her stand there in front of the mirror.

"I'm not, honey, but I'm certainly curious to see how bad a scar I'm going to have. It's right in my cleavage and it still hurts," Nancy responded.

"I guess we'll have matching scars, practically in the same spot, only mine was caused by flying debris," Nathan said with a chuckle.

"Yeah, and mine was cause by a bullet. It's going to look ugly, isn't it? I'm going to look ugly."

"You could never look ugly. You'll always be beautiful to me, inside and out."

"Oh, Nathan, that's the sweetest thing you've ever said to me. I think I'm going to cry."

"Oh, come over here and kiss me already."

Nancy slowly walked over to him while holding on to her cane for support. She bent down to him and kissed him on his lips. Nathan got carried away and grabbed her, trying to pull her down onto the bed, until Nancy screamed from the pain.

"Ouch! My stitches!" Nancy shrieked while now pulling away from him.

"Oh, I'm so, so sorry, babe, really," Nathan said in an apologetic tone.

"Shit, it felt like my stitches were being pulled apart, wow! You've got to be careful, Nathan, I'm delicate, you know."

"Again, I'm sorry, Nancy, let me make it up to you," he said with open arms.

"That's quite all right Nathan, I'll pass," Nancy said while buttoning her pajama top back up.

*
**

Hours later, near the killer's home in Sunnyside Falls, a middle-aged woman was walking her small white dog nearby on the road. The lady's dog started barking and pulling her toward the driveway of a small home. She couldn't see much since it was dark outside, even though there was a lamp post near the driveway. The woman tried to focus her eyes but she had just lost her contact lenses. As the lady approached the home, she noticed a figure laying on the ground by the foot of the steps.

"Hello, are you all right?" she asked.

"Y-es, I'm o-k. I guess I just passed out," the killer weakly said while trying to get his bearings.

"Would you like me to call for help?"

"No, thank you, I'm fine," he said while slowly getting up from the ground.

"Are you absolutely sure?" she asked as her small dog continued to bark at him.

"Yes, yes I'm fine," he said while feebly walking back toward his home.

The man slowly went inside his house and closed the door behind him, still rubbing his head from the dull headache he was now experiencing. He stood there by his front window and waited for the woman to leave his property. The woman took one last look at his front door to see if the man might change his mind, come back out, and ask for some assistance. *I guess he's all right,* the woman thought.

The lady finally turned back around and left with her dog. After seeing that the woman was finally off of his property, the killer walked into his bathroom, opened up the medicine cabinet, and took out two aspirin. The man popped the pills in his mouth and took some water from the faucet to swallow them. He looked at his watch and noticed it was nine p.m.

"Shit, I was out there all fricking day? Sonofabitch," he said to himself with a surprised look on his face.

The killer relieved himself in the toilet. He washed his hands and splashed some water on his face. The man thought about taking a shower, but he was too tired to stand up in the tub for any length of time. He decided to sit down on his living room sofa and wait for the pain to subside, before going off to bed.

*
* *

The next morning, Nathan and Nancy were waking up to the sound of the front doorbell ringing. The couple had been sleeping together upstairs in the master bedroom suite. It was the first time that Nathan had slept with anyone since Heather was murdered in the dead of winter. Nathan turned his head and looked at the alarm clock on his nightstand. Nathan tried to focus his eyes on the clock since he was still half-asleep. He noticed it was nine thirty.

"It's probably the nurse, I'll go get it," Nathan said to Nancy, while they were both half-asleep.

Nathan grabbed his cane that was near the bed. He went down the stairs toward the monitor on the wall, near the front door. Nathan looked at the monitor and noticed the screen was blank. *Shit, don't tell me the camera's out again,* he thought.

"Who is it?!" Nathan loudly asked before opening up the front door.

"It's me, Nurse Cybill Templeton, Mr. Harris," she said through

343

the front door.

Nathan cautiously opened his front door, still not trusting what he heard. *She sounds…different,* he thought.

"Good morning, Mr. Harris, or may I just call you Nathan?" Nurse Templeton coyly asked with a smile on her face, as she stood there.

"Good morning, Miss Templeton, yes, you may call me Nathan. What happened to your voice? You sound different," Nathan asked her.

"Yes, I know. I have a sore throat from screaming so loud last night."

"Why were you screaming?" Nathan asked with a concerned look on his face.

"Let's just say I had an unauthorized visitor in my apartment yesterday and he, well, he scared the living daylights out of me," she replied, while now looking flustered from vividly recalling the incident yesterday.

"I'm sorry to hear that. Did you call the police?"

"No, Mr. Harris, it wasn't that kind of a visitor. It was a mouse, right in my kitchen."

"I see, please come in," Nathan said while escorting her inside his home.

Nathan brought her into the parlor and asked her to sit down on the sofa next to him. He grabbed his smartphone from the end table. Nathan looked up the exterminator that he previously used and gave all the information to her.

CHAPTER 29

NURSE TROUBLE

Photo courtesy of Antoni Shkraba

Early Saturday morning, June twenty-four, Nurse Cybill Templeton was back at the Harris residence. It had been over a week since Miss Templeton had been taking care of Nathan Harris and Nancy Stevens in Harris Manor. Cybill had grown very fond of Nathan, even giving him special treatments, like back rubs and massages, when Nancy wasn't present in the room with them. Nancy, however, was not too impressed with their new nurse and she considered her a threat to her relationship with Nathan. Miss Templeton had figured out that the two of them were more than just brother-in-law and sister-in-law; she figured that Nathan and Nancy were lovers. *It has to be true; they're sleeping in the same room and in the same bed, for Christ's sake,* Cybill had thought.

It seemed that lately, all Nancy wanted to do was sleep. Today, Nancy was feeling rather ill when Cybill had arrived, wearing a new hairdo. Cybill also wore extra makeup to make herself look more attractive. Nathan had just informed Nurse Templeton about Nancy's condition and then he brought her upstairs to the master bedroom suite, where Nancy was lying on the bed, looking quite pale.

"Miss Templeton, I-I don't feel good, at all," Nancy barely said in a weak voice.

"My goodness, she really does look sick, Nathan," Nurse Templeton said to him.

At that moment, Nancy rolled over on the bed and spewed her entire stomach contents all over the white carpeting, the bed, and on herself. Then Nancy wiped her face on the napkin that was on the bed tray near her. Miss Templeton reached into the private bathroom for a towel.

"Here, let me help you," the nurse said while going over to clean Nancy up.

"I feel like, like I'm going to throw up again. I-I, don't know what—"

Nancy couldn't finish what she had to say. She puked once more, this time with a little blood.

"I think we should call a doctor," Nathan said with a concerned

346

look on his face.

"I don't think that's necessary, yet, Nathan. It appears to me that Miss Stevens obviously contracted a bad stomach virus. It just needs to run its course, that's all," the nurse said.

"You really think that's what it is?"

"Oh, sure, I've seen it many times before. All she needs is some good, old-fashioned, homemade chicken soup."

"What do *you* think, honey?" Nathan asked Nancy.

"I-I think she may have a point there, Na-than. I'm having stomach cramps too. I'll try it," Nancy struggled to say.

"Good, then it's settled. I'll go make her some homemade chicken soup. Let me go downstairs and check your kitchen to see if you have the ingredients I need, if not, I'll do a quick run out to the supermarket," the nurse said.

"I really don't know how to thank you, Miss Templeton," Nathan told her.

"No worries, and I told you, Nathan, call me Cybill, please," she said to Nathan, just before leaving the room.

*
**

Early that afternoon, Nurse Templeton had retuned back from the supermarket with the ingredients to make the chicken soup for Nancy. Nathan had heard her van coming. He decided to walk outside to help her with the groceries. Miss Templeton parked her van in his driveway and got out.

"I came out to help you, Cybill," Nathan said while standing there with his cane.

"Help me? Oh, no, no, no, Nathan, I'm here to help *you,* and of course, Miss Stevens. Thank you anyway," she said while walking over to him.

347

Cybill put her arms around him. She gave him a tender hug and then kissed Nathan on his neck. Nathan was shocked, to say the least. He didn't expect that from their nurse.

"Whoa, Miss Templeton, I think that maybe you've got the wrong impression. If I've sent you the wrong messages, I'm truly sorry," Nathan said with a surprised look on his face as he tried to pull away from her.

"I'm sorry, Nathan. I guess I got a little carried away. I thought you liked me. It won't happen again," she said with a look of hurt on her face, while releasing him and looking down toward the ground.

"Now *I'm* sorry. I didn't mean to hurt your feelings, Cybill. You're a very desirable young woman, any man would be lucky enough to have you, but I'm very much in love with Nancy," Nathan said while picking up her chin with a gentle hand.

"Miss Stevens? But she's your sister-in-law, Nathan."

"Ex-sister-in-law, remember? I'm a widower now. Nancy has been there for me when I needed her most. In fact, she even saved my life from a fire in my lab. If it weren't for her, I might not be here today."

"I see," Cybill said while still feeling disappointed. "Please don't report me, Nathan," she said to him with a worried look on her face.

"I won't. It'll be our little secret," Nathan told her.

Nurse Templeton told Nathan to go on inside while she brought the grocery bags into the mansion. She went to the kitchen to unpack the food items. Miss Templeton cut up the vegetables, then she cut up the small chicken she had bought with her own money. Miss Templeton put all the ingredients, along with the associated spices, into a large pot and started to cook the chicken soup for Nancy. *He really does love her. I might as well give it up, shit,* she thought. *Nathan doesn't want me; he wants her.* A lonely teardrop fell into the pot as she felt her bubble burst.

*
**

Two hours later, Nurse Templeton was finally going to bring Nancy the chicken soup she made for her. She placed the large bowl of soup on a silver tray. The nurse, without spilling a drop, gingerly carried the tray upstairs to the freshly cleaned master bedroom suite where Nancy was.

"Here you go, Miss Stevens; this may be the best chicken soup you've ever had. I made it myself from scratch from an old family recipe," the nurse said while approaching the bed with the tray of soup.

"Wow, it sure smells good, Miss Templeton. Shall I take my medicine with it now?" Nancy asked while reaching for the bottle on the nightstand.

"Oh, no, don't take any more of those!" Nurse Templeton exclaimed.

The nurse quickly put the tray containing the bowl of soup onto Nancy's bed. Then she grabbed the bottle of medicine that was on the nightstand before Nancy did.

"What was all that about?" Nancy asked with a perplexed look on her face.

"Oh, I feel it might set you back, given the state of your present condition, that's all," the nurse said with a sigh of relief while putting the bottle into her pocket.

"It was just a pain medication, right?"

"Yes, acetaminophen and codeine, which can be a little rough on the stomach. Right now, you need to build up your strength by keeping food down. You don't need anything that may be harsh on your stomach. Codeine can be a little irritating on your stomach and that's why you need to take it with food and not on an empty stomach, Miss Stevens."

"Yes, I do remember Doctor Green telling me something about that at the hospital," Nancy said as she tried to recall her conversation with the doctor.

"Have you taken any more of those pills since I left you this morning to run my errand?"

"No, I figured I'd wait till you came back with the soup, so I wouldn't have to take it on an empty stomach. Miss Templeton, is it possible that those pills were the cause of my illness in the first place?" Nancy asked her.

"No, I don't think so. What you had, Miss Stevens, was a full-blown stomach virus. It'll pass, trust me."

"I certainly hope so."

"It will. Now, why don't you try the soup? Do you need any help with it?"

"No thank you. I'm feeling a little bit better now and I'm perfectly capable of feeding myself. However, can you just prop me up with some pillows so I can eat, please?"

"Sure, Miss Stevens, *you do* look a little bit better," Miss Templeton said while grabbing some pillows to prop Nancy up in the bed.

"Thank you, Miss Templeton, that'll be all, please," Nancy said while dismissing her with a motion of her hand.

Cybill Templeton asked Nancy if she needed anything else before leaving the room. Templeton went to the downstairs bathroom and flushed the remaining medicine capsules down the toilet. Miss Templeton never saw Nathan come up from behind her. She had neglected to close the bathroom door while she was in there.

"What are you doing?" Nathan asked her with a confused look on his face.

Miss Templeton got so startled that she dropped the empty medicine bottle on the tiled bathroom floor.

"Nathan! You startled me!" Nurse Templeton shrieked.

"I'm sorry, Cybill, but why were you flushing those pills down the toilet?" Nathan asked her.

"It, it was expired, Nathan. I thought it would be safer flushing it down the toilet in case some homeless person went through your garbage," she nervously replied while picking up the bottle from the floor.

"Oh, ok, that sounds logical. May I see the bottle, please?"

"Sure, Nathan," she said while reluctantly handing him the empty plastic bottle.

Nathan looked at the label of the empty medicine bottle.

"It's Nancy's pain medicine, acetaminophen and codeine, but the label says it expires June twenty—"

"You see, it expired four days ago."

"Twenty-twenty-four, next year."

"*Really?* May I see that, please?"

"Sure, look for yourself, Cybill," Nathan said as he handed her back the empty medication bottle.

"Oh, good Lord. how'd I miss that? Jesus, maybe I *do* need glasses after all," Nurse Templeton innocently said.

"An honest mistake, but unfortunately Nancy doesn't have any more pain medication," Nathan said with a worried look on his face.

"I'm so sorry, Nathan, but you know what? I think it was upsetting her stomach, anyway. If you want, I'll go see Doctor Green personally and explain to him what happened; I'm sure he could get me a new prescription for her."

"Thanks, I'd appreciate that. Listen, I just came by to tell you that you can leave early today. I can keep an eye on Nancy from here."

"Oh, you are so sweet, thank you. I'll see you again tomorrow morning at nine," she said.

"That'll be fine, Cybill," Nathan replied.

*
**

Three days later on Tuesday, June twenty-seven, Nancy Stevens was finally recovering back to her old self again. Nurse Templeton told them that whatever stomach virus she was suffering from had finally passed. Nathan had thought about bringing her into the hospital for an evaluation, just in case.

"No, Nathan, I think that would be a big mistake. She's doing much better now, can't you see? Why put her through unnecessary added stress, right Miss Stevens?" Nurse Templeton asked her.

"Nathan, I think she's right. I am feeling much better now, and I sure as hell don't want to be sitting around for hours in a hospital waiting room," Nancy added.

"Ok, ok, I get the picture, but if God forbid you have a relapse, you are going back there, Miss Stevens, if I have to drag you there myself," Nathan firmly said.

Nurse Cybill Templeton was tremendously relieved that they both were seeing it her way. It appeared to her that none of them had suspected her of slowly poisoning Nancy Stevens. Cybill had emptied each capsule of Nancy's medication and replaced the powder with arsenic. Cybill thought that if she got Nancy out of the way, she would have Nathan all to herself. However, Nathan had made it perfectly clear to her that he was very much in love with Nancy and he didn't want anyone else, so Cybill had regrettably decided to give up her quest for Nathan, at least for now. Instead, she decided to help Nancy get well again. *I could have had it all, the man, the mansion, and the money. I still care about him and I always will, but it's pointless to try and make someone love you when they love someone else, shit,* she thought while getting ready to cook supper for them.

*
**

Outside near the gate, hidden behind the bushes, the killer was sitting in his car with his smartphone and wearing headphones, monitoring the situations that were going on in the Harris Mansion. He obviously was not impressed with Nathan and Nancy's new nurse. The killer had grown weary of the whole situation in the mansion and he knew that time was running out.

"Oh, man, this is too much! What the fuck! That stupid ass bitch! She must have had a change of heart or something. I thought she was going to make my job easier by eliminating Stevens. Shit! She ain't worth a shit! I don't need her and I don't need Stevens, just Harris," the killer angrily said to nobody but himself.

The killer turned off his smartphone and took the headphones off of his head. He entered the date and time of today's scenarios into his journal. Then the man started up his car and left the property.

*
**

The next morning on Wednesday, June twenty-eight, Nathan and Nancy were both woken from a sound sleep by the sound of the front doorbell ringing. The couple had been sleeping together upstairs in the master bedroom suite. Nathan rolled over on the bed to see what time it was on the alarm clock.

"It's nine o'clock. I guess it's Nurse Templeton again. I'll get it," Nathan said in a groggy voice, as the doorbell kept ringing with urgency.

Nathan got out of bed and left Nancy lying there half-asleep. He put on a pair of pajamas that were on the nearby chair. Nathan grabbed his cane that was leaning up near his bedside. He started walking down the stairs to the main level of the mansion. Someone was now pounding on the front door while ringing the bell. Nathan was getting very annoyed as he walked down the staircase, wondering what the hell was up with the nurse.

"Take it easy, for Christ's sake! I'm not running, shit!" Nathan shouted.

The now angry scientist was finally at the front door, opening it.

"Where the hell's the fire?! Gonzalez?! What the devil are *you* doing here this early in the morning banging on my door? What's with all the police?" Nathan asked as he noticed all the police presence in front of his home.

"There's been another murder here, Harris. Do you know this woman?" Gonzalez asked him while pointing to the body lying on his brick pathway.

"Oh, my God! That's, that's our new nurse, Miss Cybill Templeton," Nathan barely said to him.

"We got a 911 call from the phone that's still in her hand. The caller just said, "Help," and never hung up the phone. I don't believe it was her that actually made the call, since she was probably dead already, and besides, the 911 operator said it sounded like a male's voice," Gonzalez gravely said.

Cybill Templeton was laying on her back, with a big bloody gash in her neck that practically measured from ear to ear. Her blood was now blending in with the red bricks on Nathan's pathway. The morning sun had presented the horrific expression that was now frozen on the poor woman's face. Cybill was dressed in her white nursing uniform that was now soiled with her own blood. The woman's smartphone was on her stomach, as if it were just placed there by someone. There was a mysterious note that was tucked under her right hand that read, "NO WITNESSES, NO LOSE ENDS," all in caps. The note appeared to be made from pieces of letters that were all cut out from the pages of newspapers and magazines, then glued to a standard letter-sized blank sheet of paper.

"She was attacked from behind, just like Hector Delgado was," Gonzalez stated in a matter-of-fact tone.

By now, the TV, radio, and newspaper reporters were showing

up at the scene of the crime.

"Oh, shit, here come the reporters. They're like vultures, all coming to get the top stories," Gonzales said while gritting his teeth in anger.

Nancy came out of the house to see what all the commotion was about. Nancy screamed hysterically when she noticed the nurse's body lying on the pathway in the morning sun. Nathan went over to her and brought the now hysterical woman back inside to calm her. Gonzalez had followed them into the house, while the forensics team conducted their investigation.

"Oh, my God, what the hell is going on around here?! It's not safe here anymore, Nathan, it's just not safe to be here!" Nancy shrieked while Nathan held her in his arms, noticing that she was shaking with fear.

"All right you too, calm down, I need as much information as possible. You said that woman was your nurse, Mr. Harris?" Gonzalez asked.

"Yes, that's correct, Gonzalez. She's only been with us about a week and a half," Nathan answered.

"That note that was on her body, does it mean anything to you, Harris?"

"I'm sorry, I didn't notice a note, Juan."

"Well, it was right there under her right hand. It said, 'NO WITNESSES, NO LOSE ENDS.' Does that mean anything to any of you?" Gonzalez asked while staring at Nathan and Nancy cuddled together in the hallway.

"The only thing I can think of, Juan, is that it's the work of our deranged killer and somehow, someway, someday, he's coming back for us and he doesn't want anyone else around here when he does. That would be the most logical explanation that I can think of, Juan."

"Hey, not bad for an amateur detective, Harris. Keep it up and soon you can have my job."

"No thanks, Juan, I'm happy with what I have here," Nathan said while looking at Nancy.

"It's just not safe here anymore! We need police protection, Detective!" Nancy shouted out from Nathan's arms that were still holding her close to him, as if protecting her from the elements around them.

"What time was your nurse supposed to be here, you two?" Gonzalez asked them.

"She told us she'd be here around nine o'clock this morning," Nathan replied.

"Did any of you hear her arrive, or did you hear any noise from outside, besides us?"

"No, we didn't, I'm sorry," Nathan replied while gently stroking Nancy's long blonde hair and cuddling her.

"And, where were the two of you when Miss Templeton arrived?" Gonzalez asked them.

"We were both upstairs sleeping, until we heard you ringing the doorbell and banging on the door," Nancy answered while still feeling very upset.

Detective Gonzalez started to wrap things up. He realized that this time, the killer had left his calling card, in the form of a note that was on the victim. Gonzalez gave Nathan his card and told them both to call him if they remembered anything else that could help. Gonzalez also told them that he would suggest more police protection for them to his captain.

CHAPTER 30

WITNESS

𝕿hursday morning, June twenty-nine, Detective Juan Gonzalez was placing a picture of recently murdered Nurse Cybill Templeton on the murder board. *What a shame. What a waste. Another beautiful girl met this sonofabitch's wrath,* Gonzalez angrily thought while writing Templeton's name under her picture.

Detective Gonzalez knew he had a serious problem on his hands that had escalated up to epic proportions. The serial killer was adding more and more kills under his belt and the detective felt overwhelmed. *This used to be such a nice, quiet town; what the hell happened?* he thought. *He's killed four people already, almost five, but Miss Stevens survived.* What really irked the detective was the killer's elusiveness; his fingerprints where nowhere to be found in the computer system database. *It's as if the sonofabitch doesn't exist,* he thought with a confused look upon his face.

"Good morning, Juan," Gladys said as she snuck up behind him holding two large cups of coffee.

"Good morning, honey, but how did you get back here?" Gonzalez asked with a surprised look on his face.

"Your captain was nice enough to bring me back here, knowing that you'd be here."

"I see; where did he go?"

"He said he was going back to his office."

"Ok, let's go to *my* office and have some coffee," Gonzalez said while taking one of the cups from her and leading her back to his office.

*
**

Over at Harris Manor, Nancy Stevens had just woken up screaming from a horrific dream. Nancy was still hyperventilating with beads of sweat on her face, as she sat up in bed next to Nathan Harris. The scientist and inventor was so shocked that he almost fell out of bed.

"Wha-what's wrong Nancy? Why'd you scream, honey?" Nathan asked her.

"There was a man in my dream, a man in the dark, he, he shot me, Nathan; it all seemed so, so damn real. Shit!" Nancy struggled to say.

"You're remembering."

"Remembering? What the hell do you mean remembering? It was a horrible dream, but I guess it was more of a nightmare than a dream, but that's all it was, Nathan."

"No, Nancy, it wasn't a dream, or a nightmare. It was a memory, a memory of what really happened to you. You've blocked it out of your brain, your mind, and now it's finally coming back to you."

"Really, Nathan? You sound like a shrink that's trying to psychoanalyze me."

"No, really, Nancy, I think that deep down inside, you *knew* you were shot; you just didn't want to admit it to yourself, or you chose not to want to remember anything about the incident because it was so damn traumatic to you. You certainly couldn't bring up any of the details about it, up until now."

"It all seemed so horribly vivid, Nathan. Did it really happen that way?"

"Unfortunately, Nancy, yes, it did. You were shot at by that psychotic killer at point-blank range, downstairs in my foyer."

"Sonofabitch, I guess I'm lucky to be alive," Nancy said while placing her right hand over her wound.

"Yes, you are. You know what this means, honey?"

"What?"

"We're going to have to inform the police. We've got to see Detective Juan Gonzalez and let him know that you're starting to remember what happened to you. Can you remember the sound of the killer's voice?"

"I, I don't know, Nathan."

"I'll go give him a call," Nathan told her.

*
**

About an hour later, Nathan was walking toward the police station with Nancy. The two of them were both leaning on to each other and on their canes. Nathan had tried to get a closer parking spot, but they were all taken. The scientist had admired the fact that even though Nancy wasn't feeling well, she still managed to get all dolled up for her outing. The young woman wore a fancy tan blouse and a pair of snug-fitting blue jeans that helped accentuate her nice shape. Nancy even managed to put on just enough makeup to emphasize her blue eyes and her cheeks. Her blonde hair was flawlessly hanging down over her shoulders, without seeming obtrusive.

Nathan was almost the opposite; he had forgotten to shave this morning, which made him look scruffy. Nathan also wore a pair of blue jeans, but they were a tad worn. The only thing that really looked nice on him was the bright blue satin shirt he was wearing, although the scientist would have done better had he tucked it into his pants. *Hell, Captain Martinelli almost always has his shirt hanging out of his pants,* Nathan thought, as if looking for approval from someone.

"It's so dark and gloomy out; it looks like it's going to rain," Nathan said.

"Oh, Christ, I feel so old with this damn pain, Nathan. I feel like my heart is struggling to keep up with me," Nancy added.

"It's only temporary, babe. Before long, we're gonna be exercising downstairs in my gym, together, I promise," Nathan reassuringly said.

"Oh, I don't know about that, Nathan, isn't it still smokey down there?"

"Not anymore, hon. I took the liberty of hiring a cleanup crew to clean and repaint the rooms downstairs, while you were being laid up in the hospital. Hell, I even replaced the treadmill that was destroyed in the fire with a brand-new high-tech machine."

"Wow, way to go, Nathan. You know, I also noticed that the master bedroom smells a little of fresh paint; did you have that done too?"

"Yup, a couple of months ago, I had to. Heather's, well, I won't say it."

"I already know; my sister was killed in that room. I know all about her blood being splattered in there, Nathan. It gives me the creeps. I try to tune it out of my mind when we're there, so please, don't bring it up again, all right?"

"You've got it, babe," Nathan gingerly said.

"Thank you. So, I guess all that's left is rebuilding your lab, right?" Nancy carefully asked him, knowing it was a sore subject for him.

"Yeah, however, I still can't get the motorized doors to close down in the basement, and that's not going to happen until I replace the security computer down there, but without the original building plans, I don't know how the hell I'm going to be able to do that," Nathan said with a worried look on his face.

A young police officer saw them struggling as they were coming in, so he opened and held the door for them. The couple walked toward the reception counter and announced their arrival to the young female officer there. Within a minute, Captain Martinelli was coming by to greet them.

"Listen you two, I really do appreciate you coming down here in your present condition, knowing the two of you should be at home resting in bed," Martinelli sincerely said while extending his hand to Nathan.

"Yeah well, this *is* an urgent matter," Nathan said while shaking the captain's hand.

"And if it will help lock this horrible killer up, I'm ready," Nancy added.

"All right then, follow me to my office, please," Martinelli said while leading the way.

Nathan and Nancy followed the captain back to his office. When they arrived, they noticed Detective Juan Gonzalez was waiting by the door for them. Captain Martinelli had brought in some extra chairs for all of them to sit down. The captain offered them both coffee. Nathan accepted the coffee, but Nancy didn't want any, instead she wanted a cup of water from the cooler that was there in the office.

"Ok, Nathan, now, over the phone you had mentioned that Miss Stevens, here, is starting to remember the incident when she was shot in your home. How much of it do you remember, Miss Stevens?" Martinelli asked while turning his attention over to her.

"I remember being shot by someone in a dark room. I couldn't see his face, but his voice—there was something about his voice that seemed very familiar to me," Nancy said.

"Would it help if you were to hear a recording of his voice again?" Gonzalez asked her.

"Yes, yes it would," she replied.

"Captain, why don't you pull up the video I left you on your desktop," Gonzalez said.

The captain clicked on the video in his computer and turned up the speakers so Nancy could hear it. He explained that although it was a video, there really wasn't much to see.

The recording started to play:

"Hello Harris," a voice hiding in the dark said.

Nancy screamed.

"Shit! It's you again!" Nathan roared.

"That's right, your old friend, ha, ha, ha."

"Nathan, I can't see, is it the—"

"Shut the hell up, bitch! There is no light, I disabled it, and why is your ass out of jail, bitch?!"

"You destroyed my lab, what the fuck do you want now, money?!" Nathan angrily shouted.

"I told your ass what the hell I wanted, everything, everything you own, including this place!"

"You've got my time travel belt; I thought it was destroyed!" Nathan exclaimed.

"You thought wrong, asshole. I've got it now, and I know what it's capable of doing. I've read some of your research papers."

"Nathan, what the hell is he talking about?" Nancy asked while feeling very confused.

"Bitch! Shut the fuck up, or I'll shut you up, permanently!"

"You can't talk to her like that!" Nathan shouted back in Nancy's defense.

"I can and I will! I'm the one who's holding a gun on you, and this time, it's mine and it's loaded, so don't you try anything stupid, Harris, you understand?!"

"Nathan, that voice, I think I know who he is," Nancy said.

"Not for long, you fuckin stuck-up bitch!"

Martinelli stopped the playback before Nancy heard the killer shoot her. He didn't want Nancy to fall apart on him in this critical time.

"That's all you need to hear, Miss Stevens," Captain Martinelli told her with a concerned look on his face.

"That's all right, Captain, I know what was next. That's when he shot me. It's all coming back clearly to me now," Nancy told him in a disturbed tone of voice.

"Are you all right, hon?" Nathan asked her while feeling concerned about her.

"I'm ok, Nathan."

"Miss Stevens, can you identify the voice on that recording?" Martinelli asked her.

"Yes, I believe I can. I'm a legal secretary for *Johnson and Meyers Associates*. Last year at our annual office Christmas party, my coworker and friend, Joni Chandler, brought a mysterious friend with her; someone I've never seen before and quite frankly, I really don't know what the hell she saw in him," Nancy said.

"Do you remember his name?" Martinelli asked her.

"All I remember was, he called himself Billy. He wasn't much of a talker, but I *do* remember that he had tried to pick me up, even in front of his date, Joni, which pissed me off. I remember that he had a deep, gruff voice, like a smoker's voice."

"This Joni, your coworker; where is she now?"

"Sadly, she passed away a few months ago from a brain tumor. Joni was only thirty when she died."

"Just great, another bullshit lead!" Gonzalez angrily shouted.

"Hey, watch it, Gonzalez. The girl is trying her best here!" Martinelli shouted back in anger, knowing his detective was getting out of line.

"Sorry, Captain, it just pisses me off that every time we get a new lead, something or someone debunks it," Gonzalez replied in a somber tone of voice.

"Yeah, I know. No more outbursts, please. Now, Miss Stevens, can you remember anything else about this man? Can you identify him for us?" Martinelli asked her.

"Well, he was of average height and build, nothing very distinguishable about him. The man wore a black baseball cap and dark sunglasses, the large kind that cover a lot of your face—don't know why, we were indoors. It kind of seemed like he was trying to disguise himself, but in reality, it only made him more conspicuous. I don't know, he just seemed like an oddball to me. I remember him trying to light up a cigarette, until Mr. Meyers told him he couldn't smoke there," Nancy recalled.

"I see. Now, Miss Stevens, is there anything else about him, anything you can remember, like maybe the color of his hair?"

"Like I said before, Captain, he was wearing a hat, so I couldn't tell if he was bald, but from what I could see around his hat, his hair was black," Nancy said while brushing her hair away from her face with her hand.

"Do you think that you could identify him if you saw him again, Miss Stevens?"

"Yes, yes, I believe I could. For one thing, I'll never forget his voice."

"Ok, Miss Stevens, I'm gonna set you up with our police artist, if that's all right by you?"

"Sure, Captain, I'll do the best I can."

"Good! Gonzalez, take Miss Stevens over to our artist."

"Ok, Miss Stevens, come with me," Gonzalez said as he stood up from his chair.

"May I go with her?" Nathan asked, worrying if it might spark bad memories for her.

"Sure, Nathan, you can go with them," the captain said approvingly.

Nathan got up from his chair and he helped Nancy up onto her feet. Nathan held her arm with his right arm, while leaning onto his can with the other. Detective Gonzalez led them over toward the police sketch artist in the back.

***

About an hour later, Nancy was finishing up the description of her assailant to the police artist. The woman was doing the best that she could with a memory that was over six months old; it was a memory in which Nancy thought was insignificant at the time, up until now.

"You've almost got it, sir, but his cheek bones, his cheek bones were a little bit higher, I believe," Nancy told the artist.

The police artist adjusted the picture to match Nancy's perspective of her memory. Then the artist asked for her approval of his drawing.

"How's that, Miss Stevens?" the artist asked.

"Yes, I think you've hit the nail on the head. That looks like him," Nancy replied.

"How's she doing?" Captain Martinelli asked as he walked into the room with Detective Gonzalez.

"We're all done here, Captain," the artist said as he proudly displayed his drawing to him.

"Huh, it could be anyone. That's the best you could do?" Gonzalez questioned.

"Well, she said he wore a hat and wore large, dark sunglasses," the artist responded in his own defense.

365

"Ok, Gonzalez, I want you to make copies of this sketch and turn them into 'Wanted' posters. I want them on the bulletin boards of every supermarket, post office, restaurant, and on all the traffic light posts, essentially everywhere, got it?" Captain Martinelli commanded.

"All right, Captain. I'll put one up on our murder board, too," he replied.

"I'll bet you will," the captain said with a chuckle.

"Can we go home now?" Nathan asked, noticing how exhausted Nancy looked.

"Sure you two, thanks for all your help; I really appreciate it," Martinelli replied.

"What about police protection, Captain? I think we deserve that," Nancy asked.

"You're absolutely right, Miss Stevens. I'll have a man parked outside the mansion in an unmarked car."

"Thanks, Paul, I appreciate that," Nathan said as he shook the captain's hand before leaving with Nancy.

*
**

On the way back home, Nathan and Nancy had decided to stop by the hospital to arrange for a replacement nurse. When they walked into the lobby of the medical center, they noticed a breaking news story on the TV screen that was hanging on the wall of the waiting area. The sound of the television set was turned down, but they knew what the story was about.

"Look Nathan, that's your house on TV!" Nancy exclaimed to him.

"I see. Look at the news caption on the screen: *Another Murder at the Harris Mansion.* We're all over the news," Nathan replied.

The couple walked over to the reception counter and asked to speak to someone about getting another nurse to help them recover. The young woman at the counter gave them both protective masks to wear and made a call to the visiting nurse department. After that, the receptionist asked them to wait.

*
**

A few minutes later, a young, dark-skinned woman that went by the name of Judeline Augustin was coming out to greet them. Judeline had originally come from Haiti and was in the United States for only three years, but Judeline was a hard worker and quickly moved up the ranks to become a supervisor. The young Haitian woman wasn't the type to give in to rich and powerful people like Nathan Harris.

"Good afternoon, I'm Judeline Augustin, from the visiting nurse division; how may I help you?" Miss Augustin asked them.

"Hello, Miss Augustin, my name is Nathan Harris and this is Nancy Stevens. We need a replacement nurse to—"

"I'm well aware of who you are and why you have come here, but I'm sorry, I cannot help you," Miss Augustin said while scanning the two of them.

"Excuse me, but are you saying you can't or you won't help us, miss?" Nancy said while getting angry.

"I'm saying both, Miss Stevens. No one here wants to go over there, knowing that there is a killer waiting there, stalking the two of you. My nurses are scared, and for good reason. All your money could not save Nurse Templeton. Miss Templeton was a nice woman and a good nurse. She did not deserve to die like that, at your home, Mr. Harris. Again, I am truly sorry, but until the killer is caught, my hands are tied. Have a good day and good luck to you both," Miss Augustin said before leaving them.

"Nathan, what are we going to do?" Nancy asked him.

"I guess we'll just have to take care of ourselves," Nathan replied while taking her hand.

*
**

Two days later on Saturday afternoon, July first, the killer had been in the local supermarket shopping for groceries. He was standing online at the checkout register when the man noticed a few people staring at him. The killer started putting the items he had in his cart up on the counter when he noticed the cashier was now staring at him, too. The man made the mistake of wearing the same exact black baseball cap that he had on in the police sketch that Nancy had helped create. The young female cashier had a copy of that sketch in the form of a "Wanted" poster, hanging up near her cash register. She stopped ringing up his items to glance at the poster and then him again.

"That's you, isn't it?!" she shouted while pointing to the poster for him to see.

The man glanced at the picture and knew that he was in deep trouble.

"Help! Police!" the cashier screamed.

The culprit left everything there and bolted for the door. He ran as fast as he could toward his little green car, which was parked in the parking lot. A police squad car had arrived at the supermarket, but it was too late; the killer had already gotten away. *That bitch, Nancy, she must have ID'd me to the cops, fuck! She's gonna have to pay for this shit,* he thought while driving away without his much-needed groceries.

*
**

That evening, Detective Juan Gonzalez and Gladys Delgado were at their favorite Mexican restaurant, El Toro, having dinner together. The two of them were sitting opposite each other in a very cozy booth, right near the back of the restaurant. Gonzalez wore a new dark blue, pinstripe suit. He was also wearing a new powder-blue shirt with a wine-colored designer tie. The detective really wanted to look good tonight for his hot date with Gladys. He wanted it to be a very special night, especially for her. Gladys, on the other hand, didn't know her date was going to be all dressed up. She thought it was going to be just another nice evening with her boyfriend. Gladys was dressed in casual attire. The young woman was wearing a light green blouse with a pair of loose-fitting jeans on her. Gladys had her long black hair hanging down over her blouse, just the way he liked it. Gonzalez picked up his glass of dry red wine and lovingly looked at her.

"Pick up your glass, honey; I propose a toast," Gonzalez said while waiting for Gladys to pick up her glass.

"A toast to the most beautiful woman here today, who is as beautiful outside as she is on the inside," Gonzalez stated while clicking his glass with hers.

The couple took a sip of their wine and Gladys started to get choked up. She looked up at her boyfriend, wondering what he had up his sleeve. Gonzalez took a big gulp from his glass and finished all the wine, as if he were trying to derive enough courage from it to say what he wanted to say.

"Gladys, my love, I know we've only known each other for three months, but when I first met you in March, I *knew* you were the one for me. I'm not that good with words, but I just cannot imagine myself living alone without you in my life," Gonzalez softly said to her.

"What? What are you trying to say, honey?" Gladys said with tears forming in her bright green eyes.

Gonzalez reached into his right jacket pocket and pulled out a small white box.

"I'm saying, will you…will you marry me?" Gonzalez struggled to ask her while opening up the box to expose a beautiful diamond engagement ring.

"Oh, my God, oh, my God, it's beautiful. Yes, Juan, I love you with all my heart. I *will* marry you."

Gonzalez got up from his side of the booth to sit next to her. He grabbed her left hand and started to put the ring on her finger, while hoping that it fit her. Gonzalez tenderly touched her face with his hand

and then grabbed Gladys and gave her a long, sensual kiss. A kiss that would have lasted even longer, if not for the waiter coming by to ask them if they wanted dessert.

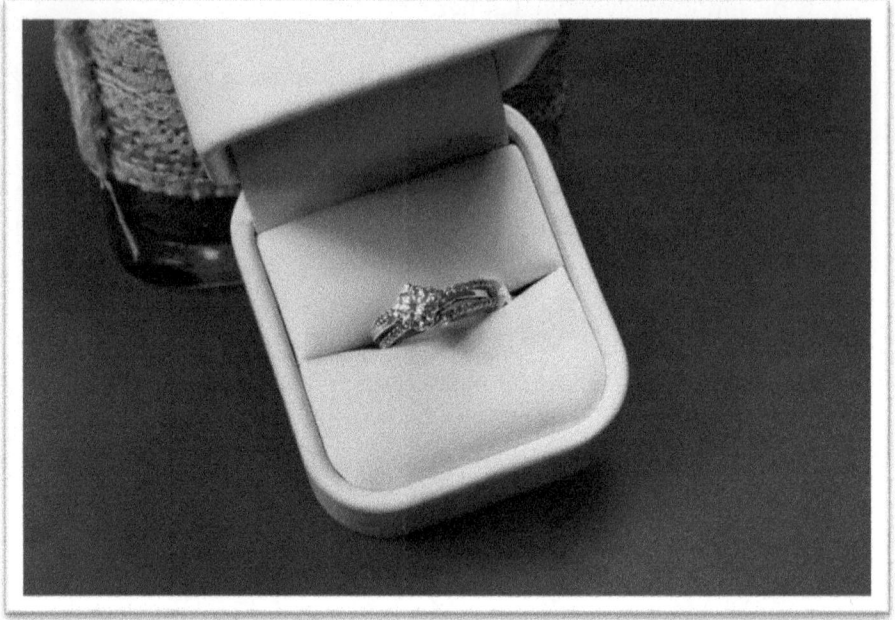

Photo courtesy of Maria Eugenia Tavera Perez

"No thanks, I already had mine," Gonzalez told him with a big smile on his face.

"I'm good, too; he is my wine, I don't need anymore," Gladys replied while smiling at Gonzalez.

The waiter gave Gonzalez the bill and he left them. Gonzalez looked at the bill, then he reached for his wallet and pulled out his credit card. Gladys offered to pay while looking at her shiny new diamond ring, but Gonzalez refused her offer. The couple got up from the booth. Gladys went to the ladies' room while he went up to the cashier to pay the tab. *I finally got me a real woman,* Gonzalez thought, but in the back of his mind, he wondered, especially after what happened with his last wife.

CHAPTER 31

I WAS POISONED

Monday morning, July third, Detective Juan Gonzalez was in his office enjoying his morning cup of coffee, courtesy of his new fiancée, Gladys Delgado. Gladys was holding up her left hand under the desk lamp, admiring the many sparkling facets of the new rock on her finger. Gonzalez gazed at the pretty young woman that was sitting next to his desk, dressed in a light pink summer dress. *She looks like a child, happy with her new toy, a very expensive toy at that, but I love her with all my heart,* he happily thought.

"I'm so glad you like it," Gonzalez said after taking a sip from his coffee.

"Like it? *Mira,* I *love it* and I *love you,*" Gladys said before getting up and giving Gonzalez a quick kiss on his lips.

"It's not as beautiful as you, my love," he said.

"Oh, that's so sweet. You know, it looks like a rainbow of colors under your lamp," she said while looking at her diamond ring again under his desk lamp.

"Well, well, well, if it isn't the happy couple again," Captain Martinelli said while walking in through the open door.

"Captain, I want to introduce you to my new fiancée, Gladys Delgado," Gonzalez proudly said to him.

"Congratulations you two! Let me see the ring!"

"Isn't it beautiful?" Gladys asked while holding up her left hand for the captain to see the ring.

"Wow! That's very nice. That must have set you back quite a bit there, Gonzalez," Martinelli said while looking at Gladys's new engagement ring.

"She's worth it, Captain."

"You know, I'm happy for you, for the two of you. Congratulations again."

"Thank you, Captain."

"So, have the two of you set a date yet?"

"No, Captain; we haven't gotten that far yet," Gonzalez told him while looking at Gladys with adoring eyes.

"Well, let me know when you do. Listen, it appears that our forensics team came across a diary that Nurse Cybill Templeton had on her phone."

"Nurse Templeton?"

"Yeah, Harris's maid, the one that just got murdered."

"So, she had a diary on her phone? That's a thing?"

"Apparently so, anyway, it was encrypted, but our techies finally got it deciphered. It appears that Templeton was obsessed with Harris, so much so that she tried to poison Nancy Stevens to get her out of the way."

"Holy shit!"

"Yup, she wanted Nathan Harris all to herself. I emailed a transcript to you; check it out when you can."

"Damn, and to think I felt sorry for her," Gonzalez said while gritting his teeth.

"Now wait a minute, Gonzalez, sure that's messed up, but Nurse Templeton didn't deserve to die like that."

"Even for attempted murder, Captain?"

"That's correct, Gonzalez. Sure, Templeton broke the law, if she really did indeed try to murder Miss Stevens, but Templeton should have served time or probably psychiatric care, not be put to death and certainly not like that," Martinelli said sympathetically.

"Really, Captain? We're talking about attempted murder here."

"Well, do we really have anything to substantiate this, or is it just some love crazed woman ranting in her so-called diary?"

"None that I could think of, Captain," Gonzalez stated while shaking his head from left to right.

"Did Harris ever complain to you about Nancy's health when you were there?"

"No, Captain, but I believe we should ask him how Miss Stevens is doing, in light of this new information."

"You're such a good detective, Juan," Gladys said while feeling impressed with her new husband-to-be.

"Yes, he is, and I'm glad he's with us. Why don't you go pay Harris a visit and see how Miss Stevens is doing, Gonzalez?" the captain said before leaving them in the office.

"You got it, Captain!" Gonzalez shouted out to his superior as he left.

*
**

Later that morning at Harris Manor, Nathan and Nancy were waking up in the master bedroom, sweating. The central air-conditioning had failed and the mansion was getting extremely warm from the summer heat outside. Nathan knew there was something wrong with the system. He got out of bed and went over to inspect the thermostat that was on the wall, near the doorway.

"Honey, it's so damn hot in here. What happened to the A/C?"

Nancy asked him.

"I don't know. I have it set at seventy degrees, but it's saying it's eighty-five in here. This shouldn't have happened. I just had it serviced two months ago," Nathan complained.

"Well, Nathan, it's a machine and machines *do* break down, usually when you need them most, like computers."

"Yeah, I know. I'll go call Solville HVAC," Nathan said while reaching for his smartphone on the dresser.

Nathan called the service department of the air conditioning company he delt with in the past. Nathan told the woman over the phone about his A/C malfunction. The dispatcher told Nathan that they were too busy to come out today, but they would send a service technician over by nine o'clock tomorrow morning. The woman also informed Nathan that since it was a holiday tomorrow, he would be charged considerably more, since it was considered emergency service after normal hours. Nathan took the appointment and hung up the phone, feeling disappointed.

"They can't get anyone over here till tomorrow morning at nine," Nathan said.

"Tomorrow?! We'll fry in here, Nathan!" Nancy exclaimed.

"I'll go down to the basement and get that big box fan I have down there. It's not air conditioning, but it's better than nothing," Nathan said.

Nathan threw on his white robe and walked out of the bedroom with his cane. He went down the stairs, but he got sidetracked by the front doorbell ringing before he made it to the basement steps. Nathan looked at the wall monitor and noticed that the screen was blank. *Shit! I forgot to have that camera repaired*, Nathan remembered.

"Who is it?!" Nathan asked by the front door.

"It's Detective Gonzalez!" he replied.

Nathan hesitantly opened up the door, wondering what the detective wanted.

"What can I do for you *this* time, Juan?" Nathan suspiciously asked him.

"I'm actually here to see how Miss Stevens is doing. May I come in?" Gonzalez asked him.

"Sure, come on in, Juan."

Nathan escorted the detective near the staircase area and called Nancy to come down. Nancy acknowledged him but said she had to get dressed first. The woman put on her light-blue nightgown and started to descend the stairs with her cane, wondering what the detective wanted from her now.

"Man, it's hot in here. What happened to you're A/C, Harris?" Gonzalez asked him.

"It's down. I called the man to service it, but he won't be here until tomorrow," Nathan said.

"Good morning, Detective Gonzalez. What do you want?" Nancy asked him with suspicion on her mind.

"Well, right to the point, eh? All right, then; I see you're doing ok now, but have you felt sick at all lately?" Gonzalez asked her with concern.

"Wow, strange that you should ask me that, because I was ill, very ill, but I'm feeling much better now, thank you very much."

"Good, because we have reason to believe that you've been poisoned, Miss Stevens."

"What?! Poisoned?! By whom?!" Nancy shrieked.

"By your ex-nurse, Miss Templeton."

"Are you sure about that, Juan?" Nathan asked him.

"Yes, Mr. Harris. It appears that your nurse kept a diary on her phone with vivid details of everything she did. Templeton was obsessed with you, Harris. From what I saw in the transcripts, she wanted Miss Stevens out of the way so she could have you all to herself."

"Wow! That explains everything," Nathan sadly said.

"You knew what she was doing to Miss Stevens?" Gonzalez asked him.

"Did you, Nathan?" Nancy asked in an accusatory way.

"No! Of course not! However, it *does* explain why she was so adamant about me taking Nancy to the hospital and having her checked out. Also, there was that time when Miss Templeton came on to me when—"

"What?! When?! You never told me that!" Nancy shrieked while growing angrier by the minute.

"I didn't want to upset you. It was nothing, hon."

"Really?! Well suppose you explain to me exactly how much of nothing happened, hon, because the way I see it—"

"She gave me a hug that day when she was bringing you the stuff to make your chicken soup."

"A hug? What else did she do, Nathan?"

"That was *it*."

"Really?"

"Yeah, really, Nancy," Nathan replied, knowing that he was in the hot seat.

"And just what did you do?"

"I, I pushed her away. I told her I was very much in love with *you* and that's the truth, Nancy."

The two of them just stared at each other for a moment, oblivious to the police detective that was watching them both intently. Nancy was trying to analyze him; she thought he was holding something back. Nathan wouldn't dare mention all the special treatment he received from Nurse Templeton. The man wouldn't dare disclose all the nice, relaxing massages and back rubs that Nurse Cybill Templeton had given him. The scientist knew that he was in enough trouble with Nancy right now.

"Excuse me, but you might still want to have yourself checked out, Miss Stevens, at least to see if you still have any more traces of arsenic in your bloodstream," Gonzalez interjected.

"Is that what she used on me, Detective, arsenic?" Nancy asked him with anger.

"Yes, it was in her diary. Templeton also stated that she stopped poisoning you because she realized that Mr. Harris only wanted you, Miss Stevens."

"Really? Is that true, Nathan?"

"You know it, babe," Nathan replied, knowing that Gonzalez just threw him a lifeline.

"Detective, under the circumstances, maybe I should have myself examined, at least by my own doctor, but it's been about a week now since I've gotten better. Do you think they could still find something in my blood?"

"It depends. If Miss Templeton used organic arsenic, most of it would be gone in a few days. However, if she used inorganic arsenic, some of it would *still* remain in your body for several months," Gonzalez stated.

"Well then, that settles it. Nathan, I want to be checked out," Nancy demanded.

"Ok, babe, call your doctor up and find out how soon he can see you; tell him it's urgent," Nathan said.

377

"Miss Stevens, you might also want to tell him it's police business, and you need a blood test for possible arsenic poisoning," Gonzalez mentioned.

"I guess the police can't do anything now, like arrest her for what she did to me, right?" Nancy asked.

"No, obviously not. She paid the ultimate price. However, you could still contact your attorney and file a civil lawsuit on her estate, but it doesn't look like Miss Templeton had very much."

"Just one more thing, Detective. Do you think this could be the handiwork of our illusive serial killer? I mean, could he have put Cybill Templeton up to this shit?" Nathan asked.

"I don't think so, Harris, not this time. There's no indication of it in her diary or anywhere else to say that she had help with this. Nope, Templeton was just—"

"Fucked up, right?" Nancy added.

"Nancy!" Nathan yelled at her.

"Well, it's true," Nancy retorted.

"*You* said it, not me," Gonzalez answered.

"Thank you, Detective, you've been most helpful," Nancy said while going upstairs to call her doctor.

Nathan thanked Detective Gonzalez and escorted him out of his home. He closed the door behind him and wondered. *I still can't believe Cybill went through all that shit just to be with me.* Nathan remembered something. *Those pills she flushed down the toilet, they were Nancy's medication.* Nathan remembered something else. *That was the day she gave me a hug and kissed my neck; that's when I told her I was very much in love with Nancy.* Nathan figured that Cybill Templeton must have had a change of heart and stopped poisoning Nancy, knowing that she couldn't have him. *I wonder; did she really want me, or was Cybill just a gold digger?* Nathan wondered.

"Right now, I just want to get out of this damn house; it's hot as hell in here," he said to himself.

Nathan climbed up the stairs to get dressed. *I hope that Nancy got her appointment with her doctor,* he thought. Nathan quickly realized that he never got the box fan from the basement. *I guess I'll get it later,* he thought as he went to check in on Nancy.

CHAPTER 32

WILLIAM

𝕿uesday, nine o'clock in the morning, July fourth, the air-conditioning service technician had just arrived at the Harris Mansion. Jerry Hang, the young Asian tech from Solville HVAC, parked his white van in the driveway and went over to where the unit was located on the left side of the house. Jerry bent down and started to inspect the compressor unit, until he noticed something quite odd.

"The power switches are turned off, why?" Jerry said to himself.

Jerry tried to turn the switches back on, but before he had a chance to complete his mission, the service tech was brutally struck on his head from behind with a heavy steel pipe. The serial killer hit Jerry so hard that he smashed his cranium, killing the technician instantly. Then, the assassin that he was, stripped the technician from his uniform and switched clothes with him. The killer dragged the technician's body back to his van. He stuck the body in the back with all the tools and drove off.

Nathan Harris had just come down the stairs in his white robe to open the front door, after hearing the van leave. He watched the van fly down his driveway. Nathan wondered why the man left without saying a word, especially since the central air conditioner was still out of order.

"Where the hell is he going? Maybe he forgot something," Nathan said to himself.

*
**

A few minutes later, the killer had stopped on a dead-end road near the edge of a high mountain cliff. He set the parking brake while the vehicle was still in drive mode with the engine running. The killer got out of the van, stuck his foot inside, and released the parking brake. He quickly slammed the driver's side door shut and watched the van roll and tumble down toward its destruction. The vehicle finally crashed at the bottom of the mountain about a thousand feet below. Within seconds, the van ultimately exploded into a ball of fire. *Well, that takes care of that,* the murderer thought. He started walking down the road, trying to get back to Harris Manor, knowing the journey was at least three miles long in the hot July sun.

*
**

Later, back at the mansion, Nancy was finally coming down the stairs to the kitchen, wearing her light-blue nightgown, after smelling the morning coffee brewing. Nathan had decided to make them breakfast. She quietly walked over to him and tenderly kissed him on the neck.

"Whoa, babe! I almost dropped the eggs; you startled me!" Nathan exclaimed.

"Sorry, honey. What you making?" Nancy asked him.

"Ham, eggs, toast, and coffee."

"Mmm, sounds and smells delicious."

"You're kind of late, baby. It's almost ten thirty in the morning."

"I was tired, what can I say? It's so damn hot in here. What happened to our air-conditioner repairman?"

"I don't know. He came by about an hour and half ago, then he just left."

"It's still not working, Nathan."

"I know. Maybe he had to go back and get a part for it or something."

"Aren't you hot in that robe?" Nancy asked.

"Yeah, but I had to put *something on* in case he came back,"

381

Nathan replied.

"I still feel a little weak from the doctor's office yesterday. My God, they must have pulled eight to ten vials of blood out of me, hon," she said while pointing to the bandage on her arm.

"Well, they have to be thorough, babe."

"Nathan, do you feel that?"

"No, what?"

"The air conditioner, it's blowing cool air again."

All of a sudden, the front doorbell rang and startled them both.

"I guess our air-conditioner repairman's back. Here, take over while get the door," Nathan said as he walked away from the stove and tied up his robe.

Nathan went over toward the front door. He looked through a nearby window to see who it was, since his camera was still out. Nathan saw part of the man's uniform, but he wanted to be sure before opening up the door.

"Who is it?!" Nathan asked through the door.

"It's Solville HVAC," the man said in a disguised voice.

"I was wondering what happened to you; I saw you leave," Nathan said as he opened up the door.

"I need to check your thermostats," he said while walking into the foyer.

Nathan looked at the man, knowing it wasn't the technician that usually comes to his home. However, there was something familiar to him about this man, but he couldn't quite place it in his mind. The tech was wearing the standard gray uniform and baseball cap with the company logo on it. He was also wearing large, dark, aviator-type sunglasses, along with a black mask, to help prevent the spread of the

COVID-19 virus. The telephone rang and Nancy picked it up in the kitchen. Nathan was just about ready to take the tech to one of the thermostats, until Nancy interrupted them.

"Nathan, it's Solville HVAC, they want to know if their service tech ever arrived here. The woman says he never checked in," Nancy reported while she was slowly coming out of the kitchen.

Nathan heard the unmistakable clicking sound of a gun that was being cocked. A gun that was now pointing at his left temple as the man grabbed him from behind.

"Hang up the phone, blondie, or your boyfriend here gets it," the killer stated in his normal, gruff-sounding voice.

"Do as he says, Nancy," Nathan told her.

Nancy obliged and hung the cordless phone back up on the wall in the kitchen. She came back out to the foyer.

"I was wondering when you'd return. What did you do with the *real* service tech?" Nathan nervously asked him.

"Don't worry about him; he's resting peacefully," the killer answered.

"You killed him, didn't you?"

"I said, don't worry about him! Now, we're all going back to that phone over there and you're calling that air-conditioning company back up. You're gonna tell them that their tech never showed up here and you wanna cancel the service call, because you had fixed it yourself, you capisce?"

"Yeah, I capisce," Nathan angrily replied.

The killer walked Nathan over to the kitchen, never releasing his grip on him. Nancy grabbed the phone off the wall and handed it to Nathan, while she was still trembling with fear for his life. Nathan called the company and told the woman on the phone to cancel the service call.

He also reported to her that their technician never arrived at his home. Then, Nathan handed the phone back to Nancy to hang it back up.

"Very good, I'm glad to see you can follow directions," the killer stated.

"You know, this is getting old, very old, and I'm sick and tired of this shit! What the *hell* do you want from me, already?! Nathan angrily shouted.

"Calm down, Harris!"

"No! I'm sick of this shit! If you're gonna kill me, then do it already, dipshit!"

"Nathan!" Nancy screamed out.

"Dipshit, eh? Now that's no way to talk to your blood relative, is it?"

"What?! What do you mean, blood relative?!"

"That's right, bro, you heard right. Can't you see the resemblance?" the killer said while pulling off his cap and dark glasses with his free hand.

Nathan turned his head and looked at him, while the intruder still kept his gun on him. Nathan *did* notice a slight resemblance on the killer's face, but it still didn't explain much to him at all.

"You're my bro-ther?" Nathan hesitantly asked him.

"Yo Moe, you just scored the double jeopardy answer of the day! I'm your half-brother, our father's bastard son, William," he bitterly replied.

"But I thought William was my imaginary friend?"

"That's what they wanted you to think, our father and your mother."

"All this time...I saw a therapist for years, for nothing. No wonder my mother was so pissed off whenever I mentioned you. Dad was cheating on her and she must have found out."

"Oh, yeah, she found out all right and threatened him with divorce, unless he stopped seeing my mother."

"Wow, I still can't believe my father had an extramarital affair with another woman. Is she still alive?"

"My mother? No, she passed away five years ago from cancer."

"Wow. That's what my mother passed away from. It was pancreatic cancer, back in 2000."

"With my mom, it was lung cancer; she loved to smoke."

"Was your mom good-looking? I mean, she had to be to pull Daddy away from my mother."

"Sylvia? Yeah, she was sweet, with a heart of gold. Our father used to send her checks every now and then to help her raise me, but it was never enough, and then he just stopped sending anything. I remember seeing a few of those checks that were made out to her, Sylvia Hooker, the ones that bounced. Mom kept those, for whatever reason. She could have sued his ass for child support, but Mom was too damn easy going and too damn nice."

"Hey, Nathan, it's nice that you two are having a family reunion here, but you *do* realize that he *still* has a gun pointing at your head, *right?*" Nancy asked.

"And I'm not about to put it down, yet. You know, brother, your taste in women sucks. You had one that cheated on you with the hired help, for Christ's sake, and *this* stuck-up bitch that can't seem to keep her damn mouth shut, shit!" William shouted.

"Don't call her that! Nancy and I have been through a lot. She saved my life when *you* tried to kill me, *damn it!*" Nathan angrily retorted.

"Let's be clear here, I never once tried to kill *you*, that was an accident. However, I didn't do anything to save your ass, either."

"But you killed my wife and—"

"She was a piece of shit! So was her boyfriend. I did you a favor, man."

"You tried to kill Nancy, too!"

"She was gonna identify me! Besides, if I really wanted her ass dead, I would have shot her more than once."

"You tried to frame me for vandalism and everything else!" Nancy shouted.

"At least I didn't poison you like that crazy-ass nurse you hired, and no, I didn't have anything to do with her," William stated.

"No, you didn't, just everyone else. Did you have to kill her?" Nathan asked.

"She got in my way, so did the others," William said while gritting his teeth.

"You've got serious anger-management issues, William."

"Look, Nate, before you try to psychoanalyze me, you've had it made here with your plush, rich-ass life, while my ass had to struggle for every damn thing. Our father took really good care of you and left my ass out to hang and dry. Shit, he renounced me. I didn't even get his fricking name. Dad made sure of that by threatening my mom, telling her that she would never get a dime from him if she mentioned him as the father. Naturally, I was envious of you. I deserved all this shit you have here and—"

"You didn't have to blow up my lab, shit!" Nathan yelled out in anger.

"I'm sorry for that. I was pissed off and I wanted you to suffer like *I* did! If I knew what the hell you built down there, I wouldn't have destroyed it."

"You know, if I knew you were my brother, I would have helped you out; all you had to do was ask!"

"I don't want your damn charity, shit! I wanted everything you had—everything *I* was cheated out of! He was my father too, but he was a piece of shit, Nate, even though he was a bigtime Wall Street executive. I'm glad he's dead. You were already four years old when I was born and I felt like an outcast! My poor mother struggled as a waitress and a part-time cleaning lady, trying her best to raise me in that old tenement that never had enough heat on in the wintertime, while you enjoyed a lavish lifestyle with our wealthy ass father and your mother!"

"Yes, it was wrong, but you didn't have to go on a damn killing spree. You fucked up your own life, Will, but you're not taking me along for the ride!"

"You wouldn't say that shit if the shoe were on the other foot! Here, I brought you a present."

William pulled out a large manilla envelope from his shirt and handed it over to Nathan.

"My research papers?" Nathan asked.

"Yup, I brought them back for you."

"What's the catch?" Nathan asked him in a suspicious tone, knowing there must be strings attached to this gesture.

"Well, I was hoping you'd rebuild your time machine again, I'd even help you."

"Time machine?" Nancy curiously asked, never knowing what Nathan had accomplished in his lab.

"Mind your damn business; I wasn't talking to you," William shot back at her.

"Let me get this shit straight, you want me to rebuild my time machine, why? What sort of a diabolical scheme did you have in mind, Will?" Nathan asked.

"I need to go back a few years to see someone, Nate."

"You mean, you need to escape the law, right?"

"Never mind, Nate. I need that machine ASAP!"

"*Well*, it's gonna take time, even with the plans. The earliest I could have a functional prototype developed would probably be around six to eight months, with your help—"

"That's too damn long! I haven't got that much time!"

"Well, what the hell did you expect, William?! You destroyed everything down in my lab, years of research—"

"Yeah, yeah, I know, I screwed up… I'm dying, Nathan. That's another reason why I'm so damn bitter. I've got a brain tumor in my head the size of a golf ball. I only have about six months left to live," William gravely said.

"Let him die, Nathan, after all the damn shit he's put us through!" Nancy yelled out until the sound of gunfire frightened her.

William shot a bullet at her, just missing her right shoulder by an inch. The bullet lodged itself in a nearby wall.

"That was just a warning shot to show you both I'm not playing here. Next time, you won't be so damn lucky, blondie," William said in a gruff voice, while pointing the gun back at Nathan.

"You hurt her again and I'm not doing *shit* for you, brother or no brother, do you hear me, Will?!" Nathan shot back to him in an angry tone.

"Yeah, I hear ya, but I'm still in charge here with a loaded gun on you both. Like I said before, I need to go back in time, ASAP. Now, if I help you get that shit back together again downstairs, working day and night, how long would it take?"

"Maybe four to five months at best, providing I could get all the parts in time."

"That's cutting it damn close. I need time to find my doctor and give him the CAT-scan images of my tumor before it gets to the size it is now. Right now, it's inoperable, but five years ago, it was pretty much non-existent."

"I see, so you think you could just go back in time with the pictures, show them to your doctor, and maybe, just maybe, he could save your life, right?"

"That's the plan, but I need to get back much sooner than five months."

"I knew there was a catch," Nathan replied.

"Hey, Nate, just so you know, I've wired up your mansion here for audio-visual transmissions to my smartphone. I'm a hacker, I can do that," William replied.

"You've been spying on us all along, haven't you?" Nancy asked him.

"That's right, blondie. I've got cameras and microphones hidden everywhere, and you'll never find them, not without a bug detector. I've also done some research on *you too,* bitch. I see you've graduated from MIT with a degree in electronics. You could be quite useful to me with this project."

"The only thing I'm gonna help you with, is putting the final nail in your damn coffin," Nancy hissed.

"You'd better straighten her ass out, Nate, because if she gets in my way, I'll waste her, so help me God."

"If we help you with this, Will, I don't ever want to see you again. I want a guarantee from you that you'll never darken these premises and bother us ever again, is that clear?" Nathan demanded.

"Agreed, now let's head on over to your computer and order the parts we need," William said as he forced them both into the family room.

Nathan grabbed the laptop from the coffee table and turned it on. He took his research papers out of the envelope. Nathan went straight to the parts list and started ordering all the components he needed for the reconstruction of the time machine.

CHAPTER 33

REBIRTH OF THE TIME TRANSPORTER

On Wednesday at eight o'clock in the morning, July fifth, Nathan's half-brother William Hooker had switched the master bedroom doorknob so that the lock/unlock knob was facing out. He confiscated both of their smartphones and locked them both in the master bedroom suite. William then went down to the basement and ripped out the master telephone cables, disabling the entire system. William had just driven to the local hardware store to pick up a stainless-steel padlock hasp and lock to put on the outside of the master bedroom door. *I've got to make sure those suckers don't get out of their room,* he thought.

Nathan was just waking up, thinking about the whole situation. He had just spent well over $15,000 on electronic and mechanical parts from several websites to rebuild his Time Transporter; he even spent extra for overnight shipping. *That sonofabitch, he's incarcerated us in my own home, shit!* Nathan angrily thought. Nancy was just waking up next to him.

"Good morning, honey," Nancy lovingly said.

"Huh? What's so damn good about it, babe? We're both imprisoned here by—"

"Your brother."

"Half-brother," Nathan reminded her.

"Oh, whatever, I thought it was all just a bad dream."

"I wish it were, sweetie."

"You know, we could be in big trouble here, harboring a criminal and aiding and abetting him. He's wanted for several murders, Nathan," Nancy logically said to him.

"I'm well aware of that, but he *does* have the advantage, you know."

"Yeah, I know, he's got the gun."

"Precisely."

"Nathan, did you *really* build a time machine?" Nancy asked inquisitively.

"Yes, I did, hon. I went back in time, trying to save your sister and our daughter from death, but I failed miserably," he sadly said, remembering what had happened the few times he went back to the past.

"Seriously? So, what the hell happened?"

"Let's just say, I found out the hard way that you can't alter the past. What's done is done, and if you try to change anything, time will ultimately balance itself out, one way or another.

*
**

At the Solville Police Department, Detective Juan Gonzalez was answering a call from his office phone.

"Solville Police, Detective Gonzalez, homicide," Gonzalez answered.

"Hello, this is Mr. John Campbell, I'm the manager over at Solville HVAC. I wanna report a missing person," the man said over the phone.

"Who's the missing person and when was he last seen?"

"It's my service tech, Jerry Hang. He was dispatched on a call yesterday morning to the home of Nathan Harris, and he never got there, according to Mr. Harris, anyway. Mr. Hang was never seen or heard from after that. I got a call from the people he was supposed to see later that day, and they also claimed that he never arrived to service their unit."

"So, you're saying that your service tech never reported to his calls?"

"That's correct and he never reported back here with the company van, either."

"Ok, Mr. Campbell, I'll stop by in a few to get a description of him. If you have a recent picture of him, that'll be helpful too," Gonzalez said before hanging up the phone.

***

Two hours later at Harris Manor, William had just returned from the hardware store with the padlock and hasp. He went downstairs to Nathan's lab and got a cordless driver/drill from the burnt-up tool cabinet. William checked the tool to make sure it was functional and then went upstairs to install the new lock and hasp on the master bedroom door. Nathan and Nancy heard the drilling.

"What are you doing, Will?! Come on now, let us out of here, we're hungry!" Nathan shouted at the locked door.

"Just a little insurance policy, bro. Give me a minute and we'll all go downstairs for some breakfast," William replied.

The doorbell rang and William put down the drill. He cautiously went down the stairs to see who it was. William looked out the nearby window and noticed the FedEx delivery truck outside. He opened up the door to greet the delivery man.

"Mr. Harris?" the FedEx delivery man asked.

"Yes, that's me," William replied.

"Sign here, please," the FedEx man said while handing him the tablet.

"Where's the packages?" William asked while signing the tablet with his finger.

"I left the boxes on your driveway over there; you've got quite a few of them," the man said as he pointed to the mountain of cartons behind him. "Have a good one," he said as he left.

Photo courtesy of Tima Miroshnichenko

William looked at the stack of packages and knew he had his work cut out for him. William went to the basement to grab the hand truck. He stacked a few boxes on the hand truck and wheeled it into the laboratory. After five trips back and forth to the lab, William was finally done and tired. *Damn, I should have had Nathan do this shit*, he thought. William went back inside to let Nathan and Nancy out. *We'll have breakfast and then we'll start this major project,* William thought as he climbed up the stairs with the keys in his hand.

William finally made it back up to the master bedroom suite. He finished securing the hasp with the remaining screws and then the man loosely hung the new padlock he had purchased onto it. William unlocked the door and opened it, completely angry at what he was seeing. Nathan was sitting on the windowsill, half out of the open window, with Nancy by his side.

"What the hell are you doing?! Trying to escape?!" William shouted at them.

"You left us in here to starve! I won't be held prisoner in my own damn home by anyone!" Nathan bellowed back at him.

"You *can* and you *will* as long as I have this gun on you. Now, get your ass back down here and close the damn window," William said while now pointing his pistol at Nathan.

Nathan climbed back inside the room and closed the window. He looked at his half-brother with complete hatred. Nancy put her arms around him, trying to calm him down, thinking that Nathan might do something foolish, like lunging at his half-brother.

"That's right, calm his ass down, blondie. That was a very *stupid thing* you were trying to do, *bro.* You *do* realize that we're up here three stories high; you would have broken your neck, then you'd have been useless to me, and we don't want that, do we?" William asked him with a devious smile on his face.

"Who was at the door?" Nathan asked him.

"Good news! FedEx just came with all our parts to rebuild our time machine."

"*Our* time machine?"

"As long as I'm helping to rebuild it, yeah. Come on you two, I brought us some breakfast sandwiches and coffee."

"How thoughtful of you," Nathan said sarcastically.

"Let's go, we've got a lot of work to do," William said while waving his gun at them.

*
**

Later that day, the three of them were down in Nathan's laboratory, unpacking all the cartons that William brought in earlier. Nathan tried to be methodical about the placement of the parts in the room, but William wanted him to hurry up. Nancy was at the workbench heating up the soldering iron, while still leaning on her cane for support.

"Why the hell do you still have that thing?! You're not crippled!" William said while pointing at Nancy's cane.

"Because of you, asshole! You shot me, remember?!" Nancy shot back at him.

"Hey, watch it, sister, or I'll—"

"Knock it off! Now, I told you, Will, if you harm her, we're done!" Nathan shouted.

"Well then, you'd better keep your damn woman here in check, bro!" William replied.

"He started it, Nathan!"

"And I'm gonna end it! Look, Nancy, the sooner we finish this project, the sooner we get rid of him, so, please, keep your cool, all right?" Nathan begged her.

"All right, Nathan, I'll do it for you," Nancy replied.

"So, bro, how is she in bed?" William asked with a devious smile on his face.

"That's none of your damn business," Nathan hissed.

***

The next morning, Nathan and Nancy were rudely awakened by the sound of drilling. Nathan slowly got out of bed to see where the noise was coming from. He went toward the windows and noticed there were now gates mounted on them. Nathan followed the sound over to the private bathroom. He spotted his half-brother, William, outside the window. William was up on the ladder, installing gates on all of the windows that were part of the master bedroom suite. Nathan went over toward the bedroom door and turned the knob to see if it was still locked.

"Shit!" Nathan exclaimed.

"What's the matter, honey?" Nancy asked in a groggy voice.

"That sonofabitch! He's installing window gates on all the damn windows."

"Well, what'd you expect, Nathan? He caught us trying to escape. I figured he'd do some shit like that."

"Really?"

"Oh, yeah, he's always been one step ahead of us," Nancy logically said to him.

"I wish I could get out there and knock his ass off that damn ladder," Nathan hissed.

"Wow, I didn't expect that from *you*, Nathan."

"Well, what the hell *did you* expect?! He's got us locked up in here like animals in a Goddamned cage!"

Nancy just looked at him, not knowing what to say.

"Look, I'm sorry I yelled at you, honey, it's just, I feel so damn helpless here and I don't like feeling like that," Nathan said apologetically.

397

Nathan walked over to her and wrapped his loving arms around her.

"We'll get out of this, Nancy, as long as we have each other," Nathan said as the two of them were comforting each other.

*
**

A few hours later while the three of them were working in the lab, the front doorbell rang. William pulled out his smartphone and looked at the image on his screen.

"It's that detective again," William said.

"You fixed my camera?" Nathan asked while looking over William's shoulder to see his phone.

"There was nothing wrong with your camera, Nate. I just temporarily disconnected it. Now, get rid of him and don't try anything stupid, or your girl here gets it, understand?" William asked while grabbing Nancy from behind and pointing the loaded gun at her.

"Yeah, I get it. The ball's in your court," Nathan helplessly replied.

"Remember, I can see and hear everything that's going on."

Nathan went upstairs to answer the door. He wondered if the detective knew what was going on. Nathan made sure his white robe was tied up before unlocking the door and turning the knob.

"Good morning, Juan. What can I do for you?" Nathan asked him.

"Morning, Mr. Harris, I tried to call you several times, but I never got an answer, so I'm here. I need to ask you some questions about Jerry Hang, the service technician from Solville HVAC. Can I come in?" Gonzalez asked.

"Well, I was really in the middle of something, Juan, but what do you wanna know?" Nathan nervously asked him as he held his ground in

398

the doorway.

"The manager at Solville HVAC claims that you were the first call on his list, two days ago on July fourth. Did he ever get here?"

"No, no, Juan, he never did, as a matter of fact, I had called them and cancelled the service call. I realized that the circuit breaker just tripped, so I just reset it myself. You know, I didn't need them anymore."

"I just find it strange that he never showed up to any of his calls and never called in, nor did he ever return the company van. From what his superiors claim, Hang was very reliable and he loved his job," Gonzalez suspiciously said.

"Yeah, well, I wish I could help you out there, Juan, but I haven't the slightest idea of where he'd be. Like I said before, I'm in the middle of something and I need to get back, so if you don't mind…"

"Another invention, Harris?"

"Yeah, you know me, I'm always building something."

"Ok, Mr. Harris, I see you're busy, but if you find out anything about Mr. Hang, please let us know," Gonzalez told him.

"Will do, Juan," Nathan said while closing the front door on him.

Nathan wished he could have motioned him to come inside, but he knew they were being watched by his half-brother, William, downstairs in the lab. Nathan watched Gonzalez get in his car and leave from the wall monitor that was now working. Then, he started his descent back down to the lab.

***

One month later on Sunday morning, August six, Nathan, Nancy, and William had just finished breakfast and were heading down to the lab. William was always walking behind them, pointing his gun at them. The three of them had been working very hard, day and night, putting in long hours, just to rebuild the Time Transporter. The machine was now about fifty percent completed and was starting to look as it did before it was destroyed in the explosion caused by William Hooker, Nathan's half-brother.

Nathan was impressed at how much they had all accomplished in such a short time, but William had grown very impatient, as his episodes of pain were getting more and more intense and more frequent. Both Nathan and Nancy had to cancel all of their doctors' appointments, since they were housebound by William. Every time they needed something like food or medicine, William would often lock them up in their bedroom and run whatever errands were needed, wearing a disguise. Nancy would frequently complain about William being a slavedriver, but Nathan just wanted to finish the project as quickly as possible, to get rid of his tyrant half-brother.

*
**

Friday afternoon, September eight, it had been well over two months since Nathan, William, and Nancy took on the project of rebuilding Nathan's Time Transporter. The machine was finally complete and ready to be tested. Both Nathan and Nancy were happy that they were finally getting rid of their unwelcomed house guest that had them imprisoned in the master bedroom suite of the mansion. Nathan powered up the main computer system and started to check the interface leading to the transporter chamber. Nathan made sure all the connections, cables, and cooling tubes were in order.

"Well, how does it look, bro?" William asked him.

"It looks like all systems are green and good to go. Do you realize that we completed this project way ahead of schedule?" Nathan asked with excitement on his face.

"Good, let's send his ass on his merry way, good riddance!" Nancy exclaimed.

"Aw, ain't you gonna miss me, blondie?" William asked.

"Shit, you have *got* to be kidding!"

"All right you two, knock it off," Nathan added.

"Nathan, give me the suit. I'm ready to go," William said.

"I think we should test it first, Will."

"There's no time for that shit! My head is killing me!" William said as he popped a couple of aspirins in his mouth as if they were just candy.

"We really should—"

"I told you there's no time!" William interrupted while pointing his gun at Nathan, again.

"Let him go, Nathan!" Nancy exclaimed.

Nathan helped William put on the navy-blue suit with its protective hood. Then William strapped on the electronic belt and walked back toward the transporter chamber. Nathan activated all of the equipment for William's trip.

"How far back in time do you want to go, Will?" Nathan asked him.

"Let's see, why don't you set it for 2018, Nate," William told him.

"Can you be a little more precise? I need a date."

"Oh, shit, I don't know... Set if for Thursday, May seventeen, at nine in the morning. I remember having my physical on that day."

"Ok, where do you want to be?"

"Put me right in front of Solville Medical Center, can you do that, Nate?"

"Sure can. I guess you don't need a return time and location, right?"

"Nope, I'm gonna change my future, for the better," William happily said to Nathan.

"Ok, you got it."

"Wait, wait, wait, give me that envelope over there on the bench, it's got my CAT scans," William said while pointing to the large manila envelope on the workbench.

Nathan grabbed the envelope and handed it over to William. Nathan set the date dials to Thursday, May seventeen, at nine o'clock in the morning. He had also set the location to be outside, in front of the Solville Medical Center. Nathan told William to walk into the transporter chamber and wait for the retractable cylindered doors to close up on him. When they did, he told William, over the intercom, to power up his controller belt and pull up on the retractable hood to cover his head. Nathan also told him to put on the dark glasses to protect his eyes from the laser beams in the machine. Nathan then placed his hand onto the touchscreen of the new remote console he added, located near the transporter chamber. He waited for the computer to respond to him.

Photo courtesy of Onur Kaya

"Hello Mr. Harris, and welcome aboard," the computer announced in its virtual female voice.

"Hello Alice, commence time travel sequence, please," Nathan replied to the computer, hoping that everything checked out.

"Affirmative, Mr. Harris, initiating time travel sequence in ten seconds."

The Time Transporter started its countdown.

"Ten, nine, eight, seven, six, five, four, three, two, one, zero," the computer stated while presenting the numbers on its LCD screen.

The overhead electrodes began to energize, followed by the halo laser that was now circulating powerful light rays around William in the tubular chamber. The transporter began operating with a loud humming sound. William Hooker began to feel strange as his body began to demolecularize from within the chamber. Then, something went terribly wrong.

"Warning! Warning! Malfunction! Danger! System overload! Malfunction!" the computer kept repeating.

William started screaming in agony as his body underwent a vicious cycle of demolecularization and remolecularization. The entire system started smoking as sparks were flying out from the transporter chamber. William kept screaming from the immense pain he was now experiencing, until the man finally collapsed, down inside the chamber.

"Nancy! Pull the main circuit breakers!" Nathan shouted as he watched his half-brother collapse on the monitor in front of him.

Nancy went over to the circuit breaker panel and shut off all the circuit breakers, leaving only the emergency back-up lights functioning on battery power. Nathan went over to the chamber and tried to pull the retractable cylindered doors open, but they were jammed shut. He went over to his tool chest and grabbed two prybars from one of the drawers.

"Nancy, I need your help!" Nathan shouted.

The two of them went over to the transporter chamber. Nathan inserted one prybar on the top portion of the cylindered doors, and the other one on the bottom portion.

"Ok, Nancy, get below me. On a count of three, we'll pull toward the back," Nathan said.

Nathan waited for Nancy to get in position and they both grabbed on to the prybars.

"One, two, three, pull!" Nathan shouted.

The two of them pulled back on the bars with all their strength, trying to open up the cylindered doors.

"Pull, Nancy, pull!" Nathan shouted.

"I'm trying," she said.

They were almost ready to give up, until finally, the doors slowly crept open. Smoke billowed out of the chamber. Nathan and Nancy were both coughing, trying to cover their mouths with the napkins that were on the nearby counter.

"I need your help, we've got to get him out of here, Nancy!" Nathan shouted to her.

Nathan and Nancy both pulled William out of the transporter chamber, as a small fire was slowly erupting from the computers and the associated equipment. Nancy had let out a big scream as the two of them looked on in horror at the remains of Nathan's half-brother, William Hooker. The body resembled a mutation of a human being, at its lowest form of life. William's body was now turned completely inside out, displaying a mixture of tendons, organs, arteries, and associated skeletal tissue, all baked together, along with William's clothing and the remote belt. William's gun was welded into the remains of his hand, as if it were a part of his appendage. The blood that had once circulated throughout the man's body was now nothing more than a charcoaled residue.

"There's nothing we can do for him, Nathan, he's gone," Nancy said.

Nathan left William's remains and rushed over to the fire extinguisher hanging on the wall. He pulled out the safety pin on the extinguisher and sprayed its contents on the fire, smothering it, before it got out of control. The overhead sprinkler system kicked in, showering them with water.

"I can't understand what the hell went wrong. I checked all the systems before he went…" Nathan trailed off in grief.

"After what he's put us through, I think he got what he deserved," Nancy coldly said.

"How could you be so callous? He was my blood relative and a human being."

"Was he really, Nathan? Was he really human? Your blood relative, as you called him, tried to kill us, remember?! William murdered several people, including my sister. Your half-brother was an evil person with nefarious intentions. Yes, it was a horrible way to go, but I'm sorry, hon, I don't feel any remorse for him at all," Nancy said without any emotion.

Nathan stared at her for a moment and then he put the empty fire extinguisher down on the floor. Nathan went over to the circuit breaker panel and shut off the breakers to all the lab equipment. He flipped the main breakers back on, restoring all the lights. After that, the scientist turned on the exhaust fan to remove the remaining smoke, while circulating fresh air into the laboratory.

"It seems like déjà vu. My time machine is completely destroyed, again," Nathan sadly said. "All that hard work and money, gone down the drain."

"Oh, Nathan, we can rebuild it again, if you'd like," Nancy said in a comforting tone.

"No, that's quite all right, I'm done with time travel," Nathan said, feeling disgusted.

Nancy would never admit to Nathan why his time machine had failed in the first place. She despised his half-brother with a passion. Nancy wanted to make sure that he would truly pay for his sins. She had made absolutely certain that William would never come back, slip through the cracks of the judicial system, and then be set free to torment them again.

When Nathan was helping William put on the navy-blue suit, Nancy had gone over to the high-voltage rectifier circuit. She turned up the voltage to extremely dangerous levels, thereby sabotaging the entire system and killing William Hooker in the process. Nancy really didn't want to destroy Nathan's invention, especially after they'd all worked so hard on rebuilding it, but she saw it as the only outlet for freedom.

William had been coming on to Nancy whenever he had a chance to. When Nathan was talking to Detective Gonzalez, over two months ago, William had gotten behind Nancy, grabbed her breasts, and started groping her, while rubbing himself on her buttocks. Nancy elbowed him and pried herself free from his grip. William came back and pulled down her jeans as he tried to rape her. Nancy stomped on his foot to break free, oblivious to the gun that was still in his hand. Nancy threatened the crazed man that she'd let Nathan know everything that just happened, if he didn't leave her alone. William agreed for a while, but unfortunately, he recently started back up again, grabbing her ass whenever Nathan wasn't looking at them. *I'm glad he's dead; he was nothing but a nasty, evil sonofabitch and I hope he rots in hell,* Nancy had thought while helping Nathan clean up.

"We have to call the police and report this, Nancy," Nathan told her.

"That's going to be a little difficult, sweetie, since William took our phones and disabled the house phones," Nancy replied.

"He took our car keys, too. God knows where he put them."

*
**

The two of them went upstairs and started searching for their cellphones and car keys. Nathan knew that William had been sleeping in his daughter's bedroom, since it was next to the master bedroom suite, where they were held prisoner. He figured William wanted to be as close as possible to them just in case something went down.

Nancy searched the dresser drawers and got emotional when she came across some keepsake items that she had previously given Alice. Nathan was looking in the nightstand drawers, but like Nancy, none of them had any luck finding their phones or keys yet. Nathan decided to take a break and lie down on the bed for a bit, and that's when he noticed the pillow seemed lumpy and hard. Nathan sat up and looked under the pillow.

"Nancy, I think I found our phones," Nathan said as he picked up the smartphones from under the pillow.

Nancy came over and picked the other pillow up.

"Well, I found our car keys too, Nathan," she said while picking them up from the bed.

The two of them laughed a little, and Nathan tried to power-up his phone.

"It figures it's dead," he said while looking at the blank screen on his phone.

"So's mine," Nancy added after checking her phone, too.

"Well, what'd you expect? It's been over two months since we were able to recharge them. I got some cellphone chargers and cables in my dresser drawer. We just need to charge them up for about ten to fifteen minutes and we can use them," Nathan told her.

*
**

A few minutes later, Nathan was calling Detective Gonzalez on his partially charged smartphone.

"Detective Gonzalez, homicide," he answered.

"Hello, Juan, this is Nathan Harris, we've found your serial killer, or rather, he found us," Nathan said.

"Really?! Don't bullshit me, Harris. Where is he?!"

"He's in my lab, oh, and you'd better send the coroner over, he's dead," Nathan said before hanging up the phone.

*
**

A half-hour later, Detective Gonzalez was ringing Nathan's doorbell. Both Nathan and Nancy had washed up and changed their clothes to look more presentable, after what happened in the laboratory earlier.

"He's here," Nathan said while combing his hair in the bathroom.

"Nathan, honey, listen, you'd better let me do the talking. I used to be a legal secretary and I've learned some things from my old boss," Nancy warned him.

"Ok," Nathan agreed.

The two of them went down the stairs to let the detective in. Nathan cautiously opened up the door, remembering what Nancy had just told him.

"Hello Harris, where is he?" Gonzalez asked him.

"Follow me, Juan. I'll take you to him," Nathan said with Nancy close behind him.

"You two look much better; no more canes?"

"Nope, we've just been dealing with emotional stress, but I think it's pretty much over now," Nathan said as he led the detective and Nancy toward the basement staircase.

The three of them walked down the stairs, past the gymnasium, and into the lab.

"Shit, it smells smokey in here. Did you have another fire, Harris?" Gonzalez asked.

"Yeah, we did, caused by him," Nathan said while pointing to the body on the floor near the transporter chamber.

"Holy shit! What is that thing?!" Gonzalez exclaimed.

"That thing, as you called it, was your serial killer; he was also my half-brother, William Hooker," Nathan sadly said.

"Your half-brother was the serial killer?"

"That's right, Juan. Believe me, it was as much of a shock to me as it is to you, especially since I didn't even know *I had* a half-brother in the first place. My father had him in an extramarital affair, without my own mother knowing about it, till later, much later."

"Sonofabitch!" Gonzalez said while going over to examine the mutation.

Nathan and Nancy looked at each other while the detective bent down and tried to get a pulse from William's remains.

"What the hell happened to him? I want details, you two," Gonzalez said while standing back up and approaching them with his book and pen in hand.

"William rang the bell this morning, posing as a delivery man. Nathan opened up the door, that's when he pulled a gun on us and forced us down here into Nathan's lab," Nancy said.

"Is that true, Harris?" Gonzalez skeptically asked.

"That's correct, Juan. He constantly had his gun on us while he made his demands," Nathan replied.

"Just what were his demands and why did he make you bring him down here to the lab, of all places?"

"William was dying of a brain tumor. He wanted me to send him back in time so his doctor could remove his tumor before it grew to the size it is now."

"Send him back in time? Oh, shit! Here we go again," Gonzalez said while shaking his head in a disgusted fashion.

"It's true, Juan. That's—"

"Why did he think you could send him back in time, Harris?"

"Because he stole my research papers, remember? He—"

"Detective, what Nathan is trying to say here is that his half-brother actually *believed* that Nathan *could* send him back in time to help him. William trained his gun on both of us. He walked into that machine over there and then he forced Nathan and me at gunpoint to activate it. Nathan warned him that the machine wasn't functional, but William was very adamant about it. He demanded to go back in time, so Nathan turned it on and the two of us watched in horror as William got fried in that contraption. Nathan quickly turned off the power and we both pulled him out. We tried to save him, but it was too late. There wasn't anything else we could do," Nancy interjected.

"So, let me get this straight, the killer had the two of you at gunpoint, while he went into that contraption over there, thinking it would send him back into time, correct, Mr. Harris?" Gonzalez asked while looking at Nathan.

"I couldn't have said it any better myself, Juan," Nathan humbly replied.

"And the two of you warned him about the dangers of the machine, correct?"

"That's correct, Juan. William had threatened to kill us both if we didn't oblige to his demands," Nathan honestly stated.

"What made the two of you think that this man here was our serial killer?"

"He confessed to everything, even killing my wife. For Christ's sake, Juan, William knew details about everything, details that only the *real* killer would have known. I mean, you see he still has the gun in his hand, for Christ's sake!"

"Yes, I see that there's a gun molded into his hand if that's what it is."

"Couldn't you get a DNA sample from him to see—"

"Get a DNA from that thing?! I'll leave that up to forensics," Gonzalez said.

"Well, you *could try*," Nancy added.

"There's just one more thing."

"What's that, Detective?" Nancy asked.

"Why did the two of you wait so long to call us?"

"William ripped out the landline cables to disable the house phones, and he confiscated our cellphones and car keys. I called you as soon as I found them," Nathan said.

"All right you two, let me call the captain and the coroner," Gonzalez said as he took out his smartphone.

*
**

Later that evening, Detective Gonzalez was knocking on Gladys Delgado's door. Gonzalez did have a date with Gladys that evening, but this was not a social call. Gladys opened up her door with a smile to greet him.

"Hello, honey, come in," Gladys said as she ushered the detective inside her home.

Juan Gonzalez stood in front of her in the doorway. He took off his hat and looked sadly at her. Gladys knew right away that something was dead wrong.

"What's wrong, honey? Why you look so glum?" Gladys asked him.

"We finally caught our serial killer; the one who killed your brother," Gonzalez solemnly said.

"Are you sure?"

"Yes, the body was badly disfigured, but we were able to pull fingerprints off of his gun. It was a match for everything else he had touched at other crime scenes."

"He's, he's dead?"

"Yeah, he died in some contraption at Harris's home."

Gladys wrapped her arms around Gonzalez and cried. She thanked him for catching her brother's killer. Gladys finally had the closure she was looking for. Juan held her tightly in his arms, wishing he could do more for her.

*
**

A few miles away at Harris Manor, Nathan had just grabbed a small white box out of his wall safe in the lab. He brought the box upstairs to where Nancy was brushing her hair in front of the mirror, in the master bedroom. Nathan went to her and kissed her on the neck.

"Well, what's that for, sweetie?" Nancy asked him.

"You saved my ass earlier with that detective. I'll never forget it. Plus, you saved my life, babe. I-I don't want to live without you," Nathan said as he got down on his knees in front of her.

"Nathan, what are you trying to say, hon?"

"I'm asking you to marry me, Nancy, will you?" Nathan asked while opening up the little white box in front of her.

"Oh, my God! Oh, my God! Yes, yes, there's nothing more I'd rather do," Nancy cried out while looking down at him.

Nathan stood up and took the beautiful diamond engagement ring out of the box. He placed the ring on her ring finger and was happy it fit. Nancy wrapped her arms around him and gave Nathan a long, sensual kiss. Then, the happy couple walked over to the king-sized bed that was eagerly waiting for them.

The End

I hope you enjoyed this story.

Manuel Rose

ABOUT THE AUTHOR

Manuel Rose, was born in Brooklyn, New York. He is the exclusive owner and CEO of MMRproductions.com. Manuel is an author of both children's books as well as adult thrillers. Manuel started his own business in 2000, which has evolved and had branched out into multiple avenues, including some of his how-to educational products. As an avid professional audio/video producer, writer, singer, and voice actor, he provided the screenwriting and narration for the instructional films that he produced, as well as character voice-overs for his line of children's audio books, including his project: "My Child Storytime VOL. 1," which is a CD that features all original stories and songs. Manuel is also a proud member of ASCAP.

Please Visit His Websites at:

https://manuelrose.com/

http://mmrproductions.com/

https://twitter.com/ManuelRose

https://www.facebook.com/Manuel-Rose-Writer-101580988342731/

https://www.youtube.com/user/MMRPRODUCTIONS

https://www.amazon.com/Manuel-Rose/e/B078J5QKVX

https://soundcloud.com/user-112846907/a-murderers-music-box-demo

https://www.goodreads.com/ManuelRose

https://www.instagram.com/manuelrosewriter/?next=%2F

Thanks so much for reading!

If you enjoyed this book, please take a minute to leave a review on Amazon.com, BarnesandNoble.com and Goodreads.com. Reviews make a huge difference to an author's sales and rankings—the more reviews I get, the more books I'll be able to write.

My readers mean the world to me, and I'd love to stay in touch. You can keep up with me on Goodreads.com https://www.goodreads.com/author/show/17650713.Manuel_Rose and Amazon.com https://www.amazon.com/Manuel-Rose/e/B078J5QKVX/ref=dp_byline_cont_pop_ebooks_1

Also from Manuel Rose

Avalina

A Murderer's Music Box

Death on the Railway, Second Edition

Coming Soon:

Beautiful, but Deranged

$30.99 U.S./$32.99 Can.

ISBN: 979-8-21-854232-0

53099

9 798218 542320

9 798218 542320